By ERIC ARVIN

Another Enchanted April
Azrael and the Light Bringer
Galley Proof
Grand Adventures (Dreamspinner Anthology)
Kid Christmas Rides Again
The Mingled Destinies of Crocodiles and Men
The Rascal
The Rest Is Illusion
Simple Men
Slight Details & Random Events (Author Anthology)
Terms We Have for Dreaming
Wave Goodbye to Charlie
Woke Up in a Strange Place

SUBSURDITY SERIES
SubSurdity
Suburbilicious
SuburbaNights

Published by DREAMSPINNER PRESS
www.dreamspinnerpress.com

TERMS
WE HAVE FOR
DREAMING

ERIC ARVIN

DREAMSPINNER
PRESS

Published by

DREAMSPINNER PRESS

5032 Capital Circle SW, Suite 2, PMB# 279, Tallahassee, FL 32305-7886 USA
www.dreamspinnerpress.com

Terms We Have for Dreaming

Cover Art

ISBN: 978-1-63533-814-0
Digital ISBN: 978-1-63533-815-7
Library of Congress Control Number: 2017904061
Published April 2017
v. 1.0
With thanks to Wilde City Press.

Printed in the United States of America

This paper meets the requirements of
ANSI/NISO Z39.48-1992 (Permanence of Paper).

FEEL HER WAKING

THREE HUNDRED souls. That is all.

The entire world, all of human existence, comes to three hundred souls born and reborn again. No more and no less. Countless billions of people share these souls, each individual with a slight piece or sliver of grace. It is as it always has been since the beginning. Humanity has a unique connection to one another in this way. No other creature has such a noble genesis. Not even us. Since untold billions are part of the three hundred, harm a stranger and you may yet harm yourself.

But we find people tend to forget things not screamed at them.

We are watching now, as the folk hero, Colm Archer, is standing naked in front of a hushed crowd, the imposing Kingdom Guard behind him in their silver uniforms. Those city-dwellers wealthy enough to afford the show, watch him with condescension drawn on their faces. Their begrudging admiration is well-hidden. Also hidden, costumed in ridiculous finery, are those the world calls sinners—fragments of Colm Archer's band of rebels, though their new leader and Archer's lover, Usker Lance, has wisely chosen not to watch. He would be spotted immediately, even in drag.

Colm Archer is a hero, yes, but not to the first ring of the inhabited Five Rings of the Immortal City. People do well here. They have plenty. They are blessed by GOD and do not care for upheaval. The sinners are a nuisance.

Colm Archer is a hero to the other four, however, and they will cry for him today, though none will see him die. Only those in the first ring have the privilege of watching executions or punishments.

He stands stoic before GOD, facing his "relocation" to the ninth and final ring, a ring well past any proper habitation, with strength and grit on his battered but still handsome face. He glares up at GOD.

"You will fall!" he cries. "You will fall! Aye, and it will be a beauty to see. I've seen it, ya see. I've seen it in my dreams."

This is his crime. Colm Archer, like many before him, is charged with spreading vicious philosophy, rumors of prophecy, and false words against GOD. They all get caught in the end. The ferrymen, GOD's dogcatchers, do their jobs well. Of late, it has been discussed, however, in the more hidden and earless realms of the Immortal City, how much longer it took for GOD to find Colm Archer than any of the other heretics and apostates before him. It was as if he had help escaping.

No one cheers for Colm Archer's release. There are no heroic or tearful last pleas. Yet no one cheers for his immediate death, either. The crowd is silent. Many do not want to see the punishment, not really. There have been too many recently. Of course, no one would dare speak this aloud.

He stands upon a gleaming stage for death that reflects the orange tinge of the cloudy sky. His arms are chained to the dramatic, large steel columns on either side. He is an anatomy specimen, muscles and flesh.

The slightest inkling of fear can be heard in his voice as he cries, "You will fall! What you do today is the first step to your own death, ya piece of shite!"

GOD is unmoved.

The Kingdom Guards get to work. A metal clamp is fixed tight around Colm Archer's scrotum and hooked to a chain brought up from a hole below Colm Archer's straddle. He closes his eyes to gather strength. Clinking and grinding begins as the chain attached to the clamp pulls his scrotum toward the burnished stage. Colm Archer does well at first as the clamp ring cuts into his tender flesh, causing dribbles of blood. He is breathing harder. His teeth are still gritted. His eyes are open now, and his glare at GOD undisturbed.

But then, he can take it no longer, and he begins to cry. His knees want to buckle, but of course, they are unable. His muscles become ever more taut as he writhes in agony. And then, as his scrotum is slowly torn from his body, he begins to scream. His screams make even us moan. He thrashes about in a frenzy. He wants to be free of the pain. We can see the lightning in his eyes, the sheer white pain as the gleaming stage is soiled with blood.

Many in the audience avert their eyes. Some cover their ears. Some even hide their tears. GOD has won.

Blood drips from the stage. Colm Archer passes out from the pain. At least there is that. He will be bandaged and taken out of the metal stocks. He will then be taken to the ninth ring, a hero no more.

We are truly concerned.

WE THOUGHT Colm Archer was the man who would open his people's eyes. We are saddened this did not come to pass. He was a good man. He had… passion. More so than any of the Great Sinners before him. Yet we are not discouraged, for we have found another. One who hears us, and regards us with more than vague curiosity.

Gemma Kerr. She will have more problems than Colm Archer. That is a given. She is a woman, after all. The humans separate their sexes and genders, but it was not always so. Once all the sexes worked together. They disregarded ancient prejudices and were becoming a more enlightened world. We were proud of them once. But then GOD manifested, and any light was blown out. GOD abhors free thought.

We tried to stay out of the affairs of man for centuries, but we cannot stand by and watch you kill yourselves. What sort of animals would we be then? What indeed?

We visit Gemma in her dreams, disguised as the ancient human goddess of light, Abrythnia.

Abrythnia. The hermaphrodite. The goddess who flooded the ancient world with understanding by unfolding her arms. Gemma knows the image well from her secret studies in her father's library, poring over actual tomes there that have not been purged or burned. Books from before the End of the World and scrolls from after. Of course, no one has any writings about the century that bestrides the two, because no writings exist.

We visit Gemma tonight as she sleeps. We meet her in the Garden of the Passions, the ruins of which still exist in another, lesser ring. But in Gemma's dream, the Garden is still beautiful, alive, and easily accessible. It pulses with life even in the night. Streams and fountainways glitter under the moonlight, though the moon rarely peeks from behind the clouds. Fresh dew settles on the tips of the tall green grass and the wide feathery ferns. Nightlight bugs flitter around us, chirping their melancholy tune. The breeze is warm and sweet with the scent of flowers and pine. We stand nude, waiting for Gemma under a weeping willow tree, our arms outstretched, our smile warm.

Gemma approaches slowly, but she is not frightened. She has seen this garden many times before in her dreams. She is a young woman now, but she has visited here since she was a child. Gemma is dark-skinned and dressed in a gown of light. Her eyes are wide, seeking as much truth about the Garden as they can accrue. Her dark hair is gathered on top of her head and adorned with white morning glories. She is barefoot and, thinking us something divine, bows as she nears. We do not require this, but she is comfortable with her tradition. She then rises to our embrace.

A kiss on the lips, and then we turn to watch the Passion spirits play in their mischievous manner on the Garden hills. They are small, with both animal and human characteristics. They delight in laughter. They tumble and trip and chase after nightlight bugs. They are gone from the Immortal City now, existing only in dreams and on friezes of ruins.

We take Gemma by the hand and lead her down a smooth, winding stone path.

"You must find us," we remind her. "You must find us outside of the city. We believe it is time."

"Past the walls?" She is a frightened child still.

"Past them all."

"But each ring stretches on and on. It would be quite a feat to travel them. I've never even been past the fourth ring, and going farther than the fifth is not permitted."

"Not permitted by whom? By GOD? Who is He to tell you what you are resigned to? This is your world, too."

She looks at us with embarrassment and shame. She has never believed in the Power of GOD, but to say so out loud would be dangerous. GOD's Tower watches and hears all. It spears the very heart of the world, built at the center of the Immortal City, domineering and invasive. You may keep no secrets from GOD. The wealthy know this and retain their wealth by staying in His favor, but the wealth disintegrates as one gets farther from the Tower. The first and smallest ring basks in His glory, enjoying the most fertile plots of land for parks and the most unpolluted water for drinking. But the second ring struggles, and the third hobbles. The fourth and the fifth merely trudge along like crippled or dying slaves. Yet those rings are where humanity may find its Salvation.

"I hear," Gemma says, "the Kingdom Guards in the walls past the fifth ring will kill any who dare approach."

"And then?"

"And then the remaining rings—the sixth through the eighth—are a No Man's Land, devoid of any life until the colony in the final ninth ring."

We stop and look at Gemma with confusion. We wonder if her own ignorance is reflective of the larger culture. "But there are twelve rings in the Immortal City, dear Gemma. Not nine."

Her eyes widen in disbelief and hurt. "Twelve?"

"The oldest is the twelfth."

"But, we have been told..." She does not need to finish the statement. "Is there life in these other rings?"

"There is. But barely."

We feel her waking. It thrills us. "Come find us," we say. "Come look for us beyond the walls."

"Twelve?" she says again, taking the word with her into the waking realm. And she thinks, *But what then, is beyond the twelfth?*

Twelve?

Gemma wakes with question on her lips. She opens her eyes and takes in her palatial surroundings. Her family lives well, thanks to her parents' connections. They are friends of GOD. Or were. Now, they are mere acquaintances. Their standing lies in their past. They have long since been uninvited from the first ring's extravagant soirées and lavish dinners.

The Kerrs live in one of the grander manses of the first ring. Like the city itself, the house is a tall untouchable thing with large wings to either side, though such ornamentation would be too heavy to ever take flight. Inside, silver and glass crystal glimmer and float down the hallways, nearly blinding the house staff with their resplendence. And while the halls of the manse are glutted with luxurious furnishings and overelaborate statuary, the walls reach so high they feel eternally empty. The ceiling frescoes have not been closely examined for years. Certain beauty must sacrifice touch to retain its luster. GOD would consider those paintings highly immoral.

Gemma rises. She is a dot in the massive room. Even the furniture pieces are distant strangers to each other. She dresses herself in something appropriate. A light blue gown suit that seems to be trending among those her age, with a thin black necktie bound delicately. She thinks of wearing a bracelet, but decides against it. Too much ostentation can garner one the wrong attention. Those in the first ring can show their station in life, but it must never seem too prideful.

Approved by GOD, the large frescoes on her walls watch her every move as she dresses. These, she has been told since childhood, are great men her parents knew during the Revolution. Great men have exceedingly mediocre faces. Their vacant expressions show no judgment of her as she dresses. They show no interest at all. They are as lifeless as those she works with every day. Yet these are not the original paintings that once hung in this old home. Those depictions of giddy Passions and lusty gods in blushing pinks and sweaty reds had been covered decades before. Maybe centuries. How long since the world ended? We are not certain. But we knew some of those delightful spirits depicted in those naughty colors, and we can swear to you, those paintings were tame.

Ten house servants are on staff, though none except the old steward Rugal have been here longer than six months. They always offer to make Gemma breakfast, to be any use at all lest her mother add them to the unemployed, but Gemma smiles and says, "No, thank you." This has always been her way. Her father, of course, needs the servants. He is ill, and her mother cannot care for him alone. But Gemma thinks of herself as a resourceful young woman. She can get what she needs, and if she cannot get it, she does not need it. It is an admirable style of thinking for a privileged child of the first ring.

"Darling," her mother had once said with natural condescension, "let the servants help you. That's what they're here for."

"I can dress myself, Mama. And I can feed myself as well."

"Very well. But you are just adding to the unemployment problem. And we cannot simply just fling them off into some other far-off ring. The destitute are resolute in their destitution."

Her mother always looks upon Gemma with an expression of concern, albeit judgmental concern. Her eyebrows are as arched as cathedral spires.

This morning, Gemma leaves the manse without seeing her mother. The large front doors open on the bright sheen of the silver street. The clouds are a white and sherbet blend and are letting a bit more light shine through than they usually do. Gemma puts on her tiny circular sunspectacles and descends the steps of the manse to join the waking city.

The first ring is alive even in the early hours of the morning. People politely parade through the pristine silver streets, the women in expensive day gowns and the men in elegant suits and hats. The serenity has an uneasiness, though, as if it is all being held together by a threat. The parks of the first ring are so lush, given only the best fertilizer from farms all over the Immortal City, they rival any from the ancient days. People enjoy them, but one hears little proof of it, even if one listens closely. The laughter of children is stifled. Even babies are trained to cry less obtrusively in the first ring. Gemma remembers snippets of her dream last night. How the Passions played exuberantly on the hills of the Garden as she and the goddess Abrythnia walked. She had wanted to join the Passions in their play. To be a child and to truly play like a child… what a delight!

Gemma is on her way to the Glass Halls. She achieved her impressive position there because of her family's standing. It is not difficult work and mostly consists of filing.

As she approaches the steel stage where Colm Archer was made a show of just yesterday, she averts her eyes. It is already spotless again, ready for the next revolutionary. Gemma never met Colm Archer, but she had felt something for him. A kinship. Familiarity. Empathy? His face appeared in her dreams sometimes. It was just as well women were not allowed front row seats to the "relocation" ceremonies. Gemma could not have watched.

As she walks, she sees the spear of GOD's Tower rising from the navel of the city, blunted at the top by a wide saucer with many windows. From there, Gemma imagines, GOD saw Colm Archer's fall. At such a height, He could probably see past at least the first two rings. It is so lofty, sometimes hidden by the orange clouds, she wonders how it ever gets cleaned. But, of course, she knows workers brought in from the lesser rings clean the first ring at night. Without them, the city would decay. Still, it is an amazing feat.

As she walks the sidewalk, she hears a carriage slowing to her side. It is large, white, and as sugared and decorated as a pastry, with gold-winged angels on its four corners and led by two pure white mastiff ponies, equine as large and imposing as any woolly bull.

"GOD is watching you, sister," says a haughty voice from inside. It is a greeting but sounds like a warning.

Gemma sees Mags Hensil, a Sister of GOD, peering at her from a window. She has a large, fleshy face, painted white. Her eyebrows are shaved clean, making her violet eyes seem like barbs.

"Of course," Gemma replies with a smile. "He watches always."

The door to the carriage swings open. "Won't you join me?" asks the Sister, her voice all angles and edges.

Gemma knows better than to turn down a Sister of GOD, so she thanks her and climbs in. "The Glass Halls," Mags commands her driver.

Gemma smiles at the Sister, trying to hide her discomfort. To say Mags Hensil is a vision in white is an affront to visions. Mags Hensil is a spectacle. She wears the garish headpiece of her order, a fanning crown of silver and white gold inlaid with sapphires and diamonds. Anyone with a smaller head would find it difficult to support, but as the Grand Mother of the Sisters of GOD Mags's head was enormous.

"You're looking very pleasant today," Mags says. "You're walking a line. Almost prideful, in fact. You must be careful, sister. Vanity is dangerous."

"And yet we still want to make ourselves presentable in the sight of GOD, do we not?"

"Remember to whom you are speaking. I am a Sister. I know GOD's laws better than you, my dear." Her eyes tear off layers of flesh.

Gemma bows her head.

"I missed you at the relocation ceremony of Colm Archer, did I not?" the Sister says.

"I did not come." She looks for an excuse. "My father had a fit, and he needed my help. My mother does what she can with the servants, but sometimes it isn't enough."

"The poor dear." Mags smirks. "And good servants are in short supply. Well, then, I am certain it is forgiven. GOD is not heartless, as your father well knows. I'll expect to see you next time, though."

"Let us hope there isn't a next time, Sister. These relocations and executions are most grieving. They put a cloud over our already clouded lives."

"Indeed." A short, snobby word. "But they are necessary to rid the world of sinners. With Colm Archer gone, GOD's people are once again safe. Who can challenge GOD's will?"

Gemma speaks, though she does not know why. "Usker Lance."

The Sister's stony face falls to the floor. "Yes. I suppose there is him, that filthy degenerate. But do not fear. He, too, will be caught and seen to just like his... lover."

Gemma does not look at Mags in the eyes.

The carriage comes to a halt, and Mags kicks the door open. "You best get to work, Gemma Kerr." She nods to the Glass Halls. "May GOD watch you."

"And you, Sister."

Gemma bows her head and climbs out of the carriage. She feels Mags Hensil watching her from behind and GOD watching her from on high. She tries to hurry inside the building.

The Glass Halls are not glass at all, but cement paneled in a slick silver. This is the way of most buildings in the first ring. The banks, the schools, and all the Churches of GOD are designed so. They are to be beautiful but strong... but mostly beautiful.

Gemma works in the Citizenry Designation & Relocation Department, which is located on the sixth floor. She was aware of Colm Archer's relocation for a bit, but she did not deal with that particular file. The offices are compact, and its cubicles are set close to one another. Every worker has a duty to report any fellow worker not performing at their highest capacity. No one has ever reported Gemma. They fear her family's connections. She is uncomfortable with this. She has no friends, and she is lonely.

Gemma can see out into the first ring from her cubicle. She steals glances whenever possible. GOD's Tower rises high into the clouds this morning. Down below the Glass Halls, carriages and pedestrians swim in a quiet ballet.

Gemma's mind wanders as she works. She thinks her dream last night is silly. How can the city ever end? A final wall is incomprehensible. She would shrug the dream off if she had not been having similar reveries for years. She trusts them.

In her dreams, Abrythnia has told her of lands beyond the final wall. Great oceans and seas thought to be only fairy tales or long extinct. Knowing these things can get one sent to the ninth city. Beliefs are policed. Gemma had asked her mother about her dreams when she was a curious child. Her mother gave her the same concerned look as always and warned her to not worry on such matters.

"And don't ever bother me with something so ridiculous again. Make every word you speak have weight, my dear. That's the only way you'll survive. You are going to need to do some climbing in this life."

But to think on things is Gemma's nature. When she was around eight years old, Gemma found a remnant of the original frescoes on her bedroom wall. It was a tiny strip in the closet corner, revealing itself as the newer fresco began to peel away. She couldn't see much or even make it out with any clarity, but those colors! It had to have been a scene of joy and merriment. Of Passions and naughtiness. She moved her coats in front of the scene so it would remain a secret to all but her, and she never let any of the servants into her closet. She would dress herself from that day forward.

She reminds herself she has work to do. She turns her attention to the new file in her hands. We are beside her. We hold a conversation with her in her mind, though she thinks she is alone.

"Cayden Lothair," she says to us. "His writing is chicken scratch."

"He annoys you?" we say.

"It's difficult for me to interpret some of the things that he writes. He does it so quickly. As if he is scared he will miss something. It seems very gluttonous writing. He wants to take down everything."

"He is taking notes?"

"He is a ferryman. It's what he does. He keeps the peace. He finds those among us who have been corrupted and infected."

"Infected?"

"By whatever old illness still exists in the world. Aside from the odd pockets of plague that pop up here and there, the Immortal City has not known illness in decades."

"But what of your father? Is he not ill?"

Gemma looks up from the file. "Yes," she whispers. Then she looks to the paper again. It is palm-stained and crinkled.

"Is he not ill?" we repeat.

"I have no answer for why he is still alive. He's barely there at all anymore. He is a vacant space since he gave up his soul."

"Perhaps he is atoning."

Gemma reads the file, page by page, as carefully as she can. Cayden Lothair's script is indeed a mess. The words are connected lines of loops and bumps, many too small to decipher. To the side, he has written his notes at a slant and these are even smaller. It is as if this ferryman was not trying to simply write a report, but instead a biography of his subject.

"He sees some importance to them," we notice. "Who are they?"

"A father and son," she replies. "Gypsies. The father seems to be ill. The boy is a child around six or seven years old. A mute. They are to be picked up and taken to the ninth ring."

"Why? What have they done?"

Gemma flips through the pages. "It does not say they've done anything at all. Or maybe I've missed it. The writing is so small."

She thinks back to years before when she had taken a walk through the lesser rings. Her mother hated when she did this, taking off on her own to the most dangerous parts of the Immortal City. Gemma remembers seeing a child, a young boy amongst a gypsy clan. Serenity and quiet is not as prized a thing in the lesser rings as it is in the first, so she heard music aplenty. Joy among the wretches. The child, she remembers, played a flute with a gypsy band, and he was just as marvelous as the adults. He danced with the flute as an audience clapped their hands and laughed. It reminded Gemma of the scene of the Passions from her fresco, the color, the vibrancy even at night. The gypsy boy had a look of delight on his face. Gemma had so wanted to join in.

She shakes the memory from her mind and prepares to rewrite and categorize the file. She has faith things will work out for this father and his son. GOD wants only what is best.

"Are you certain?" we say.

"Yes. It will mean a better life for them. I am certain."

"A better life in the ninth ring among criminals and the wretched people?"

"At least they will have a permanent home," she says as she swallows some regret. "At least they won't be wandering."

We fade away. We cannot get through to her today.

HE SPEAKS HIS DREAMS ALOUD

A TEENAGE boy made of rags and dirt swerves and dodges through the busy street of a third-ring neighborhood, past shops of pottery and trinkets, under hung laundry and through groups of hagglers and angry old men with canes. He is chased by the ferrymen who have discovered the orphans and their hideout. He is the only one they have not caught. The others, both boys and girls as young as three and as old as sixteen, are already loaded into the death wagon, their hands tied to the bars. They are all crying for mercy.

The last orphan moves quickly this way and that. He is good at hiding and evading capture. He has hidden many years. But he is out of breath and slowing down. He glances about, searching for his next step. He took care of the younger boys and girls. He was a good older brother to them, and he liked the position. But he let them down. Somehow he became relaxed, not believing he could ever be caught.

He let down his guard and a ferryman who, no doubt, was hiding in the shadows followed him back to the hideout. Now they were all going to be carted off to the ninth ring. He would cry the first chance he got, but this is not the time for it. He says his apologies in a mantra as he runs: "I'm so sorry, boys. I'm so sorry, my sisters." He names each boy and girl specifically. He sees each small tear-streaked face. "I'm so sorry."

He has lost the ferrymen who were chasing him. He isn't certain how, but he's done it. He slows now and hides behind a large basket of damp clothing. He catches his breath. The people in the streets mill about, oblivious to him. He stops himself from breaking down into tears. His family, his brothers and sisters, are being carted away. He will never see them again. But he cannot think on it.

He cannot linger. He turns to run, but his face comes into immediate contact with the ferryman's chest, as if he had formed from the shadows. He is a street demon with deep soulless eyes. He has the smell of the obscurities, of stale or lost things.

"I'm sorry, boy," the ferryman says in a voice that carries no hint of emotion. "It's time you stopped running."

The boy begs, but his pleading falls as if on deaf ears. Cayden Lothair looks unmoved as the boy's wrists are tied, and he is tossed into the death wagon with the others. The children are on their way to the ninth ring.

We watch Cayden. He walks through the streets of the Immortal City ever mindful yet never fearful of the rules. Because that is what he is, after all. The rules are all he knows or remembers: the Law of GOD. His brown hair falls loosely around his broad shoulders, over his dark eyes so that he resembles an animal stalking its prey, head down but eyes up. He wears black leather boots and a long, faded leather coat. Hidden in the coat are the hook and the scythe every ferryman carries in case more deadly force is required. He prefers shadows to men, and he knows he is one of the best ferrymen the city has ever known. Even other ferrymen are cautious around him.

He nods to a young woman in an orange wrap as he stalks a lesser street of the third ring. She follows him to the ruin he temporarily calls his home, a flat on the second floor of a multileveled death trap. She does what he pays her to do. Nothing special. No noise or signs of any real affection. No signs of life at all. They are just going through the motions. A patterned existence. He pays her and she leaves.

He goes to the broken window, which looks out onto the street below. It offers a good view for what he has come here to do. The family who just recently lived here was quickly resettled so Cayden could have this view. A child's doll with a painted-on smile still sits in the corner. He pulls up a chair, swings his feet onto the desktop with a heavy thump, and keeps watch out the window. Across the street, he sees no sign of the man he has been assigned to watch. Good for him, Cayden thinks. A few more days—a few more hours, to be true—and he'll have to say good-bye to everything he ever knew. Let him have it.

In his travels as a ferryman, Cayden has observed an elegance to the older areas of the Immortal City that the first ring could never aspire to. The structures may be old and crumbling, they may be dirty and packed too full of squalor, but they have life in them. These places have been truly lived in. They are not the superficial edifices of the first ring. Cayden wouldn't live in the first ring if GOD ordered him to. Here in the lesser rings, where residences have been built into and onto each other

for centuries until parts of the city resembles wasps' nests; this is where
he feels most comfortable. There are shadows here. Give him the muddy
and polluted waters of the River Hung over the purified spill of the first
ring any day. The River Hung still sings of some purity, even if that is an
impossibility.

"Don't let GOD hear you think that," he says quietly.

Life in the lesser rings is so much more believable. The struggle
makes it so. The everyday struggle those in the first ring have forgotten.
Why, the first ring itself is even built on higher ground so they may look
down their noses at the others. A ramp leads down into the second ring
offering an easy processional out of the first for the privileged. Yet here in
the third, having something to eat at night can be cause for a celebration
during lean months. In many districts, the food is digestible at best.

"Yet, the worse the food," says Cayden, "the louder their shouts of
celebration."

What gets them through?

"Hope. That magnificent old bitch, Hope."

We had forgotten about her. She shows up in the strangest places.
And she is radiant.

Cayden watches the residence across the street, his face as solemn
as the great statue of Iol, which still stands, though maimed, in a fountain
of filthy water nearby. The father had been smart. He was getting very ill
and trying desperately to hide it. But gypsies are nomads and live their
lives in the open. There came a point when the father, named Aidan,
feared he could no longer hide his illness. Some non-gypsy folk took
pity on him and offered he and his son, Key, a place to hide in the bottom
floor of a towering heap. But that type of secret cannot be kept for very
long. Their whereabouts were discovered, and Cayden moved onto the
street to keep an eye on them. GOD needed proof of deceit. Proof can
discourage revolution.

Cayden sees the little boy's messy brown head of hair pop out
from inside the door of the heap. The boy, his face filled with wide-
eyed wonder and fear, looks around quickly, biting his lower lip. He is
a newborn fawn, watchful of the hunter. His father has taught him to be
cautious, the first lesson children learn here. Key sprints from the door,
quick and barely noticed by the crowd. Cayden has thought for some
days now the child would make an accomplished ferryman. The boy
goes darting through the streets and is soon lost to Cayden's sight. It

would be pointless to try to follow Key. He is a gypsy. He can easily slide through the cracks and holes no adult can see.

Cayden tried to follow Key once, but the boy knows the city better than any child Cayden has yet come across. He is immune to confusion, the mazes of built-upons offering him no problems at all. They seemed to move for the boy. Cracks in walls impossible to squeeze through even for him, opened wider so Key could slide through them. Key goes anywhere, does anything, for his father, bringing back food from as far away as the forbidden and supposedly hidden Shrine of Iol, where pilgrims leave daily breads and fruits in supplication.

Cayden waits in his apartment for the boy to return. He cannot wait outside. Aidan and those helping him would know something was going on. They know they are being investigated or else they would not hide. And while Cayden blends in well with the people of the lesser rings, a stranger is still a stranger and he cannot hide in shadows during the day.

The boy returns. It was a short sprint. Under his tattered shirt, he most likely carries a vial of medicine from one of the street doctors, paid for with anything from a piece of fruit to an old trinket. Gypsies all have their favored street doctors, usually one they distrust slightly less than the others. Still, Aidan and Key chose and trusted badly. This street doctor had talked very easily to Cayden. All he required was a few drinks.

Aidan is doing everything right. He's staying well out of sight and as quiet as air. If Key isn't picked up as an orphan, this life could go on for a while. At least until Aidan dies naturally. That is, if they had not already been discovered.

Cayden realizes, of course, he needs to swoop in and pick up the pair. It is his job. He is the bringer of death. He has already watched them longer than he should. GOD's good favor shines down on him for capturing the enemy and apostate, Colm Archer, but that will only last so long.

"And you don't want to get got by Queen Mags, do ya, boy?" he says to himself. "She's in the area, and you know how she loves a good ball loppin'."

ROSSA BOUADICA stands in the shadows of the doorway until the boy returns, her hands on her hips and her emerald eyes ever cautious. She is busty, her ample breasts serving as protection of a large and tender heart. Age has not dared touch her appeal or her figure. She has a cascade of long, red curls that are the envy of many a wigmaker.

She sways in the shadows. She knows when she is being watched. She has an intuition for it. Looking the way she does, it's a feeling she has had many years to fine tune. The streets are busy today. She hopes Key is careful. Many new strangers are about, and some of them are less than savory.

She has known the child from infancy. Rossa was a good friend of the boy's mother, Claire. Claire saved Rossa's life years ago from a back-alley rapist when they were younger. She killed the man. This, in turn, cost Claire her life in the five rings. The rapist was a man of GOD, many of whom travel to the lesser rings to satisfy their desires. Of course, they ran, bringing Aidan and Key with them to the backwoods of the third ring. But they were eventually caught, and Claire was carted off to the ninth. Rossa swore she would look after Aidan and the boy. She blames herself for Claire's death, for she was surely dead by now. She apologizes to Aidan whenever she sees him. Not with words, but with her eyes. Since that attack in the alley, Rossa has taught herself to fight.

She heads to the back of the heap, passing under leaky walls and foul stenches. She resides on the ground floor with her extended family and above her are miles of tenants and rotting history. Once she leaves the front kitchen area, the light in the home hastily diminishes. She cannot afford many candles, so she uses them sparingly. The way is best known by touch and smell. Her father's area smells of onions, her brother Frulu's space has more of a rotten-egg smell. She passes into a long, narrow hallway made of stone, then through larger rooms where members of her extended family rest. There are no children here. None but Key. Her line has nearly been wiped out. They are breathing their last and they blame her for this, for she has refused to bear any children.

She passes through hole-riddled curtains that divide one area of living from the next. The Immortal City has no privacy. Not really. But there is darkness, and there is dreaming.

She comes to the very back room of the house. It is the darkest and the most secret. It smells of illness. She lights the stunted candle that sits in the small cubby hole in the wall beside the doorway. Aidan is lying on the floor on a pile of blankets, as still as a sarcophagus.

"You are awake," Rossa says. She sees his watery eyes glisten.

"Aye, I'm feeling better today," Aidan replies in a tone that is not at all encouraging. "I donna feel as though there is as such a sizable monster on my chest as there usually be."

He rises to a sitting position, perhaps too quickly, and falls back down. Rossa rushes to him.

"Be careful, ya silly basterd," she says. "How will you recover if you treat yourself so? Just you rest."

"Dearest Rossa." He kisses her knuckles. "We both know there is little hope for any kind of recovery." He coughs and the echo travels from his chest until it fills the room.

"Hush," she says. "It is a flu. A bug. What do we do with bugs? We squish 'em."

"It is Death."

She knows this is the truth, so she does not protest. She merely bites her lip and brushes back his hair.

"Will you take care of Key when I am gone, Rossa? He needs a family. I do not want him to be an orphan, to be carted away."

"Hush." She puts her hand on his shoulder. "We have been family since his birth. I am his mother now. He will have a place with me as if he were my own child. We have discussed this before. Claire... she was my... sister."

Aidan smiles in relief and relaxes. "You are a kind woman, Rossa."

Rossa watches him. He was once a strong, stout man. Not what one would call handsome, but attractive in other ways. When Claire was taken, it nearly destroyed him, but in time he mended. Then he and the boy went out adventuring in the Immortal City until just recently when he came to her, asking for help. Aidan loved life when he was well. He loved food and music and bringing up the sun in the morning. Music he loved most of all. Now, covered in sweat, he was as close to death as Rossa had ever seen him. She feels his forehead, and he groans at the touch. The man is on fire. He'll burn to cinders.

The boy comes rushing into the room, breathing heavily and pounding on his drum. He pulls a small vial of medication from a pocket in his tattered shirt and hands it to Rossa, smiling with pride. His hope breaks her heart. He has sold his shoes to get his father this useless drug. She takes it and kisses him on the forehead.

"I'll go make you both something to eat," she says as she rises. "I'll cook this fine medicine into your father's meal so he won't even be able to taste it."

The boy kneels beside his father's pallet.

"Why don't you play something for him?" Rossa says, gesturing to the small drum wrapped around his shoulder. This is Key's only possession. His only toy. It was a gift from Aidan two years back, and the boy has worn it every day.

Key seems to delight in this idea.

"But not too loud, love," Rossa reminds him. "We don't want to wake the snovelfarks."

As she leaves the boy with his dying father, she hears the soft smacking of little hands on stretched animal pelt. It is not a random beat. The boy has real talent, and she hums a wordless lullaby as she walks to the kitchen. Rossa finds she is crying.

EVENING DESCENDS on the Immortal City. The street lanterns are lit. Key has taken his drum and is strolling the streets, looking for fun or trouble: frouble. His father seemed to enjoy the song Key played for him. This lifts the boy's spirits. He left Rossa's place with a smile. Rossa did not see him go. If she had, she would have stopped him. Especially at this hour.

Key taps on the drum with his index finger as he walks, looking in wonder at the sights around him. He sees jugglers with fire, lewd puppet shows, and graceful dancers in colorful rags. Mingling with the dusk, the smells of the city are more fragrant at night. Sweets are sweeter. They even smell sticky. Breads are carried steaming and fresh to tables, and meats cook in the open at small eateries his father could never afford.

He stops in front of a café to watch a young couple. They catch his eye because they seem such an odd pairing. The blondish man is very animated and very clean. He dresses in a sharp waist coat, a clean white shirt, and a top hat, and he smiles and gestures most flagrantly at times. He must be from the first ring. What he is doing here is anyone's joke. The other man, clearly a gypsy from his dusty attire, has his back to Key. His hair is thick and black, and he sits in a slouch with his arms folded on the table. The blond man clearly means to impress, but the gypsy merely mumbles in return. Key decides they are having an argument.

"We'll be happy there," the blond man says rather loudly. "We'll be safe. My new position in the first ring is going to be the best thing for all of us. I promise ya."

The dark-haired one mumbles something that chases the smile from his companion's face.

The blond man reaches for the gypsy's hand. "Gran will be well cared for. She'll want for nothing. She might even get better."

The gypsy jerks to attention, as if the statement was an accusation. He looks around to ascertain who, if anyone, heard it. Then he hushes the blond. Everyone knows being ill in the Immortal City is a sin.

Key has wandered too close to the café as far as the owner is concerned. The boy is shooed away with a broom. Before he leaves, the blond man sees him and gives him a wink, throwing him a large slice of bread from the table. Key catches it and grins. Frouble achieved. He runs off with the warm bread between his teeth. It is the best tasting bread he has ever had. He stores some in his shirt pocket to share with his father and Rossa.

The city at night is aglow. Campfires and lanterns line the streets. Key finds a gypsy band to watch. They play a lively number on stringed instruments and a flute as a lovely pair of girls dance in cheap silks enlivened by elaborate designs. Key does not wait for an invitation to join in. He merely begins beating his drum harder and in time with the sprightly music. The gypsies smile and encourage him. Key sits on the ground nearest the guitarist and plays along. There is much laughter and merriment in the dark when GOD is not watching. The music helps to drown out the rumblings of unfed stomachs.

They applaud Key and slap him on the back with mighty guffaws when the number is over. He enjoys their gratitude, their tousling of his hair, and their invitations to return the next evening. His smile brightens the night.

Yet he starts for home when he sees a woman watching him from the crowd. He cannot miss her. She steps right in front of him, a rotund white spirit. She is a Sister of GOD. The gypsies go quiet.

"Nice playing, my boy," she says. She looks about. "Where be your parents?"

Her words are kind, but her voice is tinged with rotten juices. The smile falls from Key's face as he takes a step back from her.

"Why do you look at me so?" she says. "I am no boogeyman. Do I seem like the boogeyman? Like the snovelfark?"

She drips venom all over him. He wants nothing to do with her acidity, yet she seems to crowd around him like a fat cloud. He feels closed in. Caught.

"Key!"

Rossa's voice rips the cloud apart.

"Key," Rossa says. She wears a shawl to cover her breasts. "I have been looking for you, child. You should not have gone out so late."

Rossa looks at Mags Hensil as if she knows who she is, though she has never seen her before this night. Mags's painted white face cracks.

Key runs to Rossa.

"You should keep a closer eye on the child," says Mags. "There be all sort of beasts about at night."

"Yes, Sister," Rossa says. She and Key turn and walk away. "You need to stay with me," Rossa says. "Do not wander. At least for a few nights. You hear me?"

He nods. No more trouble.

"Good boy," Rossa says. She ruffles his hair. His arms are wrapped around her waist. He wonders if the large, painted woman is still watching them.

MAGS HENSIL watches the redheaded woman leave with the child. Her face relaxes from its false smile to a more comfortable scowl. The gypsies are making her uncomfortable. She heads for an alleyway entrance and stands, waiting and watching.

"He is not an orphan," says Cayden, stepping from the shadows just enough to be heard by Mags, but not enough to be clearly seen.

Mags looks over her shoulder at him. "Lurking, are we?" she says. "He is not an orphan. That is true."

Cayden is a quiet wall.

Mags does not move to venture near him. "You've done well today. You've rid the city of some pests, I hear. The ninth ring will cleanse them of their sins."

"Thank you, Sister."

"It wasn't meant to be a compliment, boy. Just a fact. Here are a couple other facts. You need to bathe. I can smell that whore you had from here. And then you need to do your job, ferryman."

"Sister?"

"We have more than enough proof. Bring in the father and the child. This is not like with Colm Archer. You did not need to build a relationship with this man to gain his trust. Aidan and the child should have been tossed into the wagon days ago…" She watches her volume. She does not want anyone to hear her.

"Sister, I was only—"

"Get it done, ferryman!"

"Yes, Sister," he growls.

"Watch yourself, Cayden Lothair. One might begin to think you were developing feelings for the lesser folk and the sinners."

"I will bring them in, Sister, the father and the boy."

Mags chuckles. Her whole body shakes. "Boy? If that child is a boy, so am I."

Cayden steps closer. "Sister?"

"Anyone with the sight of GOD can see it as plain as day. That child may prefer to live as male, but I have no doubt he is a third-sexer."

WE FIND interest in the pair the child saw at the café. They may be of some importance to us. We follow them home.

Duncan and Lawl lie in bed, wrapped in each other's arms. Duncan is the blond one. He is stream-lined and clean-cut, his back ever straight and proud. He is a trusting man. Lawl is shaggier of hair and attitude. He slouches and is often incoherent. He is darker in every way, both seeable and unknowable. But they are of one soul. This one night every two weeks, they can lie together and find bliss. They meld. Every night until their next engagement is fitful.

Duncan has a place of his own in the second ring. Tonight, however, they sleep in Lawl's cramped, two-room compartment in the third. It is high up and pushed deep inside the guts of a stinking ancient structure of fanged latticework and cackling stairs. Lawl's aunt Gran, his only living relation, sleeps in the other of the two rooms where the chamber pot is located. On the days Gran is feeling better and wants to be outside, Lawl helps her through the maze of rooms and hallways to one of the frail hanging-tooth balconies that look out over the city. It is dangerous for her to be seen, but she needs fresh air from time to time. Gran's feet have not touched true earth in many years, though. Gran is Lawl's full-time job.

Duncan kisses Lawl gently. Lawl is half asleep. "Think about it, won't ya?" Duncan says.

"Think about what?" Lawl says, his eyes still closed. Lawl mumbles. He does not space his words. He barely moves his lips. That is how he speaks, as if he is uncertain of anything he says, so he does not want to speak it too forcefully. Duncan finds this endearing.

"About what we were talking of earlier at the café. About you moving to the second ring to live with me. Gran, too."

Lawl opens his eyes. The sparse candlelight allows Duncan to see the wells of tender darkness there.

"I'll be making more than I've ever made now that I'm working at the Glass Halls. Cleaners are well paid, ya see. And who knows? Maybe we can get a place closer to the first ring. A nice big place with a courtyard for Gran. And you… why, you've got a great mind for makin' things, for fixin' broken things. Maybe you could open a business from our house." He is all smiles when he speaks his dreams aloud.

Lawl brings his hand to Duncan's cheek. "You're a dreamer, love," he says. "I love you for it, but the laws of society don't allow movement like that. Not anymore. You grew up better off than me. Maybe you can dream. But I can't afford to. It would break my heart."

Duncan does not like such talk. His eyes moisten with tears. "I'll get us a new life," he says. "You wait and see. We'll figure it out."

"Gran is sick," Lawl says "The fact that we have not reported her ourselves makes us unholy sinners against GOD. Living here far from the first ring, we can get away with it. But we cannot move any closer. They'd throw her in a death wagon."

Duncan has been through this argument before. He knows the danger of being with Lawl, but to be without him is a horrifying, unnatural thought. They kiss tenderly and embrace even tighter.

Gran awakens in the next room, screaming from a nightmare. Lawl goes to her. Duncan knows Lawl does not see it as a burden to care for his aunt. She is family, and she raised him. He feels shame for it, but sometimes at night when his arms are empty, Duncan thinks it might be better if Gran would die. He shuts his eyes on the thought.

He forgot to mention to Lawl that he saw some ferrymen in the area today. He wonders how he could have forgotten such a thing. But it is late, so he decides he'll tell Lawl of it in the morning.

We appear in Duncan's dreams tonight. He is high on scaffolding, cleaning the Glass Halls on a night with the moon hung low and full, as big and luminous as he has ever seen it. Not a single cloud is in the sky. The moon distracts him from his work. He seems to be the only cleaner, the only being, in the entire city. He looks around in awe. He is higher than he has ever been. As high as GOD's Tower. The stars wink at him.

And my, he can see so well. For miles and miles. Nothing moves. The city seems abandoned and pristine. And then, across the rings, farther than any human has the ability to see, Duncan sees the beauty of the Garden of the Passions. He sees the moonlit rivers curving through the green hills and past the barrows. Red and gold flowers climb the columns of the temples, and lilacs crown the statuary of the Passions.

He shivers. We appear to him as Abrythnia's twin brother, Brachnol, the god of strength, naked and virile. Our penis, ever erect, points to victory. In ancient times when gods walked the world, men could not look upon him for too long, else they would dissolve into fatal erotic self-satisfaction and forget to do anything but dream of him and spill their seed on the ground.

Duncan sees another stand beside us in the Garden, a human woman of dark skin and dressed in a white gown. He has seen her before at the Glass Halls. She works inside the building, and she arrives in the morning just as he is leaving. She is one of the few who has ever acknowledged him with a greeting. He does not know her name, but we think he will. She is Gemma Kerr.

DRAGGED DOWN THE DARK

IT IS morning again. Two days later. The Kerr household is about to receive a visitor.

Gemma is preparing once more to head to the Glass Halls. Her mother Esther has been up for hours, but has yet to make it in to see her husband in his separate room. He takes a while to wake. Sometimes he does not wake at all.

Bana Kerr is ill. He has not seen the outside world in years. The thick red velvet curtains are perpetually drawn shut over the stately large windows. The light hurts him, causes his eyes to burn. He wears overlarge sunspectacles even in bed. He is layered in clothes and blankets so he does not catch chill. Hooked up to a machine—a gift from GOD, which operates by His Power—that does his breathing for him, he has not the mobility to travel outside the manse even if he wants to. His illness has made him extremely pale. Or rather, instead of skin, he has a thick layer of transparency. The wise doctors tell him this is due to his lack of a soul. Like so many in the powerful echelon of the Immortal City, Bana has had his soul bled from him, "retracted," per GOD's request. Souls get in the way of progress, it is said.

Esther gives the door a polite knock and enters. Bana and Esther have not slept in the same room for some years. Esther, holding a lit candle, approaches her husband slowly. A short maid follows her with a white washbasin. Esther is a tall woman, stoic and stern. She does not walk. She glides like a plotting specter. She wears a long, dark, violet gown. It is long-sleeved and covers all from her neck to the obedient train behind her. Her hair is dark but streaked with gray and piled atop her head in perfect artistic mounds. She is a formidable woman, and even the cavernous bedroom she has just stepped into seems to shrink at her entrance. This perception is at odds with Bana, whose very bed envelops him.

Esther takes her seat on the settee beside the bed. The candle is placed on the stand. The maid, a perpetual annoyance named Duana, begins washing Bana. Esther takes one of her husband's gloved hands.

His own breaths are barely audible beneath the breathing apparatus and the heaving of the maid.

"Must you carry on so?" Esther hisses at Duana.

The maid swallows and tries holding her breath as she washes Bana. This only makes matters worse as Duana begins grunting and wheezing for air.

Esther rolls her eyes. "I have had enough!" she says. "Leave! Do it later, you silly girl."

The maid backs away quickly, leaving the washbasin, and scurries to the door, closing it behind her.

"You would think," Esther says, "that we have been through enough that we needn't worry about incompetent servants."

Servants have been the bane of Esther's existence for some time. It all started when that woman brought her bastard child to the door, claiming Bana was the father and that she wanted to work for them. But Esther decides not to think on this matter. It will only upset her.

Bana is perfectly still. He is awake, however. Esther can tell from his machine's breathing pattern.

"Or maybe we haven't," she says. "Maybe we're just getting started. Oh, Bana. Things have gone so badly for us faster than I ever thought possible. What happened to this new world you and I were going to help usher in? That was the whole point of buying the election, wasn't it? And the revolution afterward. It seemed so fine at first. Then you do… this… to yourself, and soon after, you get the plague. Yet the decisions we made all seemed right at the time."

She squeezes his hand. "They were the right decisions, weren't they?" she pleads, gritting her teeth. "I need you to tell me they were right."

Bana merely grumbles, and she lets go the grip on his hand.

"Sorry, dear." She resets herself. "So sorry. Sometimes, here all alone, I am left to my own thinking for far too long. I haven't left the manse in days. But I worry for Gemma. What will He do to her when you and I are no longer here? She will be of no use to Him at all. As it is, He is waiting for the two of us to pass away in some hopefully non-mysterious manner. Or at least, he wants me dead. You, I'm not so certain."

She hears a timid knock at the door.

"What is it?" Esther shouts. "I'm with my husband."

"Yes, m'lady," the maid says, "but you've a visitor is all."

The door is pushed open abruptly, and a wall of a man walks in. The maid scuttles in after him.

"Sorry, m'lady," Duana sputters, red-faced and white-knuckled. "He wouldn't stay put in the parlor like I asks him."

Esther holds up her hand. "It's fine." Her voice cannot mask her irritation. She stands to greet her guest.

"Senator General Hegart." Esther tries a smile, but he will not believe it. He will not even appreciate the effort. "How wonderful to see you. It's been too long since your last visit."

"A mere month, my lady," the senator says. His words are drowned by the excess saliva that falls from his mouth into a fine handkerchief he holds. The senator general, like Bana, was struck down by the plague, but he has recovered for the most part. The drooling is a problem, though. He is not a handsome man. Perhaps he was once. Esther cannot remember. But now, dressed in his heavy, black overcoat and loud, angry boots, his dark spiked hair at odds with his pale flesh, he is the very picture of Death. His black pupils and sharpened teeth—each one whittled to a tiny dagger—only add to the nightmarish effect. But he is a man of strength. He can shadow the sun when he gets in a rage.

"What can I do for you, Senator General?" says Esther.

"Nothing, my lady. Nothing at all." His polite voice is even more unsettling than his appearance. "I came to check on the good Senator General Kerr." He glances at the bed and lets a stream of saliva drain to the floor. "I see he is doing well."

Esther grabs the senator general's elbow and guides him away from the bed toward the door. "Yes, well, I apologize that I can't offer you a seat, Senator General," she says. The maid bows her head as they pass her. "But we have such a day ahead of us. Such a busy day."

"My lady," he protests, "I am only here because GOD is concerned for your husband's welfare. Bana holds a special place in GOD's heart."

"And now you can tell GOD no. Bana has not died." At the chamber door, she looks the senator general in the eye. "And neither have I."

"May I remind you, my lady, that GOD does not care so deeply for everyone. You are fortunate to have His attention."

"Fortunate?" She laughs. "And may I remind you, Senator General Hegart," she says, her voice the hush of weeds, "of what Bana and I have had to do to put GOD where He is."

"Do you regret it?"

"I regret nothing. I only ask for a little respect when you come to my home, you slobbering wreck of a man!"

His eyes are blazing.

"Duana," she calls for the maid. "Show the senator general to the door."

The maid hurries past them, but she stops as she sees Gemma standing at the top of the stairs that spiral down through the manse. She has been standing there for some time, listening.

"Is something wrong, Mother?" Gemma says.

"The senator general is just leaving. He came by to see your father. Wasn't that kind of him? Now he must go. The ferrymen can't look after themselves, after all."

The senator general ignores Esther. He has grown a smile as he looks on Gemma. Esther takes a deep breath.

"How lovely you have become, Lady Gemma," the man says. "How very pretty."

Gemma says nothing in reply. The air is fragile all around them.

The senator general glances at Esther, then to the maid Duana. Esther grasps the deviant in him.

"Come, Duana," he says. "Show me to the door."

Esther keeps her eyes on him as the tiny maid leads him away. Gemma joins her mother by the chamber door.

"I do not like that man, Mama," says Gemma.

"Hush, dear," Esther replies. "It's impolite to say such truths aloud, even if they are shared by those around you."

Esther looks at the outfit Gemma wears today. "You resemble a man, darling," she says as she heads back to Bana's side. Gemma follows her. "The bow tie, the blazer. It's not feminine. That style of dress will get you in trouble if you're not careful."

"What was the senator general here about, Mama?"

"Do not worry, dear." Esther takes her seat on the settee again. Bana has fallen asleep. "That man can be contained. I've dealt with foes far more cunning than him. And far more attractive as well. Your father and I were revolutionaries, after all. Hegart was only an underling in that fight."

"You were heroes."

"Indeed." The word troubles her in the context. "We have seen and done things the poor senator general can only dream of. Did I ever tell you about the hot air balloon ride Bana and I once took?"

Gemma smiles. "No."

"It was after the Revolution, before the plague, and we were assigned to take to the air and see just how much of the Immortal City survived and how much was scorched beyond repair. At that time, the balloonists had not been outlawed yet. In fact, I still know a few of them, though they have not flown since."

"What did you see, Mama?"

"I saw the city, of course. Not all nine rings of it, though. It stretches so far, you can't see everything. That's what struck me most years later." Esther stares into the air. "The streets that had been set alight by the raids glowed red hot, and the waters, too. The River Hung was filled with fiery debris. It resembled the internal workings of a body, veins and blood vessels and the like. It was quite beautiful in a horrid way. As the rivers of flame stretched below, the fires were growing. They grew on and on until they vanished from my sight. It was as if I was witnessing a…"

"…virus."

"And then came the plague, not two years later."

As a Sister of GOD, Mags Hensil has a duty to report any suspicious characters or questionable gatherings to the senator general. This is not a task the Sisters of GOD take lightly. They take nothing lightly. They are ever diligent, searching out the ghettos and lesser rings for sinners: the ill, the illegitimates, the orphans and unwanted, the unwed mothers, the same-sexers and third-sexers. Anyone who goes against the plan of GOD. The Sisters are harsh and trust rumors to be true, for the world is filled with depravity and sickness.

Once a week, the coven of nine Sisters reports its findings to Senator General Hegart, who then talks to GOD about what he has been told. GOD and GOD alone decides from His Tower which sinners are the most in need of punishment and to what severity. Nothing is done without His approval.

This very morning, the nine Sisters of GOD stand before Senator General Hegart. They are positioned in a Holy triangle in front of the senator general's large, black desk, Mags Hensil at the apex in her jeweled cowl. The Sisters are clothed in their Robes of Salvation. Like Mags Hensil's own, these are long and white, hiding any form. Unlike Mags, no jewelry or gems are allowed on the robes of the under-Sisters. They wear flat, wide headpieces with thick white veils tumbling from all sides so their faces are never clearly seen. Under the veils, they wear oval-shaped sunspectacles not only because of the glare of the sun on the silver city streets, but to avoid being blinded by the light of GOD so near his presence.

The senator general's hall is the remnant of a large, spiraling cathedral near the base of GOD's Tower. The church is no longer His house; He has evolved beyond it. Hegart sits in front of a large, mournful window of painted white glass, so when the Sisters look in his direction, they see an awe-inspiring giant silhouette. He is the Mouth of GOD, after all. His features should not be seen when speaking GOD's own words.

After the Sisters' responsibility is finished, they bow their heads and say in accord, "GOD is watching." Senator General Hegart rises and takes the list of sinners to GOD. The Sisters wait with their heads bowed, quietly, patiently, for an answer. Sometimes they have had to wait entire days. But not today.

"The old woman in District 56 of the third ring," says the senator general on his return. "She is called Gran. She is not only ill, but a third-sexer as well. Good work in finding her. She has befouled our air for too long. The gypsy family of three squatting in District 49 as well. And in District 53 of the third ring, the flesh-peddler and whore who is looking to end her pregnancy…"

He names many others. The macabre shopping list takes an hour. He excuses the Sisters and they depart.

"GOD is watching."

He uses a string of ferrymen to get the sinners list to Cayden Lothair in the third ring. They are much quicker than the Kingdom Guards and know how to slide through shadows with secrets. Cayden is in his run-down dwelling with five other ferrymen now. They are not friends. They do not speak. They are readying themselves for what they have to do. They hear a knock at the door, and the carrier slips the list inside. Cayden reads the names. He says "Gran," "Dunbar," "Duff," "Orna," and so on, each with an address following the name. Sinners. He will deal with them.

First, however, he must see to the father and the son.

AIDAN WILL not make it through the day. Rossa is sure of this. His night was fitful and filled with hallucinations. Rossa heard him call for Claire a number of times. She heard his whispered conversations with her, as if Claire were sitting on the end of his pallet. Rossa almost believed she was comforting Aidan, helping him to prepare for the next plain.

We could not see Claire. If she was there, she kept herself hidden from us. Some do. But then, we cannot see some things.

Rossa has many thoughts on her mind. She worries how she will get Aidan's body out of their home once he has passed. She will need to find a trustworthy outertaker. That will be an ordeal. She has but the boy to help her. She worries someone in her own household has told the ferrymen of her dealings. Everyone has a price, and her family lives together for necessity, not love. Her brother Frulu has been acting most peculiar, keeping close to the boy when before he wouldn't deign to be in the same room. But most of all she is worried for the child, for Key. He has a gentle heart. She does not want him to see his father die. She decides not to tell him of his father's approaching death, but instead this new day tells him to play his father a morning song on his drum.

"Your father… he's asked it of you, boy," she says, forcing a smile.

Key looks at his father, feels the sweat-soaked face with his little hands, and looks up to Rossa with some doubt.

Rossa puts her hand on Key's head. "Play, child," she urges with a whisper. "He can hear you."

Key plays his drum, but Aidan does not move. Rossa sees the concern in the child and hears it in his playing. His song has no mirth, no playfulness. Her own smile finally gives up and dies. Morning song, mourning song. He stops after a minute to stand and stare at his father. The candlelight is giving the room a funerary ambience. Rossa does not like this.

"Here, child," she says, taking Key's shoulders and turning him to face her. "Go get me some bread from the market." She takes a coin from her pocket and places it firmly in the child's hand. "Your da will be hungry when he wakes up."

Not long now, she thinks. She truly hopes it was Claire last night. She forces herself to believe it.

Key stares blankly at the coin in his hand for a moment, then looks to Rossa. Her big eyes plead. She wants to apologize, but what for?

"Hurry home," she says, pushing the boy out of the dying man's presence. "Don't ya dawdle. Just get the bread and come on back, ya hear?"

The boy walks away with his drum, head down. He is consumed by the darkness in the house. He knows.

Rossa wants to say something to lift Key's spirits, but nothing has been able to lift anyone's spirit for years. Every day has shackles. Every day is weighed down by a nauseous sense of dread, an orange sky, and an angry GOD. Yet this day, it feels even worse. There is a nervous bad excitement. From the doorway, she looks back at Aidan. They are all in danger with him here.

"He might as well be dead, foolish gal."

She hears a muffled cough and she turns. Frulu stands in the dark of the hallway. His face is in shadow, but his eyes glisten with… something. She realizes it now. Aidan and Key have indeed been betrayed. You cannot break an already broken heart, but her stomach sinks, and she wants to kill her brother. She hopes Key does not listen to her, that he does not hurry home. She hopes for his sake, he stays well away. For she knows now what is coming. And who.

KEY IS walking slowly to the market, as if his bare feet are tied together by invisible strings. He knows something is wrong. He knows Rossa is not being honest with him about his father. His drum hangs at his side. He mindlessly plays with the coin in his hand, turning it over and over between fingers. He keeps his eyes on the ground. Key doesn't want to buy bread. He wants to be with his father. To play for him and make him smile.

He looks over his shoulder as he continues to walk through the morning throng of people. He notices a strange man following and keeping an eye on him. The man is watching him like Rossa's brother, Frulu, does. Any other person might not have given the man two thoughts, but Key is a gypsy, and gypsies are taught to be ever watchful. They have a second sense… and a third and a fourth just in case that one fails them.

Key starts walking faster. The man stays with him. The boy's heart speeds up along with his feet. He is dodging quickly through buyers and sellers, easily passing between them. They hardly notice him. He sees a second man over his shoulder. He cannot get a good look at this one. He stays in the shadows under tarps and roofs, yet he is more terrifying than the others. He moves without seeming to move, as if surfing the shadows. These are ferrymen.

Distracted, Key suddenly runs into a woman in a long, orange gown. One of the local prostitutes. He has seen her before across the street. She has a pleasant smile and smells of flowers.

"Are you okay?" she says.

But she does not wait for a response. Key understands the absolute fear on her face as she surely sees the ferrymen behind him. She wraps a golden shawl over her mouth and moves very quickly away down a side street. Key follows her, but then he scampers up a set of rickety steps he has used many times before while running from bullies or venders. He races up the steps into a building, not looking behind him. He is passing through flats and hallways inhabited by others. They keep yelling at him, calling him names, but he does not slow down. He only wants to get back to Rossa's to be with his father.

He leaps from a window in a bedroom wherein a young man is romancing a young woman and onto a tarp. Rossa's place is in view. The ferrymen have stopped pursuing him. He must have lost them after he turned into the alley. Perhaps they were not chasing him after all. Key is breathing heavy, cradling his drum like a baby, as he watches the street below. He sees four more ferrymen approaching Rossa's like hungry dogs. Key wants to scream. He wants to bang his drum and make a ruckus, but something in him will not allow that. We are glad for this.

Rossa comes out of the heap onto the threshold. She looks defiant and proud. Her hands are on her hips, her chest is out, and her mouth is a straight line. One of the four ferrymen is in her face. He says something. She does not move. A crowd is gathering. He says something more. Key cannot make out the words. Again, Rossa says nothing.

In a blink of Key's eyes, Rossa is on the ground. The ferryman strikes her again. His brutal blows have no passion or emotion. She yells something hateful to him as blood flows from her lips. Key is crying from the tarp, covering his mouth so he does not make a sound.

A third strike across the face. The crowd disperses in gasps of dismay as a large black wagon with dark angels of GOD adorning each corner pulls up in front of the door to House Bouadica. The horses are frothing.

THE FERRYMAN pulls Rossa into the dimly lit heap by her hair. She is fighting and screaming, but her family is not coming to her aid. Instead, they all bow as if in supplication to the four ferrymen who bring an even deeper darkness to the place.

"We only want the gypsies," says the lead ferryman, a man with raven black hair and dark skin. He speaks without any emotion to his voice. "The man and the child. They are sinners against GOD. We do not wish to harm anyone, but this woman forces our hand. Where are the sinners?"

Rossa is kicking and screaming. Blood runs from her mouth and nose, tears from her eyes. "Don't ya say a damn thing!" she warns.

Her brother gives her a disdainful look and steps forward. "I'll show you," he says. "The father be in the back room. The child, I do not know. He left a bit ago, I think to the market."

Rossa wishes death upon her brother. Her ancient relations could draw on the power of the gods and passions, and she wishes she could summon said power to cut Frulu into pieces on the spot.

They drag her down the dark hall to just outside Aidan's room and pull her to her feet. Her arms are held behind her back by a ferryman. She sees through the darkness Aidan sprawled on the floor. At first she thinks this is the ferrymen's doing, but then she discerns the truth of it and feels a sad relief. Aidan heard the commotion and reached the threshold of the room before collapsing. Frulu stands over him, and a ferryman crouches at Aidan's side. The ferryman feels for Aidan's pulse.

"He is dead." He rises and walks over to Rossa. "Where is the child? He is an orphan now."

Rossa grins. "So, he's died before you could wheel him off, eh? What a pity. Yer sweet GOD'll be heartbroken."

The ferryman tilts his head. "Where is the child?"

"Leave him with me. He is mine. He will not be a motherless orphan."

She is expecting to be hit again, but there is a scuffle behind her. Frulu suddenly points wildly and cries, "That's 'im! That's the boy!"

Rossa turns, and the expression on Key's face at the sight of his father is enough to let loose all the tears she is holding.

Frulu races past Rossa and the ferrymen toward the boy.

And with her scream, Rossa cracks the plaster in the walls. "Run, Key!"

Key takes off like a blaze of lightning. A ferryman takes from his coat a cold, metal scythe and unfolds it. He swings, meaning to hook the boy with it, but instead tears a gash in the pelt of the drum. Frulu grabs the child's arm. As Key struggles, the scythe rips through the drum as well as Frulu's arm, sending it flying into the rest of the prostrate, huddled family Bouadica.

Rossa's heart leaps. The boy will get away! Key runs out into the streets as they throw her to the floor. The ferrymen follow the boy, leaving Rossa and her family behind. Her brother is howling, his arm lying limp on the other side of the room where his horrified family tossed it. Rossa gains the strength to get up and run into the street after Key. The ferrymen are gone, as is their death carriage. But more importantly, Key is nowhere to be seen.

Rossa looks around for any sign of the child. She knows most of his watch posts and hideouts, and he is gone. She will look for him more thoroughly when she is certain she herself is not being watched. The boy is a gypsy. He has the wits to survive on his own until then. She hopes.

She is turning to head back inside the heap. She must deal with her traitorous brother and collect her thoughts. She is in tremendous pain and shaking badly, but she sees a man in the shadows across the street. She wipes the blood from her face with the back of her hand and puts her hands on her hips. She stares this mysterious figure down. Another ferryman no doubt, but not one from inside the heap. A large caravan passes between them, and when it has gone, the man has disappeared.

THE YOUNG prostitute Orna is naked in the strange, dark room. Her orange gown hangs from a meat hook on the wall like dried beef. The room is too dark to see the street doctor to whom she was referred, but he greeted her when she entered the doorway in the back alley. She was not certain at first she had found the right place. She wondered if even an ersatz doctor's office shouldn't have more light.

"You're Orna?" he said from some secluded corner.

"Yes," she replied, trying to see a form or figure.

"Disrobe. See those pills on the table? Take 'em. I'll be with ya shortly."

She did as she was told. She has done this dance many times in bedrooms and alleys across the city.

That was an hour ago. Now she sits on the cold metal table shivering and naked, shielding her breasts from the dank chill in the room. She shakes, not just from the surroundings, but from the memory of what happened earlier today, after that small boy ran into her. She saw a ferryman, and a familiar one at that, named Cayden. He has been her client for a few weeks now and has seen every inch of her body. But never before had he looked at her like that. Like prey. Like he was a predator in the shadows. Orna had not wanted to take him on as a client. He scared her, as well he should. Ferrymen threw workers in her line of work into death wagons without qualm. But he offered her more coin than she had ever seen.

That look in his eyes. Did he know what she was planning to do?

She cannot be blamed. This is the first of these procedures she will ever have done. She has been with child once before, and it was brought to term. When the baby was born, the child had a delicate heart-shaped birthmark on her right cheek. Orna sold the little girl to a good family, she thought. It broke her heart to do it, though.

Then one day, after a particularly rough client, she stumbled into a backstreet gutter, aching and injured. Her concern with her own health melted away, for beside her lay a pale, lifeless baby with the shape of a heart on its cheek.

This world, Orna now believes, is no longer meant for children. It is hardly suitable for adults.

The pills she was told to take are making her feel light-headed and dizzy. She does not like this. She rises from where she is sitting on the old apothecary table, but nearly falls from vertigo.

"Doctor?" she calls out. "Doctor, I don't feel well."

She doesn't hear an answer. Her vision blurs.

She wonders if he's even there. She has already paid his price by third party. It was everything she had, all the money Cayden had given her. If this doctor has played the scoundrel, she is ruined. She doesn't have the coin left to make an appointment with someone new, and raising a child would mean death and starvation for them both.

Orna keeps to the walls of the dark and drab office as she continues calling for the doctor. She grows weaker and more disoriented with each step. Almost at the door, she is doubled over so far, she is nearly crawling. She can see the glow of light, but she falls to the ground.

She looks up, frantic to get out of this place. As the room spins, she is touched by shadow. Three robed figures are blocking the door, their hands folded in front of them. "GOD is watching you," says one.

"Sisters of GOD!" Orna screams as she tries to edge backward and away.

An arm locks around her neck and pulls her to her feet.

"Disgusting perversion!" the voice says. "Crawling around naked like a shameless whore. And wanting to murder your unborn child, too. Your sanity has escaped you, but we will set it right."

Orna sees the blurry image of another figure step in front of her. She cannot hold her head up.

"Orna Taith." It is Cayden. She knows the voice. "You have been found guilty of sins against GOD. You will now be taken to the ninth ring."

Orna tries to scream, but she cannot. The Sister's hold around her throat is too tight. *Cayden! Help me! Cayden, please help me!*

The Sister releases Orna. Before the girl falls to the ground, stronger arms catch her. She is falling under, into a sleep where she is half-awake. She can hear what is happening around her, but she cannot react. Orna is brought into the light. Her eyes squint as she sees the Angels of GOD on the four corners. They will judge her now as she is thrown into the death wagon.

LAWL IS headed home to Gran when he is nearly run over by a death wagon. The ferrymen are about. He has no doubt that if he had not stepped aside, the carriage would not have stopped and some poor sod would spend the day scraping his body off the road. He looked into a ferryman's eyes once, years ago when they took his neighbor away. That was when he knew how GOD steals one's soul: straight out of the eyes. There is no soul in those depths. They are drained of color and vitality.

He hurries through the streets with his prize, his stained burlap bag o' tricks holding doodads and whatnots like fire sticks and magnifiers. Today, he found some metal scraps and wires in the trash heaps and gutters around the district. He is working on an idea. He has many.

The ferrymen have him concerned. He runs up flights of stairs that zig and zag like the lines of a madman's drawing. He leaps over a couple of homeless old men who have taken refuge from the city in the stairwells. When he gets to the apartment, he calls for Gran. She is not there. Both rooms are empty, and she is not hooked up to the machine Lawl designed for her, the one which feeds her pain medication when she needs it. He is starting to panic. He puts his bag o' tricks on the bed and hurries out of their dwelling, down the long hallway of the heap. He passes many people, but dares not ask any of them if they have seen Gran. Most pay no heed to him anyway. They are content to deal with their own stinking miseries.

He finally finds her on the balcony. She stands alone, her white night shirt fluttering in the breeze, the orange sky threatening to go red above her. He sighs in relief. She looks like an angel overlooking the city from one of the forbidden books Lawl has seen. He stands beside her.

"My my! You are breathing heavier than me, love," she says. "Did I worry you?"

Her voice is a tiny, breakable thing. Like candy.

"There are ferrymen in the district, Gran," says Lawl, streaming his words together without a breath. "I was concerned…"

She lays her hand on top of his on the railing. "I'm still here. They havena got me yet. I'm feelin' good today." Then she smiles. "Or goodlier, I guess." She giggles at her made up word. This makes Lawl grin. Gran was a teacher once, many years ago when there were still a few schools left.

"I'm a bit amazed you had the strength to get out here by yourself," Lawl says.

"Me too!" She laughs and smacks the railing. "But I did it. Aye, I did. It took me near forever. But I did it. That big metal machine you put together for my pain meds is aidin' me quite a bit, darling baby boy."

Lawl has not been a baby boy in over thirty years.

"But you need to be careful, Gran. We don't know who we can trust. Neighbors turn on each other these days. We've seen it. Aye, we've seen it too much."

"I know, boy. I just wanted to feel the wind on my face this mornin'." She breathes in as deeply as she is able. "It's an obstructed wind, what with this city grown so damned tall, but it's still sweet."

"Was the Immortal City ever anything but damned tall?"

"Aye. When your daddy and me was kids, it wasn't so big and clumsy as this." She points to the west. "Way off over there, in another ring," she says, "in another time, there was a garden. Prettiest thing ever seen. It was an old relic of a place even then. There was hills and streams and big bloomin' flowers the size of your head. Me and your daddy used to play in it all day. We was pirates and Passions. The architecture of the city watched us, but only from a distance. There are places in the Immortal City GOD has not yet gotten His hands on."

"Sounds nice, Gran. I'd like to see it."

"You should go there one day."

They look at one another and silently acknowledge the hopelessness of that comment. The magic in the air is blown away like dust.

"Come on," Gran says. "Let's head in. I'm gettin' a chill."

Lawl takes her hand, and they shuffle in together.

"When do you see your sweet Duncan again?" she says. "Is he coming over tonight?"

"No, Gran. I won't see him for a week."

"You miss him, don't ya?"

"Aye, I miss him somethin' awful, Gran."

"Aw, that's the pits, darling baby boy. That's the real honest pits."

Lawl wishes he could see Duncan this moment. He wants to tell him of the ferrymen. Of Gran getting up by herself and walking to the balcony. But a week. He has to wait a whole week to say a word to him about any of it.

GOD'S POWER

WE HAVE watched her walking all night through the passageways of the derelict and deranged, past the possessed and dispossessed. Through heavy shades of anger and hate. Now it is morning, and Key is still ever present in her mind. He is all that keeps her going, keeps her safe. He is a glow around her as bright as determination and as stubborn as that bitch named Hope. Rossa Bouadica is now determined to make it to the first ring before the close of this day. She has something to do; she has something to say.

She turns her head every time she hears a child laugh. She hopes it is Key, but that idea is foolish. Key has never laughed, at least not vocally. The child is a mute. He is lost to her forever in the frustrating mazes and maddening towers of the Immortal City. He has been eaten whole by the walls. Walls that will never give him up to her.

She walks, stumbling often. She sustained many heavy bruises from her own family after the ferrymen had left. She had gone back into the heap to see to her sobbing brother, ready to rage at him, damn his arm. Frulu was already in shock when she got there. She saw to his stump as best she could, cauterized the wound, and cleaned up the mess of blood and the broken crockery scattered over the floor. Her father and uncles watched her, smoking their pipes as she worked. They did nothing to help nor spoke a single word. When she had finished, they set upon her, beating her, blaming her and cursing her for bringing shame to the family name. She cursed them in return, but they left her to soak in her own blood and told to leave. Told her she was no longer family. She was no longer Bouadica.

She rose an hour later, though she was barely able to walk at first. She dressed in her finest black and red gown. Aidan's body had already been disposed of, though she did not know where her family had dumped him.

"Good riddance to ya all, ya filthy traitorous basterds," she spit at them. She left the heap bearing not even her family name. She was now simply Rossa, bait for the ferrymen. She walked through the city streets, sore but dignified. She refused to bend to the pain the beatings caused her. She held her head as high as she was able.

She does not think of her family as she walks, nor does she think of her brother. *What good would that do?* If Frulu did not die from blood loss or infection, the ferrymen would be coming for him soon anyway. *Ferrymen take 'em all*, she thinks.

The gates to the first ring are open. A large caravan of goods is being led up the ramp wagon by wagon. Rossa easily hides in their midst. The way she looks today, she would not be let in otherwise. She passes under the high magnificent wall of the first ring, through great glass gates that almost sing. She is temporarily blinded by the magnificence of the place. She has not been here in years. She has forgotten how clean and pure everything seems even with a reflective hint of orange sky.

Citizenry of the first ring surge past her in their fine, formal attire and small circular sunspectacles. They stare at her. They judge her. She hears a few condescending whispers as she makes her way through the streets, but hardly any voices rise above casual conversation. Everyone seems to have been told to stay on their very best behavior. The place, Rossa thinks, could use some color. And she knows she is not helping matters dressed in her black gown with blood red trim. She looks and walks like a traveling mourner.

Rossa does not bend to their silent taunts. She is in more pain than she has ever been, but she will not stop and rest in front of the likes of these. She has the child to think of. He is why she is here. She won't allow herself to curl up in the gutter for a day's sleep until she has done what she set out to do. Then the ferrymen take her.

She comes to her destination. Though she has not seen the first ring for many years, she knows the way. Everyone knows the way. A map to Salvation is inside the front cover of every Bible, after all. There, rising like it wants to crush the entire city, is GOD's Tower and the Glass Halls across from it.

ESTHER IS irritated. She looks about peevishly as she emerges from Bana's bedchamber, controlling the urge to wring her hands. "Where is that foolish girl?" she says.

One of Duana's duties as housemaid is to see to Bana at the same established time every morning. Esther has done this with all the maids who have cared for Bana. She meets them outside of the bedchamber five minutes after sunrise, and they greet him together and clean up any accidents that occurred while he slept. But this morning, Bana has yet to be cleaned because she couldn't find Duana.

Esther's heels crack on the cold floors as she searches the halls. The key chain in her hand, which holds a key to every crook and corner in the manse, warns the other servants of her approach and her mood.

"Where is that girl?" she says to one after the other of them. "Where is Duana? She can expect a good beating for this lack of attention to her duties."

Only the old steward, Rugal, has seen Duana. "The last I saw her, m'lady, she was coming from sweet Gemma's room, the lovely dove." Rugal always smiles too pleasantly for Esther's taste, but at least he does what is expected of him.

"What was she doing in Gemma's room?"

"I don't rightly know, m'lady," replies the old servant, scratching his old, dried temple. "She came out in a hurry, though. Aye. And when she saw me, she went white as snow, she did. I asked her, I says, 'What are ya doing in Gemma's room, child?'"

"And her reply?"

"She did not have one for me. She made a kinda squeaking noise—" He tried to emulate it. "—covered her mouth and took off. Just plain took off."

"Where to?"

"Oh, well, beggin' your mercy, m'lady, but I didn't see on account of this crick in me neck." He places his hand on the spot. "She was gone before I could turn to get a good look."

"Oh, for the Passions!" Esther says, with a roll of her eyes. "Do you think she went outside?"

"Oh, well, yes, m'lady. She might have done." He puts his hand to work massaging his chin. "That makes good sense now that you've said something of it."

Esther walks briskly to the Front Hall, leaving the old steward to his own mumblings. "I'll take the lash to her," she says. "I'll make her bones bleed."

She opens the large arched front door of the manse. Light pours in all around her. She shields her eyes from the sky's reflection off the silver city. Squinting, she can just make out the chubby form of her maid running toward her up the manse steps. Everything else is consumed by the glare.

"I'm sorry, m'lady!" The girl is already crying. "I'm ever so sorry!"

"Foolish thing!" Esther says as she grabs Duana's arm and throws her inside. "What were you doing?"

Esther looks back and sees a male figure turn and walk away. Despairing of the city's shine, she steps back and closes the door.

"Who was that man?" she demands.

"Man, m'lady?"

"The man by the steps! Who was he?"

"There was no man, m'lady." She is sobbing. "I just went out for some more soap to wash 'is lordship. I sees we was out this morning."

"Don't lie to me, girl." Esther smacks the maid across the face. Duana falls to the ground in hysterics.

"Tell me who he is! Was that a ferryman? Are you giving him information about us? About my Gemma? Are you?"

"No… no, no…" Duana is a ball. She raises her hands to protect her face.

"Is that why you were in Gemma's room? To find information on my little girl?"

Esther towers over the maid now. Servants watch the hall from corners and through cracks in doors.

"Was he a ferryman? Is he one of the Senator General's men? One of the Kingdom Guards? Answer me!"

But it is useless. Esther sees that now, so she calms herself. "Get back to work," she says after a deep breath. "Bana needs bathing. We may speak of this later when you are… collected."

Duana crawls to her feet and is soon gone from Esther's sight, running as quickly as her stubby legs will take her.

It was the Senator General. Esther is certain of it. He plans to take the family down, and they are starting with Gemma. Oh, she is raging inside. She is a fury. Esther decides she will keep an eye on Duana. She needs proof the girl is conspiring against her. There must always be proof. And when she finds it… when she finds it, Passions help the girl.

GEMMA SITS like a stone at her desk. The quiet around her, the complete lack of any conversation from her coworkers, is distressing. She wonders why it is getting to her today. She has held the position for months now, and it has never bothered her before. Or if it has, she has successfully repressed it. She imagines the Glass Halls as a hive, and she is but one of many insignificant workers. Yet they do not hum as they work. Humming would be an extravagance. She is bored, but it is more than that. Something is itching at her. We are itching at her.

Her mother has told her since she was a little thing that "passion" is a dirty word in the Immortal City. Passionless.

Yes, she thinks. *That is exactly how I feel.*

"Have you always felt this way?" We settle in beside her.

I have always felt this way.

Something in her heart goes clink.

She looks at the file just now placed on her desk by an equally passionless mail carrier. They all wade through gray here. They choke on it until it turns their insides to clay.

The file names an older feminine-leaning third-sexer called Gran. She is suspected of knowingly passing the plague to others in her district. Gemma cannot help but think this is an absurd notion. From the notes, she sees the woman can barely walk.

Gemma looks around. Her coworkers are very busy. They are silently droning. Gemma is suddenly sickened by it all. She wants to scream, but she does not know how. She has never screamed in her life. It frightens her, this feeling of some living force in her gut aching to be let loose.

Quickly, before she explodes, she grabs the file, acting as if she needs to report something to a higher-up, and heads to the stairs. Her unexpectedness startles some, but she does not notice. As she descends the steps with increasing speed, the Voice of GOD, the Senator General comes from the loudspeakers throughout the building. It is a recording, of course. One that is played three times daily—in the morning, at midday, and at dusk.

"GOD is good," the Voice affirms in a manner that seems neither caring nor particularly healthy. "GOD is great. He only cares for you. He wants only the elimination of all sin. He wants only a paradise Earth. He built this Immortal City for you, and he wants you to enjoy its bounty. If you choose to sin, He has no choice but to punish you. GOD does not want to punish you. GOD loves all His children. GOD understands those with souls want to sin. He does not expect perfection, but GOD will persuade you to stay in His graces. GOD is good…"

There is no escaping the Voice. Not in the first ring. He is truly everywhere.

Gemma is outside. She knows of a small park at the back of the Glass Halls that goes mostly unused. No one wants to be perceived as unproductive. It has a long narrow pool of crystal clear water lined with slender, well-groomed pine trees, but there are no benches. That would encourage sitting, or worse, loitering. Gemma breathes deep, leaning against a scratchy pine tree and trying to find some quiet to think over the Voice of GOD. She knows she is most likely being watched by someone, but she does not care at the moment. And if questioned, she can simply say she was trying to be at one with the Voice. Religious fervor can be used as an acceptable excuse for anything these days.

Gemma looks up at last and sees something that makes her catch her breath. A woman is in the park just under one of the other pine trees by the pool. She is dressed in a long black gown and is staring at Gemma. She looks to be studying her. Gemma does not move, and for a moment—just the smallest dab of time—she thinks she sees the goddess Abrythnia, naked and standing behind the woman. But in a blink, we are gone.

Gemma gives the woman in black an almost imperceptible nod. The woman relaxes and gestures for Gemma to meet her by the pool. As Gemma slowly approaches, she sees the woman is in a terrible state. Though beautiful, with hair as bright as fire and eyes of green flame, she is bruised and battered. The flesh of her face is a multitude of colors. The woman does not seem beaten, though. She does not have the air of one who has been trod upon. Her back is straight. Her chin is level. She seems a general. She seems a queen.

"You must help me," the woman says resolutely. "I need to speak to someone important. I want to file a complaint, see? Are you important, my love?"

"No," says Gemma, with an embarrassed smile. "I am no one. I am a… drone. You should go see someone in the lobby. They'll know what to do."

"Don't ya think I tried that, girl? Look at me. Look at my face. They wouldna let me in." She looks around, ever vigilant. "I had to take side streets to get this far, and I don't know how I even did that with all the glass and mirror around here. And the glare! Great Passions! The glare made me stoop to thievery." She shows the small set of spectacles she has been holding in her hand. They do not need sunspectacles in the garden.

Gemma likes this woman. She likes the dance of fire in her hair and in her eyes.

"The guards chased me right away, the irritants!"

Gemma looks around. If she is being watched, the guards will surely resume their chase shortly. "What is it you need?"

The woman sighs. "I'm not quite sure, love. What I mean is, I don't know what to do now. I've spent all day and night walking from the third ring. Getting here was all I was thinkin' of. I hadna sorted it out beyond that. I need someone's help, though. I canna do it alone. It's for a child."

"A child?"

"Aye. A boy named Key. The ferrymen meant to take him, but he's a smart one. And quick. He got away, Passions protect him."

Gemma remembers the strange name from a previous case. She tightens the grip on the file in her hand.

The woman comes closer. "I trust your face, love. Will you help me?"

"I don't know what I can do. The ferrymen are beyond me. They frighten me just as much as they do you."

"I ain't a-scared of those soulless basterds. Fuck 'em. If more people thought like me, we might be able to change this world. We might be able to start a true uprising, not one of those brushfires led by Usker Lance and his band of pissed-off brats."

Gemma hushes her. "There are ears everywhere. Listen. GOD is yet speaking."

"Let him jabber on. You should listen at me. I know this is where the decisions get passed through, here at the Glass Halls. All I'm askin' is, if you see his name—Key Laren—get hold of me. My name is Rossa. I'll be around. I've no home at the moment, but I'll be around."

"What of the father? Wasn't there a father?"

Rossa looks at her suspiciously. "There was. He died before they could lay their black-sooted hands on 'im, he did. And Passions be praised for that. He was a good man. An honest man with a big heart. Do you know what a heart is, love? Do you have one? I pray to the Passions you do."

Again, the Passions are invoked in the city of GOD and again Gemma gasps. "You should not use such language here. Please."

"Maybe I was mistaken," Rossa says as she studies Gemma with an up-and-down of the eyes. "Maybe you're not who I need to see after all."

For some reason, this statement hurts Gemma more than anything anyone has ever said to her, more than the chastisements of her mother or the teasing of children when she was younger. Perhaps it is because of the type of woman who says it. The woman Rossa seems to be a tower mightier than GOD's.

"No," Gemma says quickly. "I can help. I get files like this one every day. If I see his name, if I see they are taking Key Laren to the ninth ring, I will try to find you. But I don't understand. In the ninth ring, he would have a new life, a new start to be a boy, and he would live in a comfortable home."

"Oh, you poor thing," she says. "Who's been fillin' your pretty head with such nonsense? Us folk out there, beyond this blinding prettiness, we know what really goes on there. We've all heard the rumors. That is not a place for a child, love. No, no, no."

She does not have time to explain. A pair of heavy footsteps are hurrying toward them. Rossa ducks away with a nod, and Gemma tries to greet the guards in a nonchalant manner, as if surprised to see them.

"What are you doing out here?" one of the Kingdom Guards says. His silver suit glimmers under the orange sky, but Gemma knows silver is only gray that's been glossed over. "Who was with you?"

"What? No one. I was simply—"

He does not really care. "Get back inside, miss. This is your warning. One more mess up and GOD help you."

She bows her head obediently as she passes the guards and hurries back up the steps to her cubicle. She feels something new: excitement, wonder, mystery. And in her head, Rossa's voice echoes, *We've all heard the rumors.* Her mind is suddenly flooded with images too horrible to be true.

IT IS the only mechanical lift anywhere in the Immortal City, using what is left of the current now referred to as GOD's Power. No other building has a lift but GOD's Tower, and only a select few are honored enough to ride the device. The rest, including the Children in Red who feed and care for GOD, must take the long, winding stairs.

The senator general sops up the drool at the corner of his mouth. He is on his way up the narrow stem of the Tower for his weekly meeting with GOD in His saucer-shaped home. Like the other structures of the first ring, GOD's Tower has a coat of solid silver on the outside, but inside it is lined with gold. Even the lift is a gold box. Above the door, it reads GUARDIANS OF DEMOCRACY in threatening capital letters.

But that phrase is from before the revolution, before the true faith was given to the people. Now there is but one Guardian of Democracy. One GOD. All the other would-be rulers have been successfully destroyed.

Senator General Hegart cannot help but feel envious of the lift's beauty. And the power which makes it work. The sheer technology! GOD's Power. If this technology was available to all, life would certainly be easier. Yet that kind of thinking is what brought about the End of the World in the first place. Such resources in the wrong hands can mean annihilation. It was decided long ago such great assets were to be used only by the most powerful, only those with the knowledge of how best to use it. The deciders. And GOD certainly had that gift of knowledge. He was the most feared of any leader since…

The senator general cannot remember a leader before GOD. Not one name comes to mind.

The door opens onto an enormous hall lined with obsidian and gold accents. Masterpieces line the walls, but art means nothing to the senator general. In truth, art means nothing to GOD. Not anymore. This is evidenced by their state. They need a good cleaning. Some are nearly as dark and indecipherable as the black walls.

There is little light here in GOD's Tower. The windows are all covered with metal awnings, so the senator general can barely see his way. His boots strike echoes on the cold black floor. As usual, he will not truly see GOD. He has not seen GOD's actual face in years.

He stops in front of the high chair in the center of the circular hall, and he bows on one knee. The three Children in Red, named so for their long red robes, stand silently beneath the high chair. These children are pale and ghostly, having never set foot outside the Tower. In front of them are four chairs—only three of which are occupied—for those councilors closest to GOD. The councilors say little and look nearly as ill as their missing fourth member, Bana Kerr. They stare at him with lifeless eyes and mumble incoherent whispers and giggles.

"Rise," a whispering voice hisses to him from the darkness.

The senator general peers upward to the chair atop the solid column of obsidian that flirts with the vaulted ceiling, the high chair. Stairs coil around this thick, black pole like a serpent leading up to GOD's throne. The senator general has never seen GOD use these stairs, nor move from His seat at all. GOD is great. GOD is tended to, so he has no reason to move.

Various means of ancient relay such as video, radio, and computer encircle the throne. GOD's Power. Unbeknownst to the world, GOD's eyes are not of the human variety. They are well-hidden in cracks of walls and old statuary, and if come across by the average citizen, they would be met with a shrug as a remnant of times past and most likely left as trash. Every so often, a curious sinner comes along, but the ferrymen are soon sent to see to the matter.

A long speaking trumpet decorated with deep, dark rubies, relays GOD's words from his high chair to the senator general on the floor. "What news on the outbreak, Hegart?" inquires the Guardian. It is a slow, slithering tongue, licking the ear canal.

"It is contained, my lord," says Senator General Hegart. "Your latest introduction of the virus into the population has gone very well. The weak are being weeded out. District 13 of the fourth ring has been quarantined and will soon be evacuated for the ninth. The ferrymen and your Sisters have even found a few survivors from viral outbreaks of the past."

"They do their jobs well." The voice cracks, almost like a laugh. The councilors concur with weak laughs of their own.

"Indeed, my lord."

"We all must do our part," whispers GOD. "The survival of the Immortal City depends on the sacrifices we make. The lesser people must be prepared to give up the most so the strongest of us can forge ahead. When is the next shipment scheduled?"

"The last of District 13 are being corralled as we speak." The senator general catches a stream of saliva from dripping on GOD's floor.

GOD flips a radio switch next to Him. Screaming fills the chamber. The ceiling amplifies it, causing the Children in Red to cover their ears.

"The ferrymen are doing very well, indeed, Hegart."

"Aye, my lord. We will also be taking the odd survivor from previous outbreaks to the ninth ring throughout the week. We have not rounded them all up yet."

"Excellent. And what of Bana Kerr?"

"He is yet alive, my lord. The Lady Esther sees to it. She guards him, I think, day and night, like a damn wolf cat."

GOD groans. The screaming continues over the radio. "They helped me once, but the strength of their favors has grown weak. Their pull is tiresome."

"Shall I call the Lady Esther for a meeting, my lord?"

"Not just yet. But soon. GOD is growing impatient."

"There is one other matter, my lord," the senator general says.

"Speak."

"I have discovered one of the ferrymen is fraternizing with one of the Kerr servant girls, a maid named Duana. I ask your permission to see to this matter."

"You have it." The voice is blunt and inflamed. "A ferryman in a relationship? Disgusting. His soul was taken so this would not happen. This is the second of these offenses to come to my attention. Tell me, Senator General Hegart, how does this keep occurring?"

"I can only assume, my lord, that some soul retractions do not take. Or at least, not completely."

"Mine took well enough." The voice is very irritated, rasping out words that scratch at the dark. The councilors begin to moan in fear. The Children cower.

"But you are GOD."

This is a good, strong explanation the senator general has used on numerous occasions to calm a tense situation. He does not fear GOD acting out on him as he would on his councilors or the Children in Red, but when GOD gets angry, he makes rash decisions, and those decisions slow Hegart's own plans down.

"Very well," says GOD. "Is there anything else, Senator General?"

"No, my lord."

"Then send out the wagons to the ninth city and deal with your insolent ferryman. Let me see him once you have finished. You are excused, Hegart."

The senator general bows once more and leaves the presence of this guardian. This GOD. As he steps into the lift, he hears GOD bellowing to the Children in Red. GOD is hungry.

SENATOR GENERAL Hegart descends the steep, cutting steps at the base of GOD's Tower. He wears a long black coat, large sunspectacles, and is sliding on thick, black gloves. At the foot of the steps stand two ferrymen waiting on orders. One can always tell a ferryman by his posture and carriage. There is no rise and fall of the chest, no blinking of the eyes, no fidgeting of the fingers, no licking of the lips. A ferryman loses his humanity and becomes part of the environment. That is what makes him so dangerous. He is as emotionless and as cold as stone.

The senator general stops and sizes the two men up, and then he looks about for the third. The two turn their heads in unison toward the shadow of Cayden Lothair near a tree.

"Ready the wagons," the senator general says to the two. "District 13 must be empty by nightfall. None are worth keeping there, so saith GOD."

The men say nothing. They do nothing. They are good ferrymen. Their attention is on him. Their dark spectacles hide their soulless eyes.

"One of you head on to the ninth ring and tell the good doctress Deirdre Maire to prepare for a large shipment. Beds should be prepared, and the Factory should be readied." He drools.

The two bow their heads slightly and disappear into the shining streets of the first ring, blending in admirably with the citizenry.

The Senator General turns his attention to the shadow beneath the tree. Cayden steps forward. He pushes the sandy blond hair from his eyes. He is not wearing eyewear. The Senator General removes his as well and immediately squints.

"I have heard some disturbing news from the Sisters," says the Senator General, "that you are not doing your job."

"I do my job better than any of the other ferrymen, sir."

"Then why did you linger so long on this man and his child? Surely you had enough proof. You have been surveying them for weeks. You must have had copious notes. Didn't you have copious notes?"

"They hid themselves well and had many friends. This man was not like Colm Archer."

"Indeed. You let this father linger and die, and let the child get away. GOD prefers men be offered some sort of redemption before they die, before they give their souls to him. He craves a warm… heart. But you did not allow this man that courtesy."

"I regret that. It was a mistake. My first."

"And last. I'll be watching you closely." He is spitting his words on the ferryman now. Cayden is not flinching. "This is your warning. The capture of Colm Archer has given you breathing room in the eyes of GOD. I'd have anyone else's balls torn off in the square and hang them as a trophy in my office right next to their heads. Do you understand me, ferryman?"

"Yes, sir."

The Senator General hurls a ball of phlegm in Cayden's face. Again, Cayden does not flinch even as the phlegm slowly crawls down his cheek. He does not blink, nor does he break eye contact with Hegart.

"Wipe that mess off your face," growls the Senator General. "And if you want to make up for your misstep, see if you can find Usker Lance. There's a set of balls I'd be proud to display in my collection."

He turns abruptly, puts on his sunspectacles, and leaves the ferryman at the steps.

WE TAKE Him in slowly. We are curious about this GOD.

The chamber echoes with the sounds of the raid on the district. Orders are being shouted, children are crying, and those who fight back are severely punished. Never has there been a more useless word than "please."

The only light in the GOD's chamber now comes from the screens surrounding the high chair. He is watching the Senator General converse with the ferryman. We want a better look.

We see the feeding tubes climbing out of a hole beneath His seat. It is meal time. The Children in Red have seen to GOD's feeding, but are gone. A dark gray liquid seeps into His veins.

We can see His veins now. We can see beneath His dark hood. The veins crowd his face like purple worms wriggling. His flesh is transparent, like that of Bana Kerr. He, too, has had His soul pulled from him. Even when He closes His eyes, we see the tiny puncture holes in them from where his soul was taken. His eyelids might as well not exist at all.

He is breathing heavily and coughs. Ah, we see. He is also a plague survivor. His soul is missing, yes, but we sense in Him a lack of the feminine. Some see the feminine as weakness. He has kept the masculine, though. He may, in fact, have too much of it.

GOD rasps and gasps. He is laughing. Something in the raid, some scream, some show of agony, has given him pleasure. He licks His white lips. GOD has no teeth, but he seems very capable of biting nonetheless. Of feasting, in fact.

CAYDEN LOTHAIR is walking the burnished backstreets of the first ring. There are no shadows here, and he does not like it. He feels vulnerable. His eyes dart this way and that, constantly fooled by a mirage from the silver walls around him. That is the part he usually plays, the solemn trickster, the phantasm. He is walking faster than usual. Cayden hates the first ring. It hurts his eyes, but he refuses sunspectacles. When he steps from hiding, he wants his eyes to be the first thing someone sees.

He has been thinking of Aidan Laren. The man's face will not leave his thoughts, and that disturbs him. That was why he had let the man and his son go uncollected for so long. Aidan's face held something different and yet inconspicuous from every other mark Cayden had ever been assigned to.

It had happened on the third day of Cayden's watch. Aidan looked well enough to be outside the woman's home then. He was listening contentedly to his son play on a small drum. He and the fiery woman seemed to be enjoying the day, laughing. She even danced a bit, evoking whistles and bawdy cheers from men nearby. Cayden watched them from a table that sat against a back wall across the street. He thought he was well-hidden. The canopy cast a good shadow. But he must have let his guard down, for Aidan caught him watching them. He did not jump up and move inside. No. He smiled at the ferryman. Cayden had never been smiled at, not even by the women and men he paid to pleasure him. And suddenly, somewhere deep and protected inside him, he felt a spark send shudders through his body.

Why would Aidan have done that? One does not smile at the soulless.

Cayden shuts the memory down. He sees a carriage led by four large mastiff ponies waiting on him up ahead. This is not a death wagon, though essentially the same build. This carriage is not black, but white and silver. The four angels on the corners are rejoicing, wings unfolded. Sister Mags Hensil opens her blind and peers out at Cayden. She is in full pale, painted regalia, but with small circular sunspectacles. Cayden approaches.

"Hello, ferryman," she says. "You have new orders?"

"Yes, Sister. An older woman."

"She has the plague, and she is a third-sexer."

"Yes, Sister."

"I will be there to watch the collection."

"Sister, I would prefer…"

"I did not ask what you prefer, ferryman." Her voice rises like a tide. "Would you deny a Sister of GOD?"

He does not break eye contact. "No, Sister."

"Good. I will be there to see that this collection goes off without a hitch. You don't need any more hitches, do you?"

Beneath her glasses, he knows she is looking at him with a condescending stare. He is nothing more to her than a tool.

"Get going, then," she says. "I'll see you there, ferryman Cayden Lothair. Don't disappoint your GOD again, or we could be in for quite a show in the square."

Mags hits the side of the carriage, telling the driver to pull away. Cayden remains unmoved until the carriage and all of its reflections off the city's silverworks have disappeared from view. He spies a worker's wagon headed out of the first ring and jumps in back. Ferrymen have no need to ask permission for wagon rides.

RUMORS OF the raid on District 13 and the scouring of the Immortal City for any plague survivors are flying in the wind. People are in a panic. The streets are hushed and sparsely populated as citizens hide atremble inside their homes or pubs. The Immortal City is a ghost town. From their balconies high above, some families watch the streets. Their height offers them no security. Shadows are everywhere.

Lawl is with Gran. She is not well today. Her voice is shaking and faint. Her eyes are heavy. She is hooked to the machine Lawl has made for her, but the pain medication is not working well. Lawl could only find a small amount. Most of the street doctors have gone into hiding as well.

They are getting more looks than usual from their neighbors in the last few days. He feels their eyes on the door. If asked, they will not hesitate to point the way in order to save their own skin.

"So, they're coming," Gran says. Her voice is a wisp, but Lawl hears her.

"Don't worry, Gran." He sits by her bed. His arms are crossed over his knees. "I'll think of something. Aye, I'll think of something. They'll not take ya. Besides, it's only a rumor."

"Rumors are facts round here, darling baby boy." She moans in pain, reminiscent of the sound of a heartbroken child. "I will go quietly," she says in between gasps for breath. "I'm dying anyway. There's no sense in you gettin' hurt as well."

"No, Gran." Lawl's lip trembles. "Don't give up. Don't you go."

A tremor in the air, dark and reaching like tendrils, seeps into the room. Lawl feels it. Shadows are here.

With all her effort, Gran moves her hand toward her nephew, and he takes it delicately. "You'll be ostracized after I'm gone," she says. "Kicked out of this place. That worries me so." Tears well up in the corners of her eyes.

Lawl tries a smile. "Meh." He shrugs. "It's not much of a place, Gran."

Her laugh is but a sharp intake of air.

Lawl hears a commotion at the door. For a moment, he is terrified that the ferrymen have arrived, that his neighbors have conspired against him. But he sees it is only Duncan, soaked with sweat. His face is flushed from exertion, and his breathing is quick and heavy. His eyes are ringed with tears.

"We need to get you out of here," says Duncan as he rushes toward the bed.

"What are you doing here? You're soakin' wet, fool. You should be resting. You have to work tonight."

"The ferrymen are on their way," Duncan says. "We need to get Gran somewhere else. They'll be here soon enough."

"Are you sure they're comin'?" Lawl stands, staring Duncan in the eyes and taking both hands in his own to calm his lover down.

Duncan's face breaks into a million pieces. "Oh, Lawl. Aye, I'm certain they're coming. And I'm so damn sorry. I'm so fuckin' damn sorry."

"Here." Lawl moves so Duncan can have his seat by the bed. Gran's eyes are open, but Lawl is uncertain if she is cognizant of what is happening.

Duncan is crying, his head in his hands. His breathing is still heavy, and he is shaking. Lawl strokes his hair and whispers, "Shhh."

Duncan starts to gather himself. "I've spent all day trying to get here. I ran, I hopped on wagons, I even stole a horse. I came as fast as I could. I heard the rumors last night when I was cleaning the Glass Halls. I heard there was going to be a raid."

Lawl was shaking now.

"Everything was fine at first. I heard the rumor and then mounted the scaffolding. Rumors are rumors, right? As I rose to the top, I began to have the most peculiar visions of the ferrymen. They were coming for both Gran and you. It didn't make any sense, you not being sick and all. I pushed it out of me head so I could get my work done. And then the strangest thing…"

"What?"

"I was washing the glass, and a torn edge of cloth snagged on the silver. I went to pull it away, and the silver came up like paper. Like damned paper. It wasn't silver at all. Why, it was just a pretty cover all along. And beneath it was the most hideous polluted rock I've ever seen. It was full of holes and pocks and big black pebbles that looked like boils."

Duncan looks up at Lawl. "It's all show," he says. "They want us to believe the first ring is a better place, but it's just as rotten as everywhere else. I couldn't do another thing. I came down from the scaffolding and started to run. Lawl, we have got to get out of here!"

"How can we?" Lawl says. "Gran needs her machine and her meds."

Duncan looks at Gran. His face is full of mourning. "I'm so sorry," he says.

"No need to be," replies Gran. Her eyes have grown heavy again. "You just get Lawl out of here. I'll go with the ferrymen peacefully."

"Gran, no!" Lawl says. His lip starts to quiver.

Duncan stands and kisses Gran on the forehead. He grabs Lawl's arm, but Lawl is resistant.

"No," he says. Then again, as he looks into Duncan's eyes, he says pleadingly, "No."

"Oh, for the Passions!" Gran says through tears and with all her might. "Leave! Do me this last favor, my darling baby boy, and leave. I love you. I love you."

Lawl can say nothing. The ache in his throat is too strong. The world does not feel real. He kisses Gran, and Duncan whisks him to the door.

But they are too late.

Duncan pulls Lawl out the door, but he resists to look back. Duncan is the stronger of the two, however, and is able to finally wrestle him into the hallway, both nearly falling in a pile. Lawl feels Duncan suddenly stop moving and tense up. Duncan's eyes are wide, but he seems to deflate with a long, shaking breath.

And now Lawl sees too. The hallway is empty but for a Sister of GOD followed by a trio of ferrymen. The Sister's veil is up, and she has anchored her soul-bleeding stare on them. The hallway seems too small and cramped a space to hold her. The wall candles flicker and flame out as she glides past them. Darkness and shadow follow. The ferrymen's boots bang out a death knell on the hard floor behind her.

Duncan pushes Lawl back into the apartment. "GOD is watching," the Sister greets them.

The Sister looks around the apartment as the ferrymen stand guard over Lawl and Duncan. The third, who looks to be the leader of the trio, stands near the door. She disappears, gliding like a ghost, into the second room for a moment, and then she returns.

"She's in there," the Sister says. "There is also a machine. Destroy it." She approaches Lawl and Duncan. "Nice handiwork, but illegal. It will cost you your home after this sinner has been taken."

One of the ferrymen heads into the room.

"You can't," says Lawl with a furrowed brow, a growl growing in his throat as he stares at the woman. "She'll die without those meds."

Duncan squeezes his arm, sweating profusely.

The Sister looks at Lawl with bitter amusement. "She'll die anyway, my son, my lamb. All's the better she goes now than drain us of precious resources."

The ferryman is back with Gran in his arms. She is a leaf. Lawl can see the pain on her face, but she does not make a sound. She simply stares at him, tears falling to the floor.

"To the wagon," the Sister says with an apathetic flutter of a hand.

The ferryman makes for the door with Gran. Lawl is furious. He lurches for the ferryman but is knocked back by another who holds on to him tightly.

"Do not do anything foolish," the Sister says with some irritation, mere inches from Lawl's face.

He feels he has no other recourse but to spit.

The Sister stumbles back with a disgusted cry.

"Dare you spit at a Sister of GOD?" she shrieks, wiping at the sputum as if it were acidic.

Lawl is prepared to be killed. He is certain both he and Duncan will soon be meeting that fate anyway for harboring a sinner. But then he hears Duncan vomiting behind him.

The Sister watches him momentarily, and a smile begins to curl into her thin lips, delight into her cold eyes. "Another sinner?" she says.

"No!" Lawl cries. "No. He's just nervous and fatigued. He doesna have the plague. He's healthy as a bear."

The Sister investigates. Duncan is on his knees, doubled over, and unable to speak. She touches the flesh of his cheek and feels his forehead. She bites her lower lip, pleased.

"Oh, yes. That's all the proof I need, my lamb. Take him as well, ferryman. GOD will be most pleased."

"No!" Lawl tries with some vigor to free himself, but the ferryman holds tight.

Duncan is brought to his feet. "It's okay, my love," he says to Lawl, gasping for air. "I'll look after Gran. I promise it. We'll be fine. And one day, I'll see you again. I swear it…"

"Quiet!" The Sister hits Duncan in the stomach. "Get him out of here."

He is dragged away. Lawl does not even get a final look into his lover's eyes. The Sister of GOD strikes him so hard across the face, he falls unconscious to the floor. He will be left on the street, his apartment no longer his home.

SENATOR GENERAL Hegart stands in a chamber just off the great hall where he sees the Sisters of GOD as the Voice. This room is specifically for his trophies and he is admiring them. Bronzed testicles, gold-plated penises, and cast-iron nipples delight his eyes. The heads of certain notables and would-be heroes are mounted on the wall like hunted beasts.

Those who thought they could stand up to GOD, those who thought they could defy the Senator General himself. He loved watching as their balls were ripped from them. Colm Archer's sizable golden testicles are the prize of the collection. He has designated a special place for them in a case at the center of the chamber on a bed of red velvet. The carpeted floor of this macabre museum is stained with old dark wet patches of drool.

A ferryman stands at attention in the door. Who he was before he became a ferryman is not important. At least not to Senator General Hegart, and certainly not to GOD. The soulless have a hierarchy, and the ferrymen are at the very bottom.

"You do not deny it, then," says the Senator General. He walks nearer to the ferryman, deciding on a punishment. "You do not deny that you have engaged in immoral conduct—conduct unbefitting a ferryman—with this maid?"

The ferryman could be punished in many ways. The easiest and least satisfying would be to have him shipped to the ninth ring, but Senator General Hegart sees no fun in that. He needs blood today.

"No, sir," replies the ferryman. "I do not deny it."

"You are too cool about this, Finn. Do you not realize what you have done?"

"I have sinned against GOD, sir."

"That's right." He is in the ferryman's face. Drool drops from his mouth and slides down the ferryman's chest. "Not only is it a sin for a ferryman to take a woman, it is impossible. How is it that you seem to show affection for this Duana girl? Have you a soul after all?"

"It must be so, sir. I have no other explanation for how I… feel. I must have a soul."

The Senator General squints and peers deep into the ferryman's eyes. "I wonder how far-reaching this problem is, how many ferrymen it affects. Is there perhaps a seed of it we have missed? Have any of your brethren spoken of similar feelings?"

"Ferrymen have nothing to say to one another, nor to anyone."

Senator General Hegart could have the ferryman castrated on the spot. He has done it before. The thought gives his stomach a tickle, but a ferryman's cock would be no prize. The last ferryman with this issue was impaled ass first on a wooden stake in front of his brethren. There was no titillation in the act, though. The ferryman barely reacted at all and died too soon. It was quite disappointing.

He steps back and looks Finn over. He takes his handkerchief and roughly wipes away the drool on the ferryman's uniform. This only makes the wet mark larger.

"If I were to offer you a deal—something to lessen your punishment—would you take it?"

"Sir?"

"I need someone to keep me informed on the status of the House of Kerr. I need someone on the inside who can relay to me the condition of Bana Kerr. Someone who can perhaps speed his passing if and when the time comes."

"I cannot ask Duana to do that, sir. I have a soul now." He seems proud of this.

"I didn't think you would. That's disappointing."

The Senator General walks behind the ferryman with all deliberateness. Should he slice out the man's tongue or stand atop him and pluck out an eye? Should he fuck him with the blade of his sword? The possibilities make him giddy.

"Are you familiar with sacrifice, Ferryman Finn?"

"Sir?"

"Something must be given up so that the larger scheme of things is not affected. Every true and good thing needs a sacrifice."

The Senator General grasps the hilt of his sword, which hangs on his belt.

"GOD needs a sacrifice today."

With a quick draw and slash, he cuts the ferryman in two. The body remains standing momentarily before his torso slides and disconnects from his legs, and they both fall in a bloody fount to the floor.

"Most satisfying," says Senator General Hegart.

He wipes the blade on the ferryman's uniform. He will have the mess cleaned up and the ferryman will be taken directly to GOD. A sacrifice.

Hegart steps over the oozing pile and takes another look at Colm Archer's testicles. It would be nice to have the pair of pairs. Colm Archer's balls and right next to him, those of his lover and now Great Sinner Usker Lance.

THE DAY is over, and Gemma looks for some shelter as it rains. Seated inside the small carriage, she notices how dull the silver city looks in inclement weather. It tries to retain its sheen, but the luster is soon washed away until everything is dirty gray mirrored on dirty gray. The first ring becomes one large echo of apathy, unable to hide a shrug.

Gemma is watching the people on the streets. Every one of them will be soaked before they get home. Everyone who lives in the first ring is considered "better-than," but only the wealthiest, only the most important, are allowed carriages. The faces she sees have no expressions. They are but masks. She bites her lip and wonders if any one of them has an inkling of anything more. Do they want like she secretly wants? Do they have passions?

The day has been filled with wild stories about a new outbreak in one of the far districts of the Immortal City. She knows she will be flooded with paperwork tomorrow morning. It is a depressing thought. So many people must be infected.

The boy. What was his name? Oh yes, Key. Gemma wonders if she will see his name tomorrow. She hopes not. Gemma has a climbing dread in her gut that she has been part of something altogether horrific, that she has been, in some way, responsible for something appalling. She hopes the strange, beaten woman, Rossa, finds the boy, and they start a new home somewhere far away together. She does not know why she feels such empathy for the two. Maybe because they have at last put a face on what she does every day. Every person she ships off from this day on will have the face of Rossa or the name of Key.

Is this a raindrop sliding down her cheek? How strange?

Gemma is home now. The manse is a place of echoes. Her own feet betray her on the cold floor. As always, she stops first to see her father, just a glimpse through the door. This is done out of habit, not love. Her mother is by the bed. Bana blends with the white sheets. Esther looks to the door.

"Dinner is in an hour, my dear," she says.

"Yes, Mother." Gemma curtsies and leaves.

The dining hall is not well lit. Three candles are at the center of the large table, one is near the double doors, and the servants who stand by the wall, ever at the ready, have one. There is no fuss made about food in the House of Kerr. Nutrition does not require aesthetics. Much of the food eaten in the first ring contains the government sanctioned Holy manna, a gray substance more gelatin than anything. It contains vitamins and minerals but lacks taste. Those with a bit of money or know-how can obtain spices and ingredients to make breads and soups. The Kerr house has never been without spices.

Gemma sits opposite her mother. Neither of them takes the end of the table, but instead they prefer the middle. Duana pours Gemma wine from a crystal decanter. The maid is shaking. Gemma notices her mother eyeing the maid suspiciously.

"What news of the day, daughter?" Esther says. She still eyes the maid as she drinks her wine from a tiny glass goblet. She hardly eats at all, such is her way. Gemma has never seen her mother take more than a nibble at meals. Yet she has emptied entire bottles of wine by herself in the span of an hour.

Gemma takes a small bite from her meal. The consistency is not as gelatinous today. It is more like gravy. The hint of cinnamon makes it go down easier. The food has helped curb the obesity problem that once existed in the first ring.

"There was a large outbreak," says Gemma. "In one of the farther districts."

"Was there?" Esther puts her wineglass down and now seems to have lost what appetite she had. She stares at her daughter for more information.

"Yes. I suppose I'll get some of the paperwork tomorrow." Names, each with the face of Rossa. "Then those poor people can be sent to the ninth ring where they can be helped." She looks to Esther. "I'm sure everyone gets the best treatment there. Why send them if they don't get treatment?"

"Do any of them come back?"

"I don't know. I've never thought about it. I wouldn't deal with that paperwork anyway. That would be another office somewhere."

"Somewhere," repeats Esther. "But someone does deal with it, right? For these poor souls and their reintroduction to society."

Gemma wonders about that. A bureau that helps those who have recovered like her father, must exist somewhere.

Esther answers Gemma's inner queries. "They aren't allowed to return, my silly girl."

"Surely, they aren't still in the ninth ring. Not everyone who has been taken there. Why, the sick have been taken there for years."

"As sinners," says Esther.

"But they're not sinners. They're sick."

Esther leans back in her chair. "What rot time has wrought," she mumbles. "Leave us," she says to the servants with a flick of her wrist.

Gemma feels ill. What awfulness has she been part of?

"In the end, silly girl," Esther says once they are alone, "one government is very much like any other. It might start with high hopes, with grand speeches and glorious declarations about how things will be better under new rulership, but nothing of virtue can survive intact when power is wielded by the mad. And one must be mad to rule."

Gemma's mouth is opened in shock. Her mother has never talked in such a manner. "GOD is mad?"

"GOD is an outright lunatic. If we had any guts at all, we'd oust Him before He kills everyone in the Immortal City. But people are easy to pacify if you tell them the right lies in the right way. They become complacent. I've become complacent because, for the time being, it is keeping us safe."

"But you were a revolutionary. You and father helped get rid of a government too concerned with profit. We were ruled by materialism."

"And now we are ruled by GOD. We are in need of a renaissance."

Gemma takes a sip of wine. She hates the taste. Like rotten grapes.

"I saw a woman today," Gemma says. "She had been beaten, and she was looking for a child. She said the ferrymen had come for him, but he had gotten away."

"An orphan? She will never see him again."

Gemma watches her mother rise. She has questions, but she cannot form them into words. "Excuse me, dear daughter," says Esther. "All this talk about GOD has put me off. Perhaps tomorrow you can provide more suitable conversation."

Gemma remains seated as Esther leaves the dining room. She still has questions. They roll over each other in Gemma's mind, on her tongue. It burns, this desire to know. And inside her, we see the passion, which had been but a curious seed, take root at last.

And she sees us. She sees Abrythnia sitting directly across from her where her mother had just been, and she is smiling with encouragement.

CAYDEN LOTHAIR is dreaming.

It is the first dream he has had in many years, certainly since he can remember. The setting is simple, for his mind is yet unable to construct a complicated scenario. He stands in darkness, a boy instead of the ferryman. This surprises him, because he cannot ever remember being a boy. He can only remember being Cayden Lothair, and that is a frozen memory without bookends. What is a beginning? What is an end? He is Cayden.

But the dream is assuring him, yes. You too were a child once.

And he must have had a father, because he stands right in front of him. He smiles at Cayden. He looks very proud. He looks like Aidan Laren. Cayden feels a strangeness crease across his face. A smile. He runs to hold his father. He runs and runs but can never get close enough. He is always a few feet away, his arms outstretched and aching for embrace.

And then it all stops in a sudden, violent revolution. Cayden sees his father's face go slack, and a shiny steel blade slices through Aidan's midsection. Cayden screams, yet his cries do nothing but quicken the blade as Aidan is diced into a million little pieces. Behind the minced pile of human blood and flesh stands Senator General Hegart, his sword guilty with blood. Cayden is afraid, yet he cannot look away. He peers into the Senator General's cold, hateful eyes and feels as if something has reached into his own skull and begun pulling out every bit of his insides through his eye sockets. The pain is immense. Cayden screams and screams.

And as he wakes in his dank, dark apartment in yet a different district, he sees us, if just for a moment. We smile and try to tell him everything will be all right. You will be all right.

We know he does not believe us. Not right now.

GOD HAS NOT BEEN
DOWN THIS WAY IN YEARS

THREE DAYS have passed.

Gemma wakes this morning to the round face of the maid, Duana. Her plump features are tired, her eyes swollen.

"Miss," Duana says urgently, "Miss? Are you okay?"

She shakes Gemma lightly. Gemma rises to her elbows and looks around her chamber, somewhat startled to be back in her room and out of the garden. It felt so real this time, she wonders if she might have grass stains on the bottom of her feet.

"Miss? Are you okay?"

"Yes, Duana," says Gemma. "I'm fine. Thank you."

This is not true. She wishes she were back with Abrythnia wading through the fresh streams in the Garden of the Passions, breathing the sweet humidity of an ancient afternoon. A young blond man was with her this time. She did not get his name, but he looked vaguely familiar. And they had yet sighted another visitor just as Gemma awoke. But he was in the shadow, beneath a fruit tree.

"You were talkin', miss," Duana says. "Speakin' of forbidden things." She lowers her voice to a whisper. "About Passions."

"Thank you for waking me." Her attention is now focused on the maid's face. "Have you not been sleeping well yourself, Duana?"

"Oh, miss," she says most despondently. "I've got nightmares of my own, I do."

"Don't let my mother frighten you so, Duana. I won't let her turn you out."

"She's a tyrant, there's truth in that. But she ain't the reason for my heartaches." Duana pours Gemma some water from the basin by the bed. "I have a fella, you see. Only I haven't heard from him in a few days, and I'm getting worried."

"I'm so sorry." She touches Duana's hand, and that is all Duana needs to let loose the tears. She sobs in Gemma's arms quite uncontrollably for a moment.

"He's probably found another," says Duana. "Oh, Miss Gemma, life was only bearable knowing he was gonna be there for me. Sometimes I think we are just here to suffer because of some great sin we've done forgotten all about."

"I believe…" Gemma hesitates. She wants to tell someone of her dreams.

"What do you believe, miss?" Duana's tear-streaked face urges Gemma on. Sometimes, Duana looks quite like a child.

"I believe things will soon be changing, Duana. I've been dreaming, you see. Beautiful dreams." She pulls the maid close to her, face to face. "Abrythnia is there," she says excitedly. "And there are Passions too. They tell me things."

Duana pulls back in shock and rises from the bed. "No, miss," she says. "You mustn't speak such things. That's sacrilege against GOD. It be heresy! I won't hear it. I'm sorry, but I won't."

The maid hurries from the room. Gemma stares after her, her face now fallen. She feels like she has offered someone part of her heart, and they have just dropped it to the floor in disgust. She rises to get dressed for work.

Wearing a blue satin gown of uncomfortable conformity, she takes a carriage to the Glass Halls, but does not enter the same doors she has routinely used. Instead, she enters the doors leading to the east wing. Just this once, she has chosen to use her family's name to gain a new position at the Glass Halls: in the archives of the Immortal City. This is her first day.

She does not know what she expects to find here or how she might find it, but the archives is the only place in the city that offers a glimpse of the past. Of an actual, if clouded, history. Every person who has ever lived in the city under the Guardians of Democracy, every name sent to the desks of the Glass Halls, is here. Entire lives relegated to a couple of thin sheets of paper and lost in stacks, which are then lost in boxes, miles and miles of boxes on shelves that seem as tall as the city itself and obtainable only by ladders and walkways. High above, the ceiling of glass lets in the orange tint of the sky.

She walks on, her steps echoing deeper and deeper into the archival belly. She sees no one and hears nothing but the swish of her own dress and the clack of her heels on the cement floor. The boxes have a quiet language, though. A whisper like a barely audible breeze through tree leaves. Gemma's shoes are waking them. Stirring them. Gemma stares up at the sculptural chaos above her, the shelves and ladders and walkways. She is overwhelmed.

"How will I ever…?"

"By getting to it," comes a whispering voice behind a ladder. A small, young man with large, surprised eyes steps into view. He is as pale as white glass and as thin as a sapling, and Gemma thinks it has been years since he's seen another person. "Are ya here to help me?" he says. He remains standing near the ladder, his shoulders bunched as if he thinks she might strike him. "Are we gonta be friends, Gemma Kerr?"

ESTHER KERR stands on one of the back balconies of the manse. They are stacked like doll shelves here. Every back room has a balcony. She grips the silver rails intensely. She wears her hair up so that it looks like a solid black and gray mass, not a strand out of place. The shoulder pads of her long black gown give her a severe posture. She is staring down on the servant's path, which connects the manse to the servant's paths of other families as well as the important avenues for shopping. It is not seemly for servants to amble about on the main streets. Her sunspectacles are high on the bridge of her nose. They need readjusting and are cutting her, but she is focused on the scene below.

Finally, she sees the girl leave the manse, coming out the back door in her quick, clumsy manner. This girl is too much. Too much flesh, frump, and bad attitude. Esther allows Duana to waddle off a bit before she grabs her long gray coat and wraps it around her padded shoulders. She carefully slides the fur-lined hood over her perfect hair and hurries down the steps into the servant's lane. The girl will not have gotten far. Not with those legs.

Esther had reservations about letting Gemma take a job at the Glass Halls. She wished for her to stay as near the manse as possible, preferably locked safely away in her bedchamber. But that would be pointless. If Gemma was to survive on her own after Esther and Bana were murdered by GOD, she would need to know how the world works. She would need to build a life that cannot be so easily wiped out by GOD's Holy whim. Keeping Bana alive is a task, but a necessity. When he dies, Esther knows she will follow soon after, and not by any natural means. She is only alive to keep Bana alive. A jealous GOD's will, it seems. But she also knows how quickly His Will turns. It is good Gemma is working. With any luck, it will take her away from here, away from GOD's reach. Thanks to the plague, there are many abandoned places in the Immortal City she could live unharassed.

Esther walks swiftly through the passage. If the first ring has a dangerous area, this is it. The silver and glass is scuffed, broken, and in need of polish. One can barely see their reflection. Servants glare at her as they huddle in groups on their breaks, smoking illegal coma sticks. Duana has vanished from sight, though. Esther chides herself for not paying closer attention to the girl. But then she sees her round form passing through a courtyard that lead to the proper city streets. Esther hurries to catch up, brushing past servants from other houses who apologize for having accidentally touched her.

She stops and hides behind a dying pine tree in the courtyard when she sees Duana pause and look sharply to her left. A man has appeared beside her. Duana shrinks into a ball, her head down, her hands and basket to her chest. Esther is confused as to what is happening, but she knows for certain the man is no servant. He has a different carriage altogether.

And then, as the man brings a handkerchief to his mouth with a large paw, rage overcomes Esther. "Hegart," she spits.

The Senator General says something to Duana, and the girl backs away just a bit. But then he grabs her arm and pulls her with him out into the city. Esther does not follow. There is no need to. What can she do against Hegart in the light of day anyway? While still quite angry, she is also satisfied her suspicions have been proven correct. Duana is telling secrets to the enemy.

THE WALLS of the Immortal City, rippling out hard and white from the crystal-coated center like frozen tsunamis, are eighty feet tall and thirty feet wide. They are monstrous constructions. Only the first five still retain their complete original ferocity. The outer seven not seen by citizens are crumbling ruins in areas, which makes them seem more regal than daunting. The five inner walls not only serve as barriers, but also house the guards of the Immortal City, assigned to keep the citizens protected from undefined monsters and marauders. The Kingdom Guards are a separate force from the ferrymen, though both are under the power of Senator General Hegart. They are infinitely more respected by the people and better looked after. Ferrymen are expected to find their own living arrangements. No one wants a ferryman to stay too long in their vicinity.

Each ring has but one entrance, and one major road runs through them all. The Holy Processional is a wide, paved street lined with each ring's most important buildings. However, midway through the third ring, the structures which line the Processional become less and less impressive. By the fifth ring, they are fallen hovels and shacks, some quite abandoned. GOD has not been down this way in years.

The entrances and gates themselves are great arched affairs. They are not opened unless the Kingdom Guards are given orders, or indeed, want to open them. If they do not like the look of someone, they might refuse them entry or leave. If they do not like the way someone acts, they have the authority to beat them into submission. They do not have the authority to execute, though. The punishment of death is passed down by GOD alone.

No free citizen has passed beneath the fifth wall for many years. The guards stationed there are few in number because the fear of the ninth ring is more than enough to keep the populace contained. The fifth ring itself is widely abandoned, guards posted only at intervals every few miles. The iron gate of the fifth ring is opened only for the death wagons as they speed their passengers on to the ninth ring. Beyond is ruin.

Though the wagons have no windows, Duncan is able to see bits and pieces of the ruined world he has been traveling through when the ferrymen bring them water and the gray manna. The wagon doors are opened, and Duncan sees the ancient, crumbling buildings along the Holy Processional, the homes of ghosts, and hills where homes once were.

He sees the decapitated statues of older faiths and large columned structures of such magnificence that he is stricken with awe even in his current predicament. He feels the uneasiness of this lost ring. He feels the echoes fall to whispers around him stretching in a large circle, one of three dead cities between the five and the ninth. He sees forests deeper and greener than any in the first five rings, primitive places with laws that care not for GOD. The wild has reclaimed much of these rings. Duncan sees starving wolves ogling the death wagons from the brush.

Gran has slept through most of the trip. Duncan tries to get her some water and gruel, but the pain is too intense to swallow anything without her medication. She passes out from it. One other is in the wagon with them, a young girl who rocks back and forth, holding her knees. She is a filthy mess in a torn, thin, and yellowed dress. Duncan has tried to get her to eat as well, but she does not even look at him. She only rocks and hums an occasional melody. Duncan assumes she is not well in the head, the poor little thing. No wonder she is on her way to the ninth. She does not look like she has eaten in days.

His sole comfort on the journey to the ninth ring are his dreams. We are there with him as he sleeps. It is the same dream with a few variances in detail here and there. He has descended from the Glass Towers and is in the Garden of the Passions with us and with Gemma Kerr, though he does not know her name. We are not Abrythnia with him. He sees us as Brachnol, Abrythnia's brother. He dreams of us often as he lies huddled in the wagon with Gran. He is content to stay in the Garden of the Passions and wait for his sweet Lawl there.

Lawl must come. Duncan knows Lawl would love the garden. He misses him so very much it makes us ache. It makes us glad we do not have hearts to break. He whimpers in his sleep. Alas, his lover cannot come to him. But a figure waits beneath the trees. A shadow too suspicious to join our trio. And then the shadow begins to tap its feet and hum in a dark, almost elegiac manner. Duncan always wakes then.

The sudden halt of the wagon brings Duncan to awareness. He hears voices outside that are not the leaden tongues of the ferrymen. Gran climbs to wakefulness in Duncan's arms. She is confused as she looks around.

"Where are we?" she asks, her voice as fragile as a last breath.

"I think we might be here," Duncan says. He swallows his apprehension. "We done passed through all the forbidden rings."

Gran moans in pain. Duncan holds on to her all the more tightly.

Gran looks at the girl who still rocks in the corner of the wagon. "The poor child," she whispers.

"Aye. She's been like that since the ferrymen threw her in here with us. She hasn't moved from her spot, nor has she eaten a scrap of food. She just sits there in her own filth and rocks and sings."

"She's one of the violet children," Gran says. "Beautiful souls, they are. Trapped in a world they donna understand. They keep to themselves. Their worlds are in their heads. But you are a smart girl, ain't ya?" She is talking to the child directly. The little girl at last looks up, but only for the briefest of moments. Then she returns her big brown eyes to the wagon floor once again and rocks and rocks.

"The violet children are so intelligent," Gran says. "The rest of us just aren't smart enough to understand 'em is all. I had a little girl once. She was a violet child. Her name was Elan. Never a child in the whole world was as precious as Elan."

"What happened to her?" The voices outside are getting closer.

"She got the plague, my little precious thing." Gran closes her eyes. "It took hold of her fast. She was such a pretty thing, even up to the night she died in me arms."

Duncan kisses Gran on the forehead as a tear falls down her cheek.

"I was so angry when it happened," Gran says. "There ain't no point to a blessed child dying, not in a world so starved for goodness. Her death made me question everything I ever believed, gods be damned. But now... but now... the sick are carted off to here. Just like you and me. My darling girl would have been taken from me the day she was diagnosed violet and brought here."

The wagon doors open.

"It was a blessing, Duncan," Gran says. "It was a blessing she died then. It all comes down to kindness, Duncan. One singular act of kindness can change the outcome of a life, of the whole world."

A Kingdom Guard in a dark gray uniform stands at the ready. Two ferrymen in black stand beside him. "On your feet!" the guard says.

One of the ferrymen picks up Gran as Duncan gets out of the wagon, shading his eyes from the sun. The little girl does not seem to hear the order and so continues rocking in her corner. She is forcefully pulled out by the other ferryman. This causes her to become quite agitated.

"She's just a child!" Duncan says. "Leave her be!"

He is slugged across the mouth by the guard. "Keep quiet!"

Duncan tastes the blood in his mouth. The girl is screaming in a puddle of mud on the ground where she has been dumped. Duncan looks around. At least two dozen death wagons are pulled up in front of a five floor elliptical structure. This is new architecture, not something from ancient times when the ninth ring was first inhabited. The center of the building is columned and white, with many large windows and a great cupola at its pinnacle. To either side are wings. These are not white, but dirty gray stone. Each floor has a patio that runs its length, yet other than a few Kingdom Guards, Duncan sees no people on them. The only patients Duncan can see are those being unloaded from the death-wagon caravan.

Surrounding the main structure, farther off behind the wings, Duncan sees many smaller buildings, also new. Some are clearly dormitories of some kind, while others billow angry black columns of smoke from large chimneys. The whole ring looks dead from the fallen ash with no grass, at least not in the immediate vicinity. The beauty of the older and ancient rings Duncan had glimpsed on the journey here is nowhere to be seen.

This is the ninth ring.

THE DOCTRESS Deirdre Maire stares down on the line of wagons from her perch high in the cupola. The sinners and the sick are being lined up and separated into groups according to type: the wretchedly ill, the mentally ill, the orphans, the incapacitated, and the immoralists. She sees too a single, handsome young blond man standing on his own, near the wretchedly ill and the old. She is momentarily curious.

An influx of sinners and the plague-ridden has been arriving for the past few days. GOD wants his due, Deirdre supposes. But exactly what is He due? The question has been nagging at her lately.

She watches as the doctors beneath her, for she is the high warden, walk out to inspect what the cavalry hath brought. She knows nothing personal about her fellow doctors. They are not friends. They are hardly colleagues. They eye her, not with respect, but with extreme caution and fear. Deirdre has been known to lose her temper and order spontaneous lobotomies. Only one of the other doctors, Sara, tries to offer her any true kindness.

Deirdre Maire has very little contact with anyone on a personal level. The Kingdom Guards and the ferrymen are tools of the ninth ring, and the nurses? They mill around in their faded gray uniforms and do as they are told, saying nothing. Five of them stand behind her in the cupola now, their hands at their sides, their blank faces awaiting orders... or expression. Of course, every last one of them is a lobotomized sinner, mostly immoralists. The doctress looks back at them. Some of them might even be considered pretty if they could still smile.

Of humanity—but that is the wrong word—of humankind, Deirdre sees just one man, and that is a rare thing. Senator General Hegart occasionally sees fit to visit the doctress. Only then does Deirdre know some type of limited human contact.

She catches her reflection in the glass of the cupola window as she thinks on the Senator General. Her hand instinctively goes to her mouth. She had once been a beautiful woman. Her golden hair trapped many a young hero, and her laugh was as disarming and playful as a Passion. Now, the left side of her face is a mutilated waste. Her upper lip is shorn off, and her mouth widened years ago by a butcher knife so that she now frowns eternally. An eye, too, was ripped away, and the lone brown eye she is left with is paired with an orb of milky glass blue. The Senator General's rage has increased over the years. He is, at times, uncontrollable.

He had not always been so vile. Deirdre remembered when they had first met. He had at least guarded his temper, though he always claimed to never have a soul. But he was also ambitious, and when the Revolution happened, he aligned himself with the Guardians of Democracy. Deirdre started seeing the change in him then. He no longer asked, but took. Instead of looking at her, he watched her, Deirdre Maire, the third-sex beauty. He had never had issues with those of the third-sex before serving GOD. But now he talked of soul extractions and feminine cleansing.

"The feminine is the weaker gender," he had told her once as he towered over her. "We must have it removed, all of us, if we are to be strong and fight for our way of life."

The Senator General himself went through the soul extraction, "just to be sure," he had said. Deirdre did not see it done, but she saw the blankness of his eyes after. He scared her then. After some time, she decided to end things with the Senator General. She went to his new office in the old cathedral at the base of GOD's Tower and found him waiting for her. He was seated on a stiff, tall black chair as she walked in the door, and he was silhouetted by the light through the glass behind him. She smiled nervously. Her lovely smile had once the power to make even the hardest of things acceptable and more easily done.

But in a split second, the Senator General was on top of her, a long stream of drool pouring from his mouth on her face like putrid molasses.

She screamed and passed out. When she awoke in the newly built patient's ward and hospital of the ninth ring, she had been disfigured. Not facially. That came later. But Deirdre Maire would never know sex again. Not in the way she had. Half of her sexual being had been cut away, and in its place, she had been left with a wicked scar in the shape of a smile. She was given the position as the high warden and doctress of the ninth ring once she had undergone sufficient reprogramming.

But that all seems ages ago.

"Nurses," Deirdre says, refocusing her attention on the caravan below. "Let's go see who they've brought for us, shall we? What goodies shall I be playing with today?"

ORNA STANDS in line with the others collected. She is grouped with three other women and two men, all of them young and, as apparent from their colorful dress, all of them in the same line of work as Orna herself. They look to one another for some support and encouragement, but there is little to be had. Orna is shaking, and she is biting her lip. The season has grown colder, and she wraps her arms around her waist for warmth. The once vibrant orange gown she wears, has become torn and filthy in a very short time.

A blonde woman in a long, fitted black coat and skirt descends from the large steps of the building. She looks exceedingly unhappy. Her face is a twisted wreck. Orna decides not to watch her and instead looks to the brown earth at her feet. It is dull, spoiled earth, she notes. Little can grow in this soil. She knows this because before the Kingdom Guards had forced her and her family off the land and she turned to flesh peddling, she had lived on a farm near the outskirts of the fourth ring. She wishes she was there now.

The unhappy woman is introducing herself as the high warden and head doctress. "You will be given a place to stay, good care, and two meals a day," the woman says as she speaks from the steps. Her voice is flat and emotionless. "Do what is expected of you, and there will be little reason to worry."

What did that mean? Orna wonders.

The warden doctress is now on the ground, inspecting like cattle those the ferrymen have brought to the ninth ring. The little girl who has been causing such an uproar since the wagons arrived is taken away at once by the doctress's orders, not to the hospital but somewhere beyond it. Orna can hear the doctress speaking to the other doctors. Some of the collected are to be housed in dorms and will work in the fields and mines. Some will be put to work in the Factory. Some will be given rooms in the hospital. And some will be "prepared." Orna does not like the sound of that last one. She holds her breath.

Terrified… terrified…

The warden doctress comes to the group Orna stands with. Each of them is inspected. This is nothing new to Orna. Her clients did this often back in the five rings. She is product, not personage. The doctress lifts her chin. Orna is forced to look at the ugly, disfigured face. She flinches at the sight of the unnatural milky blue eye and quickly looks away.

"This one and the two young men will make good nurses, I believe," the doctress says to the doctors behind her. "Yes, indeed."

Orna is relieved. She is happy not to have to work in the mines or some factory. A nurse sounds so much better. Respectable, even. She does not know what gives her the courage to speak up, but speak up she does.

"Thank you, Warden Doctress," she says, trying to look the woman in the face. "Thank you so much."

The doctress smiles, but Orna doesn't feel comforted. Her smile is stretched and cynical. "Why, you're very welcome, my dear," she says. "And tell me, why are you so grateful to be one of my nurses?"

The doctress gestures behind her to where a group of nurses stand.

"Well," she says, studying them. Taking them in. "I'm pregnant, you see, and a factory or mine would…" They are mute, unmoving, slack-jawed. Standing as if hanging on hooks.

"Oh, you're so right," says the doctress. "The mines are no place for an expectant mother. Not yet anyway." The doctress brushes Orna's cheek with her hand. "And I promise you, your labor will be so easy you won't even feel it. Nor, indeed, will you feel much of anything else."

Orna is confused. The doctress's smile disappears.

"Take her at once," she says.

The nurses come to life as if turned on by a key. A guard takes Orna by the wrist and pulls her to them. The nurses crowd around her on all sides. Their faces are blank, their eyes are pits of darkness. They reach for her and scratch at her as she tries to get away, but it is no use.

"Please!" she screams to the air, to anyone who will listen. "Please, help me!"

But who can help her? Who would dare? She is quickly taken toward the main building, the hospital, and we lose sight of her.

ROSSA HAS been wandering the Immortal City for days. Her bruises have faded, the pain laid on her by her family and the ferrymen has lessened, but her mind is ever on the child, Key. She has searched the darkest places of the city, down cavernous alleyways and inside rotting buildings. She keeps her eyes open, and her ears to the ground. She has much to be cautious about.

Rossa was thrown out of the first ring her first night. The guards did not even bother to ask her why she was there or where she was from. With her beaten face and her style of dress, they needed no more proof she did not belong. After her exile, she walked along the city walls, hoping for a crack she might crawl through. But, of course, she didn't see one. Even the River Hung, which runs through the ring wall, is guarded by a cluster of men and gated with steel bars. In time, wary of the suspicious glances she was receiving by those who saw her studying the ring wall, she decided she had to search for the boy. She has now given up on ever hearing back from the girl Gemma. Rossa has disappeared into the bowels of the second ring.

Her days are spent wandering the most derelict of homes and neighborhoods. Key is a smart child. He knows how to hide even in the most dangerous of places. He could be squatting at the top of one of the massive tenant halls or hidden away in the dank dungeons of some ancient dance palace. Or somewhere much worse. Key is also a curious child, and that curiosity concerns Rossa the most. Rossa has seen things she wishes she could unsee done to children. She wishes those memories could be removed from her head for good by whatever painful means necessary.

Rossa no longer has a home or a family, yet she needs to look like she does to escape the suspicion of tattlers and the hands of the ferrymen. She will not hide from a ferryman or a Sister of GOD if she passes one in the street. No. She walks upright and proud. While this attracts attention, trying to scurry and hide in a crowded boulevard would be her death. Tattlers are all around.

She keeps herself clean, and her gown washed, down by a small stream that branches off from the River Hung in an older and less vital area of the second ring. The stream etches through a small grove of dying trees, but the water is clean and good. At night she sleeps in any abandoned structure she can find, along with the other homeless and destitute who the ferrymen have not yet come upon. It will only be a matter of time before they do, however, so Rossa keeps moving and looking for Key. In her most desperate moments at night, she huddles up in her gown on some cold and filthy floor and shames herself for not taking care of Key like she promised Aidan, and not taking care of Aidan as she promised Claire.

She finds herself now at the gate of the second-ring wall. It should be easier to get to by now. Each successive wall after the first is less guarded, less taken care of. While she didn't think she'd see any cracks in the second-ring wall, Rossa knew of at least one in the third. It was kept a great secret, but she had seen it once used by some orphans running from the ferrymen.

"And what do you need, my pretty lady?" a guardsman says to her as she approaches the gate. She knows his condescending yet lascivious look too well.

Her hand is on her hip, her chin is up, and her swagger is out. "I aim to get through that gate, sir," she says.

The guardsman smiles and continues looking her over. "Flan," he calls to another guard. "This one wants to get through to the third ring."

The other guard stands beside the first. He wears a similar condescending grin and gray uniform. "Aye? And pray, why should we let you through, gal?" he says.

"Because I need to be there. 'Tis none of your business, the why."

The two look at each other and begin laughing. "Saucy, this one," the first guard says. "But what if we don't want you to go? What if we want to keep your pretty lil' face right here with us?" He reaches his hand out and touches her hair.

Rossa pulls away as they laugh. "Let me through."

"You ain't getting through, missus," says the second. "Not without a favor. You do us a favor, and we'll do one for you."

"Do yourselves your favors, ass boils."

She turns and walks away, still proud, still Rossa, as the guardsmen laugh and tease her with naughty words. Soon they are back to the gate, however, as a large wagon pulls up needing passage. Rossa watches from afar. Some gardener or farmer for the city, it seems, is showing the guards what he carries. There are bags of dirt and an assortment of small trees, bushes, and flowers. Satisfied he is not smuggling goods, the guardsmen walk with him back to the front of the wagon, cracking wise about the gardener's distorted gait as they go. They are distracted, so Rossa takes a chance.

She looks around to make certain she is not being watched too closely, and then she calmly and quickly walks to the wagon, sits graciously on the open tail like a lady in need of a momentary rest, and scoots herself securely beneath the larger trees and bushes. She waits as she hears the gate opening and lies still beneath the shade of the plant life as the wagon moves forward. There are a few seconds of complete darkness as the wagon passes beneath the ring, and then she hears the gate close behind her.

As she squirms her way down the wagon bed so she might hop off and begin her search anew in the third ring, the gardener says in a quiet, ominous tone, "You might want to stay put just a bit longer, dearie."

Rossa freezes.

"There be ferrymen just up ahead, and it would be a shame to get yourself caught by them after pulling such a great one over on the Kingdom Guards."

She does not move.

GEMMA'S BROWN eyes hurt. She has been poring over files for days in the dim light of the archives, making certain things are in correct, if befuddling, order. When she has a spare moment, she carefully wanders off to her own investigations. She wears seeing spectacles in the archives, not because she needs them for the filing, but because she is wary of Tully. The archivist keeps his eyes on her. He looks harmless enough.

When she catches him watching her from high on a crosswalk, his big moony eyes seem more frightened than threatening, but still Gemma is beginning to realize from her file readings that one can never be too careful. Tully seems to blend into the shelves and files, appearing suddenly and disappearing just as quickly. He is such a thin creature, Gemma jests to herself that he hides in the file folders just waiting for her to pass.

Gemma found the files for Aidan and the child easily enough. Tully has a strange system of archiving, but once she figured it out—the more destitute the sinner, the higher they were shelved according to gender, age, and, sometimes, health—Gemma was able to locate whatever file she needed. The trick for her was finding the time. The archives are vast and the walkways, she has discovered, are never in the same position from hour to hour. Tully likes to keep things moving. She sometimes catches glimpses of him racing along a walkway as if running from the light.

There was not much to see in the child Key's file. What trouble could a child less than ten years cause? Perhaps none at all. But he is an orphan now and that is enough for the powers that be in the Immortal City.

Next to Aidan's name in his own file was stamped the word PREPARE. This word was not there when she had first seen the file back in the offices of the Citizenry Designation & Relocation Department. She has seen this same stamp now numerous times in the archives in various files, most of those belonging to the sick and dying. Her first thought was that it was a note reminding those in the ninth ring that the sinner was soon to die and so they should be prepared for this. If the stamp did not look so angry, so large, capitalized, and blood red, Gemma might have been content in believing this. But PREPARE read more ominous than compassionate. There was a hungry smile behind that word.

She looked deeper in the archives for any information that might exist on her own family. She dug into the files in the basement where the more respected names strangely were kept. But that was yesterday, and she has not found a single mention of the Kerr name, nor of Bana or Esther. She puts a folder back on shelf and sighs. Trying to find any information on her family's ties to GOD or the whereabouts of the child, Key, is an overwhelming prospect. Her mind is flooded with names, addresses, sins, and punishments. That is what hurts her head the most. Each file is as heavy as if it were soaked in blood. Very few people, it seems, meet happy endings.

Suddenly, Tully is standing next to her, having slipped out of hiding. His eyes are wide and locked into hers. They glow in the sparse light. She is startled and fells a shelf trying to steady herself.

Tully grabs her by the arm. His touch is light, barely there. "I know what you're doin'," he says. "Come with me."

Gemma is frightened. "No. I promise I'll get back to work. I was just... I was..."

"Shhh," he says, as if others are around. "Come with me. I can help ya, I can. Someone else has gotta know it. Someone besides me."

He loosens his grip and slides his palm down her arm until they are holding hands. He pulls her with him into a passageway she had not even seen, though it was but two feet in front of her. He leads her past still older files heavy with dust. Again and again he pulls her through passages that seem dead ends until they are upon them. The great iron shelves seem to part like interlocking gates, letting them through. They are in an area now that is totally new to Gemma, on a walkway above a deep chasm in the earth. She can see nothing but darkness far down, but there is a faint light ahead of them behind very high shelving of ancient books.

They enter a room constructed from shelves and very old, very large books. Gemma cannot believe what she is seeing. The walls, if they can be called such, are lit with candles. Atlases and books of maps with names of places she has never heard of before speak back to her.

"Books," she says quietly, as if speaking too loudly might bring the room down around them. "Books are forbidden."

"Knowledge is forbidden," Tully responds. "Books are nothing to those what can't read 'em."

Gemma glides her fingers across the covers and bindings. Tully is right. She is one of the few who has been given some sort of education. She was deemed good enough at some point long ago. Most in the Immortal City would not know what to do with these books. They would be good only for hearths and campfires.

Gemma is surprised to see an uncomfortable looking bed in a corner of the room. It is but a hay mattress supported on a wood frame and covered with a torn old quilt that is a tragedy. "You live here?" she says, removing her seeing spectacles and looking at him.

"It's not so bad. I'm surrounded by what I love, and I have company."

Movement across the room catches her eye. From behind the bed a great white figure rises from the floor where it had been resting. She thought it was a pile of pelts, but it is a beast the likes of which Gemma has never seen. A dog of monstrous size with a pure white coat of fur. Gemma is immediately terrified as it moves toward them, but Tully calms her.

"Don't worry," says the archivist. "He is my friend as well. My first and only friend until you. His name is Madden. Madden, say hi to Gemma."

The dog sniffs at Gemma, nearly staring her eye to eye, and then he licks her face with a long wet strip of a tongue. Gemma laughs, and at once, her fear is quelled.

Tully grabs Madden by the ears and gives the beast a big kiss between its eyes. Madden's long tail swings wildly, snuffing out candles and disturbing papers.

"He's caused fires wagging his tail like that, he has," Tully says, looking at the dog with the affection of a parent.

"He is a very quiet dog," Gemma notes. "I've not heard a bark since I've been working here."

Tully's face drops. "That's a sad bit of the tale. My brother says to me that the only way I can keep him with me is if he remains quiet as a mouse. To ensure this, the basterd had his barker removed."

"That's dreadful."

"Aye, it is... Now," says Tully, "to the reason I brought you down here."

He hands her a folder, thicker than most she has yet seen. "Have a seat," he says, gesturing to the room's only chair, a sickly green beat-up reading chaise with thin, wasted cushions. A candle sits beside it on a stack of thick tomes.

She sits and looks through the folder. "This is my father's file," she says. She looks to Tully for explanation. He has seated himself on the floor across from her, leaning back onto Madden behind him, who is acting as a sofa.

"It's all about him, missus. Read on. Read on."

"I'm suddenly very wary to, Mr. Tully."

"You've good reason to be, missus, but if it's the truth you're after..."

She nods and puts her seeing spectacles on again. Much of what she is reading she knows. Bana was a revolutionary for the Guardians of Democracy. He and her mother, Esther, were key participants in gaining control of the government by somewhat questionable tactics, including many assassinations and murders, and even more attempts at such. Freedoms were curtailed for the good of the people, for their safety. Others beside her parents were involved as well, though Gemma does not know them, nor has she ever heard their names. Even in these files, they are only initials. She supposes Senator General Hegart is one of these initials.

She notices quite a few instances of dispute between Bana and H. Between Esther and H. Between Bana and Esther and T. T is mentioned more than any other initial in the file. Esther is marked down as "someone to watch." Then, sometime after Gemma is born, Esther goes from an annoyance to an absolute enemy.

T wants her gone.

H wants her gone.

The other participants in the revolution are silent. Their initials have suddenly vanished without reason. Gemma wonders if the answers to their disappearance are other files.

And then she begins to read some rather curious and cryptic entries.

The plague has worked.

Soul retraction is a success.

And then Bana is sick, having been struck down with the plague. T is furious. Gemma remembers those days. Her mother's hands were white from wringing.

The next words catch Gemma off guard. She reads them aloud. "Gender-milking unsuccessful. Esther Kerr to be terminated for interrupting procedure. Esther Kerr to be terminated."

Gemma's eyes are wide as she once again looks at Tully. "I don't understand," she says. "What does any of this mean? This file is at least ten years old, and my mother is still with me. She looks after my father."

"Maybe that's why she's still alive."

"Maybe that's why *we're* still alive." She removes her seeing spectacles. "She realized the only way to keep us alive was to make certain Father stayed alive as well. But why? GOD kills indiscriminately, does He not? Why would He care if Father lived or died? My parents' relationship with Him seems to have grayed quite a bit since the Revolution. I don't understand any of this, Mr. Tully."

"Nor do I, missus, and I'm right under GOD's nose."

"Why have you shown me this? These are not answers, only more questions."

"Because you were looking for it. Because these questions need to be asked so someone will find answers. And because somebody has to do something. Somebody has to stop what's going on in the ninth ring. Somebody with more courage than a lowly archivist with a mute doggy."

"Mr. Tully," she says warily, "what happens in the ninth ring?"

With his unnaturally large eyes, he gives her a look of such sorrow as to make her throat close up. "Ah, Miss Gemma, such horrible things. You see, I know now," he says, tears welling, "I know that GOD is nothing but a heartless devil. When you head out, Miss Gemma, when you leave for the ninth, which is what you must do, take Madden here with you, won't ya? He's a good dog and he's been a good friend." Tully reaches behind him and rubs the beast behind the ears. "He deserves better than this. Better than me."

"The ninth ring," Gemma repeats. She does not think it a preposterous idea at all. She knows she should, but it sinks into her as something she wants to do. For some reason, it matches this notion of immoral passion she's been playing with. "You won't go to the ninth ring with me?"

"Oh no, miss. I'm a coward, you see, a skinny little flitter-cat. I barely escaped what my brother did to the rest of my family. He slit our grandmother's throat, you know. And the baby. What he did to my sister's baby." He squeezes his eyes tight as large tears tumble down. "I've not left the archives in five years."

Gemma rises from her seat and puts a hand on Tully's shoulder as she kneels beside him.

"Who is this wretched creature? Who is your brother?" Gemma says.

"Why, the Senator General, missus. Hegart."

Her mouth drops, but she collects herself. "He will not harm you, not so much as touch you, when you're with me. If I leave for the ninth ring, you must come out into the world again. Just once. I will take Madden, but you will meet me outside on the steps with him."

"I don't know, miss…"

"Yes, you do, Mr. Tully. You know this is exactly how it is supposed to happen."

A WOMAN in Esther Kerr's situation, surrounded by assassination plots and rumors of deceit, needs to know how to protect herself. Esther has books, secret books on self-preservation, written by ancient killers. She knows how to make a strangulation look like a suicide or a push from a balcony seem a careless misstep. She has become more conniving and illusory than many who have tried to deceive her. She lives in a manse, yet in truth the whole thing could go to blazes for all she cares. She only holds two things dear: her daughter and her rage. Their extremes balance her out.

Duana is frightened when she finds Esther standing in her bedchamber. "M'lady," she says, clutching at her heart. "What are you doin' in this part of the manse?" She sniffs.

"It's my house, dear," Esther says. "I can go where I wish. I was concerned about you. You look as if you've been crying."

Duana's face is flushed and haggard, her eyes wet. Her apron is a mess, wrinkled and soaked from her tears. "Aye, missus. I have. This day has not been kind." She crumples into a weeping mess whose blubbers and words of explanation are meaningless.

"Calm yourself, girl," Esther says. Her words are as sharp as the angles of her shoulder pads. "Have a seat on your bed here. I've had Rugal make some tea to calm your nerves."

"Th-thank you, m'lady," she says, shocked. She takes the fine porcelain cup from Esther as she sits down. The tea is still steaming. The scent of cinnamon seems to calm the girl.

Esther slowly begins to circle around the small room, eyeing it with little interest. "I hope you enjoy the cinnamon. I wouldn't normally give it to the servants, but you looked as though you needed it. Don't crack the porcelain, please."

Duana drinks carefully from the cup.

"Would you like to tell me the matter, Duana?" The servants' quarters has no décor. No paintings are allowed. Only gray wall. Esther notices Duana's walls are in need of a new coat of paint. "I saw you earlier," she says, "speaking with Senator General Hegart."

"Oh, no, m'lady!" Duana turns to the mistress so suddenly, she nearly drops the cup. Only a little of the tea is spilt. "I wasn't talkin'. Honest. He only told me somethin'… somethin' awful… just awful…" She has another fit of tears.

Esther gives the girl a minute to compose herself again. She continues her slow circle about the room. "What did he tell you?"

"He told me… He says… that my Finn has died. That he executed my Finn."

"A lover." This is not a question. "And a ferryman at that, I take it, or else why would Hegart care." She smiles, finding this most humorous. The ferrymen seem to be regaining their souls.

"Yes, ma'am." She takes another sip of her tea. "But he weren't like the others, m'lady. He weren't. He was becoming a good, decent man."

"And why did the Senator General tell you this? What does he want from you?"

The girl coughs as if she has a tickle in her throat. "He says to me… Wait… Oh, m'lady, I feel so dizzy…"

"What does he want from you?"

"He says to me that he'll do the same murdering on me if I don't do what he wants… what he wants and report your movements… to him…"

"And what are your plans to that?" Esther is at the chamber door, her back to the maid. The door is wide open.

Duana cannot answer. Over her shoulder, Esther hears the girl's choking, her gasps for air. The porcelain falls to the floor and breaks.

"Silly girl," says Esther. "You broke my porcelain. I'm terribly sorry, Duana, but I'm afraid I'm going to have to let you go."

She waits to hear the final desperate gasp for air and then leaves Duana dead on her chamber floor.

About Passion

LAWL HAS been wandering for days, staggering around with the other unknowns of the Immortal City. Without Duncan, his is an untethered life. He is lost and fumbling, stumbling and falling into mud puddles and disregarding the rules of safety on the busy avenues and boulevards.

He is not careful. He would invite the ferrymen to take him to the ninth ring. Then he would at least be with Duncan and Gran. But the ferrymen have all disappeared. He has not seen one black-coated bastard in all his wanderings since Gran and Duncan were ripped from him. Where's a ferryman when you need one?

The Kingdom Guards only laugh at him. It is not their job to take a man to the ninth. They remind him of this, and then they hit and kick him and then laugh at him some more. They have so little entertainment, these guards. Perhaps they will keep him around. Everyone needs a good laugh.

Lawl does everything wrong. He sleeps in gutters. He sits in the middle of streets. He steals food from vendors and does not even run. He only eats a bite or two of his pillage before he tosses the rest to a passing child or horse. In the past few days, he has been hit and thrashed more times than he can count.

Duncan remains with him. He is smiling in Lawl's dreams. He is crying in Lawl's nightmares. He asks for forgiveness. But why?

Lawl realizes he has not been meandering aimlessly through the Immortal City at all, but only taking the long way 'round to a specific destination. And he is here. His legs quake as he stands directly in front of Duncan's apartment in a nicer district of the second ring. He bites his lip to keep from crying. His dirty face is already painted with tear tracks. He pushes his unwashed dark hair back from his forehead and approaches the place. Residents of the district eye him with disgust.

"Someone call a ferryman," he hears a woman say.

"Aye," he replies in a low mumble. "Please do."

The steps up to Duncan's apartment are cleaner than those back in the third ring and not as awkwardly spaced as the places in the older areas of the city. Lawl sees a family has already moved into Duncan's apartment. He rests his head against the wall and collects himself, pouring tears to soothe his rage.

An older man stands at the door where once Duncan had carried him in with a romantic flourish. "What do you want?" the old man says gruffly, smoking on a pipe. "We want nothing to do with you. Get gone."

"The man who once lived here," Lawl says, trying to speak clearly. "Where are his things? His furniture? Art? What've ya done with his things?"

The man looks Lawl over. "They was taken first day. He had the plague, they say. Most everything was burnt, I suspect."

Lawl cannot help but let a small cry loose, a hand slipping from a ledge.

"No, Daddy," a young boy says. "Some of his clothes is still down in the courtyard."

Lawl gasps, feeling a reprieve. "Thank you!" he says to the boy, and then he races down the steps to the courtyard. The residents are kind enough to give him wide berth.

Lawl recognizes every thread of the small pile of clothes lying in the courtyard. People huff, puff, and swear as he kneels at the pile, clutching the first shirt he sees—part of Duncan's Glass Halls uniform. He holds it to his face and breathes in Duncan's scent as if it is the first drink of water he has had in days. It is life for him. The scent moves through his being, every vein, every artery. The smell is every memory, good or bad, since they became one. And now he knows what he must do.

He strips off his own clothes. He takes his time, as if the people standing near him were nothing at all. Slowly he dresses in Duncan's uniform. He feels better surrounded by Duncan's scent, as if the smell were Duncan's unfaltering optimism. Lawl has decided he is going to stop moping and find some answers, and the only way to find answers in the Immortal City was to get into the first ring. Duncan and Gran may yet be alive. He will wash his face, clean up, and then he will walk through the first-ring gate when the laborers are let in at night as a worker for the Glass Halls. From there he will find his answers. Yes, he tells himself. For Duncan and Gran, he will find answers.

THE DOCTRESS warden Deirdre Maire is walking the Preparation Ward of the Great Medical Hall of the ninth ring. It is a daily routine, checking in on the patients who are soon to die, making certain they are prepared for their trip to the Factory. The Preparation Ward is a long hall on the third floor of the East Wing. Much light comes from the tall windows, and the ward does not smell of death but of more pleasant things such as flowers brought in daily from some unnamed farm in the five rings. Deirdre demanded the flowers. They seem to comfort and calm the patients, and that, in turn, makes her job much less stressful.

Twenty-four of sixty beds in the hall are filled. Last week every bed was filled. Those still alive now are hooked up to pain medicines and are fed through tubes. Deirdre inspects each of these feeding tubes. A few of the patients watch her, but they turn away when she glances in their direction. They do not wish to see her face. But then, she does not wish to see theirs, either.

She comes to the third-sex plague victim, the one named Gran. Deirdre hasn't come upon another third-sexer in a while. Doctress Sara is looking at Gran's charts at the end of the bed. Deirdre tolerates Sara because Sara is different from the others. She seems to care. Naturally, this will only lead to mental instability in a place like this, but under all her resentment and condescension, Deirdre appreciates it all the same. She wonders if Sara realizes she will be filling one of these beds someday.

"How is she?" Deirdre says, looking at Gran.

"She's well," Sara says in her gentle voice. "But she had a rough evening last night. I do not see how she is still here. She's a tough ol' thing."

"She's a third-sex. We have to be tough."

"She keeps asking for a Duncan. A son maybe?"

"I believe that's the name of young man she came in with. He may be her son. The guards had to pry the two apart at the entrance before taking him to be branded."

"Perhaps we could find a way for them to be together?"

"Don't be ridiculous. He is in quarantine, and she is to be prepared. When she finally dies, how do you think he would react to us taking her off to the Factory?"

Sara's voice went to a whisper. "He doesn't need to know about that."

Gran opens her eyes and stares at Deirdre. Deirdre cannot help but fidget, and she moves her face so Gran can see the good side and is spared the ugliness. Gran motions for her to come nearer. This surprises the doctress, but she complies stiffly.

"Do you need something?" Deirdre says, standing fully erect over Gran's bed and looking down at her. "Do you have enough pain medication? We can increase the dosage."

"No, no, sweetie," Gran says, barely audible. "Come closer, ma dear."

Deirdre leans down hesitantly, and Gran touches the scarred side of her face. This gives Deirdre a start. The feeling of the old woman's delicate hand against her face causes her to stand straight up again and step back. Her heart blossoms in beats, and she puts a hand to her chest.

"Doctress?" Sara looks concerned. She always looks concerned.

"I'm fine," Deirdre nearly yells. Gran has fallen back to sleep. Her pain medication offers her but a few minutes of sporadic lucidity.

Deirdre walks to the west wing of the hospital. She wants to feel where the old woman had touched her, but she dare not. There are so many people around her, and a few of the doctors study her ardently, always looking for her failings so that they might have reason to replace her.

The Quarantine Ward looks much the same as the Preparation Ward. The main difference is that the patients are allowed to roam about and even to go out on the veranda if they first ask permission. The doctors and their lobotomized nursing staff wear masks against any strain of virus. Deirdre is handed a mask by one of the vacant nurses, a young man who might at one time have had a mischievous grin.

Duncan is sitting on his bed. His face shows signs of exhaustion. He has bags under his eyes, and his skin looks pale and oily. Still, he is an attractive man. He reminds Deirdre of the young men who once courted her and chased her through the streets of the Immortal City back when she was a beauty. He slowly looks up to her as she approaches his bed. He is rubbing his forearm where he has been branded with the mark of GOD, a circle with five rings.

"You're Duncan?" she says.

He stands. "Aye. Is there something wrong with Gran?"

The look on his face speaks of concern... and something else. Guilt. She sees that look every morning in her own reflection.

"She's fine," she says, not bothering to shield her ugliness from him. "I just wanted to tell you, she's fine."

Why? Why did she want to tell him this?

"Can I see her?" he says, hope straining in his voice.

She says nothing as she turns around and leaves quarantine, her black skirt like a trail of death in her wake. It is all she can take of this place today. The quarantined are never made better. Not here.

ROSSA THINKS the sky is clearer than it has ever been, even seeing a hint of blue through the orange. She quite likes that about her stay with the gardener in his thatch-roofed home on the outskirts of the third ring. Here, the tall city buildings are only a mark on the horizon. The greatest height belongs to the trees, the largest area to the fields and the gardens. Far off in the distance, one can barely make out the third-ring wall. She loves looking look up and not seeing heaps of cumbersome architecture twisting to and fro with lacing iron walkways and rope bridges as high as the eye can see. Nothing impedes her vision of the sky here. She drinks in the air as she stands over the outside kiln making dinner—fresh vegetables, manna, and fresh meat, most likely squirrel the gardener has caught and skinned.

The gardener made her an offer the first night she arrived at his home. Cook for him, clean for him, and she could stay and recuperate for a bit. She agreed, perhaps too eagerly. The old man got a greedy stare in his eyes. But no matter. Rossa needed this. She was even given a new wardrobe. The old man's former maid had left in a hurry, it seemed, and hadn't cared to take any of her clothes. Rossa did not ask any questions, but she kept her eyes open.

"She was ungrateful," the gardener told her. "So, so ungrateful, and after all I had done for her. She owed me. Yes. Yes. The little slut owed me. Mmmm."

He gave her a single rule to follow: "I don't want to ever see you in the garden," said he. "My friends, my masterpieces, require absolute quiet and care, and they won't get it with the likes of you whorin' about. Mine are the only hands that will tend them. Do you understand, missy?"

Of course she did.

He inspects her now, with one eye wide open and the other nearly closed due to some abnormality as she stirs the stew at the kiln. Every day he seems to inspect her more. He holds a pipe, and his lip has a twitch. His garments are dirty, patched rags the years have faded apathetic colors. Rossa keeps a good distance between them. Men have looked at her with just such an expression before, and it has never turned out well. If the gardener were to ever try anything, though, she knows she can easily overpower him.

"What is your name?" she asked him the first day there.

"I be a gardener," he said, rather reproachfully. "That's all you need to know. Mmmm. There be not much to know after that."

She knew then she would not be staying with him for too long. The looks he gives her are not healthy. They are not safe or sane.

She stirs the stew, and the scents waft into the air around her. The gardener has a varied collection of spices. More than Rossa has ever seen. Cumin, cinnamon, hosterscent, garlic, and guren powder to name but a few. She could open a shop with the dishes she could make if she were back in her district.

A wagon is pulling up the road. Rossa saw it coming through the trees, but she assumed it would pass them by. Now that it is closer, she sees it is a death wagon. Have they come for her? Has the gardener given her up? She cannot go with them until she sees that Key is safe. She drops the spoon in the soup and prepares to hide.

"Calm yourself, girl," the gardener says. "They're just bringin' me some tools for me work, for me art. My garden gets the best food from the ferrymen. Mmmm."

The death wagon comes to a stop just yards from them. A ferryman jumps down and opens the back. The gardener hobbles to the wagon, saying something to the ferryman, though inaudible to Rossa. The gardener looks at her as he is speaking to the ferryman. This makes Rossa uneasy, but the ferryman seems to be uninterested in anything the gardener is saying. Instead, he pulls out a long burlap bag as the old man is prattling on. It is a cumbersome thing and falls to the ground at the gardener's feet. The gardener, having said whatever it was he had to say, drags the bag off toward the garden as the ferryman mounts the death wagon and heads back down the road taking no notice of Rossa. The gardener looks back at her, though, as he works the brown bag through the garden gates, his eye ever-inspecting.

Rossa does not know what type of plant food is in the bag. She does not know what type of plants the gardener is feeding. But she knows what type of business the ferrymen deal in, and this knowledge makes her shiver. Something is not right.

"THE SOUP is tasteless," says Esther Kerr as she sits at her large dining room table. She is pleased Gemma is home for lunch. Her daughter's new position in the archives gives her more freedom, though, Esther is certain, no less attention. GOD's eyes are everywhere. "I am missing Duana more with each passing meal. She wasn't much of a housekeeper, but she was at least a decent cook." Esther looks over her shoulder at the new cook, a young man who seems terrified already. Sweat drips from his brow. "I hope you have plans to better yourself, or you won't last long here."

"It's not so bad, Momma," Gemma says. "Not so bad at all. Don't scare him so."

"But the soup, my dear. The soup is tasteless."

"You barely eat anyway, Momma." Gemma was not touching her own meal very much, either. She sat with her hands on her lap, her back straight against the chair. "Besides, it fits right in. Many things are tasteless, Momma. I am finding the whole world altogether bland."

Esther takes a sip of her wine and eyes the girl suspiciously. She dangles and dances her dainty wineglass in the air between thumb and forefinger. "Is there something you wish to say, child?"

Gemma pauses. "I'm just puzzled. Why would Duana kill herself?"

"Who can say?" Esther takes her silver spoon and plays with her soup, circles and circles and circles. "Perhaps she was pining over a lost love. And too, she was a thief. She had some of my porcelain in her room. Perhaps she felt guilty."

"Or harassed."

Esther does not like the path her daughter's conversation is taking, nor does she like the tone of that path. "It's about passion, darling girl. Passion is always our undoing. We want, then we strive, and when we cannot obtain, we fall apart. And we always fall apart."

"Surely, Momma, you had passion once. You were a revolutionary. You can't change the world without passion."

The servants are fidgeting. The word makes them uncomfortable.

"Once I did. Maybe. But it caused me nothing but pain." She is back to the wine, swirling it in her glass, watching the red liquid dance near the lip. "Our revolution was a noble idea. But in the end, a government led by theocracy is no different than one led any other way. We set ourselves up, thinking our beliefs would better this world. That people would see it in time and embrace it. But our democratic theocracy… well, it's fallen apart, hasn't it, darling girl, because it is something that can never exist. Now GOD sits on His throne, a mad monarch."

The new cook gasps.

Esther looks over her shoulder and eyes the man. "He'll have to go," she says.

"Excuse me, Momma," says Gemma. "But I don't know if I see the nobility in the Revolution anymore. Not from the files I've been reading in the archives. They are heavy with blood."

"Some would call those sacrifices." Esther studies her daughter with slight apprehension. "Your eyes look tired, my dear. Do the archives not have sufficient lighting? Perhaps you should seek other employment."

"Momma," Gemma says. "Sacrifices? The revolutionaries killed anyone who they perceived as different. They killed children. I saw the orders. Your name was on them, as was Father's, and some person called T—"

Esther is a striking snake. She stands at once. "What did you see? What files did you see?"

The servants have all gone quite pale.

"The archives, Momma," Gemma says, cowering under her mother's glare. She is quieter now. "They say so much. All these horrible things…"

"What do you know of this person T?" Esther begins to shout. Her eyes are wide with rage.

Gemma stands. "I think I'll head back to the archives. I'm not very hungry today. Excuse me."

"Gemma!" Esther cries after her as her daughter rounds the table and leaves the dining room. "Gemma! You have no idea what I've had to do for you. To protect you. I know sacrifice too, darling girl."

Her daughter does not answer as she leaves out the front door.

"Don't believe what you read about me in those files," she says, though she knows it is useless. "Don't believe any of it."

The room is silent for a moment before Esther screams and swipes the table with her arms and the wineglasses, bowls, and candles clatter and crash to the floor.

"You!" she screams at the cook, her breaths shaking and quick. "Clean this up. Then get out of my house, you worthless toad."

DEIRDRE STARES out her office window. She dares to look at her reflection. Mirrors are a thing of the past for her. She has not seen one in years, nor does she allow them in the hospital, but she can do nothing about windows. She is feeling the scarred side of her face where the old woman touched her. She feels that touch still, the gentleness, the compassion, surging from the old woman's fingertips into her being. For the briefest of moments, she glimpsed her other life, the more contented one before the Revolution. She had danced then. Many men and women had touched her face gently, had kissed her tenderly. She remembers smiling and laughing until her face hurt. Surely all that is not a dream. Surely it happened.

Her smile once charmed rabid dogs.

Senator General Hegart has sent a note with a ferryman. He will not be able to come and see her as he has promised. This is no surprise. He has not seen her for longer than she can remember. Something always comes up. This time, it is a new outbreak of the plague. Last time, it was the orphans running wild in the city. But she is relieved, for what would she do if he came? Hate has made her ugly. She can see that much in her reflection in the window. And she does hate him. It festers in her, eating away at her insides and causing her painful cramps. She shakes so awfully at times that she finds it impossible to do any work. More than one lobotomy has been botched because of her pain, her hate.

Deirdre remembers the last time she was with the Senator General. There was no conversation. Words are for pages are for books are for history. There was only fucking. She did not move at all as he grunted and hit at her, inside and out. As he cursed her for being "so damn ugly" and then fucked her harder for it, soaking her with drool. After they were through, the bed was wet and sticky from his saliva alone.

She would have cried if she cared or noticed the pain anymore. She had no sensation in her private areas. Not since the Senator General's slipshod operation on her. Her only pleasure from the sexual experience with him was the touch—even his touch—on her face. "I'm still here," she would say to herself. "Aye, that's my face, that's my flesh. I can still be touched."

Deirdre breathes deeply. "Time to stop your daydreaming, you fool," she says. "There's work to do. Fill your day so you don't think of such things."

She is good at filling her days. Her mind rarely wanders except when she is alone. The old woman has distracted her, but it is over now. Yes. She is quite fine. She has a new nurse to lobotomize. Hospitals do not run themselves.

IT IS dusk and light is fading. The sky is so golden as to make GOD envious. Something has been troubling Rossa ever since she saw the ferryman with the gardener. Something is dark, very dark, here. She tries to shake the foreboding. Never mind her suspicions of the old man, she has to leave this place and resume her search for Key. Her rest has been sufficient. Her bruises have healed. She made promises to Claire and Aidan, and she intends to keep them as far as she is able. If the child still lives, Rossa will find him. She is certain she is the only one looking specifically for him. GOD does not care for lost children.

After searching the house and the barns, Rossa realizes the gardener must be with his masterpieces. She knows the gardener has warned her about disturbing the peace of the garden, but she intends to leave this night and has no desire to wait for him to return to the house in the wee hours of the morning as is his habit. She will chance an angry spat.

The black cast-iron gate feels cold and heavy as she pushes it open. Everything grows around her in silhouette. The fading light gives form, but no definition. She feels watched by the larger plants and trees. Their closed blooms and bulbs follow her like eyes on stems. She walks proudly, but watchful. This is no ordinary garden. It is expansive and overgrown, and has a unique stench Rossa can almost place. This odor is so strong, she is forced to put her hand to her nose.

She dares not call out for the gardener. Who knows what might answer? She hears a steady undertone, a growl in the dusk that seems to come from the plants themselves. She tries not to listen, lest she hears words that parallel memories from her childhood nightmares of snovelfarks and boogeymen.

The garden is guarded by scarecrows. There is one for every crop in this field. They stand, arms outstretched against the now-darkened sky. They glisten from the rain, only it has not rained for days. Rossa is drawn to a scarecrow that guards a field of leafy cornbean stalks as tall as she. She pushes past the stalks, her hand still to her nose and mouth. She is continuously tripped up underfoot by the strange, lumpy roots of the vegetables. She stands beneath the scarecrow and looks into his eyes. His eyes. These are not buttons sewn into a cloth sack. These are actual eyes, filmed over with white and surrounded by pale, rotting flesh. From the clothing, Rossa sees that this was once a Kingdom Guard, an expression of horror still set on his face.

Rossa stifles a scream and turns to run. She sees field after field, each one with a rotting corpse to keep the crows' attention elsewhere. Why bother with vegetation when there is fresh meat?

Suddenly, Rossa hears movement toward her in the stalks. She tries to run but is tripped by the roots and falls. But then she observes with a gasp, these are not roots at all. Severed hands and feet litter the ground. Rossa vomits at the sight of half a child's face sticking up from the earth, glaring at her.

She cannot see the gardener coming up behind her, but she can hear him. She hears his dragging movement through the stalks. She hears his hoarse whispers to his plants. He says, "Shhh. Everything will be all right. Aye, it's all going to be just fine."

But not for Rossa. She is frozen in fear. Her mind flashes back to an alley many years ago and a man of GOD. The gardener's feet shuffle along the ground behind her. She hears the dull thud of hands and feet being kicked out of the way, of bones being stepped on and broken. She hears him rear back, ready to strike her with something. But then she thinks of Claire and forces herself to act.

She ducks and rolls away from the strike, crawling under the stalks. He comes after her. She is confused and heads to the scarecrow, crawling over the muck and the rot, disallowing the faces and arms and legs to register in her mind. She gives the scarecrow a mighty push from behind. The gardener is caught unaware as the corpse falls on top of him. Rossa knocks the rake from his hand, and the moment he stands free again, Rossa swings the rake with all her strength. The gardener's cry is a sad thing, not befitting a death. She drives the rake through his temple and face, its sharp prongs sunk in deep. He falls to the ground, his large eye still staring up at her.

Rossa runs from the field and the garden, tripping over death and decay. Once past the iron gate, she collapses to the ground, retching and stripping the soiled garments from her body.

She lies on the grass for a while, naked and staring into the night sky. She is shivering from what she has seen. But she will forge new armor from this trauma. She urges herself to rise and go inside the house.

"You are stronger now," she says. "You've brand new skin."

She bathes, washing away the filth and stench of the garden, washing away the complacency of a woman she can no longer be. This does not take her long. She wants to be rid of this place soon.

When she is done bathing, she finds a new wardrobe. Rossa is through with skirts and long dresses and the designs she is supposed to wear. She finds them cumbersome. Their very idea is confining. She searches for items of clothing that will be easier to move about in because she suddenly realizes she will need to fight. She knows now what happened to the last maid, and the one before that and so on. She wonders what field each of them watches over. She refuses to think on that too deeply now, though. Instead, she focuses on all the clothes that have been left behind. She chooses a pair of dark riding pants and a lace blouse, which shows her ample chest. Over this, she wears a long black coat, buttoned at her waist, and she finds a pair of thin black boots that extend to her knees. In the mirror, she sees that she is Death. She bundles her long red hair and pins a large black hat slightly askew on her head.

Before she leaves the house, she finds a satchel and fills it with food. She grabs a large knife from the kitchen and sticks it in her belt, with another in her boot. They will do until she can find a proper sword. She wanders into the gardener's bedchamber—it smells of manure—and finds his coin purse.

Finally, Rossa heads to the barn. She finds two horses: one of pure white and one of gray. She sets the white horse free in the garden but saddles up the gray. "How would you like to come with me?" she says.

The horse seems content to oblige.

"Good. Because I didn't trust your sister. White has never been my color, lass. I'm gray through and through. I don't know if that crazy man gave you a name, but I think I'll call you Claire. You don't mind that, do ya?"

Rossa, once of the House Bouadica, with the satchel on her back, leads the horse outside and mounts it with ease. "How about we find our boy, Claire?" she whispers in its ear before they take off on a night road toward a part of the city more urban but no less dangerous.

KEY IS sniffling by the fire on the rooftop. He is alone, but that is fine. If he joined up with one of the orphan bands, he would be more easily caught by the ferrymen. His will be a lonely life. He accepts this, but not without nightly tears.

He ran after he saw his father dead, just as Rossa told him to do. He ran without thinking, his mind a blank slate, acting as a buffer from the pain, not letting it all sink in so very soon. He just ran, dodging through people and stalls, into homes and down long alleyways with secret doors and secret stairs. He was carried by his feet, the rest of him too numb to do much else. He ran up to the highest of the buildings and heaps in the most abandoned areas of the city. The air became thinner as he climbed, but he did not stop until at last he collapsed on the ramshackle ruins of what was once a luxury apartment above the clouds. Then, with his arms wrapped around his broken drum, he slept and he cried.

He has been safe here. No one has come looking for him. Most have forgotten the city still reaches this high into the clouds. No structure is allowed to be higher than GOD's Tower, yet one or two in the ghost towns of the second and third rings manage to escape notice. In vestiges of play, Key pretends he is high in a fortress sometimes. The broken blocks and splintered wood beams of crumbled walls allow him this fantasy. At night, he lets his legs dangle over the edge, and he tries to peer past the thick dark blue clouds to the city down below.

He is an angel without a soul to look after.

Sometimes the wind is a comfort. He almost discerns a language in it.

When he is hungry, he is careful to take the most secret of stairs. From there, he sneaks into a local home that has not yet been abandoned. If he's lucky, he gets past a lost vendor and tries to steal something. He is usually successful.

But not tonight. Tonight, he goes to bed hungry and sad. The wind is no comfort. Only his small fire offers him any warmth of heart.

He sniffles, the wind whistles, and then, quite surprisingly, he hears another sound just before he nods off. A faint shuffling. Someone is here. Someone else has found Key's fortress. With his little heart racing, he suffocates the fire and waits, remaining perfectly still against a stone wall beneath the scant moonlight. The shuffling gets closer. The remains of the arched doorway is like a stage, on which Key is certain he will soon see the most horrible things.

But no monster comes forward. It is a man in a uniform. He carries a bag over his shoulders. He looks around the ruins but does not see Key. The man walks cautiously to the edge of Key's tower. The wind rushes through his dark hair as he stands above the field of night clouds. All is still and quiet. Then the man turns.

"Hello?" he says. "Is someone there?"

Key jumps up with his drum and tries to flee, but the man is quick and closer to the door. He catches the child. Key pelts him with fists and kicks. He releases Key and stumbles backward. Key wipes at his tears, sure he is soon to be killed.

The man massages his shin. "You got me good," he says. He is holding the other hand out, palm open, a sign of friendship. "It's okay, boy. I'm not one of them. Whoever you're scurred of, I ain't them."

Key is unsoothed. He is on his feet and ready to run, breathing heavy and shifting his weight from foot to foot.

"I'm just lookin' for a place to hide, see? Like you. My name is Lawl. I had planned to get into the first ring, but there was a chase. Ol' Queen Mags was after me, the frigid bitch. I just need a place to hide out. Just for a wee bit. I've been climbing all day, and this looks like the safest place I've seen. Do ya think ya could stand sharing the space with me? Just for the night? I promise ya, I'll be gone come mornin'. I've no reason to stay around here. None at all."

Key does not know if he should trust this man. He eyes him warily.

"Look," Lawl says, digging into his bag. "I've got food." He pulls out an apple and a slice of bread. "You're welcome to share it with me. It'll be my rent."

Key inches forward. His eyes never leave the man's face, but his hand reaches for the bread. Like a timid, wild puppy, he snatches the slice and hurriedly devours it. Lawl waits for him to finish, then offers the apple.

"There's more," he says.

Key takes the apple and walks back to the smoldering ruins of his fire. Lawl approaches slowly and sits opposite the boy. Key starts the fire again quickly, and Lawl brings from his bag a whole loaf of bread. The boy looks at the bag in wonder.

"I was born a gypsy meself," Lawl says with a lopsided grin.

If Key could giggle, he surely would as he tears into the bread. Lawl is smiling.

"You build a good fire," Lawl says. He warms his hands over the flame. "Do you play, then?" he asks, nodding to the drum.

Key holds the drum closely. He fingers the tear where it had been ripped as he ran from the ferrymen.

Lawl is once again digging around in his bag. He comes up with a large ball of adhesive. It is thicker than any Key has seen.

"May I see your drum?" Lawl asks.

Key warily hands the drum over to the man.

"Everything can be fixed, boy," says Lawl, as he rips a strip off the ball. "Aye. Everything that is broken can come back better, stronger. There's no point in having a song you can't sing or a drum you can't beat."

Lawl hands the drum back to Key. The boy drops his bread on the floor and examines the instrument. It looks almost new, but for a small line where the tear once was. He drops a single beat. Then another. Then a whole series of ecstatic drumbeats as he smiles a toothy grin. Lawl is smiling as well. Key nearly tackles him in an embrace.

"Play something, boy," Lawl says. "Me and the clouds be your audience."

Key needs no more encouragement than this. He fills the abandoned tower with his drumsong, the sound of a heart quickened. It spills out into the night and bounces among the clouds. No thunderstorm has ever given such a show as this.

THREATS BENEATH THE HUSH

GEMMA HAS decided to steal away tonight.

Last night she had a dream. Abrythnia stood in the open door of the manse. It was dark outside. The goddess would not enter but instead held her arms wide, beckoning the girl to her with divine light emanating from her face. Gemma awoke knowing this was the last she would ever see of the first ring. Tonight, she would be leaving for the ninth ring and then for the edge of the world. To find us there.

She has things to do, however. After getting dressed in a long brown coat over a matching drab skirt, she writes a brief letter to her mother. She cannot contain the drops of resentment in the words as she writes: *Have gone to find the Passions. Do not look for me. I love you, but this is not my place. We both know it never was.*

She does not sign it. The note is left on her pillow. Her mother hardly ever comes into Gemma's bedchamber, so unless curiosity overtakes Esther, a servant will find it and give it to her.

In the archives, down in the forbidden room of books, she explains her plan to Tully. He is hesitant, but he agrees to meet her outside tonight so she might take Madden with her on the journey.

"I'll miss that dog," says the archivist, his saucer eyes already awash in tears. Gemma wonders if he will survive alone.

Now, she has but to wait. She stops in at a local pub across from the Glass Halls and hears the city humming along. She is surprised she has not seen the monotony here until recently, the patterns of straight-line boredom. Everything is so quiet, but not peaceful. Threats lie beneath the hush. These threats are made vocal when the Voice of GOD repeats His daily diatribe unto the world. Everything once seemed so clean and orderly, but now all Gemma wants to do is throw away her sunspectacles. To never have to see the world through tinted frames again.

She hides at curfew in the garden behind the Glass Halls where she met Rossa. She hopes the woman has found the child. Her stomach churns as she thinks she may be responsible for his death. When it is safe, she hurries to the archives and waits at the back door for Tully to appear. She is concerned he will not show. But then, she assures herself, he knows she must get to the ninth ring. He feels this strange push and pull of dreams and augury as deeply as she. She finds a place to hide behind a muscular statue meant to resemble GOD. If it does, no one knows, for who can look upon the face of the Almighty?

It is night now. The streets are empty save for the Kingdom Guard on their patrols. Gemma knows the impossibility of hiding in the first ring even at night. The crystal and glass give the slightest movement away. It is so frustrating, she wants to smash the whole city and she feels no shame in this. Not after reading the files in the archives.

She has been waiting for some time, growing restless, when the door squeaks open. Tully peeks out, his glowing bulbous eyes searching for Gemma in the darkness. He clearly has no plans to actually step from the building, but Madden does not know this. The huge white hound bounds out the door, free for the first time in his life. He knocks Tully to the ground in the process, and the archive door shuts with an echoing bang and locks behind them.

Tully stands and seems unsure whether to run after Madden or try to get back into the archives. Gemma comes to his aide.

"He'll be fine," she assures Tully quietly, taking his arm. "He's a dog. They are the most loyal creatures in the world. Madden has just gone to play for a bit. Can you blame him, after being for most of his life such a big dog in such a small space?"

"He'll be back?"

"I won't leave without him," she promises.

Tully examines his surroundings. "It's darker than I remember."

Gemma is uncertain if this is a joke, so she stifles a laugh.

"Are you ready?" Tully says. He is holding onto her arm so tightly it hurts. His eyes are the size of grapefruits.

"I am. I'm more ready for this than I've been for anything I can remember. I'm ready and I'm absolutely terrified."

"You there!" A Kingdom Guard has spotted them, drawn by the slam of the door. He motions for another, and the pair approach Gemma and Tully with wide, quick strides.

Tully begins to shake.

"Stay calm," Gemma whispers.

"What are you doing out past curfew?" The guard has an uncomfortable leer. Gemma suspects he means harm no matter how she answers. He is pockmarked and angry.

"We've been locked out—"

"Not you," he says. "You." He points a sword at Tully's throat.

"We've done nothing," Gemma says. "Please. Just let us be on our way."

A large hand swats her so hard across the face, she goes flying to the ground. The sting leaves her deaf to all else around her for a few moments. When she finally regains her composure, she sees Tully on the ground as well. The guards are kicking him and laughing about it. Tully is begging for mercy but getting none. He looks to Gemma, his eyes holding such misery she has to look away. *What have I done?* she thinks to herself. *They're going to kill him and it will be my fault.*

She looks back just in time to see the heavier of the two guards leap into the air and jump on Tully's back. Tully cries in agony for help, for mercy, for death, for a GOD that doesn't care.

Gemma rises. She may not be able to do much against these two, but she will not stand by and watch as a friend is trampled on like manure in the field. Death is near, and she feels it is coming for her. She runs toward the attack, but a great flash of white knocks her again to the ground. She hears more screams, but now it is the guards. Heavy drops of blood rain down around Gemma as Madden rips into the second guard. The first man is a bloody, lifeless pulp against the archive door. Tully looks up at Madden in astonishment from his fetal position on the ground. An arm lands near his head, and he flinches.

Gemma runs to Tully. "We haven't got time to waste now!" she says, grabbing his arm and pulling him up regardless of his pained protests. "Other guards will be here soon. We need to hide."

Madden licks his bloody teeth and is soon at the ready. Gemma puts Tully on Madden's back.

"You're a good dog," Tully says as he strokes the dog's coat.

"Hold on to him," Gemma says. "Hold on to each other."

Tully mumbles something as his eyes close.

"Stay awake, Tully," Gemma says as they hurry through the city streets, her heels echoing on the cobblestones. "We'll find you a doctor soon, but you must stay awake. It will do no good if you go into shock."

But where will they go? Gemma knows nothing of the seedier parts of the Immortal City. She has no idea where to go. All she knows is the gate, so that is the direction in which she heads.

Sirens are blaring. The guards have been discovered. In the streets ahead, a large group of Kingdom Guards gathers. They have not spotted the three of them yet, but it is only a matter of seconds. She pauses, uncertain what to do. Her head is dizzy, her heart races. She looks around for some route to take. And then she sees it.

To her right, a large portion of wall suddenly vanishes, pulling back and revealing a dark doorway. A man and a woman appear, ushering them to follow. Gemma sees no other course and no time to object. Madden bares his teeth but follows Gemma just the same. The wall grumbles closed behind them once they are out of sight.

Inside the wall, it is dark and cramped. At least five others are here along with Gemma, Tully, and Madden, but there is no time for introductions. In complete darkness, they are being hurried down what Gemma can only assume is an old sewer system, remnants of an older order.

They are led on for a while without a word from the wall people. Gemma is becoming concerned for Tully. She has not heard him whimper or moan since they were first brought in. She continuously feels for his pulse.

At last, they come to a stop. A torch is lit, and Gemma sees they are in a small spherical room most likely meant for storage in some ancient past. The bricks are rust-colored, but solid. Having some light, she immediately checks on Tully.

"He'll be fine," comes the gruff voice of a man, apparently the leader of the group. "We've got some of the best street doctors in the whole of the city. They can bring back the dead, they can."

Gemma studies the man. He has long black hair and a beard tied into many thick braids. He wears a patch over his left eye and a great scar across his right cheek. His clothes are those of combat, but ancient combat. He wears a silver breast plate over his muscular torso and a green and black kilt signifying nothing to Gemma, but most likely everything to him. She knows who he is before he introduces himself.

"I be Usker Lance," says the man. "I've taken the title of Great Sinner after my friend and my life Colm Archer was taken from me by that great ass polyp GOD. You be Gemma Kerr, and we've been waitin' for you, lass. Aye. The whole stinkin' Immortal City has."

GRAN IS screaming in pain. One of the nurses has forgotten to refill the medication. Such is the problem with a lobotomized nursing staff. They tend to forget a lot.

Deirdre is the only doctor on duty. It is early morning, still dark out. She doesn't chide the nurse; it wouldn't stick. She simply stares at Gran stupidly, confusion marking her expression. Deirdre refills the bag and taps the IV, making certain it is now flowing into Gran's system. She wonders how long the old woman can hang on. She should be dead by now. Deirdre has seen much stronger people die within a day of the illness, but Gran seems to be almost improving at times. One person's miracle is another's curse.

Things are calming. Gran moans quietly. The medicine works fast. Deirdre sits on the bed beside the old woman. She excuses the nurse, and the young woman shuffles away mechanically. Her name was Orna. She miscarried yesterday, but that is for the best. If born, the child would have been sent to GOD to be one of the Children in Red and then, at around ten years, he would have been sent back to the ninth… and to the Factory.

"Why are you still here?" Deirdre whispers to the old woman. "Why hang on to all this pain? Why not just let go?"

Gran opens her eyes, surprising the doctress. Deirdre instinctively tries to hide her face.

Gran reaches out for her. "Oh, no, my baby girl," Gran says in a delicate hush of a voice. "My precious Elan, you are beautiful, child. Don't you ever let anyone tell you different. You a lovely angel, that's what you be."

She places her hand firmly but softly on the scarred side of Deirdre's face.

"I-I am not Elan," Deirdre says, her voice beginning to shake.

"Of course you are. You are my beautiful baby girl. Beautiful…" she says. "Beautiful… beautiful…"

Every recitation of the word is like a blossom in Deirdre's soul.

Gran's hand falls away as the medicine takes over. She is now asleep and out of pain once more.

Deirdre wants to burst out and cry and yell. She feels a flood of emotions surging inside, searching for some way out, some form of expression. She rises and heads to the balcony. Once outside, she does not go to the rails but clings to the wall, fearing she might fly away if she gets too close to the balustrade. She cups her mouth, and she allows herself to scream into her hands. And suddenly, she feels a tear, the first she has cried in many years, rolling down her cheek.

Beautiful... beautiful...

GEMMA STANDS in a plaza far beneath the Immortal City. She does not know how old it is, but she is certain it is older than the most ancient acknowledged districts of the five rings.

She and Madden have been led down miles of narrow causeways, tunnels, and stairs until at last the walls began to grow farther apart, allowing more freedom to move. Soon, wall sconces with candles began to appear and gave more light. They were walking among street ruins, among complete structures beneath an earthen sky. The architecture became more poetic as they journeyed on, etched with artistic flourishes. Faces of Passions and statues of gods looked this way and that. They blew kisses with full ripe lips and groped one another playfully and obscenely. Most of the statues were broken and fissured, but the artistry of those who carved them eons ago was ever apparent.

As they walked on, Gemma saw life and even more light. A small horde of people began to emerge from ancient homes and structures, following Usker Lance and his small parade with whispered awes. Some pointed at Gemma, which made her extremely uncomfortable. She held tightly to Madden's fur as she walked beside him.

They came to the plaza. The fountain in the center was a representation of the goddess Abrythnia holding out her arms in welcome. A hand was missing, having most likely fallen off years before, but that was all the damage the goddess has taken. Torches lit the cavern, almost as if a festival were underway and above them was not earth but the night sky.

Now, Gemma tries to take it all in, but it is too much. This underground contains a whole history she has never dreamed existed, not discussed even in the secret, banned books. The Immortal City is not as old as all are led to believe, if walkways and plazas are beneath it. Murmurs heighten as the small city of ragged underground dwellers surround her.

Usker Lance jumps up to the fountain and stands beside Abrythnia on her pedestal. Those assembled hush. "This is Gemma Kerr," he says. "I bring her before ye so that ye can see the dreams we've all been having are real. Can any of ye deny it now?" He squints at the crowd with his good eye, as if in warning.

Gemma glances around.

"I didna think so, ye crazy basterds!"

Everyone laughs. Usker grins, his smile fragmented but joyful.

"Tend to the lad's wounds," he says, gesturing to Tully. "And someone grow some balls and feed that massive beast. He's a hero too, after all. I'm guessin' our lady friend here needs some food in her belly as well. If not, well then, she can watch me fill mine, cuz I'm hungrier than a horned-up dragon."

He jumps down and offers Gemma his tattooed arm, as strong and solid as an oak tree. "To the pub, eh?"

She accepts his offer with a smile, but she watches until they take Tully carefully down from Madden's back and carry him into a columned forum. The hound goes with him, excited by the sudden number of people. The crowd is awestruck by the massive animal, the children especially. His tail wags uncontrollably as he creates a small dust storm around them.

Gemma is now sitting at a stone table. She imagines it has been in this very structure since the world began, long before the Immortal City, long before GOD. Even the air smells of primeval understanding. The pub is lit brightly with candles and lanterns stolen from the city above, and it looks clean and well kept. The same lyrical architecture from outside carries through in here. She sees an old hearth opposite them, the walls painted in joyous frescoes resembling the fragment in her bedchamber back at the House of Kerr.

"It's so much nicer down here," Gemma says. Usker has seated himself opposite her, slumping a bit the way comfortable men do. His shoulders are wide and thick, those of a hero, and others lean on him as they crowd around the table. She is introduced to a few of these, with names like Sary and Royce.

"Up in the Immortal City," she continues, "I can barely see for the glare or breathe for fear it will be my last."

"You never need go back there, Miss Gemma," Usker says. "You be done with their sort now."

Plates of vegetables, breads, and meats are set before them. Gemma is stunned by the quantity and, indeed, the quality.

"We've got the best thieves in the city providing for us." Usker grins as he tears into a bird leg. His good eye is locked on her, not with lust but with deep interest. "But ye won't be stayin' with us long, will ya?"

"No," Gemma answers. She takes some bread and dips it into her wine. This is not her mother's wine. This is real wine. As sweet as a Passion's kiss. She relishes it, lets it play on her tongue. "I'm heading for the ninth ring."

"And you've caused a stir, ye have. It's a good thing that hound don't bark, else we'd all be in a big mastiff pony shit pile, we would."

"Thank you for your help," she says. "I don't know what we would have done if you hadn't found us."

"We've been watching ye for some time," Usker says. "Nothin' gonna happen to ye on my watch. We've even had to dispense of a few Kingdom Guards for your sake. Ye realize there is a certain Holy contingent that would like nothing more than to see ye dead. And worse."

"I realize that now." Gemma does not, however, realize assassins have been out to get her for some time. If Rossa had not met her behind the Glass Halls, disrupting an assassin's plan, Gemma would surely be dead by now.

"They won't harm your mother, the Lady Esther," Usker assures her. "Not yet. They need her for somethin'. We haven't figured that part out."

"My father, Bana," she says. "They need my mother to care for my father. When he dies, so does she. But why would GOD care if my father lives or dies? That's what I can't figure out. He was just one of many in the Revolution and most of the others are dead now, if the archives can be trusted."

Usker stares at her as he chews. He does not say anything for a few moments. Those around the table echo his actions. Finally, Usker says, "Fuck my hole, I wish Colm was here. He'd know the answer. He'd know what to do."

"Was Colm Archer important to you?" Gemma says.

Usker's eye drops to the table. "Aye. There will never be another like him. He was the basterd what found this city under the earth. Our whole movement owes a debt to him. There have been other Great

Sinners, of course, but none as great as he. He kept us safe and fed, and he kept up the fight."

"You loved him," Gemma says, her hand finding his across the table.

"We had a covenant, he and I. We even had a ceremony out there beneath Abrythnia's Embrace." He takes his thumb and wipes the corner of his eye. "We'll be together again someday in whatever afterlife is fit for buggars like us. I swear that. Until then, I fight."

She wonders if Usker was somewhere hidden in the audience of spectators when Colm Archer was castrated. She hopes not.

"We can get you as far as the third ring," says Usker. "This ancient place stretches that far, we know. Probably farther, but none have discovered passages yet, and not everyone has balls as big as mine to go explorin'."

"This city has been here all this time?"

"And it's not alone. There be a city beneath this, and deeper still, another city. Man builds and builds until he forgets his past. Until he forgets he has anything to be guilty for cuz it's been buried so deep. Then he shits new shit on the old shit and soon, all you're left with is petrified shit."

"Why are you helping me?"

"Let me ask you, lass, why are you going to the ninth ring?"

She knows the words. Now she only needs to set them free. "I need… I feel… I have a… passion…"

Usker laughs hardily and toasts the air with his wooden mug. "There be the word. See, now. You… you have balls as big as mine. That's for certain." He raises his mug again. "To Gemma's balls!"

The crowd repeats in raucous consensus and everyone drinks as Gemma laughs.

"Tell us of this passion," Usker encourages.

She clears her throat. "When I was a young girl, I began to have dreams, but they were more than dreams. They felt like… like lessons. Like things I was supposed to remember of places lost and forgotten." She looks around. "Maybe even this place. My dreams are filled with the Passions, with the green men and faeries, and more recently with the goddess Abrythnia, looking very much like she does in that fountain in the plaza. Strange. So strange." She takes a drink of the sweet wine.

"What is?"

"That I would dream of a goddess exiled, and yet here she is under the city all along, and so close to me. In my dreams, I walk the Garden of the Passions with her and two others. Both of them are men, though. Not gods."

"Do ye see them here, these men?" Usker says.

She looks around. "No."

"Then you'll see them soon enough. All of us here have dreamed these dreams ye speak of. Some of us dream them harder than others, with more clarity, but dream them we do. You see Abrythnia in the Garden, but others see her brother, Brochnol. And yet still others see the Passion King, Mungoran. I meself see the god of fire, Helix. They are all the same spirit, it seems, pushing us to some great end and new beginning. We all walk with the gods in different places, but we believe the destination is the same. The only thing our dreams seem to have in common, my sweet, is you."

Gemma coughs up her wine. "Me?"

"Aye. Why do ye think everyone is looking at ye so?"

"You've seen me in your dreams?"

"Every one of us. We're old friends, you and I. And you and Sary, and you and Royce…" Usker points around the pub. "You're as clear to us then as ye are now. Granted, this is the first any of us has heard ye speak, so forgive us our ogling. And, oh yeah, forgive Royce most of all. Methinks he has a crush on ye and may have taken some liberties with his dreamin', if you get my meanin'."

Laughter laps in a small wave.

"So, these are visions everyone has been having."

"Visions, insights, glimpses… Whatever you want to call 'em. They're just terms we have for dreaming. And we've all dreamed of you, lass."

"What do we do?" Gemma says, suddenly feeling a great weight thrust on top of her small shoulders. "What do we do now?"

"You have but to walk to the ninth ring. We ragged band of rebels and heathens, we shall follow ye. And I, the Great Sinner, I will protect ye by any means possible." Usker holds up his large mug. "Let's drink to it. Let's drink to freedom."

And the air of the place is rife with a joy Gemma has never sensed before as cheers and the knocking and clanging of mugs and stolen silver chalices fills the room and grows outward until all the Undercity is alive. The dead have risen.

ESTHER SOMETIMES wishes—in fact, she goes as far as to fantasize—that Bana would die. Or she could kill him. She is certainly capable of it, and the man, she assures herself, deserves death. But that would be a mercy for him. Best let him waste away here in this bed. Alive, he ensures her own survival, and that, in turn, ensures Gemma lives as well.

Where is that girl, anyway?

Esther sits beside Bana's bed, watching him. Sometimes his thin eyelids flutter open, and he looks over at her suspiciously. This is how they relate, through icy stares in a house of lies and suspicion. She gave up pleasantries years ago. She does not even smile at him. Now, after working in the archives, neither will Gemma.

She did not hear Gemma rise this morning, nor leave for the archives. Esther has asked a servant girl to go wake her daughter, but the servant has yet to return. She's going to need a new belt for servant lashings at the rate she uses it. Gemma has been distant since she began working at the archives. Not that they have ever been confidantes, but at least the girl would smile at her mother. Gemma's is the only genuine smile in the first ring, she warrants. Now Esther barely receives a glance from her daughter. Maybe that is a good thing. Building walls and setting up barriers means less chance of pain in the future.

The old steward Rugal is at the chamber door, knocking as light as a cautious bird.

"Yes?"

"Pardon me, m'lady, but a gentleman is at the front door. Methinks he may be the new cook."

Esther rises. "What is he doing using the front door?" No answer is required. She quickly passes by the old man. "Go find that silly maid I sent to wake Gemma," she says. "And then you wake up Gemma. I'll receive the new cook."

"Yes, m'lady."

Esther has about had it with servants these days. They seem to grow more ignorant and irritating with every passing day. There are rules in the first ring. Servants use the back door. How hard is that to remember? But then, they are lesser folk after all.

She slides on her sunspectacles and opens the large front door. Standing on the steps are two individuals, not one: a dark-haired young man dressed in a worker's uniform, and a small boy, as clean as a whistle and carrying a drum. They are both wearing a lesser quality of sunspectacles than she.

"Good afternoon, miss," says the man. He tries to bow. "I'm Lawl, and this be Key. We was wondering if—"

"Come in," Esther says bluntly. "And for now on, use the servants entrance if you don't want the lash."

Lawl looks confused and turns to the boy.

"Well, do you want the job as my cook or not? I can't have you standing on the stoop all day."

"Y-yes, miss," he says. He and the boy move past her into the manse. "Sorry, miss."

Once inside, they take off their sunspectacles, clearly amazed by the grandeur of the place. She notices the man tense up almost immediately as they stand in the hall.

"And who is this?" She looks at the child, towering over him. "I asked only for a cook, which I imagine is you."

"H-he… why, he's the best cook's assistant I've ever had."

"Assistant? Why would a cook need an assistant?" She gives Lawl an oblique stare. "Isn't the cook any good?"

"Why, I'm the best, miss. None better, I swear it. And that little scrapper is one of the reasons why. He has ways of bargaining for some of the best ingredients in the whole city. Now, I don't ask how he does it. I just let him do his thing. He's a little genius, that one."

"Very well," she says with a sigh. "He can also act as a maid. I'm about to need a new one. And you." She points at Lawl with her sunspectacles still in her hand. "You mumble. Do not mumble when you address me. Are we clear?"

"Yes. Ma'am."

She leads them through the manse, explaining the rules and introducing what staff she remembers, which is but Rugal. She walks ahead of them with a stiff, high-nosed air and a feminine glide, gesturing fluidly with a curl of the wrist or finger.

"You take your orders from me. No one else," she says. "If you disappoint me, consequences can be severe. I expect this home to be run with liquid ease. I have much to look after with my husband Bana's ill health, so I do not need impediments. You will not be dealing with him, anyway." She turns to Key with an arched eyebrow. "But you might." Then back around as she leads them through the kitchen. "You, Mr....?"

"Lawl."

"What an odd name. You, Mr. Lawl, will cater to my daughter Gemma and myself."

"Twill be an honor, miss."

"Yes. It will."

They make a circle of the large room, filled with more brass and copper than any family of their size could ever use. Esther is bored by the shine. She leads them up the connecting staircase, which is a narrow passage to the servants' quarters. The quarters are dimly lit and suffocating. Esther hates being here. She opens the room where Duana just recently died and motions them in before her.

"This is where you will sleep. Both of you."

"That's fine, miss," says Lawl. "We'd prefer to be together anyway."

"Well, I'm glad I could please you." She is not certain how she feels about this man. But then, he is only a servant. She reminds herself she never feels anything for that class of people.

"M'lady."

Esther turns to see Rugal at the end of the hall with the young servant girl in front of him. They both look peculiar.

"Well?" Esther says, walking toward them slowly. Candlewicks tremble with flame as she passes them. "Is Gemma awake?"

The servant girl keeps her head bowed and eyes to the floor as she offers up a small scrap of paper.

"She says it was on the bed, m'lady," Rugal says. "She says Miss Gemma—the precious dove—is gone."

CLAIRE WHINNIES and neighs as Rossa rides her through the congested street. Rossa has forgotten until now how much she loves being on a horse. Her family had owned a fine stallion once, but it had to be sold, like everything else. The price of living is high and allows few luxuries. That stallion had been secretly named by her Askerth, after the passion of fury. No one else in the family dared call the horse by its name, though. To do so in the Immortal City would take some courage.

Now, as Rossa sits high on this new beautiful gray mare, she feels the respect of those around her in the street. Most have never had horses of their own, and Rossa, so newly attired and out of the fire, shines regal and stunning. Beneath the broad-rimmed black hat, her red hair is a crown of flames. Children smile at her, and she smiles back and even winks.

The respect is kind, but it is not why she is here. If she were a small orphan child, a gypsy who knew the city better than anyone, where would she be hiding? She keeps her senses peeled. She has searched what remains of the orphan dens of the third ring and has asked questions, but people are tight-lipped. The ones who do talk to her have nothing to say of Key.

Rossa has climbed the abandoned mills by the River Hung, and has knocked on the doors of the homes of the darkest districts, looking for answers. Nothing. But she has only rummaged through a small portion of things worth rummaging. She will find the boy. She is more certain of that than ever. Key is alive and free of the ferrymen, for Rossa has seen truly awful places in her search for the boy, but none of these have come close to the horrors of the dead Garden. And because of that Rossa knows the search is not in vain.

She hears a stir behind her and feels the heavy breaths of the mastiff ponies before she glances over her shoulder and sees the great white carriage. All traffic on the street has pulled to the side to let pass the Sister of GOD. Rossa would rather spit in her eye, but relents. Claire seems just as put out as she.

The carriage stops beside Rossa, and the blinds are pulled up. It is Mags Hensil herself, her face as wide and white as the ancient moon. The woman's sneer makes Rossa feel all the prouder, for if you can annoy a Sister of GOD, you must be in the right.

Her veil is raised. She gives Rossa the once-over. "GOD is watching you," she says. "You carry yourself like a queen." It is not a compliment.

"Perhaps, I am," says Rossa. This elicits gasps from those who can hear the conversation, those who are on their knees in supplication. She steadies Claire as the horse seems uncomfortable in the presence of the Sister.

"Such haughtiness will not go unpunished by GOD, my child. You will pay for it in time. I saw you riding and I thought to myself, yes. There is a woman who is given to sin."

"And how would you know this, dear Sister?"

"The manner of your dress, my child." Her condescension is deadlier than a snake. "You need to be cleansed. My guards shall take you now."

Rossa laughs. "And are you the one who thinks she can cleanse me? Sister, your sins far outweigh my own."

A great cry comes from the crowd. Mags's face drops. Her lip trembles in rage. "Dare you! A common whore in the coat of a ferryman mocks a Sister of GOD! Guards!"

Mags intends to get out of the carriage, but Claire does not allow it. The horse blows its nose in the Sister's face, and Mags falls backward with a thump and a grunt. The guards come at Rossa, but Claire turns about and bounds past them, knocking one to the ground. Rossa is laughing as they gallop away, looking over her shoulder to see the street that had been cleared for the passage of the Sister and her carriage fill up once more before Mags Hensil can call out for pursuit.

"Good lady!" she says in Claire's ear. "I'll have to remember that trick."

GEMMA HAS spent the day with Usker. He has explained to her how they will move, and with what speed. With the number of people, the obstructions in their way, and the danger of being underground, the journey will take longer. Many plan to come with them, but some will stay behind with the children. Usker has designated a couple of the sinners as carriers who will get word from the marchers to those left behind if something urgent were to occur. How many will stay with the march beyond the third ring, however, is unclear. Though Usker himself has sworn to Gemma he will see her through to the end.

"And when we get there," he says, "we're gonna have us one hell of a party. There'll be a-drinkin' and a-fuckin' about as has never been seen. The first fella I see walkin' round with a tight ass is mine. You can have the second."

Usker makes Gemma laugh harder than anyone she has ever met. His is a refreshing personality, especially given what he has been through.

"Laughter is a drug," he says. "It'll keep your head above the shit."

The plans have finally been made. They will start on the march this very night. Gemma finds Tully bandaged up and seated by the fountain in the plaza. He has a swath of cloth wrapped around his head and another on his broken hand. Both eyes are colored, though the right is more severely purple, and his bottom lip is busted. His face is wet with tears. Still, he smiles when he sees her.

"Is it very painful?" Gemma asks, sitting beside him on the fountain's edge. She dries his tears with dabs from her scarf.

"It is," he says, holding to his side where he was kicked by the guards. "But these are na tears of pain." He gestures out into the plaza.

Madden is playing with the children and having a time of it. Their laughter spurs on his leaping and bounding, his tail-wagging and licking. His tongue is as big as the children's heads. They are taking turns riding on his back, and he races around the plaza with them, creating small cyclones.

"I've never seen him so happy," says Tully. "If only he could bark."

"I think you've done well by him," says Gemma. "He's alive because of you."

"He's the best friend I ever had. Until you, Madden was the only friend I ever had, or ever dreamed to have."

"Can I ask you about your dreams?" Gemma says.

He looks at her curiously.

"Am I in them? Usker Lance was telling me that many people are having dreams like mine. Dreams with the goddess Abrythnia and the Passions in the Garden. But he also says that I appear in a lot of other people's dreams. Am I in yours?"

Tully grins big. So big it hurts his face and he grimaces. "Aye. You're my dream girl, you are."

"Truly?" Gemma laughs.

"Aye. We walk in the gardens, the three of us. I see Abrythnia as well, you see. She be a huntress, but she's a gentle goddess. Sometimes I see others I don't know. I can't make out their faces yet. Only the goddess and you are clear to me. See, that's how I knew you would be my friend. When I saw you walk into the archives, why, Miss Gemma, my heart skipped right out of my chest. 'That's her!' I says to meself. 'That's the girl of my dreams!' I got them warm fuzzy chills all over, and I knew something big was gonna happen, and soon." He pauses and shudders in pain. "I just didn't realize it was gonna hurt quite so much."

Gemma puts her hand on his. "I'm heading out tonight," she says. "Usker and many others are escorting me through the Undercity as far as the third ring. I need to say my good-byes to you soon. I won't ever be coming back this way. I feel that. I'm certain of it."

Tully is looking at her in confusion with his big bruised eyes. "Why would we need to say good-bye, Miss Gemma?"

"I just assumed you would want to stay behind and recuperate."

"No, missus." He is shaking his head most adamantly. His voice is now stronger than when they had first met, but just by a fraction. "You assumed wrong. I'm out now. Out of the archives. I might as well see this thing through, eh?"

Gemma smiles. "I'm so glad."

"Yes, ma'am," he says, turning back to watch Madden and the children playing in front of them. "You assumed wrong."

A SINNER'S MARCH

DAYS HAVE passed. Whispers from the Undercity bubble to the surface and are snatched up by the wind, kicked about by hooves and feet. There is a march, they say. Something is rising. Someone is rising. At first this hero has no name. Like all heroes, this one is only an idea, a faceless notion in the back of the head or an ear tickle. It is Hope.

"I hear ol' Usker Lance is coming up from the fires below to seek his revenge for the death of Colm Archer."

"No. 'Tis Archer himself. He's risen from the dead, he has, to reclaim his balls and brings with him a demon horde."

"It's the Passions," some dare to whisper. "The Passions have woken the gods and goddesses. Abrythnia and Brochnol lead the way."

"It is but the plague, coming up in the form of Death herself to eat us all!"

"Gods be with us!"

"Passions guard us!"

"Revolution!"

And yet the hero at last is getting an identity. The House of Kerr is an important family even if they have been shunned, and servants talk. If an important person goes missing from any such family, well, there must be an important reason for it.

Senator General Hegart has come before GOD in the Tower to discuss the matter of the rebel sinners. He believes this uprising, like all the others, shall be easily put down. But the Senator General thinks it is best to discuss such things anyway. After all, the very Revolution that put GOD on His high chair was once met with shrugs and eye rolls by those in power.

Hegart is standing before GOD. He holds his handkerchief to his face, not only to catch his drool, but to stifle the stench that permeates the room. The air is a moist, heavy soup that smells of rot and decay. The two halves of the half-eaten corpse of the ferryman Finn lay like offerings at the foot of the high chair, where the Children in Red squat and hold each other, pale and nauseated.

Only two of the council are still left alive. The third, who sits next to the empty chair of Bana Kerr, is slumped over, his arm stretched out like a thin, transparent stalk and a blue tongue bloating from his mouth. The Senator General is tasting vomit in his saliva. He cannot spit it out fast enough. He speaks quickly, trying to breathe in as little air as possible.

"This march," the Senator General says, "it is being aided, it seems, by various heathens and hidden sinners. I have some of my best ferrymen looking into it. They see people setting food and drink out in strange places, at the old temples of the Passions and cathedrals of the gods." He pauses to smother himself with the handkerchief before he continues. "They do this in places that, quite frankly, we have forgotten even existed. Places that have not been accessorized with your Power so that you may keep an eye on them. They have that over on us, at least."

GOD is angry. "GOD must be all, see all, know all!" he hisses down the pipe.

The Children are nervous. One of them vomits.

"Yes, my lord. I do apologize. But we are taking names, and soon we'll do a roundup and a mass execution of those that help this march— with your permission, of course—like they have never seen."

Hegart would have salivated excessively at this thought, but all he tastes is bile.

"Word is, the Great Sinner himself, Usker Lance, is on the march with the group. If he means to exact revenge, he doesn't know what he's in for. I'll skewer the dick lover and put his balls on display in my collection. But it is this new hero the people speak of that has me—"

He doubles over, vomiting up his morning meal. GOD waits, breathing heavily down the pipe.

"The march, it is being said, will emerge soon somewhere in the third ring. We haven't learned exactly where. The Undercity has all but been forgotten. The maps are in the archives, but the archives have been categorized so that only my brother Tully can find them."

"No matter," GOD says, His wrath subsiding. "We will easily squash this group of marching fools. Get your brother to find me those maps anyway."

The Senator General swallows. He grimaces as the acid and bile burns down his throat. "But my lord, my brother is with the march."

The Children in Red hold their breaths. The council begins to moan.

"And one other thing, my lord, you may find distressing, but the name of the new hero is Gemma Kerr."

GOD takes in a lungful. "Well, now," He finally says. "That is something I did not expect. Yes. That is something else altogether."

This area of the Immortal City, the ferryman notes, has been abandoned for some time. Far from the Holy Road and the gate, it sees only the occasional orphan or feral cat. The most excitement the ferryman has seen is the wind sweeping up dead leaves or a tattered cloth. The structures sag and collapse in depressed surrender. It is a district of light grays and browns, the colors having nearly given up their hold and interest. After the plague, this place has been left to de-exist.

And yet…

Cayden Lothair watches for sinners from a broken window inside what was once a small pub. The bar still stands, though the glass of the liquor cabinets is shattered and the shelves empty. These are the places he prefers of late. Near humanity, but not of it.

Their drop-off point, he has discerned, is in an alley just diagonal to the pub. He has seen four citizens cautiously step into that alley carrying bowls and water jugs. They are not cautious enough. They seek to feed the Great Sinner and the new hero. Cayden notes their stupid bravery. He cannot help but admire these soulkeepers.

Cayden does not believe this is where the march will emerge. It does not look an ancient enough space to hide an entrance to the forgotten Undercity. But he has gotten word from Senator General Hegart himself that he is to find where the sinner's march in and keep track of them. Mirror their route above ground. He has been given six Kingdom Guards. They are to follow his orders. He can tell by their expressions they resent this command, and so has set them to watching various other sections of the district to free him of their indignant faces.

Follow the marchers. Just watch. Do nothing. Something about this new hero, the girl, had the Senator General a little nervous. Nervous. Cayden wants to laugh, but he does not know how.

Even in his dreams, Cayden is watching the girl. She has been given a name now, but how did he know her face before? And it is a pretty face. In his dreams, her eyes rise to meet his like the moon climbs the night. She sees him even as he hides in the shadows of a willow tree. She walks through the Garden of the Passions with the god of anger, Thunkill. Thunkill's ugliness only accentuating the girl's beauty. Shrouded in the skins of his enemies, he drags his great bloody scythe behind him, but does not harm her. A third visitor comes in the Garden now. He is familiar to the ferryman. He is the young man Cayden had arrested with the sickly old woman. He greets Gemma and Thunkill and they walk together. They wait for him, but he stays in the shadows.

A young woman is taking what looks to be a bundle of bread or a cake into the alleyway across from the pub. She looks kind. Kindness will get her killed. But not today and not by him. Cayden plays the shadow monster, and he will keep to his shade.

LAWL FINDS cooking for Esther Kerr to be the easiest job he has ever had. The woman does not eat. Not really. She will have a nibble of bread or fruit every so often, but she seems quite content with a bottle of wine for every meal. In that respect, Lawl has done very well. He has her glass filled before she sits at the large, lonely table, and she never has to ask for a top-up.

His days are tedious. They are filled with thinking of Duncan and Gran, watching Key play his drum in the courtyard behind the manse, and wandering the halls of the House of Kerr. Sometimes Key will join him on his investigations. On those occasions, they look at each other, smile, and shake their heads at the extravagances of the manse. Today, however, Lawl decides to leave the kitchen and wander through the halls alone. Now that he is in the first ring, there must be answers somewhere.

Esther is nowhere to be seen, so Lawl climbs the great spilling tongue of the main stairs and tours the second floor where the family's bedrooms are located. As with the rest of the manse, the halls are so large they feel mocking and derisive. How, Lawl wonders, can there be so much house in this house? Even the furniture, as stacked and crowded as it is, feels like filth and lint lost in corners.

He tries a few doors on the east wing. They are not locked. Most open easily. These are private rooms and guest quarters. They are florid and lovely, with large beds and sofas, but they have not been used in some time. They all smell of stale air except one, in which Lawl finds a hint of perfume in the air. Lawl stands at the door and looks at the bed and the furniture, all of it quite ordinary. Much nicer than anything he has owned, but ordinary. This is the hero's bedchamber?

He laughs to himself. "And how exactly is she a hero, this rich girl? What has she done that makes her so?"

He closes the door and walks away.

To the west of the stairs, he comes upon Bana Kerr's chamber almost immediately. One does not need a sense of sight to notice the man is ill. The room has a smell, an odor that spurns. Rot. Waste. Vomit. Lawl sees the machinery, the pumps and tanks keeping the man alive. This is the Power of GOD. If he had these for poor Gran, she could live another few years. But there is nothing for it. She has likely already died.

This man is far worse off than Gran. His eyes are open, watching Lawl as he nears the bed and slowly walks around it. He seems to beg for some kind of mercy. Or is that fear? Lawl is uncertain. He has never been the cause of much fear. His mumbling elicits just the opposite from people. The man is so wired into the machines, and his skin has such a nightmarish transparent quality, that it is hard to separate man from bed. Indeed, he resembles a hideous mutation or disastrous experiment. He is tied to the bed by the very thing that keeps him alive, completely immobile.

"Explain to me what you are doing in my husband's chamber." Esther's voice cuts through the sour air of the room. She stands in the doorway as demanding as a Kingdom Guard. "You are supposed to be in the kitchen. You are the cook. Did you come to see if my husband would like something different? As you can see, he is quite the picky eater. Only the best strained gruel for him."

Lawl bows his head. "I'm sorry, m'lady."

"I don't need an apology," she says, stepping into the chamber, her black gown soaking up the light. "But I would like an explanation before you get the lash."

He looks her in the eyes. "I was curious, m'lady."

"Speak up! No mumbling."

"I says, I was curious. He is sick. Sicker than I ever saw anyone. Sicker than anyone alive has a right to be."

"Yes. You are right about that." Her stare leaves Lawl's face and focuses on Bana. "He has absolutely no right to be alive. It's the plague that did it, you see. But we are the House of Kerr, and that name offers us special attention. We have options the likes of you do not."

"Ah, clearly, m'lady. You are soaking in options."

Her eyes are back on his.

"But, m'lady," he says, "what ails him is not only the plague. I know what the plague looks like. I've lived among the poor victims of the plague for many years. No plague can make a man's skin fade away so. He is a chained ghost. There be somethin' else at work here, aye."

Her gaze remains fixed on his. She is trying to unlock doors. "Observant. Or just courageous and stupid to speak the truth. All I will say is that my dear husband Bana has made some terrible mistakes in his life."

"He seems to be paying for them."

"Not in full. Not yet. He hasn't been moved from this room, from that bed, in years."

"Sounds like a prison."

"For us both."

"And now you wish to punish me as well? For my curiosity?"

Lawl matches her stare.

"Why are you not afraid? I promise, it will hurt. The lash has thorns and a biting temper."

"I'm certain. But once a soul has lost everything they love, what is there to fear from a strap of leather? Besides, I have access to somethin' you might be interested in, m'lady."

She raises an eyebrow. "Oh? What could you have that would possibly interest me?"

"I talk to the other servants from the other houses, you see? We talk about many things, but these days one topic is on everyone's lips: the sinner's march and the new hero. Your daughter Gemma."

He hears Esther's breath catch, though her face is not less severe.

"Some of these servants, they know things. They have friends on the inside. Friends who are rebels. Revolutionaries. Sinners. I can tell you what I know of her progress, where she's been. I can tell you things you can never find out yourself."

"Why would you offer to do this for me?"

He shrugs and looks at Bana Kerr. "Because I have lost someone, too. Because searching seems to be my new hobby. Because... well, why not?"

"Do you know where she's at now? Where is she going?"

"No one knows where the march is at, specifically. That would dangerous. But she is said to be moving with Usker Lance to the third ring."

"The Great Sinner?" She seems appalled.

"Aye, m'lady. So he's called, though I've never had the pleasure of his sinful company."

Esther looks as if she wants to chastise him, but she refrains. "Very well," she says. "You do this for me, you keep me informed on the whereabouts of my daughter, and I shall spare you the lash."

"And Key as well?"

"And the child."

"Most kind, m'lady."

"Nothing of the sort."

USKER LANCE and a silent group of sixty are marching with Gemma Kerr through the haunted streets of the Undercity. Half faces, shadows, and ghosts are in the windows, and behind every pillar, a phantasm. They have been marching for days. They are silent and in the dark, fearing echoes might give their whereabouts away. Sometimes, this uncanny silence threatens to drive Gemma mad. Other times, it is welcome for contemplation.

Usker leads the march. He wears a different kilt now, long, black and red. The material is thick, with a slit up the front giving his muscular legs some air. Gemma walks at her own pace with Tully and Madden always nearby. The children of the Undercity hated seeing the massive hound leave them, but Tully promised they would be back one day. It was the first lie he had ever told, and he felt terrible for it.

Scouts keep watch on things up above. They report often on the latest rumors or tall tales being told by those in the Immortal City about the march. As they are watched, so are they watching.

"The Kingdom Guards, O massive asswipes of GOD, have been given a promotion," Usker explained to Gemma after the most recent scout's visit, "from giant twits to giant twats. Give a man enough praise, and he's your whore for life, eh?"

"Did the scout say anything else?" she asked, hoping for news of her mother.

"Only the newest imagining of who ye really are." He grinned, his worn face suddenly seeming new.

"And who is that?"

"Why, you're the goddess Abrythnia herself. Didn't ye know?"

They walk now in an ancient boneyard. The torches give the giant statuary permission to make faces at the marchers. The silence here especially is unsettling. The silent screams of the dead are more frightening than those of the living. Though they wish to pass through as quickly as possible, their fears cause most to walk more slowly. Magnificent stone sculptures of fire dogs and horned demons line the causeway, some standing fifty feet tall with fangs set to tear a man apart. Others are faceless beings in capes, but no less disturbing or ominous.

Gemma looks back at Tully. His hand is buried in Madden's fur, and his eyes are wide and glowing as he looks around.

Usker has come back to walk with Gemma. He glances at poor Tully as well. "He looks bloody terrified," says the Great Sinner.

"It's a terrifying place," Gemma responds quietly. Her whisper echoes. "I don't like it here at all. I wish us away from this boneyard. There is no good here."

"Aye," says Usker. "This was most likely a boneyard for murderers and rapists. These demons and snovelfarks be here to keep the damned souls in line, no doubt. But have faith, my love, they can't harm the likes of us." Usker spots a nude statue of a vampire demon and walks up to it. He looks to Gemma with a smirk and nonchalantly slaps the stone phallus to the ground, where it shatters. "Yet we can harm them. Did you see what I just did, miss? I slapped this old basterd's wanker right off. Did you see me? Did ya?"

Gemma stifles her laughter. She looks again at Tully, and he is now grinning like a child. He saw it.

"Naw, miss," says Usker, coming back to her side, "those statues are not the ones ye need be fearin'. There are other beings made of flesh and bone who are far more cunnin' than stone and just as cold. Now, listen at me well, Miss Gemma. There are those who will pretend to be your friend on this journey, but they'll sell ye to the Guardian before you've had time to blink."

Gemma has grown introspective as they continue walking. "I am no judge of character. How will I know who to trust?"

"You'll have me to help ye out, ye will. Others as well. But I'm the best now that my Colm is gone." He smiles again. "There be many who would do ye ill, be it for madness or glory, but there are also some who will want to join this march. Some of them good basterds and basterdesses will. You'll see. Ye won't be alone."

"But why will they follow me? I am no leader. I am no hero. I have lived a privileged life, and until recently I haven't even thought of sinners and how they have been wronged. Why would anyone follow me?"

"To many of these folk, ye be true hope. The first spot of it in some time. They dream of ye, and those who don't dream of ye want to. Ye be Abrythnia, whether ye want to be or no."

She looks at his proud chin, his regal warrior's countenance. He wears every struggle and defeat, every scar and pain, like badge of honor. This man should be the hero of the people, not her.

"Besides," he adds, "marchin' is good for a body. It keeps a man in shape and keeps a mind from foolishly thinkin' it be satisfied with the awful world. Marchin' is so much better than standin' still, don't ye think?"

"I KNOW you are not ill," Deirdre Maire says to Duncan as she leads him down the long hall to what she has told him are his new quarters. Even silence has an echo here. "Though, for the time being, you will remain on the hospital grounds."

Her voice is flat. Duncan does not pick up a hint of emotion, either irritation or disgust. Her heels are clacking away on the cold floor.

"Soon, I don't know when," she continues, "but soon you will be given lodging out there with the other workers. Now, and until I decide otherwise, you are needed here, however."

Needed?

They pass the long narrow windows that look out on the balcony. The windows are closed due to the change in weather, but all we can see is brown mud, a dying orchard, guards, and the future.

The doctress opens a door at the end of the wing and stands to the side so Duncan might pass. He sees two beds and a large window. Little else. "It's a private room," Duncan says.

"You will be in this room with Gran until she dies." Her hands are at her sides. She exudes no warmth.

"With Gran?" Duncan's heart races, and his stomach churns.

"Yes. She will be brought in shortly. I have also found you a job at the Factory. It is hard work, but it will keep you away from the Kingdom Guards. They tend to be bullies, though I'm sure you already know this. A word of warning about the Factory," she says. "You will see things that will disturb you. You might, in fact, go completely insane. In which case, you will be right at home here."

"Why are you doing this for me?" He studies her good eye.

"I'm not. Not for you, anyway." She turns to leave. "You start at the Factory tomorrow," she says as she walks away. "Prepare yourself."

Gran. He will see Gran again and have the chance keep the promise he made to Lawl. He will be able to… to…

He retches on the floor. His guilt is acidic.

He remembers the night well. It is sculpted into his past like a frieze. Perhaps it was selfish, but he only wanted to make things easier for Lawl. Easier for them both. Once Gran was being taken care of by qualified individuals like doctors and nurses, he and Lawl could have their perfect life together. One day he was certain they would even have that place in the first ring he always wanted. Duncan was a hard worker, and Lawl was a smart man. Together they would be unstoppable.

How silly that all seems now. As if true mobility existed.

Duncan got to the specified location early that evening, a small café two districts from where he lived. The place was dim, but not unsavory. The food smelled eatable, which is always a good sign. He waited, tapping his fingernails on the wood table when he was through eating. He had many moments of doubt. He had even attempted to leave once, but the thought of him and Lawl living happily in the first ring made him sit back down.

When the woman arrived, Duncan imagined the place had gotten the tiniest bit chilly. Mags Hensil was not dressed as a Sister of GOD, but as a simple woman in gray garb. She still retained the air, though. She cast shadows where none were needed. She wore no makeup, and she seemed all the more frightening for it.

"Will she be treated well?" Duncan had asked. "She'll be looked after, right?"

"Of course, of course," said Mags with a smile that seemed to creep up from the bottom of her face. "I am a Sister of GOD. I can promise you, she will be seen to."

Looking back, Duncan cannot believe he fell for her line. He is angry at himself for not listening to his inner voice telling him to run. He cannot believe how foolish he has been all his life. How trusting. And it was right before him. The whole grand lie was right there the whole time.

To hold Lawl just once more, that would be all he would ask before he dies.

He falls to the floor and retches again. When he looks up, a nurse— the woman who used to be Orna the flesh-peddler—is looking at him, face drawn and emotionless, arms limp at her side. She is there to clean up the vomit.

ESTHER IS finding Lawl's presence most distracting. She has followed him like a shadow ever since he told her he could offer news concerning the whereabouts of Gemma. She has tried to go about her daily routine, but that is near impossible. She would even go as far as to lower herself and take dinner with him if he might recall even the tiniest fragment that someone has passed along about her daughter. All that keeps her nerves from straying too near the edge is the glass of bitter wine she constantly carries with her, a liquid comfort.

Lawl approaches her as she watches him from the kitchen door and tells her he has an idea to make Bana more mobile. She is not overly enthusiastic.

"Why would he need to be mobile?" she says with her arms crossed and the wineglass close to her lips. "Where does he need to go?"

And yet it would be much easier for her to watch the new cook if he was in the same space as her husband. She would be able to keep an eye on them both more easily.

"All right," she says before Lawl can turn around and head back to the unlit stove, over which he has strewn strange sketches and blue prints. "Yes. Let's do make my husband more… mobile, as you say. One never knows when that mobility may come in handy."

So, Esther watches from Bana's chamber doorway as Lawl and the child measure things: the bed, the sheets, Bana. She hears words like "retractable" and "wheels" and "wrench," but they mean nothing to her. The two are working most diligently, though. She sips from her wine and slowly nears the work. Lawl takes quick glances her way with his brooding eyes, but seems unperturbed for the most part. Bana watches her, too. She can feel his faded eyes and their ice-cold stare without even looking at him. Yet she is only truly concerned with Lawl.

The child with the drum ever strapped around his torso is a quick worker. He listens well to Lawl's instructions. He is a pretty child. Some gypsy woman was lucky to have had him. Or not. The lower classes do not appreciate beauty the way those in the first ring do. Gypsy art is far from the perfect straight-lined form and balance of first-ring artists like Degat or O'Noyle. Gypsy art is wild and untamed.

Lawl has caught her watching the boy. "Got some news for ya," he says, as he sketches some measurements down on a pad.

Esther nearly chokes on her wine. "Yes?"

"The Kingdom Guards killed outside the archives the other night, word is Gemma had some doin' in that."

"Ridiculous," she spits. "Those guards were torn apart. My daughter is not a fire dog or a wolf demon."

"I don't know the hows and whyfors, missus. That's just what I hear. Gemma had somethin' to do with the archive murders."

"Who is telling you these horrendous lies? They must stop at once."

He stops writing and looks up at her. "I've upset ya. I'm sorry, miss. Would ya like for me to stop? To not report to ya what I hear?"

"No!" She speaks too quickly. Now the two of them know who has the upper hand. "No. I want to know even the lies. Tell me every tall tale you hear, Mr. Lawl. Every one."

"Aye, missus."

Esther gently shakes her wineglass. "Boy," she says to Key. "My cup is empty. Go get me some more wine, pretty little boy."

Key looks to Lawl, who nods. Quicker than Esther can notice, the boy takes her glass and runs from the room. She finds his speed mildly disconcerting.

"That child runs faster than light. He's been taught well."

"Not by me," Lawl says in a mumble. He realizes his mistake at once and looks up from his sketching.

"You are not the boy's father."

"In all honesty, I never claimed to be, missus."

"True. But all the same," she says, as Key comes racing back into the room with the wineglass, "he is an orphan. We both know how GOD feels about orphans."

Key draws close to Lawl, looking up at Esther in fear.

"Yes, well," Lawl says, "GOD is a little too nosey for my liking. If you're going to report him, you'll have to report me, and then where will ya get information on your sweet Gemma?"

"I have no intention of reporting you, Mr. Lawl." She takes a sip of the new wine. "I just needed you to understand how easy it is for me to know things. I am certain I could effortlessly find someone else who would know the whereabouts of my girl. Don't you forget that."

"With all due respect, missus, you couldn't. Your reputation among the servants, aye, even among those uppity-ups of your own class is dire. I've seen the dust on the crystal. Nobody's been to a dinner party here in years. And the servants you haven't already cast out don't want to be let go for havin' met secretly with you on the whereabouts of your daughter, the hero. No, missus. I'm all ya got."

She wants to lash out, to scream, but he is right. No one likes the House of Kerr. She is wildly unpopular. She turns around slowly and walks from the room. She will go to her own chamber now, where she can rage into the mirror.

NIGHT IS falling on the Immortal City. Most living things search for shelter. The farther one travels from the first ring, the more one has to fear. Ferrymen and Kingdom Guards are not all that prowl the night, especially in the abandoned districts of the city. Before the Dark Angels of GOD came up with their soul-sucking contraption, both seen and unseen creatures provided the same service, only with sharper teeth.

Rossa has settled for the night with Claire not far from the third-ring wall. It rises in the distance like a shadow wave creeping ever closer. It is distinguishable from the night sky only because the darkness it collects is of a deeper shade. Rossa has shielded herself well in an old stable, half of which has caved in. She keeps watch from the drooping stable door. A small campfire glows behind her.

This is an old district, abandoned long before the Revolution or any of the plagues. This place existed and thrived when each district had a name, long forgotten now, like a village within the larger collective of the city. Much like the rural districts—a flashing memory of the gardener gives her a chill—they seem more content places. Or would have been once. Places filled with laughter and children and the smells of good food. But so much has happened since these streets last saw any joy. There have been rumors of snovelfarks and fire dogs and crawlers. There have been famines and wars and plagues and hate piled upon hate. Every god, every new faith, every bully regime, takes a bite out of the soul of these places.

GOD is the mightiest bully of them all. Of course, Rossa barely remembers any other before Him. She was a girl when the Revolution took place. But in the history books, if some daring fool still writes them, Rossa is certain this regime is by far the most devastating. And the laws and rules and those who make them are ridiculous and monstrous. There are no better angels here. Only less dangerous devils.

She discovered from an orphan she has befriended that GOD has decreed all horses now belong to Him. She laughed when she heard this. She is certain she is the cause. Mags Hensil wants some revenge for Claire's nostril full of snot in her face.

"Let her try to take ya from me," Rossa said to Claire, her face against the equine's brow. "I be a lunatic murderess now. Don't she know that?"

From her stance at the stable door, Rossa notices movement on the far end of the ancient street. She steps forward cautiously to take a closer look, holding to the collars of her long coat. Her hair is now pulled back in a long braid. She has given the hat up, traded it with an orphan for a bowl of soup. She has the coin from the gardener's purse, of course, but the orphan girl wanted that hat so bad and would only take it if traded fair.

Shadows are rising from below the street. Many of them. They are hushed and without torches, but Rossa sees they are no ordinary citizens. She crouches behind a broken statue. Soon the street is filled with people. She cannot yet see their faces, but their secretive actions tell her they are no friends of GOD. And if that be true, they are indeed friends of hers. There seem to be around sixty in all.

She decides to rise and meet them, but is distracted. Suddenly, from all sides comes the sound of a charging army. The Kingdom Guard and ferrymen descend on the group, cutting off their retreat from whence they came. The people do not surrender, however. These are fighters. They do not care that the guards are on horseback and have mighty weapons. They begin hacking and sawing their way through the assault. Their battle cries mute the commands of the guards. Some in the shadow group are easily taken. The death wagons appear as if by magic, and the rebels are thrown into them.

Yet this is not as easy a fight as the guards most likely wish it to be. A great white hound is silently tearing through the guards like they are rag dolls, and a young man rides on its back. They are trying to protect someone. In fact, the entire group, or what is left of it, is guarding one individual. Rossa strains to see past the fighting and flailing. She struggles to adapt her eyes to the darkness. And then she sees. The girl's face gives Rossa a start. Recognition shoots through her like an electric current. She runs to Claire in the old stable, mounts her quickly, and rides into the fight.

ALL IS caterwaul and confusion. Gemma is overwhelmed by it. She has never seen such a frenzy of panic. The attack seems to have caught even Usker Lance by surprise. The night is so dark and the sound of attack so all-encompassing, it is hard for any of them to get their bearings.

Gemma is being pushed back behind rows of sinners.

"Stay there!" Usker yells at her as he stands with his long sword, preparing to strike down ferrymen and Kingdom Guard alike.

Gemma cannot see much of the action. She hears men on horseback charging them, probably Kingdom Guards. She hears the agitated hooves and screams of the horses, but it's the cries of those in the march that disturb her most. She is dizzied by the fighting going on around her. The sinners are armed with ancient swords, spikes, and scythes. They use them wildly. But their opponents are better versed in fighting. Gemma sees some of her marchers fall. Another is caught by a ferryman's hook, which tears his jaw clear away. And still another has her throat ripped out as she prepares to run. Those who fall and yet live are quickly arrested by the ferrymen and dragged screaming to waiting death wagons.

Usker Lance is the loudest and most furious of the sinners, shouting with rage and ecstasy at every swing of his blade. He uses his broadsword to slice the leg from a guard on a horse. When the rider falls from his mount, Usker finishes the job with a swift decapitation.

"Get her out of here!" he looks back and cries to his fellow sinners.

Royce and Sary Cledes grab Gemma and pull her away from the madness. "Tully!" she screams. "Where's Mr. Tully?"

She sees him still on the back of Madden. "Go!" Tully screams to her. "Get outta here!"

Madden has a screaming guard in his mouth. His powerful jaws clamp and crunch amidst an explosion of blood. Tully is blinded by some droplets and falls from Madden. The ferrymen drag him away, his eyes large orbs of terror as they fade into the dark. Gemma screams. Madden is too busy chewing on another guard to notice.

Gemma is being pushed on by the sinners, though she keeps a horrified watch to her aft. As she turns about, a Kingdom Guard bears down on the three of them. She is frozen to the spot. Her fear has turned her to ice. The sinners pull at her, screaming that she must move, but she cannot. The hooves are drawing closer. She falls to her knees. What was she thinking? She is no hero.

Yet as the guard is upon her, a blade slices through him, sending his head tumbling to her feet. His body slumps forward, and the horse runs past. Gemma looks up and sees the woman Rossa healed of her bruises and on a horse.

"Get her out of here now, ye basterds!" yells Usker as he hacks at a ferryman.

"Come with me!" Rossa says.

Madden races to Gemma. She grabs his fur and hoists herself onto his woolly back. Other sinners run with them. Some capture the horses of the dead guards and ride with Rossa and Gemma. Many, though, stay behind and fight the guards and the ferrymen.

Gemma looks back at the battle, at Usker Lance now fighting three ferrymen at once. "He must run!" she says, tears stinging her eyes. "Why don't they run?"

Rossa is racing beside her. "Every cause has its sacrifices."

But Usker and Tully... Gemma is not certain she can live with those sacrifices.

FRAGMENTS OF SOULS

GEMMA IS with us again. We are Abrythnia, and we are in the Garden of the Passions. Yet things are different, not pleasant at all. The dark sky is threatening with violent streaks of silver and great claps of thunder. The lightning brings forth shapes in the dark clouds, like an army of sky gods charging the heavens and letting forth blasts of wind with their battle cries. Trees and statuary have been toppled, uprooted, and ruined.

We are sitting at a stone table in the middle of the once-beautiful garden. It is all but destroyed now and centuries done. Instead of lush greens and climbing vines, the garden is colored dust brown and the vines are but twigs, seasons past their youth. Nothing grows here anymore.

Our clothes are in tatters. They barely stay on our forms.

"I'm scared," says Gemma, looking around at the devastation.

"We know this," we say. "It is natural to fear. It is a good thing."

"What will happen to my friends? To Mr. Tully and Usker Lance?"

"They will play their parts." We try to be comforting, but we realize there are no comforts in nightmares. "They have been waiting for you. They knew things would become dangerous."

"Then they are the true heroes. Not me."

We are in the wind now, drifting high above the Garden, but still seated at the table. Below us, the world moves. Around us, the sky churns and flashes.

"Why me?" she says. "Why have I been chosen?"

"We like you."

"But why?"

"We like you."

"What if I refuse to play my part? What if I go home?"

We smile tenderly. "They would kill you. You know this. And they would kill everyone you now hold dear. We know we ask a heavy task of you. But the world will be better for it if you hold true. All victories begin with a simple action, word—or person."

There is a blinding flash, and a man sits with us now. His hair is long and shaggy, and he wears a black coat. He stares straight ahead, as if neither of us is there.

"When he comes to you," we say to her, gesturing to the man, "listen to him."

"Who is he?"

"I am a boy without a father," says Cayden Lothair. "I am a man without a soul."

We touch his hand. "No. Your soul is not gone. Only hidden. We made sure of that. Yet it will be returned to you."

"This is the man from the shadows in the Garden," Gemma says.

He turns to her, his eyes glassed over. "I think I know how this ends," he says.

"How what ends?"

But another blinding flash takes him away.

"I don't like this dream," Gemma says. "Not at all. It is too strange."

"You will not be harmed here. This is your place, your mind. All you need do is calm your thoughts, and the agitation will go away."

She listens to us. Her face relaxes, and we are once again back on the ground in a beautiful garden. The clouds have gone and the sun is shining over fields and fields of green. Passions play like children beneath the trees.

"Who are you?" We have been waiting for this question. "Are you truly the goddess Abrythnia? Are you a Passion or a demon of light?"

"Like you, we have many different names and many different worlds. Unlike you, we are able to see them, to live them, and be aware of them, all at once."

"You speak in riddles," the girl says. "I do not understand."

"We are the Something Else. That great Other you feel when you are at your most alone and scared. We, sweet girl, are fragments of your souls, and you are figments of our imaginations. We are here to guide you."

"Guide us? Where?"

"To guide you out of your self-made prisons."

CAYDEN LIES uncomfortably on the makeshift bed and stares at the ceiling. Again, his sleep has been interrupted by dreaming. And again, it is the girl, the one they call "hero." He nearly had her tonight. She should have been easily caught. Rebels can fight, but she is no rebel. She is just a girl. How did she get away and with at least thirty others? Was it the hound? The woman rider? Usker Lance? Or was it something altogether different?

He found an ancient stable nearby to bed down for the night. Someone has recently used it, leaving fresh hay on the ground and the remains of a small fire. He thought that things would be clearer in the morning after a good sleep. But he has dreamed.

The girl was in the dream, seated across from the god Helix, who was immersed in blue flame, his face black ash. Thunkill is nowhere to be seen this time. They were above an expansive ocean, bluer and greater than any known to man. They sped over it, the white clouds above them like passing cities. Cayden spoke in the dream, and this disturbed him. "I am a boy without a father. I am a man without a soul."

And then came a flash of light, and he saw himself as a child standing above his father's motionless and bloodied body. Or what remained of it. His father's corpse was in bits. Like a puzzle that proved too difficult to put together and was shredded to pieces in anger. There lay a hand. There lay an eye. A feral dog was lapping up blood and another was tearing at the flesh on his father's face. If someone were ever to ask Cayden when he had lost his soul, he would say it occurred when he saw his father's remains being feasted on. And yet this is a new memory. Who knows what other horrible things he has chosen to forget? Who knows when they will resurface? Already flashes of a separate life are firing in his brain like a synaptic slide-show. He remembers a mother's presence. He remembers Senator General Hegart and a sword. He remembers seeing the ninth ring for the first time.

He remembers fear.

Cayden rises. The dreams have a way of making him think. He much prefers the nights when he does not dream, does not think. Everything has been numb for so long. Why are things becoming painful just now? Why do these memories have an edge?

He digs in his trench coat for a match and strikes it. He looks around the stable and finds a broken shard of glass. He has a feeling something is different. Strange. He picks the shard up and angles it so that he can see his reflection. But it is not him he sees.

The match burns his fingers and he drops it, quickly stamping out the flame in the hay. The wind outside begins to howl. He remembers fear. He strikes another match and returns his gaze to the glass. There is his face, some might say oddly handsome and rugged, but it is not him. At least, not the eyes he has known. It is a frightening peculiarity, as if someone is hiding behind a mask of his face. There is something else, someone else, in the eyes looking back at him, studying him. And it occurs to Cayden: That is just it. There is something in the eyes when all his life he has been so used to seeing nothing.

He remembers Helix's words in the dream: Your soul is not gone. Only hidden. We made sure of that. Yet it will be returned to you.

Cayden drops the shard and the lit match to the floor. He leaves before the stable goes up in a cloud of smoke.

IT IS morning, and Senator General Hegart stands in front of a crowd in the third ring. The square is filled to capacity. People are leaning from their windows to get a view of the executions. For once these are taking place not in the glass heart of the Immortal City, but in the midst of the lesser folk. The faces of the people are an amalgam of emotions. Some are angry, some are excited, some are grief-stricken, and some have no feelings at all. It is quiet. Five of the rebel sinners have been hung—three men and two women—their bodies suspended behind Hegart, swinging gently. Yet they are mere appetizers. Usker Lance is to be the main course. The big show.

"This is your folly," the Senator General growls at those assembled from the stage. "This is your doing. Not mine. GOD does not enjoy this. We find no delight in the death of those who once were our brethren." The air smells of lies. "But these were sinners. They sought to corrupt, and those who seek to corrupt must be dealt with. When a nail comes loose, one must never fear to hammer it back in place. Any one of you caught collaborating or helping these sinners, these rebels, these corruptors, will meet this same end… or worse." He cannot hide the pleasure he takes in this. A smile appears where none should be.

"Bring him out!" the Senator General yells.

Usker Lance is brought forth from a death wagon. He is naked and beaten, wounds and bruises coloring his muscular frame. His hair is roughly shaved, every braid gone and gouges of flesh taken from his bloodied scalp, and his eye patch is gone as well, revealing a deep black hole. He struggles, but he has been weakened by the abuse, and he stumbles forward. He is forced facedown on a small block of a table. His arms are fastened to the side with chains, his legs spread wide and fastened as well. The crowd is still silent. Some turn away, expecting a beheading.

"Here is the lover of Colm Archer," says the Senator General in a mocking tone. "See how your heretical heroes fall one after another like dominoes. And yet we are not heartless. No. For we have been moved by the Great Sinner's plight, his need for vengeance. We understand it."

The crowd is confused.

"And to show that GOD is indeed love, we will love Usker Lance." A line of ten Kingdom Guards line up behind the Great Sinner. "We will love him to death, in fact. Men," Hegart says to his guards, "love this sinner."

And the first guard unfastens his belt, pulls out his large penis, and inserts it between Usker's legs forcefully. The Great Sinner grits his teeth, but he does not make a sound, even as the guard goes deeper and deeper inside him. One by one, the guards take their turns to spill their seed inside the Great Sinner, the people's hero. They are not kind lovers. They are angry and degrade him as they fuck, with words and fists. They show him no mercy. The Senator General has asked for only those guards with the largest and most dangerous penises to step forward, and that is exactly what he got. These men, who rarely got the chance to be inside of anyone, were free to stretch the Great Sinner as wide as they pleased and in front of a crowd. Hegart watches, salivating with each thrust, lusting after every strike from the guards.

Usker Lance is in pain, but he is brave. Tears stream from his eyes, but he refuses to so much as whimper. The veins in his forehead are large and engorged. We do not know how much longer he can bear this. And so we let him see us. He sees Colm Archer standing in the midst of the crowd. Colm is bright and healthy. He is smiling with love and compassion. He extends his hand to his soul mate. Thus, we make Usker forget the pain. He forgets the horror that is happening to him, and he smiles. His eyes now fill with new tears. Tears of joy.

Senator General Hegart sees this, as does everyone watching. The senator calls a halt to the proceedings, and the ninth guard reluctantly pulls out of the Great Sinner before he comes.

Hegart crouches down and spits in Usker's ear, "What are you smiling at, man lover?"

"I see…" he stutters, "I see… me lad Colm."

The Senator General looks up and into the crowd, searching, searching. "There's no one there but the righteous and those you've led astray, fool."

"Oh no, ya daft basterd," says Usker, not taking his eyes from us. "Me lad Colm is standing right there. He… he be with the dead." Usker strains to look up at the Senator General. "And they be marchin' with our gal, Gemma."

The crowd stirs. His words carry like wildfire through the throng, whispered from one ear to the next.

"Ridiculous," Hegart snarls. "You ridiculous fool. I'm through with your ass and so are my men."

With those words, he runs his sword up Usker's rectum. Only then does Usker Lance make a noise, a short scream followed by a sigh. When he lowers his face in death, he wears a smile.

The Senator General draws his sword out and, with a quick swipe, takes off Usker's balls, holding them up triumphantly before the plaza. The crowd does not seem impressed. They are whispering, humming. Senator General Hegart looks out at them. Their faces are filled with disgust, though not for Usker Lance, the Great Sinner. No. They are looking directly at the Senator General himself.

ROSSA, BORN of the name Bouadica, led them out of the third ring by means of a great fissure in the monstrous wall. The small group had ridden the whole night, staying clear of districts and roads known to be heavily guarded. GOD would be hunting them now, seeking His vengeance. Everyone kept watch as they rode, even Gemma, though her thoughts were visibly elsewhere.

The fissure was guarded by a pack of orphans Rossa had befriended. They could be angry and vicious, but they were honest. When Rossa arrived near the abandoned village, the orphans were initially inclined to turn them away.

"There be thirty of ya!" said a pudgy little girl three feet high who had been charged to keep watch that night behind a thick spotted pine. She carried a small knife and had a breastplate of wood. "And ya got horses and…" She looked at Madden with amazement. "Wow!" she gushed. "Okay. C'mon, then. The doggie first!"

The motley crew was then led through the fissure by the small band of orphans. The little girl walked beside Gemma and Madden the whole time, staring at the hound in amazement. "I got some food. Not much, but he can have it if he's hungry."

Gemma smiled and thanked the child.

"My name is Eight, on account of me bein' the eighth kid born to me ma. That up there," she said, pointing to an older boy around thirteen or fourteen who kept looking back at Madden nervously, "he's Two. He's me brother. He's not rude or nothin', miss. He's just shy and slow. Ma dropped him when he was a babe, and he ne'er got better."

Once safely through, the five orphans led the party to Dingy Hall, an old dance palace at the edge of the fourth ring. They led the horses into the building as well, where they could rest and be fed. Eight kept her word and gave Madden her meager dinner. Her little mouth hung wide with awe between two plump cheeks as she watched the beast scarf the food down.

Now, days later, they are sitting in the center of the dance floor. Thirty sinners, Gemma, Rossa, the hound Madden, four horses, and nine orphans. All of them are brothers and sisters to Eight and Two, and every one of them is named numerically.

The dance hall itself still holds a dying beauty, like fading laughter. At one time it was a spectacle of a place. Now all the gold and silver has been stripped away, and any statuary that adorned it is either broken or stolen. A faint swirling design decorates the wood floor, at the center of which sits Gemma and Rossa.

It is the sinner Royce who is speaking. He is a fairly ordinary-looking man, which helps when he needs to not be noticed. He and Sary Cledes doubled back after the attack and attended the executions of Usker Lance and their five brothers and sisters. Sary is still unable to speak of what she saw. She stares at the floor with an expression of seared angst. Royce, though, is heavy with anger, with rage. His face is red, his eyes crazed.

"…and what they did to the Great Sinner before that final moment… Nine guards. Nine! They raped him in front of the whole crowd. Right there in front of all. Sweet Passions, have mercy." The room is dim and weighted by the tale he is telling.

Gemma looks as if she might crumble into dust at his words.

"But he won at the last," Royce says with a grin. "He took away the Senator General's thunder. Snatched it away with a smile. He says he saw Colm Archer."

Gasps from his small audience. Mouths dropping.

"Aye!" says the teller, looking around to every set of eyes. "He says that Colm and all the dead are marching with us."

He looks to Gemma.

Rossa nods. "Of course they march with us." She is proud of the path she is on. "Don't ya see?" she says, looking around the room. "This is proof. This is the Passions proof that we are on the right side of things."

"Is it?" Gemma is not certain. "In my dreams lately, when I speak with Abrythnia, she responds in riddles. I ask her who she is, what she wants of me, and she says nothing of godship or Passions. She refers to herself as the Something Else. As if she is but another being, invisible. As if she is but a part of my own soul, my own self. I do not think I even believe in the divine anymore."

"I think it impossible for her to be an inner echo," Rossa says. "For you are not the only one to see her, Gemma Kerr. And as for the possibility she may be but some underseen invisible entity who has the talent to invade your dreams, who is saddened by the way we treat one another and is determined to do something about it… well, I thank her for her kind interruption then. Seems to me someone had to get this ball rollin'. Seems to me it's been teeterin' for far too long."

"Aye," say Royce.

"Aye!" echo the sinners.

Gemma is watching the girl Eight and her brother Two play on and around the lounging mountain of fur that is Madden. The world the way it is has no place for these children. Gemma is not yet certain what happens to orphans once they are taken by the ferrymen, but she has a gut feeling that when she discovers the truth it will shatter her. She is already cracking.

"I've not heard anything more about the child you asked me to look for," Gemma tells Rossa. "Key."

"I didna think you would, but I had to ask. He is a good boy. A smart boy. He knows how to get lost and how to stay lost." Her eyes are wells of stifled emotion. "But I'll find him yet."

Gemma looks to her. "Can we do this? Can a group of thirty rebels and sinners hold against GOD's might?"

"Aye," Rossa says. "We know secrets that GOD has forgotten. Look around. We have friends. And if Usker Lance was right, we have the dead on our side as well."

"And our number will grow even more once word gets out of what happened in the third ring, of what they done to Usker," Royce promises.

"GOD's a basterd!" seethes Sary Cledes. She looks up from the floor. "He gives a bad name to true basterds everywhere."

"See there?" Rossa smiles. "Sinners, rebels, and basterds. We've got one hell of an army already."

"And us!" Eight is standing with her brothers and sisters now. "Us little kids is tired of being pushed around."

Gemma smiles. "This won't be easy," she says. "I know the Senator General. He will be furious. Some of us might die. He'll send ferrymen, Kingdom Guards, even Mags Hensil herself after us."

"He sends an army for us, then we need to build an army to defend ourselves." Rossa's voice is reason. "But you leave that ol' bitch Mags for me." This brought snickers from the group and whickers from Claire. "I owe her a good bash to the face, I do."

"We would need armor and weapons."

"Leave that to the orphans," says One, Eight's oldest sibling, a young lady with tired gray eyes. "There be all sorts of buried things you come across when you're an orphan. There be pockets of true might in the forests. GOD's done forgot His own history."

THE HOWLING WOODS

TODAY A crisp wind comes from the east. The doctress is dressed in her heavy wool coat. It bunches around her throat and makes her look as if she has no neck, but it was a gift from Hegart years ago on one of those rare occasions when he still thought to give them. No matter. The wind still bites.

The sinners lined up in front of the hospital are not as warmly dressed as she. Rebelling is hard work. It builds up a sweat. But once the moment of revolution is gone, one is left in the cold, naked and vulnerable. If these poor fools would just do as they were asked by GOD, they might have simpler lives. They might never be sent to the ninth ring. It is their own doing, really, the fools. They might never… they might… might…

Her thoughts are elsewhere as she looks over these new apostates. She sees their stubborn faces, each one looking her in the eye, but their pride means nothing to her. They are bound, every one, hands tied, and all show signs of being beaten, some more severely than others. She does not inspect them as thoroughly as she normally would. She simply rattles off where each is to be sent. It is random assigning at best. She sees only two who will make nurses. The rest will be sent to the Factory… in one form or another. She has her orders to have most of them "prepared." This means nothing to her.

She believes the lies she tells herself now.

Gran was supposed to be "prepared" as well. In fact, the old thing should be long gone by now. Deirdre watches her sometimes when Duncan has left for the Factory. Gran sleeps quite a bit, but she will open her eyes occasionally and even smile. Smile! A smile in the ninth ring is rare indeed.

Once Deirdre even sat beside the bed, and the old woman reached for her hand. They remained like that for some time. They didn't speak, but the feeling, the sensation of being touched, was glorious and familiar. Like a rush of nostalgia that broke Deirdre's heart. Yet she was grateful for it. For so long, she has been afraid she has no more heart to break.

The doctress is jarred back to the now by the face in front of her, like a solid emerging from a shape in a cloud. This is a young man she knows, or rather, knew in another life. Her jaw remains set, but her good eye is wide in shock. The young man looks at her in much the same manner, though his eyes are certainly wider. He always had such abnormally large eyes. Hegart has sent her his brother. Hegart has sent her Tully.

"What have you done?" she whispers. "What have you done?"

And she knows what Hegart expects her to do. It is her job, after all. She has to play executioner and have this gentle young man killed.

THEY CROSS the River Hung warily at midnight. Night is blinding, but the ferrymen can see just as well in the dark.

The orphans have led Gemma, Rossa, and the sinners to another of the abandoned districts of the fourth ring. The river cuts through it like a blade with no bridge to span it. The orphans use rafts instead. They are old and look dilapidated, but they are the only way across. The water is cold, dark, and deep, and large things swim in its depths. They coil about the legs and slowly drag one down until one is planted in the mud, and the corpse is a standing smorgasbord.

The crossing is slow going with two rafts and near forty fools to cross, along with frightened horses and the giant hound. Madden seems anxious to get to the forested other side of the river. He jumps into the current with Two and Eight on his back, and he paddles quickly across. The sinners watch with bated breath until they are safely on the other side. The hound and the children wait for the others.

The past two days have not been without incident. Since arriving in the fourth ring, they have been spotted by the Kingdom Guards or their informants. They have been chased and nearly caught more than once. Sary Cledes has begun to show signs of mental decline. She raves at the ferrymen and guards, daring them to follow her, daring them to come for her. She spends the days muttering and raging, her eyes darting to and fro. At night, she slashes and jabs at anyone who comes too near.

The small march now on the other side of the River Hung, they disappear into the thick, ancient foliage. It will be easier now to hide from GOD. The trees are tall, thick, and gnarled. Their roots resemble the knuckles of giants. They have grown close to one another, affording cover for wild animal or phantom man. The sounds of the forest are what have given the place its name. Not Ring Four, District 17, but the Howling Woods. Ghosts live here. It is known.

They have made camp deep in the woods on a hill. Rossa and Royce are keeping watch. Madden keeps Royce company, as Claire does the same for Rossa. Gemma is unable to sleep. She walks around the camp, taking in her haunted surroundings and the resting marchers. She settles on a slope of hill and sits. She cannot see beyond the dense forest and the dark, but the lamp bugs give light and make the world slightly less ominous. She is not frightened. She is in wonder. The earthy smells of dew on leaves relaxes her, and though it is chilly, she feels no desire to bundle up. She has nothing to bundle up with anyway.

She sees a blue glow to her left. Too large to be a lamp bug, it was faint at first, but then it intensified. For an instant, Abrythnia is walking naked up the hill toward her. Then she changes and becomes Usker Lance, the Great Sinner, naked and grinning. His muscles are etched and deepened by the light he is exuding, and his manhood swings mightily from side to side. Gemma notices he now has two eyes.

"This hill had a great lookout tower once upon a time, it did," he says as he sits down beside her. He is a massive man.

She is smiling and crying. "Here?"

"Aye. This very spot. But that was centuries ago. Things change. Nothin' ever looks the same all its long existence."

"Are you truly him? Because if you are truly Usker Lance, I would like to say how sorry I am to have gotten you killed." Her eyes are pools. "But you're not him, are you? You're Abrythnia or Brochnol or some other god. You're not truly Usker Lance."

He looks at her aghast. "I am so, ye daft bitch!" he says. "Well, I am and I amn't. I'm more Usker Lance than I ever was, in fact. I'm back in the fold, ye see. I know the secrets. But I can be Abrythnia again if ye want, if it'll make ye more comfortable."

"No. Please don't go."

"All right, then. Good. Because, honestly, I like being Usker Lance. I like walking around nekkid and havin' a wee." He gestures to his groin. "And look at this wee! Magnificent, eh? No wonder Hegart wanted it so bad. I gots the balls of a bull and the cock of mastiff pony. I've always been blessed like this."

Gemma laughs. "It's very nice. Colm Archer must have surely appreciated it."

"Aye, and he does still."

She gives him a questioning stare.

"Well, he's here as well, in the fold with me, with Abrythnia, with our soul family. Me and Colm, I always told the cocksucker we was one soul. He didn't truly believe me until he left his form. Then he gets here and he's all, 'Well, what do ya know?' and I was all, 'I told ye so, ye ass bandit.' He always had a thick head on him."

"We're all one soul, then?"

"Not all of us. There are three hundred true souls and we all have a home in one of them folds. Until we get the chance to move on and adventure again, that is. Then, after a time, we come home once more. 'Tis a cycle and it never ends."

"I cannot believe Senator General Hegart has a soul home anywhere."

"And you'd be right there, soul sister. But that be from his own doing. Some souls rot away, but the senator had what tiny bit of soul he had forcibly removed. When a soul is taken like that, it can't never find a new home. It floats, is all. It floats on forever and becomes an angry story parents tell their children."

Gemma looses a tear. "Like my father."

"Aye. Like yer dad."

"So, what am I doing?" Gemma says. "Why am I on this march, Usker?"

"Ye need to save your souls, lass, and your souls will save ye."

Gemma hears movement below amongst the trees. Usker Lance vanishes. She stands, ready to run back to the others in the camp. If the ferrymen have found them in the forest, things could turn confusing very fast.

But it is not a ferryman. It is an orphan boy. Behind him is another, and behind that one is a grown man and an older woman. More and more appear, dressed in tatters and surrounded by lamp bugs. They look at her with the same confusion she bestows on them.

"Who are you?" Gemma asks quietly.

"We're the Ghosts of the Howling Woods," an older man comes forward and says. "And if you be Gemma Kerr, we want to march with you."

DUNCAN MINDS the mixer, but he will not look into it. He does his job, but he refuses to see it being done. Madness waits for him in the corners of his mind, and it is soaked in red, bruised violet, sickly white, and a gooey peach. He must not think on what he is doing. He tries to think only of Lawl's face. That and that alone will keep him from falling over into the mixer himself.

The smell was the first thing he noticed. How can it be missed? It is the smell of rotting flesh, death, and chemicals. He did not know what sort of chemicals until he was inside. Then he realized it was acidic, to strip the muscle from the bone. The window frames of the Factory have no glass, allowing the stench to escape rather than be trapped inside with the workers.

The Factory is a tall building far from the hospital. One must ride many miles on a rickety wagon with other workers to reach it. Some of these looked like the nurses, walking dead; some twitched and shook; some seemed as if they had given up. But others looked as scared as he.

"I don't want to go in," a frightened woman said to Duncan as they rode past fields of dried dead things. She rocked back and forth like the child he and Gran rode with on the way to the ninth ring. "I don't want to go in." Her voice was brittle, and what color she once had was now leeched from her face.

They went into the Factory in a line. Once Duncan was inside, the smell was overwhelming. The frightened woman retched. Duncan nearly followed suit. He saw workers in strange dirty yellow leather uniforms, which covered their entire forms and made each person seem twice as thick as they were. They wore hideous hoods that resembled evil birds, each with a long yellow beak and two large black holes for eyes. The whole place was devoid of any emotion. Duncan was given a uniform by a listless worker and told to put it on. He discovered the hood helped defeat some of the smell as it was laced with floral scent inside.

Corpses hung from hooks from the ceiling like beef. Rows and rows of the dead, most of them upside down, their arms reaching for the floor and mouths wide and gaping. The yellow carrion indifferently pushed around bins full of stray arms and legs and decapitated heads. There were babies… there were babies… That was when Duncan decided not to look, to keep his eyes to the floor as much as he could, to stave off the insanity as long as he was able. It would get him in the end. He knew this. But he would fight until Gran passed.

"Do ye know what they're doin' with everyone?" the frightened woman asked him a few days later as they rode once again to the Factory. Her voice trembled and made her stutter. "D-do ye know what they do with all the dead folk? They're bein' reused, reincarnated." She giggled. "They're GOD's food now."

"GOD's food?"

"Num num," she said, making a quick, greedy eating gesture with her hands to her mouth that caused Duncan's heart to race. "GOD eats people right up."

"Why would GOD eat people?"

She leaned in closer and whispered in his ear, "Because He lost His soul and wants all of ours. Soul is in the bones, ye see. It's in the flesh and blood too, but mostly in the bones. And He wants it."

"But a soul leaves the body at the moment of death."

"Does it?" She became agitated and angry and pushed herself away from him. "How do ye know? Ye don't know! Ye don't know anything t'all!"

The dead weighty eyes of the mindless workers were on him. They stared at him for the rest of the ride that day.

"It's not all bad," the frightened woman said. "I gots to meet Colm Archer. Aye, the Great Sinner himself. He was dead, but I still gots to meet 'im. I shook his hand, and then I took his hand." She laughed. "It's funny. Heroes blend in the mixer just the same as orphans and whores. You'd think there'd be a difference. And GOD is gracious, too. Why, he shares his food with the whole of the Immortal City."

Duncan felt a surge of disgust run through him. "What do you mean?"

"He's been sharin' His dinner with us for years. He puts it in the gruel and bread mixes. There's more than enough extra soul to go around."

He couldn't breathe for a moment after hearing that.

Now he simply stands at the mixer. Things have not improved since those first days. He hopes he never feels as apathetic as some of the other workers. But which is worse? Apathy or insanity?

Just don't look at the bodies. Don't look at the mixing. Don't watch those who have been prepared.

The frightened woman is with him at the mixer, a large bowl in the floor run by GOD's Power. She has been staring into it for a while, her great yellow beak pointed down, down, down. Something is in the air. Duncan tries to get her attention, but she does not respond. She seems too interested in the blades as they mulch flesh and bone. She is too close to the edge. Much, much too close. But before Duncan can get to her, she is already gone. She screams briefly, and then he hears a great crunch followed by a silence. Duncan dares not look.

CAYDEN CLIMBS the ancient steps in the Howling Woods to get a good look at Gemma Kerr. Her marchers are making decent time, their number so small getting through the dense woods is more easily done than he expected. The stairway on which Cayden now travels must once have been an elegant procession up the hill between old homes and businesses. Now, it is covered with thick black vines and bright green moss. Instead of architecture, the stairs are crowded by trees with limbs that block the midday sun as they embrace one another overhead. Below his feet, the fibrous roots threaten to dig up the heavy stone steps.

Losing the Kingdom Guards assigned to him on the other side of the River Hung was an easy feat. They are probably only now realizing he is gone. They are worthless drones and easily deceived. Cayden cut his hair short and changed into a tan tunic and brown pants, but he is not certain that was even necessary. The change in his eyes would have been enough. If he simply holds himself differently, back straight and eyes forward, he has discovered no one suspects a thing. The master of disguise has learned a new trick. To look human.

Cayden wants to see the girl eye to eye. He has seen her in his dreams, these new and disturbing nighttime wanderings, but he wants to see the heroine herself. He's heard rumors in the Immortal City that she is ten foot tall and wields an axe made from the bones of ferrymen. This, of course, is ridiculous, but Cayden's curiosity has gotten the best of him anyway. He wonders if he ever felt like this as a child.

So, he has watched the orphans. He has watched any movement in the night that might lead him to Gemma and her sinners. He is the best tracker in the Immortal City, and he blends well. Colm Archer is evidence of that. But in the end—and this is a truth that eats at him—his tracking abilities have not helped him find the sinners. It is the dreams.

More specifically, it is Father in his dreams, smiling gently and leading him through the woods on the very trail he now climbs. And he emerges, just as in the dream, onto an ancient ruined plaza in the middle of the Howling Woods.

The forest has taken over, but once it was a great place. He can see stone walls evidenced through the vines and foliage, crumbled heaps of blocks and stone and the sad remains of a well in the center. A large oak tree chokes it now. He does not see Gemma, but the plaza is crowded with near one hundred marchers. Much more than Cayden initially thought. This does not dismay him, though. In fact, he finds the march even more impressive for this fact. He hides in the shadows behind one of the larger trees as he espies the camp of marchers: orphans, sinners, revolutionaries, and nonconformists.

"I know you," comes a voice from behind.

This startles Cayden, for it seems his shadow god has betrayed him. No one has ever come upon him unaware before. He turns and sees Gemma Kerr. He cannot help but notice the serenity in her deep blue eyes and how her tranquility is made only lovelier by the smudges of dirt on her face.

"I know you from my dreams," she says. She is holding an armful of fruit from foraging. "I was told to listen to you. What is your name?"

With all the warmth he can muster, he says, "Cayden." The moment is becoming strange for him. The dreams themselves cause him great distress, but even more disturbing, she has them as well. She sees him in her dreams. No one is supposed to see him. He has an oath with the shadows.

She is at ease now and steps closer to him. "You are of the forest people. Do you see Abrythnia in your dreams?"

"No," he responds. Gemma is making him nervous, though not in a manner he is familiar with. This feels more like a caress.

"Abrythnia told me I should listen to you when we meet. But you don't talk much, do you?"

Listen to him? Why would Gemma be told to listen to him, even in a dream?

"Your dream goddess is mistaken," he says. "I am a weak conversationalist. I have nothing to say to you."

"Which only means what you do say is important, right?"

He is caught in her eyes. She is right in front of him. He could end this march right now with a snap of her neck. But...

Gemma hears a commotion in the plaza. Royce and Sary Cledes are bringing in two new faces. Kingdom Guards. The crowd gasps, and the marchers are on alert, grabbing what weapons they can find. Madden's hairs bristle. Cayden pulls Gemma behind the tree with him as they watch. Cayden listens closely.

Rossa approaches the guards as regal as a warrior queen. "What's this?"

"We caught 'em sniffin' around the woods," says Royce. "There may be more. These two say they want to join up with us."

"It's a trick!" Sary is shrill. She is hanging on by a thread. "They mean to kill us."

Royce hands Rossa the guards' swords. "They handed these over when we found 'em."

Rossa studies the two guards. Both of them are young and nervous. "What say you? Is this true? You want to be a sinner?"

"Y-yes, miss," the short, portly one says. He does not look her in the eyes.

"Why?"

"Because we've had enough. Because GOD... He's killing us, every one. Because we are ordered to slaughter babes and grandmothers and people that ain't done nothin' to us. The Immortal City is full of rot, miss."

Rossa laughs. "This one is smart," she says to a slow mumble of agreement from the marchers. She turns to the other, a sad-looking man with no hair. "And you? What say you?"

This one is looking her in the eyes. Good, thinks Cayden.

"I was there... I was part of the guard when my mother and father were arrested and sent to the ninth ring. They never done nothin' wrong. They weren't even sick. I couldna help 'em. The last I saw of me ma was her lookin' at me, pleadin' with me to help them, right before they was put in a death wagon and wheeled off."

"Tricksters!" Sary Cledes shouts. "They're tryin' to trick us. Let me kill 'em like they killed Usker."

"That wasn't us," the portly one defends. "The Senator General, he's gone insane. He does things to people that..."

"One guard is the same as another." Sary raises her sword.

"Enough, Sary!" Rossa yells, holding out her arm. "These men are under my watch and my protection now. They may be able to help us on our way to the ninth."

"You can't be serious, miss. We should do 'em like they done us."

"We should, aye," Rossa says. "But then we'd be no better than they. If they cross me, you can be assured I'll run 'em through meself."

The argument continues, but Cayden needs hear no more.

The ninth. That is where they are headed. The realization strikes Cayden as a given, yet it is slightly surprising as well. He pulls away slowly from the tree and Gemma. The girl hero is still listening to what is happening before her. Enrapt, she is. Cayden is tempted to tell her she needs to be in the midst of the marchers, not collecting fruit. She is not safe, even in the Howling Woods. He is proof of that. But he says nothing more to her. He steals a final glance at her, wishing he could get a last look into those eyes, feeling that pull, and then once again, he fades into the shadows.

MOTHER MAISY'S VENGEANCE

THE MARCH is growing as does the density of the forest around them. They have been walking for days, well-shielded from the eyes of GOD. Entire tribes of the forgotten live in the Howling Woods. Gemma is seen, sometimes riding atop Madden, sometimes walking in step with Rossa, who leads the march through the mists of the woods and the vines of the ancient trees. By the time the march reaches the fifth ring, the number of followers has grown to near three hundred strong.

"We need protection and soon," Rossa says. "The larger we grow, the harder it will be to hide."

The orphans lead them through the crumbled remains of the wall into an older and less traversed fallen city. Here the trees reach higher still, and unfamiliar creatures prowl and snarl in the dark. This too was once a great city, but now its cathedrals are mere trellis work for ivy and vines. They pass statues of strange gods and goddesses and men and women of valor whose names are now lost. Locked to their pedestals by thick tendrils and moss, they peer at the new visitors with grimaces.

The going is slower here to assure the horses do not trip on the massive roots or crumbled stones marking the paths. Many of the new marchers from the forest believe the Passions, if they still exist, live here amongst the wild and untamed beasts of the world. For some, this is a comforting thought. Passions are mischievous spirits, but never malevolent. For others, a spirit is a spirit, no different from GOD and His ferrymen.

The orphans lead the march past the cathedrals and the skeletons of dead architecture to a massive structure. At first it seems only to be a cliff face, but upon closer inspection, they find a doorway beneath the vines and the snakes. Once they pry the door open, Death seems to be huffing stale, dead air in their faces. Rossa stares the darkness down, draws her sword, and rides Claire inside. Torch carriers follow. Scant light peeks through cracks and what were once windows. After she hears and sees nothing of ill intent, she dismounts and lets her eyes adjust to the darkness.

The ruins are strewn with gold and silver and bronze. The light catches on blades and sends rainbows across the ancient hall.

"What is this place?" Gemma wonders.

"It seems to be a museum," says Rossa. "There hasn't been a museum in the Immortal City since I was a wee thing."

The Kingdom Guard named Hedric agrees. "Aye," he says, "but these weapons were old even for these people. These be more ancient than ancient."

"Can they still be used?" Rossa says as she examines a battle axe that has fallen off the wall.

"Aye. These be goodly made. They need to be cared for, sharpened, but there's still life to them."

Birds scatter in the rafters overhead and give everyone a start.

"Grab what ya can, then," Rossa says. "We need any weapon we can find. We'll have an army yet."

The marchers carefully pilfer the hall. Rossa puts the battle axe in the strap over her shoulder where she keeps her sword. She also grabs a set of daggers as well, which she plans to give to the orphans. Children need their toys too, she thinks.

As she walks the halls of the museum, she cannot decide if this place celebrates death and carnage or simply remembers victories. She sees contraptions used for flaying men alive and some for slicing men in half, and she cannot help but think how they play into the darker side of human nature, the deep-rooted and curious sadism.

A wall ahead has completely fallen away, exposing more forest, though not as dense as that from which they have just come. Rossa even sees beams of sunlight poking through. Gemma with the orphans Two and Eight ride for it on Madden. Rossa wants to say something, but she knows they will be careful. Having Madden with them eases her mind. And if they run into trouble, this is the perfect time for her to try out her new battle axe. How many heads has this sweet monster lopped off? What did they look like? Did they deserve it?

Rossa hears raised voices behind her. She jumps on Claire and rides through the halls, torch in hand, racing past dead and decaying history until she finds Sary Cledes brandishing a spear at Hedric. Royce is trying to calm Sary, but the woman is shaking and her teeth are bared and gritted. Her eyes are demonic. Hedric has a slash on his forearm, and blood is streaming onto the ground.

"Sary Cledes!" Rossa thunders, jumping down from Claire. "Put that spear aside."

"He means to kill us!" Sary spits out. "He means to kill us all."

"Please," Hedric says. "We only came to help."

"Liar!" She jabs at the man's side, and he crumples to his knees.

"Enough!" Rossa shouts. "Give me the spear, Sary."

But then Sary seems to turn on her as well, pointing the weapon in Rossa's face. Gasps of disbelief fill the hall. "You're one of them, ain't ya? You show up in the dead of night on a horse just as we come out from the Undercity… I shoulda seen it a long time ago."

"Sary…"

There is no warning. Sary thrusts the spear at Rossa, but her aim is off. The unhinged woman is twitching and shaking too badly to do harm. With her own sword drawn, Rossa knocks Sary's weapon away. It clatters to the ground. The mad woman is running now. She darts past orphans and sinners down a long hall, screaming like a displaced spirit as she runs into the shadows. Some people call for her to stop and some run after her for a bit, but she cannot be found.

"Was anyone else harmed?" Rossa asks as she kneels to look at Hedric's arm.

The injured guard looks up at her, then nods at the other Kingdom Guard with a spear through his belly.

OUTSIDE THE old antiquities hall, Gemma walks beneath the trees with Madden and the brother and sister, Two and Eight. There is a sharp decline to what might have been a road or even a creek, and then more level ground punctuated by large rocks and great roots. The trees are not so crowded here. They can wander without needing to squeeze between trunks. Ivy climbs the statuary and broken columns of forgotten structures. These statues are different than any they have passed on their march. They seem happier. Indeed, Gemma makes out smiles on a few of the sculptures, as if they are merely playing with the vines and roots that invade them. Gemma sees something familiar about these faces, as if she knows them.

Madden and the orphans play on one of the surrounding forested hills as Gemma stands and studies a small stone Passion in front of her, a smiling sprite with fox-like features. She cannot help but return the creature's mischievous grin as it looks to be running from something. Its arm is missing so whatever the fox once held is now gone forever.

"Sneaky lil' buggers, eh?" comes a voice from behind her.

She recognizes it before she turns. "Foxes are known to be quite mischievous, yes."

Usker Lance stands again in all his naked glory. "They're not the most clever, though. Not by far."

"And who might that title go to?"

The Great Sinner raises his arms to the sky. "Usker Lance. Now, he's a tricky lil' cum-licker."

She laughs. "Little? I wouldn't say that. I remember him being as big as life."

They are walking the forest now, toward the children and Madden at play. "Big dog! Big dog!" Two is shouting affectionately between laughs. They are the only words he has said since seeing Madden. Anything else is pointless to him.

"Do ye recognize this place?" Usker says.

"Should I?"

"Aye. Ye come here enough. You've seen it since ye were a wee thing. Every night."

"The Garden of the Passions!" She stops and looks around, a broad smile forming on her face. And she recognizes it, true enough. The hills are overgrown with trees, but she sees the remains of the fountain beneath bush and ivy, and one solitary willow tree, perhaps all that remains of the family that once dominated the Garden. Gemma's eyes fill with tears. She looks down and finds the small stone table she sat at in many of the dreams. It is cracked in half and nearly swallowed by the forest, but she knows it at once. A sense of sadness and despair comes over her. "I do not know what I am doing here," she says.

"Ye be marchin'."

"I am walking."

"Ye be leadin'."

"I am no leader. Rossa is a leader. I am just a silly girl who had this crazy idea that maybe I could change something if I found the root of the problem. And that wasn't even my idea. It was given me by you... or Abrythnia... or whoever..."

"Sweet girl," says Usker, holding her chin between his thumb and forefinger, "No true hero believes they are a hero. They simply want to do what's right."

"I'm no hero. You… you are a hero."

Usker's face is sad. His eyes become gentle pillows. "Ye will be the greatest hero the Immortal City ever saw, Gemma Kerr. I guarantee that. But I won't lie to ye, missy. Bein' a hero… it's painful work, and the sacrifices, aye, the sacrifices seem too much to bear at times. And maybe they are. At least to the individual. But to the soul, those nasty ugly sacrifices are beautiful things because they inspire growth."

Gemma embraces him. "Why is there such awfulness in the world?"

"Ah, sweet girl," says the Great Sinner, "no one knows the answer to that. Not even Abrythnia."

LAWL IS looking at himself in the prop mirror. He decides right there in the middle of the scene that he is a pretty man. Duncan always told him so, but one should never trust those they love to give them the truth about beauty. And yet with the stage makeup and sharpened brows, with his dark hair lacquered up and pulled back into a ponytail, with his pursed lips and his seductive pose in the big frilly tunic, he can see it now. And the small crowd gathered to see Mother Maisy's Traveling Tribe of Wonders seems to be quite enamored with him. The young ladies and some of the young men are swooning. This is a new experience for him. He flashes a little thigh in comic jest, and the gasps are audible. It is the easiest work he has ever had… except for the smiling. Mother Maisy is always having to get on him about the smiling.

"Brooding is fine, to an extent," she tells him. "But a smile, my lad, a smile will get you so much farther. With that pretty face of yours, you should be makin' your mother very wealthy very fast, my sweet little flesh dumplin'. And we're gonna need every bit of that wealth if we intends to get where we intends to get."

At least he did not need to speak. His mumbling did not travel so well in crowds. Esther Kerr, however, had gotten used to it by the time he and the child left the manse.

The troupe on this tour of the Immortal City consists of three other people. Mother Maisy is, of course, the Mistress of Ceremony. She is a squat woman in sequined black suits of her own design. She wears a top hat with not so much a veil as a drape hanging heavily from its brim. She flicks her wrist with a showman's liquid ease, and her voice thunders over crowds in waves. Her two sons, now called Anger and Spite, are scarcely clad muscular eunuchs who wrestle and box and perform feats of strength to the amusement of the crowd. They are twins and have little use of language, able to communicate quite well with each other. They have auburn hair and awkward stares, the kind that burrow deep, looking for an honest heart in the filth. To one another, they are brother and lover and comforter. Lawl likes them. If the whole city were as silent as these two, it would be a better place.

Lawl had heard about the Traveling Tribe through excited whispers building in the courtyard behind the manse. The show itself would never be allowed into the first ring due to its bawdy nature, but it was just outside, at the first-ring wall. The servants were abuzz, giddy.

"Can ya believe they dare come so close?"

"I want to see 'em. I wonder if I could sneak away."

"This is gonna be the best tour yet, I hear. Mother Maisy intends to head to the ninth ring."

"How's she plan to do that?"

"How should I know? I'm not fool enough to head up there with 'er. Word is, though, she be in league with the sinner's march."

Lawl decided he had been in the first ring as long as he needed to be. This was something new. This was a chance. He thought of Duncan and Gran, and that afternoon, he set to readying himself for departure. He planned to leave Key well behind and safe in the first ring, but the child seemed to know something was up. He was in the bedchamber with his drum, ready to go before Lawl even got there. His face had an expression of little-boy challenge, and Lawl knew he would not stay put. And how would Lady Esther treat the child without Lawl around?

They waited that evening until Esther had no more use for them, and then they quietly left through the servant's entrance and snuck out onto the courtyard. Esther would wake in the morning wanting news of her daughter from Lawl, but she would be served a cold plate. Lawl was done with her. They left through the first-ring gates with the evening's last group of workers who lived in the lesser rings.

Mother Maisy's Traveling Tribe of Wonders was easy to find. The stage and wagon were set up against the first-ring wall as if they were merely an extension of the great structure. By night, one might assume the stage had been there all along. The massive twins, Anger and Spite, were outside doing their job and courting interest in the show. A throng of people watched the two do nothing but leer and pose. They were identical, so Lawl had trouble telling them apart.

They were like flesh statues welcoming the citizens in for a look. One stood by the wagon with a meaty leg upon a step, and the other in a similar pose near the stage. They were dressed very much the same as well. Sleeveless white tunics to better show their mountainous arms, black velvet sashes around their waists to give them more shape, body-hugging striped white and red tights to accentuate not only their legs but also the elements of their bodies that made them such oddities, and big black boots. Each also wore a beret. Lawl would later learn Anger wore the red, Spite wore the redder. Lawl and Key passed Spite on their way into the wagon to see the Mistress. He gave Lawl a quick once-over and returned his attention to an adoring trio of young men who nervously touched his arms.

Mother Maisy sat behind a large dark wood desk. Lawl was uncertain if she saw them behind her veil of black, though she faced their direction. She did not say anything, so they waited at the door to be asked in.

"Are you going to stand there all night, boys, or would you like to come in?" she said in a commanding voice. She might make a child cry by simply wishing him a good morning.

"What do you want? What can I do for you? Mother Maisy lives to entertain the Immortal City."

Lawl looked around the dark, candlelit wagon. The wagon was filled with gaudy knickknacks and souvenirs. Mammoth bone and Passion fur and things from the outside world before its fall.

"My name be Lawl. We heard you was headin' to the ninth," he said quietly.

She did not respond. She was very still. Was she looking at him? Had she heard him?

"And why would you want to go to the ninth ring?"

"Because they took the most important people in my life there in those damn death wagons, and I plan to get 'em back, I do. And as for my little friend here, they killed his pa."

"I see." She continued her stoicism. "There is nothing so beautiful as a game of vengeance well-played, Mr. Lawl," Mother Maisy said. "I cannot take you all the way to the ninth. None go past the fifth ring 'cept the ferrymen and their charges. But I can take you to the sinner's march as long as they're still there."

"That'll do," said Lawl.

Mother Maisy leaned forward over her desk. "Give me your face," she said. "I must see your talent with my hands."

Hesitantly, Lawl put his face into her hands. These were not soft hands. They had been hardened and felt as cold as stone. "Oh, yes. You're a pretty one. We can definitely use you." She sat down once more. "And the child? What can he do?"

"His name is Key. He has a drum."

"Play for me, child."

Key tapped and pounded on the drum, a slow, wary syncopation. It was very much something of a death march.

"How insane are you, Mr. Lawl?" said the woman.

"Not at all, miss."

"Oh, come now. To have survived your grief, you must be somewhat insane. When you dream, do you deal in nightmares? I do. Mine are horrific. I wake screaming every night. You'll hear it."

"Are you insane, miss?"

"Aye. Very much so. It's the only thing that keeps me going, that and my boys. But, you see, they're one and the same, really. My boys are a product of insanity."

"How so, miss?" He felt the darkness close around him. The wagon was drowning in rage.

"I have run this troupe for many years, Mr. Lawl. Those first few years were good. I had a husband then, and a little girl and my boys. We were one of the best troupes ever to cross the River Hung." She cracked her black-gloved knuckles one by one.

"We were performing in the first ring one day, when a Sister of GOD caught our show and reported us as base and immoral. I will admit, my troupe is a bit bawdy, but it's all in good fun. Ol' Queen Mags didn't think so, though. The next day, my husband was taken off to the ninth, and our wagon was burned. You would have thought that would be enough. But no…"

Lawl's skin was crawling. Key had curled up beside him, leaning fiercely into his ribs.

"The Senator General raped and murdered my little girl right there in front of me. Slit her throat, he did. Then he took my boys and had his Kingdom Guard hack their willies right off. I was forced to watch all of this before they tore my eyes out with serving spoons. Then they threw us out of the first ring and gave us a night to crawl away. They said if we had not disappeared by the morning, we'd be joining my husband in the ninth."

Lawl breathed in the cold rage around him. "Vengeance," he whispered. "Vengeance."

Now, Lawl gives the audience a wink and blows a kiss before leaving the stage. He is naked but for the white tunic, which comes down to just above his knees. He watches as Key steps to the stage with his drum. A nine-foot talon bear dressed in the torn uniform of a Kingdom Guard dances behind the child. Lawl was nervous for the boy when Mother Maisy suggested the routine, but Key was not frightened and the bear, Lolly, playfully dances along to the beats of the drum. The crowd loves it, as does Key if his smile is any indication. When the routine is finished, Key giggles and bows and the bear roars. The twins are next.

"We should be careful," Lawl tells Mother as he watches off-stage. Mother Maisy is ever curtain-ready. "I saw a Sister of GOD and a couple of guards in the audience."

"Good," Mother says. "That means my sweet angry boys can have some fun tonight. It's been so long since they've had any fun."

"But shouldn't we be headin' out?"

"Aye. We will, Mr. Lawl. It won't take long. By the time the little Sister waddles her way back here with more guards, we'll be good and gone. It's a dance we know by heart."

The twins wear nothing but brown sackcloths around their waists. They circle one another, pectorals dancing, eyes aflame, and then they tear off their sackcloths, revealing large, low-hanging testicles but only a small slit where a penis should be. The crowd roars with disgust, intrigue, and lust. The twins grapple with one another and the stage shakes with their throws and holds. They are so very much alike, it is as if one man is fighting himself. Their wrestling is a ballet more than a sport, without a grunt or groan heard from either of them.

There is a winner, though, and he straddles his brother's chest and kisses his lips. Lawl watches, mesmerized, as both men rise from the stage and jump into the audience. Admirers touch their arms and legs and fondle their testicles as they part the crowd. Lawl knows what they are doing. They are looking for their fun. Having found what they are looking for, they give a nod to the lucky audience member to follow them into the shadows behind the wagon.

Mother Maisy takes to the stage. "Gentle people of the Immortal City," she bellows sarcastically, "I pray you've had your fun tonight."

The crowd roars its approval.

"Good," the blind woman says. "Very good. I am afraid, however, it is time for us to part. Please come see us again if you hear our wagon wheels on your cobblestones. We're ever so much fun. We won't bite. Well"—she points in the direction of Lolly—"most of us won't."

Laughter.

"Good night." And darkness. The crowd is dispersing.

As Lawl and Key help Mother Maisy pack up, Lawl sees the twins, now completely clothed, disassembling the stage in a matter of minutes. "Where are the guards?" he says.

"My boys probably tired them out. They're so much fun." Then she leans in closer to his ear and whispers, "Vengeance." Her word is made from smoke and ashes.

The wagon looks ordinary as Mother Maisy's Traveling Tribe of Wonders makes its way down the main road of the second ring toward ring three. No one would ever suspect that inside the boxy structure is a bear and a stage. The twins are at the reins, dressed in long brown capes. Lawl and Key sit with Mother Maisy behind them. They are on their way now.

Vengeance.

DUNCAN SITS beside the bed, holding Gran's delicate hand. Any second now, the heaviness of what he just admitted to her will make her skin fall away and her bones to wither to dust. He cannot look at her, so he keeps his eyes on a fold of her bedsheet and the small shadow it casts. He is crying. The pain is deep and cutting, but he feels relief as well.

"I'm sorry," he says, struggling for breath. "I'm so sorry, Gran. I thought it would make everything better. I didn't know what this place was, didn't know what they do here. I thought it would be a better life for you and me. Ah, it was selfish, I know, but I thought Lawl could come live with me and…"

Gran pulls her hand from his light grasp. This, the most forced movement she has made in some time. He looks up to see her turn from him, her eyes closed tight to lessen the tears.

"Please… please, forgive me…"

She dismisses him with a slight gesture of her wrist, something that could be construed as a jumpy nerve. He does not want to leave. The guilt burrows into him like a dull blade, digging and digging. He sits for a moment more before getting to his feet.

"I'm sorry," he whispers one last time.

Duncan turns to see the doctress at the door. She stares at him in the same manner she always has. He is a drone among many. He feels judged by her and quickly leaves the room, stumbling down the hallway of the hospital with blurred vision and an ache in his throat. The orange sky outside shines in and paints the slick floors and tall white walls in flame. Duncan sees nurses pass him, but he is as uninterested in them as they are of him. They, too, are painted orange.

He finds himself on the balcony. His world ends here. If he were at the Factory, he could make quick work of his misery's end by pitching himself into a mixer. The pain could never be as intense as the guilt he feels now. He looks up to the swirling orange clouds sucked into the direction of an unseen sun. If only he could be like that. Sucked away into oblivion, ignorant to all. He would not then be forced to think of what he has done, of how he has betrayed Gran and Lawl… Sweet Lawl…

Duncan gasps for air and sobs as he climbs upon the banister. His bare feet clutch at the cold railing. He feels eyes on him. Some of the nurses have sensed movement and come to watch his fall. He balances, arms spread for flight. He imagines the steps below already brilliant with his blood. Bright red on screaming orange. He closes his eyes.

"Sweet Lawl," he whispers as he gives up.

But he does not fall.

Someone grabs him and pulls him back down onto the balcony, where he lands with a thud. He is in a daze now. I should be falling. I should have fallen. I should be dying. I should be dead.

But, no. A young man looks down at him. Duncan has never seen this boy before. He is saying something, but Duncan hears only echoes as if he is in a dream tunnel. And the young man is strange-looking. Distorted. His eyes are way too large for his thin face. Duncan thinks he is hallucinating.

Finally, through the haze, Duncan hears the clarity of words. "Don't do it," the young man is exclaiming. "Don't ya give 'em what they want! Fight! Fight! Fight! And by the Passions, I'll fight with ya."

THE FIFTH ring is mostly forest and plains, a few hills and wide acres of ruins. Its villages and cities are no longer populated, and most of the citizenry live in tribes in the wooded lands or in the more fertile valleys. They live in small earthen huts, though some prefer tents so they may pick up and roam at will. The fifth ring is home to nomads who love the wilderness and have no interest in the affairs of the first four rings, which is not to say they are not plagued by GOD.

He persecutes every sinner, and those who would worship false gods are seen to at once. Those in the fifth ring worship the Passions and elder gods as if it were still the ancient days. Some even erect carved wooden images deep in the forest and pray for the sprites to return. A few of these tribes have now joined the march, though more have stayed behind, hidden from the eyes of GOD by the dense forest. Those who have come march behind the main group in their own smaller bands of twenty or thirty, and they are conspicuously adorned in little else but colorful beads and small loincloths. Some mark their faces with tattoos and paints. Others wear great silver discs through their lips and ears.

"These are Usker's people," Royce told Rossa and Gemma. "He was from these same forests, but stolen for a rich pair of first ringers. They thought he was precious, cute lil' bugger. They didna think so after he bit off the old man's dick."

The march settles for a rest at the edge of the forest. Gemma and Rossa take Claire for a graze on a rolling grassland. Evening is coming, turning the orange sky a blood red. The winter chill rolls over the hills like a whisper. Rossa likes the touch of the cold on her face. Cold feels like new.

"And ya trust this stranger ya met in the woods, do ya?" Rossa asks. "He hid and then snuck away. That would not elicit my trust, dear Gemma."

"He was in my dreams," Gemma says. "The ones with Abrythnia before Usker Lance started visiting me. Abrythnia told me to listen to him."

"What did he say? Was it of any importance?"

Claire whinnies and shakes her mane in contentment as she munches on the long grass behind them.

"Nothing I can think of. But there was something… something about his eyes…"

Rossa crosses her arms. "I don't know, Hero Girl. I do not trust it. Maybe he is a spy. Maybe he is a herald of GOD. Maybe he is a fucking demon."

"I want to trust him. Can't there be anyone I can trust?" She seems irritated.

"No." Rossa knows when to be blunt. This is no time for subtle charm. "Trust belongs back in those old museums. Trust leads to death."

Gemma is silent for a moment. "That disturbs me," she says. "I never much liked the people around me. Not even my parents, really. But I always trusted them. Now you're telling me that was folly. I feel such anger welling up in me." She clenches her fists. "I think I understand Sary Cledes."

"Sary Cledes is insane now, gal."

"Maybe I am as well. Maybe you are."

"Maybe we all are, and this whole walled city is a figment of some creature's bizarre and complex imagination."

"That's what Abrythnia told me, that we are figments of her imagination, that she is a fragment of our souls."

"So, we're puppets then." Rossa does not like that thought. Despite everything, she believes people make their own ways. Free will to fuck up their lives how best they see fit. If that does not exist, if everything is preordained, then no matter how hard she searches and what tragedies befall her, she might never find the child Key. If some higher spirit or creator has chosen to strike the child down or make it so their paths never cross… She does not wish to think on this. We feel a stab of resentment from her.

"Passions protect us!" she says suddenly.

Across the rolling plains, she sees a band of riders on horses racing toward them. They are coming too quickly for her and Gemma to mount Claire. She pulls her sword and axe, and Gemma pulls a small blade she has taken from the museum.

"Kingdom Guards?" Gemma says.

"They be the only ones with any horses these days, if what I'm hearin' is right. That's all thanks to yours truly."

Yet as the riders approach, Rossa sees no uniforms. In fact, they are wearing clothes of the common man. And women and younger folk are among their number as well. Rossa is not less threatened as the riders surround them. They have weapons, but they are not drawn.

"Are you the Lady Rossa?" a large man with a tattoo over half his face says.

"I am Rossa," she replies. "But a lady I am not, sir."

"And a sir I am not, m'lady. We have been looking for you." He looks to Gemma with wide-eyed interest. "And her."

"Who be ya?"

"We're horsemen, and we want to join your march. So, put your sword away. You have no need of it."

Rossa relaxes a bit and looks at the steeds. "Horsemen? Has GOD not taken them from ya?"

"He tried, but some of us managed to get away with our most prized mounts."

Claire looks a rag doll compared to the horsemen's steeds.

"We've lost twenty riders trying to find you," he says. "Lorien is me name." He looks about the plains. "Where be the others in your march?"

"Back in the forest," Gemma answers.

"What news from the rings?" Rossa says. "If you can find us so easily, is the Senator General far behind?"

"He's coming hard for you, miss," says a young woman with short dark hair. "They're setting fire to the forest and flaying and hanging those who get in their way. Women and children along with the men."

"They impale the bodies along the road as warnings to others," says Lorien. "It's a bloody mess."

Rossa's heart sinks. She tries to keep up her walls so that nothing might affect her, but she sometimes fails. She notices Gemma's jaw tense. There is rage in the girl, not grief.

"Come back to the forest with us," Gemma says with a new look of resolve. "We shall have a feast tonight. We shall remember those who died for us, and then we shall collect our anger and march on. They will not have died for nothing. We will succeed, and we will bring GOD down."

THE SENATOR General has called upon the House of Kerr once again. He sits in the parlor with a cup of tea he has yet to taste. The place looks dismal and dim, as if it hasn't been cleaned in days. Dust is an inch thick on the shelving and tables. Shards of broken dishes are scattered over the floor of the parlor and in the hall, as if a small cyclone had been released. One lit candle sits atop the mantel in the parlor. Esther herself answered the door, looking haggard but no less haughty. Where are her servants? Hegart wondered. There is the old man who brought the tea, but that is all. Odd.

Esther Kerr sits slouched in her chair across from him. Her hair is straggly and hanging lazy from its usual knot, her gown is wrinkled, and her eyes seem tired. Very tired. Hegart has hope for some sort of victory here. He cannot help but grin.

"Wipe that ugly smile off your face," she says. "I told you, you will never see my husband again. Ever. He is through with you and GOD. You lose."

"I lose?" he says, deciding to keep his grin all the same. "Pardon me for saying so, but by the looks of things, it seems as if you have lost. You are swimming in darkness, dear lady."

She watches him intently. Scrutinizing. As if she expects him to do something. But what?

The manse creaks and knocks around them, ready to be done with it, to be done with the Kerrs, done with the entire city. Hegart would gladly put the place to the torch, and the lady of the house with it. To hear her screams would be akin to a lullaby.

"Are we to be drowned by your odious voice indefinitely?" she says.

The Voice of GOD has been playing throughout the first ring all day, the same few sentences on an endless loop.

"GOD's affirmations are a comfort to His people," says the Senator General. He slurps back a stream of saliva.

"Do you really think threats will quell an uprising? You are a fool, and so is GOD."

"'Tis no uprising, lady. 'Tis but a squabble."

Esther's sharp laughter surprises him. He has never heard it before. She keeps her eyes on his cup of tea. She takes a sip from a wineglass that sits on the floor beside her chair. "This is no mere squabble, Hegart," she assures him. "I hear the sinner's march is swelling in numbers, as is support for it. People go in search of it. Why, even here in the first ring we have had these so-called 'squabbles.' Can't you recognize the truth? This is revolution. It has taken a different form than the one we anchored, but things are changing and they're about to get very, very nasty. For you, for me, and for the damned Almighty."

Hegart loses his smile. He knows the truth in what she says. Some of his own guards have defected, slipped away in the night. When he regains control of the city, he will skin the insolent guards and hang their corpses from the gates as a warning. Perhaps a weekly flaying would do the inhabitants good. He could do it by lottery.

Esther clambers to her feet. She nearly trips as she walks to the large window that looks out over the empty nighttime street. She throws her wineglass to the floor where it does not shatter but rolls into a corner like a frightened pet. "Won't you take a sip of your tea, Senator? It's good tea. Would be a shame to see it go to waste."

"Lady Esther, where is your daughter? Where is Gemma?"

"She's out. Out and about doing this, doing that. Sometimes doing this and that. She's quite popular these days."

"With all the wrong people. I think it would be best if you told her to come home to mommy."

Esther laughs again, but it is a deflated laugh, lost of all strength. "Oh, that I could. But you see, Hegart, I am just as lost as you." She turns to face the man again. She is but a silhouette. "I assure you, I have not the slightest idea where my little revolutionary has got to. But I can tell you this. I'm very proud of her. She's got more balls than every man in your loathsome guard combined."

She glances at the cup again. "Have some tea," she says. "I made it just for you."

The Senator General looks at the cup suspiciously. "You have it," he says as he flings the hot liquid at her.

She is quick to jump away as the acid in the tea lands on the carpet near her and begins to eat away at the fibers. Her eyes are white with fury. Esther grabs a lamp and swings it at the man, gashing his forehead. He is on top of her, choking her, soaking her with drool and rage. He wants her to die. He has wanted it for so long that he does not even remember why. But it feels good, orgasmic. It feels marvelous to dig his fingers in her throat. This is what he loves. This breaking, this crushing, this finality. And yet...

She is smiling. She wants this, too. She wants him to kill her. His thoughts turn to GOD. He would not want this. He wants Bana alive, and Bana would surely die for lack of care without Esther.

Hegart releases her throat and stands. She is choking on the floor, clutching at her neck and hacking.

"Coward!" she yells coarsely. "You can't... even kill... a woman."

"Too easy," he says, his eyes gone white and his filed teeth bared like a monster from a folk tale. He wipes the drool from his mouth with the sleeve of his coat. "What you need, miss, is a long imprisonment. Just you and Bana. I'll be taking your old valet with me, and I'll be posting guards at your doors. You will never set foot outside of this manse again. And when you die, I'm going to rape your corpse and hang you on the gate for all to see your rotting pussy. Best hope Bana outlives me, Lady Esther. If not, you'll be joining him the minute he dies, and in the most excruciating manner I can come up with."

THE LIBRARY

THE KINGDOM Guards are screaming, but in the fourth ring, they think it is part of the show. Mother Maisy is known for her gory brand of theater effects. The woman can do anything, they say. She owns the best traveling show in all the Immortal City.

Lawl watched Anger and Spite from behind the stage curtain as they seduced the two unfortunate guards. The twins gestured for them to follow, their muscular glutes in striped tights giving an open invitation as they led the way. Mother Maisy was with Key, decorating his face like a warrior with the makeup Lawl used every night. He looked fierce when she was finished. Finely applied black vines half-mooned his eyes and beneath them were swaths of red and black. At the center of his forehead was a red triangle. Lawl did not know what it meant, if anything at all, but the child looked only half as innocent as he was. How the old blind woman had managed to paint his small face so precisely was a mystery as well. Lawl was curious, but thought the answer best left to the enigmas and the shadows.

In an alley nearby, the twins were both completely naked, lying on their backs head to head on a couple of large wooden crates as the guards fucked them. Anger and Spite held each other's hands over their heads as the guards tore into them angrily, punching and cursing at the twins as they fucked. The boys testicles were thoroughly abused, but they showed no signs of distress. Their faces were emotionless, but their eyes… They both turned to Lawl and watched him until he suddenly felt ashamed for having witnessed their rape and turned back for the wagon. Their expressions haunted him, so much rage in them that he was certain the only color they ever saw was deep red.

And they are getting plenty of it tonight. The guards are part of the show, and they are bleeding their sins away. They are screaming for an end, but the crowd sees only effects and a dazzling display of grotesquerie.

When Lawl saw that the guards were still with the troupe, only now bound and naked, he knew he would need to close his eyes at some point. The guards were whimpering for someone to help them, anyone. The crowd laughed and threw scorn and derision their way. When the naked twins, with bruises on their bodies from the night before, whipped out a large, sharp blade and hacked off the members of the two men, the crowd cried in wonder and horror. The guards bellowed and screamed. The twins, however, assuring the crowd that it was all a show, gestured to their own missing members as if they had not put up that much of a fuss. The crowd laughed.

And now they have brought out Lolly in her cage. The twins throw her the severed penises, and she eats them like candy. Lawl knows to close his eyes. He tries to tell himself the guards brought this on themselves, but empathy will not abandon him. Key does not watch, either. He buries his face in Lawl's stomach as Lolly roars, the guards scream, and the crowd cheers. Lawl knows he will never forget those screams.

Now the shows are through and Mother Maisy's Traveling Tribe of Wonders is back on the road. They travel on the side roads. That is the only way to get to the fifth ring without attracting unwanted attention. The main road is being carefully watched since the sinner's march made it to the fifth. There are so many holes in the fourth-ring wall, though, that any blind woman could throw a rock and find one. The wagon itself does not go into the fifth ring. The twins take their government-rented steeds into the forest. Lawl rides with Spite, Key with Anger. Lawl feels safe with Spite, as if behind a wall where no one can get to him. Mother Maisy stands on the wagon steps calling, "Vengeance! Blood and vengeance!" She is an apocalyptic town crier. Lawl watches her as they slip into the wall. She is the maddest person he has ever met, and the angriest.

Orphans meet them on the other side. They seem familiar with the silent giants on horseback, asking them to flex as they travel alongside them on the densely forested trail. The twins oblige. The night is so dark, Lawl wonders how any of them can see their way, but they do. They slip in between trees and boulders and ruins like shadows and shades.

They travel all night, and come morning they arrive at a small encampment of men and women. The leader of the group nods at Lawl. "Ya wish to march?" he says to Lawl.

"We both do," Lawl replies, gesturing to Key. The boy is still wearing the face paint Mother Maisy had decorated him with.

The twins dismount and help Lawl and Key from the horses.

"We'll get some breakfast for ya, then," says the man. "I imagine you're hungry after the night's ride. Then we'll make for the march. My name's Royce."

"I'm Lawl. This is Key."

Royce nods, then looks to the twins. "You fellas come get ya some food, too. Ya do good work."

Lawl couldn't tell whether the twins appreciated his words or not, but they and the orphans join everyone else around the campfire. A few of those in the camp are forest folk who cook whatever Royce and his hunters bring back from the hunt. One of the cooks, an old woman with as many wrinkles as years, takes immediately to Key, admiring his painted face.

"You've found us at an impasse," Royce says to Lawl as they are sitting on a log by the fire. "The march has stalled until we find a way through the fifth wall."

"But a way will be found, right?"

"Oh, aye. Don't doubt it. We've got a queen leading us." He tears into a roasted giant rat leg.

"Gemma Kerr."

"No. The other one. The redhead. Gemma's a lovely hero, no doubt about it. But it's Queen Rose who's keepin' us going. That woman can fight."

They leave for the sinner's march. The twins and the orphans are thanked for their help. Lawl watches as Anger and Spite disappear into the woods surrounded by children on their mounts. Such rage and innocence, such a human thing.

They journey through dark vales and creek beds, over barrows and the remains of once proud homes. They come to the march at last and are greeted by the hero herself, the girl Gemma. Lawl is surprised when he sees her. She looks nothing like her mother. Whereas her mother scowled with condescension, Gemma smiles with compassion. She takes both Lawl and Key into her arms at once.

"Welcome," she says. "To the future."

Lawl takes in his surroundings. The marchers have built a moveable city. And their number far exceeds what he imagined. A twinge in his gut tells him that this will lead to trouble. The larger the number, the harder it will be to hide. There will be death. Best keep the child close by.

Key is making friends with Eight and Two and Madden when at last the redheaded woman appears. She has been out scouting on her horse, Lawl is told. She is every bit the queen and leads her gray mare as assuredly as any of the horselords around the camp. All look at her with respect. Some of the forest folk even bow.

Lawl notices Key paying special attention to Queen Rose. His mouth drops, and a tear runs down his cheek. The queen notices him as well. She squints, and then her eyes widen and well up.

"My boy!" she cries as she runs to embrace him. Key is hugging her so tight, Lawl believes he might hurt her. The child is sobbing, taking in huge gasps of air, and the queen herself is covering him with kisses. Others in the crowd cheer and begin to weep openly at the reunion as well.

"Well done," Royce says to Lawl. "The queen at last has found her prince."

GOD IS dining.

Senator General Hegart stands below the high chair and hears the slurps and tongue-smacking as His Holiness masticates another soul. The Senator General wonders who has the honor of being digested by GOD. Is it an orphan? Perhaps an elderly gypsy? Or maybe even a baby? Theirs were the purest of souls, GOD has assured Hegart. Abandoned babies are hard to come by, however. They die so quickly on their own. But remnants of soul might still be in their tiny bones.

No Children in Red are in the chamber now. Hegart notices too the empty council chairs as he waits on GOD to finish eating. Not one of the four is filled. They have all died and most likely been incinerated. Their bodies were useless, having lost their souls years ago. What does a soulless body taste like, he wonders.

GOD finishes His meal with a long aching moan and then silence. The darkness of the chamber is oppressive and heavy.

After a few more minutes, a whisper crawls toward Hegart's ears. "What news of the realm, Senator General?"

"The people are restless, Your Worship."

"I have seen that much from my monitors." GOD's hushed voice crawls down the trumpet like a snake slithering. "Even here in the first ring, there have been uprisings."

"Begging your mercy, but not uprisings. Only easily quelled dustups."

"Still, should I be looking for a new Senator General?"

This strikes Hegart to the gut. "I beg Your Worship, Your Almighty, please give me another chance. I have served you well. Better than most. We can increase the public executions—"

"The executions only seem to be making the citizenry more irritable. And aside from that, at the rate you are killing the sinners, I will have a serious dent in my food supply before long. I can only consume those who are freshly deceased, those who still have soul to spare." GOD is not happy. He creaks and groans in his chair, each sound coming down the trumpet like a slap to Hegart's face. "Are the rumors true?" GOD says. "Is this march that you believe so insignificant headed for the ninth ring?"

"That is what we believe, yes."

"Why do you think that is their destination?"

"We do not know yet. But I have our best ferryman on it. Cayden Lothair is following the march."

"Ah, good. The hero killer."

Indeed, thinks Hegart. But he feels something is amiss with Cayden of late. The man has disappeared in the jungles, not reporting back to his guards for days. Hegart grows suspicious.

"It will save us time if the sinners take themselves to the ninth. Time and strength. We shall have an army waiting for them when they arrive. Make that happen. I want the healthiest taken alive. Kill all the others at your whim." GOD's whispers are taking on a high, excited quality. "But continue tracking them. It would be best if we arrested this march before they reach the ninth, otherwise we look weak. I look weak. You may use our other means to stop these sinners since it looks as if the forests and wilderness of the fifth ring are proving to be such a barrier for you."

"The fire dogs and the hungry men?" Hegart smiles, his lips rising like a fleshy curtain over his sharpened teeth.

"Yes. But keep them under control. I don't want a repeat of the Third-Ring Massacre."

"I won't let you down."

"Best not. Not again, anyway. If you still had a soul, I would have already had you on my table, Hegart."

"Y-yes, sir."

"Now, what about this woman from the march that you captured?"

"Sary Cledes. The woman is absolutely gone, Your Worship. There is nothing left of her mind. She refuses to speak and only screams unintelligible gibberish when we put her to the question."

"Is she otherwise healthy?"

"Aye."

"Then send her to the ninth… but first, cut her tongue out. I'll have it mixed and served with peppers and onions."

DEEP IN the forest, near the fifth-ring wall, is an ancient city hub. Its plaza and forum were once filled with people, not trees and jungle creatures. Structures surround the plaza, and those that have not crumbled to piles of detritus stand stubborn and proud against the giant trees and creeping tendrils. The sinners pour onto the plaza in search of some place to rest or explore. Whenever they come across ruins, they go in search of weapons or anything else that might prove useful. Many of the marchers choose to station themselves by the remains of wells or under the branches of strong trees. Lawl is exploring with Key and Rossa. The child holds both their hands. Gemma follows with Madden and the orphans, Two and Eight, riding the beast's back.

Of all the structures surrounding the plaza, the one that has weathered the storms of time with the most grace is a domed structure with large steps leading up to a columned portico. Half of the dome itself has given away, and large branches crawl from it like new life from an egg. Vines are so thick on the portico that those passing need to be careful where they step.

Once inside, past the arched doorway and rotted remains of rusted double doors, it is quite apparent, at least to Lawl, where they are.

"It's a library," he says, staring in awe.

In the center of the building grows the massive, twisting tree that has broken the dome. It has taken root on a map, now unreadable, painted on the tile. Tables in various stages of decomposition are scattered across the first level. Leather book covers litter the floor. To either side of the entrance are ornate, curving staircases with Passions as banister heads— one a wolf, the other a lizard. The second level is a half moon of tall bookshelves, some of them even containing the scrolls and works they last held when people were yet using the library, but most now holding but shadows and squirrels. The wind moans through the place like a ghost reader mourning the loss of pages and stories.

"Sweet Passions," Gemma remarks, her eyes wide. "Tully would have loved this, wouldn't he, Madden?"

Lawl decides to make camp with Key and Rossa on the portico. People have collected firewood and assembled into small groups throughout the plaza. Night descends on a low hum of activity. There will be ghosts tonight.

Lawl watches Key snuggled into Rossa across the firelight. The child has not stopped smiling since he saw her. Lawl is glad of this, though, admittedly, he's somewhat jealous. He rather liked looking after Key. He even imagined a future where the child would join he, Duncan, and Gran somewhere, perhaps in one of Duncan's dreamed-of homes in the first ring. Key catches Lawl looking at him and smiles. He drums out a light rhythm on his instrument. A thank-you.

"You're an amazing man, Mr. Lawl," says Rossa, her arm around the child as she leans back on a column. "I be in your debt for findin' the boy and bringin' him to me safely."

"No debts. How could anyone look at that face and turn the stinker away?"

"Indeed." Rossa smiles and kisses Key on the forehead. In the firelight, she is majestic. "How did ya find him? Where have ya been hidin' out?"

Lawl thinks about telling Rossa of Esther Kerr, he thinks that he should certainly tell Gemma, but why? From what he heard, Gemma has no intention of ever returning to her mother. Like him, she wants nothing more to do with the first ring. If he tells her of Esther, of how close the woman is to the edge, he fears Gemma might give up on the march, abandon everything she has come so far for with one foolish rash decision. It is a selfish reason and he knows this.

In response to her question, he says, "We hid away in a very big house with a very angry, lonely woman. And then, when the time seemed right, we skipped away with Mother Maisy and her twins."

"Another angry, lonely woman."

"Aye. Just so."

The camp is asleep but for Lawl and those assigned to lookout. Rossa and Key are huddled together. The faint glow of perishing campfires is all that is clear through the dense forest. Lawl realizes sleep will not come tonight. He has slept very little without Duncan's comforting arms to hold him. He might die of exhaustion someday. He rises and wanders into the library.

Scant light sifts in from the broken dome, giving everything a blue death pallor. Lawl lights the firestick he carries in his bag and searches through this newly discovered tomb. Little is left of actual writings. Time has destroyed much of the parchment and only the leather covers of some of the volumes are even legible. There is some ancient Quakespeare, some forgotten Shaucer, a scrap of what was once a grand volume of Romer. Few in the Immortal City know those names, but Lawl recognizes them. Gran taught him from her own library before it was burned for heat when he was a child. That had broken her heart, and he remembered her gazing into the fire with wet eyes. She wanted to burn with her books, he could see that.

Beneath the massive tree under the broken dome, Lawl finds a table strewn with books, scrolls, and ledgers, which have been nearly petrified. He digs through the works as best he can, but finds not a single written word to prove they had been books at all. As he clears the books and scrolls from the table, piling them neatly on the floor, he notices a crack in the slab. He follows it with his finger and discovers it widening as he goes. He realizes this is not a table at all. This is a coffin.

He pushes the remaining debris to the ground, then stands back and takes it in. The tree has grown up around it, so it has been here for quite some time. There is wording on the coffin. It is nearly perfect, having been protected from the elements for centuries. He blows away the dust and he reads:

Here he lies, the King of Last Hope, the One Born to Save Us.
We leave the world a forgotten people, though once great.
We who have doomed ourselves to being forgotten.
We who have brought about the End of the World.
We who relied too heavily, proudly on our technology.
We who gave up the written word and instead put all to devices.
We who lost the ability to tame nature and so lost our history,
Our culture, our lives, when the End of the World was upon us.
If any will read this, please remember us, please come find us.
We are gone to the outer world.

You must go there too. Do not linger here. This is no place for
humanity.

This is no place for the living.
You must breach the walls.
We are gone today.
We will be waiting for you.

MAGS HENSIL is feeling suffocated, but she goes where GOD bids her
to go. She is a Sister, and a Sister has no purpose but to obey GOD. To
do what He bids, for He knows what is best in all things. GOD cares for
all sinners, even these before her now on their knees in the Undercity.

The place smells foul. It is old and useless. To think, she has been
walking above these derelicts and heathens for years without even
knowing it. But GOD knew. He has to have known. GOD knows all. For
some reason, He simply saw reason to keep this sinner's hole a secret.
She will not question His reasoning.

Something itches. She scratches her head, but it is a deeper itch
than that. She cannot get to it. Like a tickling hair in the ear.

These ancient underground structures, remnants of some lesser
world, will be destroyed once they have the sinners carted off. All for
the better. But it will take time as the Undercity runs for miles and miles.
It may take years for the whole nether landscape to be discovered and
eradicated. Even the sinners have only been living in a small part of a
grander underworld. This city's history will be forgotten again.

Mags has commanded all statuary of the gods and Passions be
wrecked on sight. The statue of Abrythnia in the fountain was the first to
meet its fate. Mags hears about a whole burial path ahead with terrible
demons as high as any building up above, and she wants them destroyed
before she has to look at them. Those who have been buried there are
disremembered anyway. Why would they need a demon to announce
their unimportance?

The same is being done to the old barrows and stone gardens up
above. The Passion statuary is being smashed to gravel and dust. The
Immortal City will have no signs of false gods anywhere within or
beneath it. This should have been done long ago.

"Your gods have abandoned you," she says to those sinners who did not march. She is the White Mother above the flock of fallen. "Do you wish to repent?"

"It was our choice to stay behind," says an older man with dirty gray facial hair. "We had the honor of relayin' what bastardry you and your fuckin' tyrant god got up to."

"Why must they always talk back?" Mags asks herself aloud. She nods to a Kingdom Guard, and he buries a spear in the old man's ribs. "Send the rest to the ninth ring. A gift for GOD."

"And what of those that escaped into the lower levels," asks another guard. "Women and children."

"You can't find them?"

"No, Sister. We've been lookin', but they know the Undercity too well."

"That's a shame. The babies have the purest of souls." She sighs in disappointment. "No matter. Set fire to what is flammable, and then seal off the exits. This is their hell."

"Yes, Sister," says the guard. He turns and relays the orders to his underlings.

"The rest of you get these vermin off their knees and into my wagons. The ninth ring will be waiting for them, I'm sure, with much eagerness."

THEY ARE prepared to fight. Every one of them, from old to young, from lame to healthy. Rossa sees this and she is proud, if sad. They are willing to die for the march, for their passion. Even if it looks pointless, at least they are making a stand. Perhaps after them, when they have all been slaughtered, the next brave souls to make such a stand will succeed. Perhaps they will have been inspired by this sinner's march.

Rossa sits in a small circle on the library portico with those who have volunteered to lead in the fight should they come across guards and ferrymen. Beside her sit Gemma and Royce, Lorien the horseman, and a few of the forest folk. Around them are the sounds of training, the clanging of old swords and battle axes. The guard that Sary Cledes didn't manage to kill is doing his best to instruct the marchers on the ways of GOD's Army.

"He's doin' well," Royce says. "The children seem to pick up his techniques goodly and quickly."

Key is close by, keeping his own against both Eight and Two. Theirs is more play than fight, but learning is going on through the grins and laughter.

Every time Two is struck, he frowns and shouts, "Bad dog!" Then he smiles again and takes up the fight once more.

"Aye," Rossa agrees. "But fightin' the Kingdom Guards with their own tactics will not win us any battles. We need to think differently."

"No need to worry there, lady," says a forest elder named Gol. "We can swing through the trees. We can fly. They'll not see us comin'."

"But what if there are no trees around us when Hegart decides to attack?" says Gemma. "What if we're on the grass plains?"

"We can adapt their guerilla tactics," Lorien says. "It can be easily done. The element of surprise is much needed against so large an army. It's the only hope we have, I think."

"Agreed." Rossa pops a berry into her mouth from the bushel brought to the meeting by the forest folk. "We must play nasty against so nasty a foe. One can't survive these days by playin' by the rules. Those basterds was the ones who set up the rules in the first place. Gol, how soon can ya begin showin' us your way of fightin'?"

"Now. Right now, lady. There ain't no time to waste as I sees it."

"Good. We'll start as soon as we're done here." She turns to Royce. "How many of the guards did ya see on your scoutin' at the ring wall?"

"Not many, though some may've been out of sight. The wall is so damn big. We counted five."

"So few?" Gemma says.

"It's a remote section of the wall in a remote part of the fifth ring," replies Royce. "In that, we be lucky. They most likely see no reason to add more guards here. The forest folk have never been any trouble to them, and no one else has ever tried to get through in so large a number."

Rossa turns to Gol again. "And ya believe the explosives you've come up with will be enough to get us through the wall?"

"Aye," Gol says proudly. "We know many secrets. The forest gives us the ingredients. We only have to bake the cake. And then, when those guards open their door, Happy Birthday! BOOM!"

Royce laughs. "Twisted basterd."

"Must there be death?" Gemma says. "Must someone die? There's already been too much."

"It's revolution, my friend," says Rossa. "And revenge. Neither happens without bloodshed or else the point be missed."

Lawl approaches the group from below. The look on his face tells Rossa something exciting has happened. He is not shuffling as usual. He has been out exploring more of the ancient city. The child Key sees him and stops his play with the orphans. He runs to Lawl's side with the drum and gives a drumroll on the instrument as if in anticipation. On cue, Lawl holds up a thick tube of wire to Rossa.

"Vengeance," Lawl hisses.

"What's this?" Rossa says, taking the wire.

"I was adventurin' along a path, and I stumbled across this piece of tubin'. It's copper mostly." He looks at it with a mischievous grin. "It looks like trash, but I know better. Aye, I searched until I found its source, an uprooted copper tube pokin' up beside a stone walkway. I followed it for a bit. Other tubes were shootin' off this way and that, but the main tube kept headin' in the same direction."

"What is it, Lawl?" Gemma says.

"It's a communication tube," he says in a revelatory whisper. "Power. What they called electricity in the ancient days, and I'll wager that large tube goes all the way back to the first ring."

"An ancient technology that helped bring about the End of the World," says Lorien. "What good is it to us?"

Lawl crouched down beside the horseman's ear. "Plenty. Ya see, when I bent to dissect a bit of the tube, I encountered quite a shock from my knife. Why, it threw me back a couple of feet. Oh, it hurt, but I couldna help but laugh."

Rossa's eyes lit. "It's live?"

"It's live." Lawl grinned.

"But how?"

"I don't know," Lawl says with a near laugh. "But I think this could be used to our advantage. I have a bit of technical expertise, if ya wanna call it that."

"What would ya suggest we do, Mr. Lawl?" says Rossa.

Lawl looks to Gemma slyly, and Key gives another drumroll. "Gemma, sweets. How be your speakin' voice?"

THE CHILDREN are marching through the forest to the fifth-ring wall. Key leads them proudly with his drum. Behind him march Eight and Two, their brothers and sisters, and the other orphans and children of the forest. They are streaked with war paint of charcoal and flower stains, and marching to a BOOM BOOM BOOM born of Key's rhythmic mind and let loose on the skin. He is enjoying this. He knows his father would approve. His father would be marching right alongside him. In fact, Key believes he is. He has seen his father in the trees, watching him in the night.

Key pounds louder and with more passion the nearer the march gets until at last they come out of the forest and face the wall, still marching in place. The other children call for the guards in the wall as Key continues his BOOM BOOM BOOM.

"Come and face us, cowards!" cries Eight as fierce as she can.

Two simply roars as if he is a bear. The other orphans follow suit.

The forest children hoot and holler like monkeys and birds.

A stone door in the wall slides open, and two guards walk out. They are unimpressed and smiling. They have not even bothered to raise their weapons.

"What is this?" one of them says. "What sort of bother wakes me from my nap? Get on home before you hurt yourselves, children. Go back to your trees."

Key continues to play his drum. His face is solemn and unwavering.

"I said git," says the guard. The smile falls from his face. "You are not a march worth my time."

The children do not move. They do quiet, however. They hush and stare. Key thumps a low drumroll. It sounds like a mumble of nerves.

"Creepy little shit," the guard says as he raises his sword. He comes for Key, but he stops as the children part behind the boy and reveal the massive hound that crouches there.

Madden drools and rises.

"Fuck!" the guard says, his eyes revealing deep fear.

"Indeed," Rossa says as she slips out of the forest beside the guard, holding a knife to his throat. "Now drop the sword."

Key smiles up at the guard, and the sword falls to the ground. Key takes it for himself.

Behind Rossa, Royce is on the other guard by the wall.

"Well done, children," says Rossa. "You are now our prisoners," she says to the guards. "Now, where be your brethren?"

He says nothing, but spits. Key kicks him in the shins.

"Not talkin'? No matter. We're more than a match for ya."

A tumult in the forest announces the marchers, a face behind every tree and every bush. Both guards are taken aback.

"It's the sinners," says the guard held by Royce. "It's the sinner's march."

"Aye," says Rossa. "Now we'd like a little tour of your facilities."

Inside the wall, it is dark but for a few candles. The fireplace has not seen use in years, but it would not help keep things warm anyway. The walls separating room from room have long since fallen or are in the process of falling. The place might have been grand at one time, but now there is little but gloom and a never-ending darkness of hallway. A candle glows on a half-standing table where a half-eaten plate of slosh sits. Flies decorate it now.

The march begins to move through. The place gives Key the shivers. He dare not touch his drum. He fears things are hiding here. Forgotten things waiting to be called upon. Even his father might not be able to save him from them.

There is a commotion. The guard has elbowed Rossa in the stomach and is running down the darkness, screaming for the other guards. Lorien quickly strings an arrow and brings the guard down. Three more guards appear suddenly from the dark, staring at the marchers in fear and confusion. They do not run. Instead, perhaps instilled with a false sense of GODly protection, they charge. Lorien shoots another through the neck. The downed guard sprawls across the table, knocking the slosh to the ground.

Madden opens his great jaws on another and carries him screaming into shadow. The third comes swinging for Rossa. He strikes, but she is quick and avoids his blade. She swings her sword, and he blocks. The sound of metal against metal fills the hall as the guard strikes with maddening frenzy at Rossa. She grabs her axe as well. His fury and zeal seem too much at times. Key watches from behind Lawl, wanting to do something to help. It is all brought to a quick end, however, as Gemma steps from out of the crowd and stabs the guard through the back with a knife. The man gasps and falls dead.

"We have precious little time," she says. She is shaking. Her eyes seem lost. "We must get through the wall."

They load Gol's explosives into the ring, and the marchers file back out to a safe distance, a sense of accomplishment sweeping through them. Key feels it. This… this is the beginning. This is where it all starts to end.

"Light the fuses," says Rossa from Claire's back.

And with that, the Immortal City is rocked by an explosion the likes of which has not been heard since the End of the World. The children cover their ears. Some close their eyes. But the anticipation of what lies on the other side of the fifth wall heightens everyone's senses. The smoke slowly clears and before them is a new way. The sixth ring. A new world.

Pray for Plague

"Dear Bana. I'm going to have to kill you."

Esther is intoxicated. She has had nothing but bitter wine since being imprisoned in her home with her husband, and it has served only to darken the dimly lit rooms she walks through. She is a disheveled mess. She will not look at herself in a mirror, for she knows what will be staring back at her. Not a lady, but a beggar. She feels her eyes are as dry as sand, and her color must be that of paste. Her gown sags like a servant's uniform. And the only voice she has heard aside from her own has been the Voice of GOD echoing outside, tormenting the first ring with thinly veiled threats. She occasionally finds herself shouting out the windows, cursing the Voice with language she had never dared to use before. People have gawked, but let them. They are all just as dead as she is on the inside. She prays for plague.

"You see, my darling," she continues speaking to Bana, "I am quite suffocating. You and this life, this government, you have all quite pulled the pillow over my face." She smiles, laying her head on the pillow beside her husband, watching Bana's fearful eyes. "Is that how you would have me do it? Should I smother you with a pillow? Or is that too humane? I think so. I think you deserve something more terrible. You realize, my sweet love, that they will kill our brave daughter Gemma when they catch her. You see that, right? Without my girl…" She is tearing up. She blames it on the wine and throws the glass across the room. It shatters against a cedar chest. "…I see no reason to live any longer. I see no reason for either of us to live. Especially now that I just broke my last wineglass. I think you should die first. You've sacrificed so little else."

She can tell Bana wants to scream. His eyes are enormous.

She wraps her hands around his throat and applies pressure. Just a little at first.

"You should indeed have a bloodier death, but this will have to do." The Voice of GOD hammers His word into the streets outside. "And my, won't GOD be angry, won't He be horrified when He finds you dead… with me."

She squeezes harder. Bana is doing his best to struggle. He moves his fingers, fluttering them in meager defense. "What a lovely shade of violet your face has become. Gemma loves this color. Maybe I should have—"

She eases up, distracted. The Voice has changed. It has stopped and now... and now a feminine voice takes over. Esther cannot hear the words, but the tone is altogether familiar. She rushes to a window and flings it open, letting the cold morning air into the chamber. The light causes Bana to moan in pain, but Esther has no interest in him any longer. She is focused on this new Voice. A sweet Voice. Her daughter's voice:

Rise up. Rise up and unite against GOD. He has led you astray. I am Gemma Kerr.

I am with the Sinner's march, and we can offer you hope. We can offer you

freedom from the oppressive, terrifying tyranny of GOD and Senator General

Hegart. They are but bullies, and you have the real power. We have the real power.

Rise up. Rise up. I am with you. Abrythnia is with you. Bring forth the Passions.

Bring forth your righteous anger. You shall not be abandoned. It is time we left the

Immortal City. It is time we destroyed it. Rise up. Rise up. Join us at the ninth.

We have the power.

Esther is in hysterics. She has never been more happy or more proud or more sad. She laughs as she looks out the window onto the street below, as she looks at the guards watching her and sees the dumbfounded people of the city waking. Slowly waking.

"What do you know," she says loudly and coherently. "Maybe we're not so dead after all."

THE CHILDREN in Red cower, running for shadows far from the high chair of GOD. Senator General Hegart stands at attention before Him. He does not flinch, but on the floor, he sees the bloody mess that was once a child in a red robe. A ferryman stands expressionless over the mutilated corpse. Hegart lets his drool creep down the side of his mouth and form a stream on his black coat. Best not to move when GOD is seething.

GOD screeches. He throws a fit, seizing in his chair, thrashing his head this way then that, screaming unintelligible things. Every word is a high-pitched scratch on the air. It flays at the mind. The Children in Red are hiding and sobbing. One of their own has just been killed in front of them. When GOD gets angry, He looks for an outlet. With ferrymen at His beck and call, He finds that outlet quite easily.

Hegart watches GOD shake and tremble. It has never been this bad before. GOD has never raged so long and so very loud. Is it weakness, Hegart wonders, that causes Him to carry on so? Surely a GOD should be able to more comfortably control Himself. Yet this one seems quick to anger. As quick to anger as… well, as Hegart himself would be in the situation. Is then GOD only as human as everyone else after all? Heresy. That is heresy to think. And yet…

Senator General Hegart wonders for the briefest of moments if he could be a GOD. If all it required was passing judgments and a certain quantity of blinding bloodlust, Hegart has that in copious amounts. What would happen if the Children of GOD suddenly stopped feeding His Holiness? How long might it take for GOD to waste away to nothing as his councilors have done? As Bana Kerr is doing?

GOD has stopped screaming. The children still sob, and the ferryman stands as if waiting further instruction. The Voice of Gemma has now replaced that of Hegart's, and is being piped over the speakers. At least all of GOD's carrying-on has given Hegart respite from Gemma's constant sticky sweet droning.

GOD'S voice is ragged. It shakes now as He finally speaks. "Find the marchers," He says, "and burn them! Bind them wrapped in the copper they have used to make this blasphemy happen and then melt them down! If my people want misery, I'll give it to them. Send out the carriages with the ferrymen. Round up every person who's even seen a riot and take them away. Take them to the ninth ring. I want to be feasting on souls before the week is out."

"But Your Holiness, won't that be—"

"Go!" cries GOD. "Go now! Strip their souls from their bones. Make them cry before they die."

THE GATES have opened with a heavy steel clamor that fills the landscape with angry echoes. At once the death wagons pour forth. Twenty black carriages led by ebony stallions, each one with angels on their rooftops and devils locked inside, screaming, crying. More will follow. These twenty are but a taste. Royce and Lorien watch them, hidden in the treescape, with the marchers who have been sent by Rossa to keep an eye on the fifth-ring gate.

Reports have come in that GOD is growing more volatile. That He is rounding up as many sinners and degenerates as He can to send to the ninth ring. Rossa intends to put a cog in His Holy wheels. GOD would not expect them to be anywhere near the main road. He would expect them to hide while He carries on with His play, with His torments. GOD is mistaken. GOD has grown too proud.

Royce and Lorien count the number of ferrymen and Kingdom Guards with the horde. Lorien looks down at Royce from his steed and grins. "We will smash them." He draws an arrow from his quiver and aims it at the lead ferryman. Royce draws his sword. The forest folk with their arrows and spears and throwing stones do not need to be told when to charge. As soon as Lorien lets his arrow fly, they know to attack. Gol has stayed behind with Gemma and Rossa, but he has left very capable warriors in charge.

The death wagon approaches, and Lorien concentrates. Aim for the ferrymen, he knows. The guards are often clumsy cowards, easily dealt with. First the sinners must see to the ferrymen. There are nine with the wagons.

Lorien shoots.

Eight. Eight ferrymen now with the wagons.

The forest folk are upon the dark caravan. Lorien dispatches another ferryman, and the wagon flips over, throwing the guard to the ground. Royce is upon him, thrusting a sword through his gullet. The ferrymen react swiftly, jumping from their carriages and bringing out their long scythes. Two of the forest folk are immediately decapitated as they attack a ferryman, but he is brought down by one of the horsemen as they gallop through the carnage shooting arrows. Those inside the death wagons are shouting, confused as to what is happening. It is all dust and arrows, blood and screams.

Lorien stays in the forest, picking off guards and ferrymen. Some are not dying immediately, so he is shooting them more than once. One ferryman looks like a porcupine before he falls expressionless and bloody to the ground.

Horsemen and warriors are providing cover as the forest folk break open the carriages and free those locked inside. Some are not able to escape. Some are already dead. Those who can run off to the forest and are soon swallowed up by the trees. And with that, having done all they can do, the horsemen ride off. Not a guard is left standing. Everyone behind on the road is dead or dying. The marchers have had to leave some of their own. Cries of pain and anguish follow them through the forest. Lorien meets up with everyone at a designated ancient causeway in the jungle. They free their prisoners, who express their gratitude to their rescuers with confusion and relief.

Royce has not returned. Lorien saw him cut through the gut by a ferryman at the end of the battle. There is nothing for it now. If he is not already dead, he will be soon.

The horseman leads on with a heavy heart.

CAYDEN SITS alone in the ancient library. The sinner's march has moved on, and he has followed them. He does not know why he is drawn to the library, but it has called to him. Here, for the first time, he has a sense of home, of belonging. These tattered remains of old books are whispers of friends.

He has shaken off the guards. He does not care where they are as long as they leave him be. They will most likely be lost in the jungles without him, dinner for a Helix wolf or a briar cat. Since losing them, he has seen the strange ruins of the world before the Fall. He has seen large pictureless frames attached to beds of keys painted with symbols; he has seen rusting mechanical men in various states of repose. His curiosity grows with each new discovery.

Cayden does not feel like following after the marchers tonight. He will catch up to them later. Their group is so large, they will be easy to locate. If he cared. He finds that he develops a kinship with the girl.

Kinship. Another new idea.

He sits cross-legged on the floor in the center of the library beneath the massive tree. His eyes are closed. He is asleep, but not really, just as he is alone, but not really. Cayden has only ever been half of anything—half asleep, half alone, half a man, half a monster. He is perfectly balanced by the other half.

This night, as has occurred the three previous nights, a new visitor comes to see him. The god Thunkill is no longer in his dreams, but has taken the form of Cayden's father, a fair-haired young man with a wistful smile and sad green eyes. Cayden did not know how to react when he saw his father on that first night, so he did not react at all. He simply woke up. But then the next night, his father came near to him and touched him on the forearm. The feel of his flesh, so gentle and easy, made sleeping memories race to the fore, and Cayden felt his first tear crawl down his cheek. Now he remembers his father, the poet. The artist. The man who tried to give Cayden some type of education, and that is what got him killed.

"Ya still wish to learn," his father says as they sit opposite one another in the darkness of the library. Strained moonlight pours through the roof. "Why else would ya be here? Why else would ya feel the call?"

"I doona understand any of this," Cayden says. "Who are ya? Me father has been dead for years. I saw him cut to ribbons right in front of me."

"Ya saw a man's body cut up, aye. But a man's soul was not taken." He is smiling, such gentleness and patience.

"Mine was. Mine was sucked right out of me eyes. I remember now. They took me to a dark room and attached tubes to me eyes. I was screamin'. I was cryin' for you…"

"But I couldna be there. Not in physical form. But I saw what they did to ya, and I knew one day ya would wake up like you're doin' now."

"Wake up?"

"From your long nightmare. Gemma Kerr is not the only hero in this tale, Cayden. You are her, she is you. Ya will complete one another."

Cayden looks at his father—at us—with a pinched brow. "I am a monster. I am asleep."

"No. You are a hero. We all make mistakes."

"Breakin' a dish is a mistake. Breakin' a man's neck is somethin' worse."

"And now ya recognize that. Do ya see? You are waking."

He is stunned by this realization. More light appears in his eyes now. Even more than five minutes ago.

"Ya were a poet," he says. "Ya were a great poet."

"I tried to give ya that poetry as well."

"Ya failed. It did not take."

His father laughs lightly. "My sweet boy, the seed was planted. It is inside ya still, just waitin' to sprout. You're lettin' in the sun with every new moment of realization. Soon ya will feel it within ya. Keep practicin'. Keep recitin' your poetry and ya will see. Your soul, your beautiful soul, will be replenished."

"Why do I need a soul? Those with souls seem only to find hurt."

"Because ya need to live in order to die. And ya need to die stuffed full of soul to be with me, with all of us who are waitin' for ya outside the Immortal City."

Cayden's eyes are glistening. "What's it like? Out there?"

"No words," his father whispers. "There are no words." He looks up to the top of the tree, then back down to Cayden. "But ya need to go now. Ya need to find the march. To join them. They need ya, my son. Some of them may not like ya at first, but they need ya."

His father leans in and gives Cayden's forehead a delicate kiss.

"G'night, Da," he says.

We smile. "G'night, son." And then we fade.

THE FORESTS and jungles of the sixth ring fade in density the closer the marchers get to the wall. The Plains of Coirean stretch out for miles, and during the day, the golds and greens wave in the winds like a groundswell under the orange sky. At night, the fields are sucked into the line of a blushing horizon.

The march is resting as the dusklight fades into dark. Rossa has situated herself on a hill above the marchers so she might keep watch. Lorien and others keep guard with her. Gemma has wandered away a bit. She is wading through the tall grass, deep in her own thoughts. She walks with Usker Lance.

"I want to get away," she says, catching the grass between her fingers as she strolls.

"Away?"

"From the march. From all of this."

"Ye want to abandon the march?" Usker says, no judgment in his voice.

"Not abandon. No. I just… I'm wondering if I even need to be with the marchers anymore. They know what to do now. They know where to go. And all this rage… I feel their rage. Sometimes I have such rage that it scares me. I feel as if I am soaking up all the anger around me like a dirty sponge. I killed a man, Usker. That guard in the wall. I killed him. Me."

"He was gonna kill Rossa."

"I know, and I know it had to be done. But when I slid the knife into him, I felt nothing." Her eyes water. "I took a human life and felt nothing. Doesn't that make me some kind of monster?"

"Every man and woman is a monster, Gemma girl. Aye, and every man and woman is a kind spirit as well. Both light and dark are in us all. Whichever of those two shows up in any situation, that's when a man knows who he truly is. Ye protected your friend by killin' that man. Ye had to reach into yourself and call forth the dark, but then when it was done, ye put the darkness back, didn't ye, gal?"

"But I feel different," she whispers.

"Aye. Many things be different now. You'll never be the same. You'll never see your ma again. Nor will ye see the first ring. Do ye want to?"

She is silent for a moment, walking on through the grass. "No."

"Well then, what ye moanin' about, ye silly girl?"

"Change, even if it's for the best, it's very strange."

"Aye. 'specially if the change is more about who ye are than where ye are."

"And who am I?"

"Gemma Kerr." The voice catches her off guard because it is new to the conversation. Usker Lance has disappeared and in front of her, under a small tree, is the man she met in the forest, Cayden. They connect without coming any nearer to one another or saying a word. They know one another as well as family somehow. The night wind blows around them, the sounds of the tall grass being swept by the breeze is whispered conversation.

And then the horn sounds.

Gemma is startled and looks back toward camp. "That's Gol's battle horn," she says.

"You're under attack, miss," Cayden replies.

And they race back to the camp.

CAYDEN SEES what is happening before he hears the cries of terror. There is mass confusion in the darkness below the hill. He sees the fire dogs—great snarling beasts that streak the night with the glow of flames lit on the thick quills of their backs. They are on leashes, but leashes of such length the ferrymen are able to stay back from the confusion on the fringes as the beasts rip into the marchers.

The marchers overturn the camp as they flee. But Cayden notices the fire dogs and the ferrymen are not the only nightmare unleashed here.

Hungry men, a breed of man once created by GOD that Cayden thought extinct are on leashes, enormous naked men made of enhanced and grotesque muscle and vascularity. With drooling mouths and penises, they have nothing but an unquenchable appetite for the taste of sex and flesh. They roar through the camp led by their bloodlust, snatching up mostly the old and the young and ripping into them, tearing them apart, for sex and hunger.

Cayden pushes Gemma back into the grass. "Head to the forest," he tells her. "Now!"

He does not have the time to see if she listens. He charges into the confusion. The horsemen who have joined the marchers are doing their best to repel the fire dogs, but the beasts are full of anger. Cayden sees the tail of a horse catch on a fire dog's quills and both horse and rider are engulfed in flame. Nothing can be done for either of them as they run howling into the night.

Cayden stealthily grabs a leash and wraps it around a ferryman's neck, killing him instantly. He steals the ferryman's scythe and gives those too far gone mercy from their misery as they are being mauled or burned. Looking back, he sees some hungry men are already making a meal of the strangled ferryman even as one fucks the corpse.

Another ferryman comes for Cayden, pausing as if in recognition, allowing Cayden the time to slice him through and steal his scythe as well. From here Cayden carves through fire dogs, hungry men, and ferrymen alike. The screams around him are deafening, yet there is plenty of light. The fire dogs provide that easily.

A horseman has come to Cayden's aid, fighting beside him. The leader of the march, the queen called Rossa, is up ahead. She is cornered by a group of hungry men, but neither she nor her horse seem ready to give up as she slashes and the horse kicks. Cayden is uncertain if he can make it to her in time.

Suddenly, he feels teeth sinking into his shoulder blades with a vicious pain. He twirls around and comes face to face with a hungry man, eyes as red and crazed as a demon of hell, veins like blood worms beneath his skin. The massive hungry man reaches for him with crooked, long fingers, scratching at his cheek, but Cayden takes both scythes and separates the man into quarters.

Ahead of him a large white dog has taken the hungry men's attention from the queen and allowed her to escape. A small boy rides on her saddle. The large white dog then bounds away from the hungry men with a couple of orphans on its back. As the white dog leaps, a fire dog snaps its jaws down on one of its legs, causing the older child to fall off.

"Two!" the little girl screams.

Cayden is up. He beheads the fire dog with ease, allowing the white hound to escape. The little girl is still crying "Two" as she races away. A hungry man pulls up the boy by his hair. "Bad dog! Bad dog! Bad dog!" the boy is crying. The hungry man opens his maw, but Cayden slices the top of his skull clean off, and the boy falls back to the ground. Cayden picks up the child and hands him to the horseman.

"Make for the trees," he says. "This is lost."

And it is true. Looking around, all he sees is death. Cayden does a ballet of the macabre as he fights on. He will take out as many as he can, indiscriminately. Ferrymen, fire dogs, hungry men—and marchers. It will be doing them a kindness, these marchers. He is the swordsmen now, cutting fathers into ribbons before their sons. But unlike Hegart, he will have mercy. He will kill the sons as well.

REASON & RHYME

GEMMA WATCHES from her seat, cross-legged on top of the ancient pyramid in the middle of the forest. The march is regrouping. Survivors have been filing in all day. The pyramid—far away from any of the other ruins and more ancient than most—was designated a point of convergence if anything were to ever happen. Like an attack by cannibals and fire dogs. The squat pyramid has room inside to treat the wounded. The survivors are straggling, bloody and limping. Some will most likely not survive the day. Two-thirds of their number were killed last night while Gemma stood watching on the hill where Cayden had shoved her. She felt helpless there. Useless. She still does. She has felt useless her whole life, but since she has known worth for the briefest of moments, the feeling is worse than ever before.

She recognizes some of the stragglers and is relieved to see them. Madden, though wounded, came to the pyramid carrying Eight. Lorien was followed by a few of his horsemen. He carried the boy Two, looking dazed and hurt, with him. When Eight saw her brother, she ran to him screaming with joy, "Bubby! Bubby!" and then tackled him with an embrace. Rossa and Key rode in on Claire. Lawl came later in the day with a group of forest folk and Usker's original sinners. Gol was torn apart by a hungry man and a fire dog. And finally a group of orphans and other children, including three of Eight and Two's siblings, found their way to the pyramid. Behind them limped Cayden, his stolen scythes strapped to his sides. He received some worried glances, some whispers of suspicion. Gemma knows what he is now. Everyone knows what he is. Or was.

"He be a changed man," says Usker, sitting behind her.

"Can a ferryman change?" Her eyes are glazed over. She is still in shock.

"Anything with a soul can change, sweet girl."

"I thought that was the whole point of ferrymen. To be soulless."

"That's what GOD wanted, aye, but that's not the truth of it. They got souls just like you and me. They's just hidden, is all. They's beaten back. Truthfully, it be a hoax, this business of soul-takin'. Ye can be born without one like Senator General Hegart claims he was, and ye can bleed it out your ass like GOD, but a soul canna ever be taken."

The remaining hungry men and fire dogs were easily killed. The forest folk have positioned sentries with bows and arrows in the treetops to shoot the monsters between the eyes at the first sight of any more. None have yet broken through.

A sweet breeze makes its way through the canopy and gives Gemma a momentary respite from her thoughts. It is like a cool balm on her skin. She prefers this solitude, this loneliness, to all the confusion below. She knows now she is a loner. She could live quite contentedly as a hermit, away from everyone. She has tried to fight that inclination to be alone all of her life because she was told it was wrong. Her mother scolded her that one should want to be part of the city, part of the structure. But Gemma never felt she fit in there. She is not part of any structure. Not even this march that she has helped create.

"Just ye hold on a wee bit longer," Usker says. "Then ye can go."

"I can be alone?"

"If ye want. But just wait. You've still got some work to do, sweet thing. There still be those what depend on ye."

She is looking down at the wounded mass convening on the ancient grounds. Cayden stands alone, looking around at the human debris. And as if feeling her eyes on him, he glances up to her.

"Just wait," repeats Usker.

SHE IS their leader, but she will not say queen.

The former is a title she has taken hesitantly, but Queen Rose does not set well with her. It stinks too much of another woman with a put-upon royal title, Queen Mags. Yet the marchers look on her as their leader, their queen. Some even address her in that manner, bowing and refusing to look her in the eyes. She has given up correcting them. In their minds, she has already had her coronation by fire and blood.

She makes certain to see every person who has returned from the attack. Every survivor is important. She greets them all with a smile laden with honey. For some, hers will be the last smile they will ever see. Those closest to death lie inside the pyramid, resting on the stone slabs and empty wall shelves that once held the bones of ancient heroes and angels. The inside of the pyramid is lit as well as can be expected, and the dimness helps shield Rossa's face. Those who have given their lives should see no sadness at the moment of their death. They have all died as heroes, and deserve trumpets and fanfare.

Outside, as Rossa walks the grounds, marchers bow to her. She wants no such supplication. Yet how can the people help but bend their knees at the sight of her? She is a regal and commanding presence even with a smudged face, unkempt and wild hair, and torn clothes. She is the Queen of Angels. She smiles politely, aware that she is not the true leader. She is not Gemma Kerr. Gemma Kerr sits atop the pyramid, inert and silent. She is becoming more aloof with each passing day.

Rossa spies Cayden, the rehabilitated ferryman, lying in the bow of a candelabra tree. He is watching Gemma. Rossa knows for certain the ferryman can see her as well, but he is not concerned with the queen. His attention is focused like an arrow upon the Messiah.

Rossa finds Lorien, the horseman, tending to the horses. He is bloodied and bruised, but unconcerned about his wounds. "What do we know of the ferryman?" she asks him. "I doona trust him."

"Nor do I," says the horseman, looking back in the direction of the candelabra tree. "And I would be the first to say kill the basterd if I hadna seen him decimate six of his own kind, as well as a half-dozen fire dogs, and near twenty hungry men."

"Why do ya suppose he would do that? Go against his orders?"

"I've got no answer for ya, Queen. All I know is that he saved most of the orphans, and that's not a story I've ever heard told of a ferryman before."

True, but she will never trust a ferryman. Her eyes will be on him at all times. He is the epitome of her rage.

"Rossa," comes a call from behind. Lawl makes his way to her in hurried, if dragging, steps. He speaks better now. Clearer, if not clearly. But he looks concerned. "Have ya seen Key?" he asks. "I canna find him."

Lorien promises to keep his eyes open for the child if he should pass by, and Lawl and Rossa head off to search the forest and the ruins.

"He's probably just playin' with some of the other orphans, but I'd feel better if I knew where he was," says Lawl.

"Agreed," says Rossa. "Even with his gypsy blood, he's no match for a hungry man or a fire dog."

They have split up, calling after Key as they go, but keeping vigilant for danger. Rossa is so grateful to Lawl for what he has done. For bringing back Key to her. She wants to thank him, but she has no idea how to do that. Words have never been easy for her. When she lived in the city, she would show her gratitude through cooking or hospitality, but how does one show hospitality without a home?

The brush and bramble are thick. If Key is asleep or hiding beneath a fern tree, he might go completely unseen. She gives sharp whistles as she searches. Better to sound like a bird than a word.

At last, Lawl calls her name from somewhere nearby. His stance when she catches up to him is one of caution and alarm. His back is straight, and his knife is drawn. He looks at her with a questioning stare.

"What do we do about this?" he says in a whisper.

Key is sitting on the ground, the drum between his bare legs, as a fire dog nibbles on a bone beside him. The dog looks up at the two adults, ears pointed, but then loses interest and returns its attention to the bone. Key grins from ear to ear.

"I think he means to take the beast as a pet," Lawl says in a low voice. "It looks wounded and half starved, the poor thing."

"Aye," Rossa says. "Where'd ya get the bone, darlin' child?"

The child points back to the camp.

Lawl understands. "The forest folk. They keep bones of their kills as charms to ward off demons."

"Demons like fire dogs."

"Aye. So?" Lawl looks at her with a slight grin. "What do we do, Ma?"

"It's a fire dog," she says. "It should be killed."

Key does not like that one bit. He grabs hold of a quill on the fire dog's back as if he will never let go. The dog gives the child a lick on the face, then returns to crunching, snapping the large bone.

"You'll break the boy's heart, miss," says Lawl.

She realizes she has lost this one before the argument even begins. Besides, having a fire dog and a ferryman on the march, if both of these demons are indeed with the march, might not be so bad.

"Well, name the thing, then," says Rossa. "I doona trust anything that don't have a name. What will it be?"

Key smiles, full of victory. He gnashes his teeth together.

"Crunch? Cruncher?" says Lawl.

Rossa sighs. "He's your responsibility, lad. Ya get to introduce him to Madden and to the rest of the marchers. And if he comes near Claire with those jaws, he's a dead dog, got it?"

The boy nodded violently.

"Aww," Lawl says. "Look at ya. You're a good ma."

CAYDEN MOVES with the marchers. They dare not stay too long in any one location. GOD is after them, and He is sending demons as heralds this time. Whenever Cayden has the opportunity, he finds a secluded patch of woods and retreats into his mind, juggling words and colors and meanings. He is practicing poetry today, lying on his back and staring into the tree limbs and the spots of sky peeking through.

"Sky," he mumbles. "Sky. Orange sky. Fly. We fly in the sky."

He does not understand the use of poetry. He can hear rhyme, though. He can hear rhythm. The child with the drum knows rhythm as well.

"Drummin'. Hummin'. Singin'." He is stuck. "Singin'. Singin'?"

"Breathing."

Cayden sits up. He is not surprised Gemma Kerr is standing beside a tree watching him. She has been there for some time. He did not expect her to offer any conversation, however. She is a small, quiet woman. The forest would eat her up and she would allow it.

"Breathin' doesna rhyme with singin'," he says.

"It's not a perfect rhyme," she says, approaching him and sitting on the ground beside him. "But some of the best poems don't rhyme at all. Not even close."

"Truly?" He finds this curious.

"There is no rhyme or reason to life. To force it into art is… manipulative."

"Life is manipulation."

She smiles. "That's a very dire assessment."

"I am a ferryman, miss."

"Yes. We know. The boogeyman of the Immortal City."

"Aye. And the worst of them. Or the best. I caught Colm Archer."

"I would not let Lorien or Rossa know that. He was a great man. Besides, now that the hungry men have returned, you and your brethren ferrymen have slipped down to Boogeyman Number Two."

She pushes back a strand of blonde hair from his brow. He is surprised by the touch.

"Why poetry?" she says. "What purpose does poetry hold for a ferryman?"

"None, but for a young boy, poetry once had very deep meanin'."

The smile she gives him sets fire to his insides. He wonders if she could douse it with the tears now forming in her eyes.

"You've found your soul," she says.

Has he? He wonders. He has found something, he sees it in his own eyes. Do souls come bursting out of hiding like flowers in spring?

"What are you lookin' to find, Gemma Kerr?" he says. "Ya stray farther and farther from the march each day. Everyone sees it. They all whisper about their hero."

She plays with a blade of grass by her knee. "Not this," she says. "I'm not looking for this. I am happy for these people. They say I am a hero, but I am nothing of the sort. Yet if it helps them free themselves, I suppose I can play the part. But all this horror, all these awful things that happen on a daily basis…"

"Real life."

"Yes, well, real life is so grounding, and all I want to do is fly. I want to be alone. Truly alone. I want to see beautiful things and oceans. I want the sky to be blue like it is in the fairy tales. I want to see every impossible thing that has never existed. I bet you've seen some amazing things, haven't you?"

He shrugs. "If seen by my new eyes now they might seem amazin', aye. But when I saw them as a ferryman, they were nothin' to me. This… this march is amazin' to me. These people follow ya because they love ya, they trust ya. They do not fear ya. I find myself inexplicably drawn to them."

"So, we are on opposite ends then. I want to get away and you want to get closer. And there is a barrier stopping either from happening."

"So we meet in the middle."

She surprises him. She leans in and gives him a hug. He tenses up but finds himself melting into her embrace. He swallows a breath and a warm sensation ripples through his body.

"I was told to listen to what you had to tell me," she says as she unlocks her arms from around him and stands. "I am glad I did, Cayden Lothair."

She will be leaving soon. He knows this somehow. She will want to go and adventure on her own, and her people will wail and cry over her departure. She will become a legend.

THE SISTERS' carriages are being drawn by wooly bulls, not the regal equine bred for the duty. The bulls are loud and cantankerous and lumbering, but they are very large and make anyone with foul intentions think twice. The Sisters of GOD had to leave the first ring in such a hurry, they didn't have time to hook up the proper carriages to their magnificent steeds. Instead, once they escaped the anger erupting in the first ring, Mags Hensil had to search for suitable means of travel.

The Holy Processional makes the traveling easy, and they are making good time. For these first miles, the Sisters will tolerate the company of the Kingdom Guards and the wooly bulls. After that, however, they will need to go it alone, just the Sisters of GOD. The citizens of the Immortal City watch them pass. They are showing the Sisters little reverence, but at least their anger is not apparent. The third ring has been less GODly, but also less violent than the first two rings. Mags can breathe now without fear of death from some fool or fiend.

The Sisters were on their way to GOD's Tower to see His Holiness when the uprising blew up before them. The Glass Halls shattered and fell, and an angry mob came storming toward the Sisters. The Kingdom Guards were their only protection, and the nine Sisters were quickly ushered down alleyways like waste water. One of the Sisters was hit on the head by a large rock, but she was seen to once they were safely out of the first ring. She sits beside Mags now in the carriage. She is bandaged and dazed.

"Do not worry so," says Mags Hensil. Her veil hangs over her face. "Your pain will be assuaged, Sister."

The Sister looks to her. She is silent. She has taken no vows. All the Sisters just simply have so little to say. They let Mags speak for them.

"We are taking matters into our own hands," Mags continues. "GOD would want it so. I know this. I am His Sister after all. He is trusting that we are out here doing His Will, doing what He would do if He had not been trapped in His Tower. We must not let Him down, Sister."

The faces of those in the third ring are growing more and more hateful as the carriages pass. They are starving and they are grief-stricken. But how is that her fault? How is that the fault of GOD? It is not. The fault is theirs and theirs alone. They should work harder, and they might know better lives. It is as simple as that.

"There is only one way to quell this uprising, Sister, and Senator General Hegart, in his buffoonery, has looked right over it. We will find the sinner's march ourselves. and then we will find the girl." She takes a deep breath through her nose. It stings her nostrils with hate. "And we will kill her. She will be the Lord's Sacrifice."

BY NOW, thinks Cayden Lothair, GOD should be upon them. Granted, Cayden was the best of the ferrymen who now has abandoned GOD's Army, but still, other ferrymen should have easily been able to track down the sinner's march. He finds it curious that the marchers are so near the ninth ring.

They are a forlorn group, struggling and downhearted after the hungry men's attack. Yet here they are in the open street of an ancient stone city. The standing buildings here are the colors of dust and sand. They might have indeed been proud structures once, long before time licked them dry. Cayden walks behind the marchers as they trudge silently between the crumbling buildings. If GOD swept down on them now, would they even care? Would they fight or simply let the dogs and the hungry men tear them apart?

A thought grabs him. Cayden is walking past the marchers now. They see him. Some seem slightly curious, but most are drowning in sorrow and pain over lost friends and family. The ferryman sees the boy with the drum near the front of the march. He remembers the boy. He knew who he was since he first laid eyes upon him in the Howling Woods. This is Key. This is the gypsy child whom he watched for too long. This is the child that brought back to his memory that first inkling of his own relationship with his father. Cayden slides through the crowd with ease, approaching the child with an idea. Something, anything to awaken the march once more.

Lorien and his horse come between Cayden and the boy, however. There is warning in Lorien's eyes. Rossa is watching Cayden as well from atop her gray horse. At least the child is well protected. The fire dog marches faithfully beside him and beside Madden, who it seems to be quite taken with.

Cayden falls back and slips to the side. He marches forward until he is some feet away from the child but in the boy's line of sight. Key notices him and stares curiously as he walks. Cayden rhythmically taps on his thighs, keeping his eyes on the child. Rossa is watching Cayden with caution, but she is more confused than concerned at the moment. Cayden does not bother with her. He sees Gemma, however, who rides atop Madden, and she understands. She smiles and begins to hum.

Good, Cayden thinks. Humming. That's good.

He is humming now as well, but not a true melody. Not at first. But soon both of their voices come together in something resembling a song. Others look up from the ground, hearing it and wondering where it is coming from, for it is disturbing the silent march.

And then the drum.

Key begins quietly at first. One… two… three… But then he hears the rhythm, and the song becomes a true march. Gemma sings higher and Cayden tries to match her. The marchers raise their heads with slight smiles, a few of them humming along as well, getting in rhythm with the little drummer boy. The orphans and forest children around Key begin to stomp and march, almost as if choreographed. This in turn sends ripples of giggles and laughter through the crowd, and even the adults try their hand at the dance. The march is going at a swifter rate now, the song and the drum carrying it along. And now they are all marching and humming, they are as one, smiles throughout. Cayden sees the smiles even on the faces of Rossa and Lorien. He sees smiles on Lawl and the drummer boy, Key. Most of all, he sees a smile from Gemma Kerr. She winks at him as the music leads them out of the ancient city. They are singing, they are dancing, the spirit is returning.

Yes. He has done it. He has found his soul.

Perhaps this is why he cannot sleep tonight. The march has camped on a hill above the valley city. Though Cayden now finds more marchers comfortable around him—the children think he is the most interesting man they have ever seen—he still knows to give them space. He sleeps away from most, choosing a rotted trunk as his bunk. Yet something new hampers his sleep. A sense of… what? Happiness? Yes. That must be it. Cayden feels happy he has lifted the spirit of the march.

"The valley is quiet," says his father, squatting down next to him. "There will be no trouble this night. Come, my boy. I want to show ya somethin'."

Cayden rises to follow, bringing his blades just in case there be trouble. Most of the marchers are sleeping, but a few are on sentry and some are down in the valley keeping an eye on the ruins. But the campfires are out and sleeping bodies sprawl on the ground or, in the case of the forest folk, in the trees. The great beast Madden snores beneath a giant oak and curled up with him are the fire dog and the drummer boy. Two of Lorien's horsemen eye Cayden as he passes. He disappears into the shadows too quickly for them to say anything.

He is being led over a hill and then down the wide, cracked steps of a grand staircase with what seem to be the remnants of burial crypts on either side. The place is crawling with vines, a place of death now once more a place for living things. Nightbirds and midget monkeys hoot and scamper around the crypts. A pink moon hangs full overhead, giving the crypts a warm glow. Cayden needs no lantern or torch to see at night. The ferrymen have to be adept at nightsight. They are, after all, catchers and most catching is done in the dark. Such has always been the way of the ferrymen.

At the base of the steps, in what seems a pitch formed by other stone staircases on all sides, is a large tomb. Beneath the plant growth, something catches the light from the moon and Cayden tears the vines away, revealing an obsidian coffin, not rectangular but round. In the center of the coffin shine silver words: ERUNG FERRY.

"Do ya know who this be?" asks Cayden's father.

Cayden places a flattened palm on the silver words as if to absorb them, and looks to his father for explanation.

"I be named after him."

At last, Cayden remembers his father's name. Erung. Yet he still does not know who lies within this tomb.

"Erung Ferry was the first of the ferrymen, my boy."

Cayden is startled and looks down at the sheen of the coffin. "He received a burial?"

"Of course he did. As everyone should."

"But he was a ferryman, Da. We be unworthy—"

"Doona say it. If ya knew the history of your tribe, those thoughts would never dare cross your mind, boy. The ferrymen were protectors of the Immortal City. They were the Knights, brave, beloved, and true. They were adventurers and poets. They were artists and lovers. They were us. And then, through manipulation and dark arts, they were twisted to serve other purposes. They were forced to forget who they were and where they came from. They were taught to believe they were dogs to the master's bidding."

Cayden is breathless. He is no monster after all. "I am a ferryman," he says. "Still."

"You are a true ferryman." The father smiles.

"And GOD must pay for what He's done to us. To all of us." And for the first time in his life, Cayden feels anger, rage.

"Aye. He must." Rossa speaks from behind Cayden on the steps.

Erung has vanished. Rossa is bathed in the pink glow of the moon. She stands with a hand on the hilt of a sword at her waist. She descends the steps slowly as he backs up to give her space. She studies his eyes and then the silver inscription on the coffin.

"The first ferryman," Cayden explains. "A good man. A true man. Beloved. We were all lied to."

"So it would seem," she says. "And yet ya be the only one of your kind to see it."

"There may be others."

"Doubtful."

"There is always hope?"

A smile darts across her face, but quickly vanishes. "I appreciate what ya did. Lorien says ya proved quite the hero, especially towards the children. Quite the knight. But you'll forgive me, sir, if I canna bring myself to trust ya."

"I will continue to prove myself, miss. To prove my worth."

She pauses and takes a deep breath. "I'll not mince words. I want to kill ya, sir. I want to hack your handsome head right off."

"I warrant I'd deserve it."

"Aye, ya would. But I will not kill without provocation. So, perhaps it might be better for us both if ya just left the march. Ya lifted our spirits today. But there be nothin' more for ya here."

He does not respond. Not at first. Rossa is ascending the steps when Cayden says, "Perhaps, my queen. Perhaps I should go like ya say. But I won't. I won't."

She stops and looks back at him. The expression on her face is a strange mix of anger and appreciation.

SENATOR GENERAL Hegart leads GOD's Army—an army that, in truth, he has always seen as his own—through the seventh ring on its way to the ninth. It is substantial and slow moving, stretching on the road from one end to the other in a wide band of black and silver. It crawls quietly across the land like oozing oil. Hegart watches from a hill above the main road, a road that can no longer be called the Holy Processional. He has led most the way, but he likes to see his army's progress and so stops occasionally for updates from his field commanders.

He now sits on an angry black steed with as many scars as the Senator General himself, talking with his lead commander, a large pockfaced man by the name of Wendrif. Behind them lag three other Kingdom Guards and two ferrymen. Hegart draws his hand across his jaw and flings a string of heavy saliva to the ground.

"There has been no more sign of Cayden Lothair," answers Wendrif to the Senator General's question. "He is either lost or dead."

"I doubt the former, and we can only hope for the latter." Hegart has felt badly toward Cayden lately. The ferryman seemed to have acquired an independent streak.

"His guards have been found and put to the question per your orders."

"And?"

"Nothing, sir. The three that survived the jungle spoke of little but wolves and cats before they were driven through. They were half mad from wandering."

Hegart snarls. "It seems you need better trained men, Commander."

"With respect, sir," Wendrif says, caution evident in his thin voice, "my men have never had to deal with the forests and jungles of the Immortal City. At least, not those beyond the third ring. Wild, evil creatures are in the trees, and as the rings stretch, things only become more wild and more evil."

"Cayden Lothair was the best ferryman I had, Commander. I want him found. If he is found dead, so be it. But I want him found just the same." He is thinking of his collection of gilded prizes.

"Is this GOD's command?"

Hegart gives the man a sly look. He almost hisses through his pointed teeth. "It is. Yes. It is indeed."

"Then we will not rest until we find him."

"What of the sinner's march? Have you found any more sign of it?"

"All over the place, sir. They… they seem to be everywhere."

Hegart looks at the commander with a warning glare. "What do you mean?"

Wendrif swallows his fear. "We'll hear news of some commotion in a region, but when we head off to check on matters, there is nothing to be seen, no one to be caught. And then we get news of another commotion in the opposite direction. Once we heard of three different spots along the fourth-ring wall supposedly under attack at once. Senator General, sir, there be uprisings, or rumors of them, all over the place."

"Nonsense! The march is a tiny thing. Insignificant. At their highest number, they are said to be no more than five hundred." His attention returns to his army's progression before him. "Again, Commander, it seems your guards could do with better training. You may take that as a threat."

The commander says not another word. Hegart is certain the sinner's march will be handled easily. The random and sporadic attacks on the wall are most likely nothing more than young men seeking to be made heroes. They will be castrated and made to eat their own balls. When he is GOD, Hegart will see to that. And Hegart knows he will be GOD. After the march is annihilated and those who started it executed, the Senator General will institute a new kingdom. He will let GOD starve in His Tower, locking Him up but flooding the place with light so that every moment for the former GOD will be torture, and Hegart will have the Sisters burned as the prophets of a fallen GOD. Traitors. It will be delicious.

Senator General Hegart leads his commanders and ferrymen from the hill down to his army. Hegart's army. This is the beginning. This is where it all begins to turn. Even we can see that.

WHISPERS OF HOPE

DUNCAN HAS been working nights at the Factory. He is in the wagon with the others now, riding back to the barracks. He will get special leave, as always, to see Gran at the hospital. Then it is back to the filthy bunks and infested walls of the shacks with Tully and all the others in his new family of sinners and wretches.

The sky is a faint morning orange, like blood being washed away. Additional wagons pass them by, some carrying workers as downcast as themselves, others stacked high with dead bodies, pale and nude. Duncan has trained himself to see the bodies as one big mass of flesh. This way he does not have to recognize the faces of friends or the lifeless hands of a child.

He has not been completely successful in fooling his eyes today, however. Sary Cledes, the rumored marcher and madwoman, was dumped at his feet this morning. The guards and the government tried to keep her identity a secret, but they failed. The captured marchers, those of this new revolution, have come pouring into the ninth ring. They are still coming in daily. With them come whispers of hope. To quell this, they are being exterminated and sent to the Factory at an alarming, horrifying rate. Bodies are piled up like firewood.

Duncan looks around the wagon. They can only look at one another now. No talking is allowed anymore. You can lose your tongue that way. But the eyes can say more anyway, and unless the guards start blindfolding the workers to and from the Factory, long conversations will still be taking place. Duncan finds Tully's eyes to impart some bit of information, and Tully nods in agreement. Tully finds another set of eyes in the wagon and gets the same reply. Not all the eyes are trustworthy. Not everyone in the wagon is in on the plan, but those who are fill the wagon with a buoyancy, an excitement. Hope. And that, Duncan surmises, is a strange and refreshing feeling, even if it is all for naught.

They drop Duncan off at the hospital. He will need to walk to the barracks on his own after his visit with Gran. He will most likely be harassed by guards, but the fists do not seem to have much punch anymore. Or rather, he feels he deserves them. They are his penance.

He does not sit beside Gran's bed as he once did, but stands to her left. He says not a word. All his apologies are drained away now. She knows he is sorry, and even if Gran does want to say the words "You are forgiven," she cannot. And oh how Duncan would love to hear that phrase! But she can no more talk than open her eyes. She will be dead soon. And then… and then the Factory…. His stomach churns at the idea. How he has failed Lawl. He looks over his shoulder. The doctress stands watching him. She doesn't allow him in the room alone with Gran, since he broke the old woman's heart. She too knows Gran will be dead soon. He cannot imagine she feels anything for Gran.

He is back at the barracks now. The sky is swirls of orange clouds. By the look of it, the world will end soon. A true end. Bright lights and kaboom. Tully is the only one awake and waiting for Duncan. The thin man sits on the end of his straw mattress on the floor. The shack is dark and made from rotted wood. It is getting colder, and Duncan does not believe Tully will survive it. But he is here now, and he is a true friend. The two of them have kept one another sane. When it rains, the roof leaks between their mattresses. Drops of rain hit the floor in steady, maddening increments. You can either talk over it or go mad because of it.

Duncan sits down on his mattress opposite Tully. Tully looks about to make certain no one sees them and rolls back his own mattress to reveal the rotted floor beneath torn up, and a pit dug. In that pit are steel pipes, wooden stakes, and anything else that might possibly be used as a bludgeoning weapon. Duncan pulls down his pants and unties the rope from his thigh where he had fastened a long, thin leg bone, that of a woman. While he was working the mixer, he slowed it just enough to grab the bone before it was pulverized. He throws it in with the other weapons, and Tully rolls his mattress back over the pit once more.

Sary Cledes will have her revenge after all.

THE YOUNG, affable doctress Sara stands behind Deirdre Maire at a long tall window on the second floor of the hospital, the so-called "recovery wing." The windows are pulling in the tinted colors of the sky, bleeding all over the floor, the chairs, and the nurses.

"The army will be here soon," Sara says. From the reflection in the window, Deirdre can see Sara's expression of concern. The poor thing struggles so with her guilt. She shakes. She will lose her grip soon.

"Yes," Deirdre says. "Hegart sours the air with his advance. I can smell him, can't you? He smells like a thousand corpses."

Sara does not disagree.

He is not yet on the horizon, though. On the road ahead, at least from this window at this height, Deirdre sees only the dry landscape of dust and gravel, and then, farther off, the lifeless orchard planted centuries past. No longer trees, it was now only claws reaching to the sky to choke some careless god. Deirdre's heart sinks deeper and deeper. It has been sinking since she was informed Hegart would be visiting the ninth ring. She is trapped. They are all trapped.

"He'll want the beds empty," Sara says. "All of them."

"I realize this, Doctress. Thank you."

Sara gives a nervous bow of her head in the reflection, then turns and walks away.

Deirdre knows what Sara is implying. All of the beds will be emptied, including Gran's. Especially Gran's if Hegart ever finds out the affection Deirdre feels for the old woman. And that old woman is dying anyway, dying very soon… but still… after she dies, what then?

Trapped. Trapped and shaking and desperate.

Deirdre has barely made it to her office. She quickly slams her door so that none, not even the mindless nurses, may see her. With her back against the door, she slides to the floor, her shoulders lurching as she tries desperately to hold in her sobs. Her rib cage might bust open, but she will not let a single snivel escape. Not a sound from her mouth. She bites her lip, drawing blood, and she shakes violently, her hands in tight fists drained of color.

She cannot kill the old woman. She will not. So what then? Must Deirdre kill herself to avoid knowing what must happen? Will the darkness accept her? Will she at least find peace in that final sleep?

She crawls toward the medicine cabinet beside her desk. The pills therein are a wide variety of death candy. But her throat is burning. She cannot breathe for her refusal to cry. Oh, but she wants to cry. And then, not a foot from the cabinet, she can suffer it no longer, and she collapses in a great horrible bellow, a hurricane of howling and tears. She lies on the floor, her cheek cold from its hard touch. Hopeless.

Yet the room is changing. She feels then sees it dim, the harsh light relaxing to a warm glow. And the astringent scent of the hospital is replaced by lilacs and grass, and a cool breeze makes her rise to her knees. She is still quaking from the aftershocks of devastation, but her hand goes to her heart as she looks about. This is not her office. This is a garden, a Holy place with a fountain of Passions just ahead of her and little birds playing in the pure, clean water.

And then she sees us. Abrythnia. We are the goddess of the third-sex.

Deirdre gasps, her arms reaching out in a gesture of both awe and fear.

"Come no closer!" Deirdre pleads. "I am unholy. I am unfit."

She is crying again. Her tears flow as freely as the fountain in front of her.

We approach her. We are nude. We take her hand in ours and show her love. More than she has ever known. And she smiles, the warmth echoing through her being.

"You should smile more," we tell her. "It is beautiful."

Her bottom lip is trembling. "But I have nothing to smile about. The world is now so very sad. Why did you abandon me?"

"Rise, daughter," we say and pull her to her feet. "You were not abandoned. But for some time, we could but watch. You were not open to us. And now, you have a very important part to play here."

"What? Why am I here? What is my part?"

"You are going to be a gateway, sweet Deirdre Maire… if you wish. That is your immediate purpose. As for a larger scheme, we do not yet know."

"But you are the goddess Abrythnia. You know all."

"To think that any creature is omniscient or omnipotent is a mistake. Just as you question the universe about your purpose, so does the universe ask you about its own." We kiss her on the forehead and we whisper, "But together we may yet discover our new beginning."

And we are gone.

She is standing in front of her desk, looking out her office window before she realizes it. Her face is wet, but it carries a remnant of a smile.

"Doctress?" Sara has poked her head into the office. "Are you okay, Doctress? We heard a cry."

Deirdre does not turn. "Yes, Sara. I am much better now, thank you. Thank you, Sara."

STRANGE DAYS and getting stranger. Two Children in Red were at the door. Were because they are now standing before Esther and Bana in the dark parlor. Esther cannot get over the fact that they are here at all. The Children in Red never leave GOD's presence, so something absolutely wonderful and awful must be happening. Esther wheeled Bana into the parlor with a grin so he too could hear whatever it was the Children in Red had to say. Thank goodness Lawl engineered Bana's bed to move. Life is so much easier for it.

The children stand wide-eyed, frightened as baby deer. They have most likely never set foot outside the Tower. The poor things are trembling. A boy and a girl, it looks like. Yes. Both so very thin. Too thin.

"Doesn't He feed you, children?" she says. "Does GOD not allow his Children even a morsel of bread?" She takes a drink from a bottle of wine as if she is at the theater and the children are her show.

The children are confused and look at one another.

"Never mind, never mind. Have all the ferrymen gone? Are there no more Kingdom Guards so that GOD must now send out His precious Children in Red?"

"It is dangerous, miss," the boy says. "Everyone is running or hiding. Even the guards."

"Not you."

"No, miss. We are little and unimportant."

Esther grins. She feels something like her old self again. Her hair is done up, and she is wearing a gown. She thinks it is the gown she was married in, but she cannot be certain. It is white and stains easily, though. This she knows. "Yes. And being little and unimportant means you can maneuver nicely through streets unseen, doesn't it?"

"Yes, miss."

"Yes, miss," she says, mocking them. "Tell me, children, I no longer hear my own daughter's sweet voice piped through the city. Why is that?"

The little girl responds this time. "The guards have destroyed the source, miss."

"You mean they've destroyed the means by which the Voice was relayed. For, you see, sweet girl, they can never destroy the source. My dear Gemma is a hero, and she will live forever."

"She is the reason we have been sent, miss," the boy says.

"Of course, she is, silly child. Why else would you be here? So, get on with it. What does GOD want of my daughter now?" Esther elbows Bana in the ribs and he moans. "Listen closely, Bana dear. They speaketh. From the mouths of babes."

The girl says, "GOD… He commands you to bring your daughter home, miss… please."

"So polite." Esther leans forward. "But no. I am afraid I shall have to decline His Holy Commandment."

The children are quite disturbed. They look as if they might break into tears. "GOD promises Lady Gemma shall not be harmed," says the boy, his voice rising. "That is not something which He can see to if she is so far away."

"Ah, yes. Well, it would be better if GOD had all of His troublemakers where He could keep His big fat eye on them, wouldn't it?"

"GOD recalls how the House of Kerr helped smash the sinners who once ruled the Immortal City, how you helped Him put them all to the flame."

"As do I. The city stank of charred flesh for weeks after."

"But, miss, you…" The boy is having trouble saying the words he has been told to say. "You have no more power. Best do what GOD says… please."

Esther raises an eyebrow and smiles. She snuggles the wine bottle between Bana's thighs roughly. "Children," she says, every bit the schoolmarm, "do you know who your GOD truly is? Not who He claims to be or acts to be, but who He truly is?" She rises and walks toward them, straight-backed and in control. "Because I do, children. I know every little thing about Him, and I can swear to you on whatever god or Passion you hold dear, He is not who you think He is. GOD is a lie."

The children are shaking below her, staring up at her with eyes as blue as myth. "He…" the little girl whispers. "He will be mean to us if we return without the answer He desires."

"Yes, I know." She touches the girl's cheek with the back of her hand. "Which is why I will not be sending you back to Him."

"He will starve without us," the girl says.

"What will you do to us?"

"Let Him rot… and painfully." Looking to the boy, she says, "To you? I will do nothing to you. No, for you see, it has just come to me as sudden as that why you are truly here. You are to be part of my hero daughter's great revolution. You will be the littlest revolutionaries, yes. Isn't that marvelous? Don't you feel special? Take off these glaring robes, children. We shall find you more suitable attire. You have a long trip ahead of you."

"Where are we going?" asks the girl.

"You are going to see a man about a balloon. Doesn't that sound fun?"

THEY HAVE made camp along the River Hung, north of the seventh-ring wall where the waters have cut through the stone like liquid steel. The wall was once a line of artistic arches over the river, but as years passed and with no one left to care for the stones, the structure was eaten away and it collapsed into the rushing channel. Along the river's banks are densely forested hills and stone remnants of ancient docks. And in the center of the wide River Hung is a hilled island of thin white-barked trees most certainly haunted, so say the forest folk. But these rumors did not stop Gemma from crossing over once she found a hidden jetty just beneath the current that connected the banks to the island. She crossed the waters, disappeared into the ghost forest, and has not been seen for hours.

The rain starts as Lawl and Key cross the jetty themselves, followed loyally by Cruncher. Rossa and Lawl are glad of the ugly fire dog. He is very protective of the child and does not let him out of his sight.

Lawl marvels at the island as they walk beneath the trees. It seemed as dense as any forest in the Immortal City at first view, but once actually in the woods, Lawl feels at ease and the claustrophobia the rest of the world encourages slips away here. The trees are tall, white, and thin. They have only branches near the very top where they fan out like wings. Even in this colder season, they are crowned with silver leaves so that only a few drops of rain make their way to the firmament. This explains why the ground is but dirt and struggling tufts in some areas.

The ruins of the island hold some religious significance and hardly seem like ruins at all. They are most definitely of older stone, but they look to be still in use. Lawl stands in front of the statue of a Passion holding out both palms, a trickster grin on its face. Is it giving, receiving, or teasing?

As if a sudden rush of wind is blowing through the trees, Lawl hears whispers. Loud and urgent, they seem to come from everywhere at once. He grabs the child, and they hide behind a statue that is not as dry as the others. Raindrops fall from above. Cruncher whines in curiosity, but stays beside the child. They get wet together, the three of them.

And Lawl sees Gemma by a grand stone arch, but she is not alone. She is talking to a couple of very tiny people. These are the whisperers, or at least two of them. Lawl squints to see them. They are no more than two feet tall, dressed in robes of silvery white and blue. Their faces are strange, almost catlike, with what seem to be black whiskers at the sides of their noses and small black eyes, and their hands are more paws than anything. Yet they are people. There is no denying they have skin, not fur. Lawl and Key seem to realize the same truth at once and that truth causes them to gasp. Passions?

Yet Lawl is unable to think on the matter anymore. From behind him comes a fierce ripping sound and a snarl he had hoped to not hear ever again. The icy tendrils of fear rush through him. He turns just in time to see it.

"Run, Key!" he screams at the boy as the hungry man races toward them, howling. Cruncher leaps at the cannibal, but an arrow finds the hungry man's head first, throwing it back and nailing it to one of the white trees where it flails and spasms until finally dying.

"Put an end to his hunger, didn't I?" Holding a bow is an older man with a burn scar on the left side of his face. He is dressed like the forest folk, but speaks with a noble tongue.

The fire dog growls at the arrowman and sidles up to Key.

Gemma is there now, confused by all the commotion. The Passions are not with her. "What has happened?"

"One more day we're not dinner," Lawl says as he breathes a sigh of relief and slides down to the ground, his back against the statue. The rain is falling faster and harder now. "Might I inquire of my hero's name?"

Ten others stand behind the man, all equally bowed and nearly as old. "You can call me the Old Man. Everyone else does. Who be you?"

"I be Lawl of the Curious Dead Cats. This here be Key and Cruncher, and that be Gemma Kerr."

The Old Man is taken aback. He stares at Gemma in awe and walks to her. His mind seems to be working out something. The others follow him. "You be the girl Gemma that the whole world has heard tale of?"

She nods. Lawl can see she does not want to be this Gemma girl anymore. She wants to crawl into a hole.

"Then you have our arrows," says the Old Man, bowing to her on one knee. His followers do the same. "Many years ago, we were prisoners of the ninth ring. There were more of us then. Much more. Our number has dwindled lately. But if you can use us in the march, we are yours, miss."

The girl hates this. Lawl can see that. She would rather be anywhere but here. And Lawl suddenly gets a creeping feeling that Gemma will very soon leave the march. *There be darkness ahead.*

TWILIGHT SETS the scene, and one by one they arrive, drifting through the valley city and over the forested hill to the burial crypts. Ferrymen in search of the march discover the black obsidian coffin with silver lettering, and then they stop. Not one has gone on since reading the name ERUNG FERRY. It echoes back their memories.

Eleven of them are here in total. Silent black phantoms standing stoic and thinking, remembering beneath the moonlight. The newest to arrive stand nearest the coffin. The very first of them stands back on a stair, yet still facing the obsidian box. None fidget or glance about to other faces for reassurance. The ferrymen decipher things as they have always done: alone in the dark paths of their own minds.

And yet those paths are lighting up like fireworks parades. Those paths are trickling with first memories. Of faces they should know. Of events they have seen. The ferrymen are remembering who they are, who they were, and who they were meant to be. Who Erung Ferry meant them to be. The coffin has been cleaned off meticulously by Cayden Lothair so this would happen. Just so.

Eleven are here. More will come. Those who do not will be told. Shadows make it easy for secrets to fly unseen.

Miles away, as Mags Hensil watches the march from a distance, she feels some change as well. She does not like it. It is but her and the Sisters now. The guards have gone on ahead to the ninth ring, and the lone ferryman who had helped her locate the march has silently and quite abruptly slipped away.

Mags shrugs off her concerns for now. She watches the ferryman Cayden Lothair as he recites, as he rhymes and chimes, as he paces in a circle. She slips away before he notices her, back to her Sisters at the circle in the woods where they have made camp.

"Tomorrow," Mags says. "Tomorrow, my Sisters, we shall make quick work of it."

THE SILVER SEA

IT IS morning, a cold miserable day. The ride back from the Factory was spent trying to keep warm in the rags they are given for clothes. Duncan would have tried to sneak out one of the horrifying beaked suits if they didn't smell of death and shit. The sinners are not allowed to huddle for warmth. The guards are wary of uprisings and plots these days, as if plotting is done anywhere near a guard. Duncan did not find a weapon this day. Everything went in the mixer too quickly, and guards have increased their patrols. They suspect something.

Duncan stands now in the hospital, having been dropped off for his daily visit to Gran. He stands in her doorway in shock, looking at the empty bed, the empty room. His heart spikes and then sinks. His breath shortens, and his insides turn to jelly.

"Where is she?" he whispers to no one. "Gran?"

"She is dead, the poor dear." The head doctress stands behind him. He has heard nothing but his own thoughts for a few minutes and so did not hear her approach. Selective hearing. "It's for the best," she says. There is a slight strain in her voice. A picked chord.

Duncan floods with ice. "Where has she been taken, miss? Please…" He is facing her now, his mouth a quiver. "Please, doona let them…"

Deirdre raises her eyebrow to remind him of her supremacy, then gently pushes him backward into the room. "Listen to me," she says sternly yet quietly. "Doctress Sara waits for you in the Thorn Fields." She stares through him with her one good eye.

"But I need to find Gran before—"

"Doctress Sara waits for you," she says each word emphatically, "in the Thorn Fields."

Duncan is confused. What is this new expression the doctress seems to be wearing? Concern?

"You must go to the Thorn Fields at once and help her. Do you understand?"

He thinks so. He thinks he understands.

"Do you understand?"

"Y-yes. I think so. The Thorn Fields."

"Yes. The Thorn Fields. Out back, a nurse driver is ready to take you in the wagon. She knows the way. But that is all she knows. That is all she'll ever know."

Duncan wants to thank the doctress, but words do not come and an embrace would be cause for alarm.

"Get going," she says. "But go slowly."

The Thorn Fields are just that. They start ten miles to the rear of the hospital and from there encircle the entirety of the ninth ring, a barrier and a trap to any escapees fleeing toward the ninth-ring wall or the end of the world beyond it. The Fields start out as rather harmless briar bushes, but within a mile, they grow thicker and taller, with thorns that could impale a man… and have. A few, however, know of secret paths through the thorns, and it is on one of these that Doctress Sara is waiting.

Duncan is not taken all the way into the thorns. The silent nurse driver halts quite suddenly and stares blankly forward until he realizes he must walk the rest of the angry path alone. Though it is a dreary day, he feels confident he can find his way. If it were night, he would be a dead man. The thorns would strip him of his flesh.

Lawl had told him a story as they were cuddled up in bed one night years ago. It was a children's tale he'd heard from Gran about a little boy named Alex who chased a white boxyboo through a thorny thicket and down a burrow. "Are ya the boxyboo?" he asks Doctress Sara as he comes upon her in her white coat.

She smiles, apparently familiar with the tale, then looks down at dear old Gran who is lying serenely on a wood plank, an old discarded door. One hand is on the silver doorknob, as if she is ready to give it a turn.

Duncan puts a hand to his forehead. He is trying not to get very emotional. He is trying to beat back the guilt and regret. He grins above it. "Not quite the pyre ya deserve…" He collapses to a crouch and sobs. Sara waits patiently. She does not look away. Here in the ninth, this emotion is something rare and beautiful to see.

Duncan collects himself and kisses Gran on the forehead. "I'll bring your Lawl here to say good-bye," he whispers. "I promise ya."

And as they bury her, Duncan makes mental notes of the surroundings. Of the shape of the vines and thorns. Of their thickness. Of their curvature and color. And as he and the doctress make their way back to the wagon and the nurse driver, he tries to commit puddles and small jumps in the path to memory. Sara helps him, pointing out odd anomalies of outcroppings and large boulders. Otherwise, she is silent. The ride back to the hospital past the noon hour is hushed one. Duncan does not want to be distracted or think of anything else but the way back to Gran. He plans to write it all down once at the barracks.

As the wagon pulls up to the hospital, there is static in the air. The foregrounds are a flood of silver and black made up of Kingdom Guards and horses, woolly bulls and wagons. And they are still pouring in from the long orchard path. How will the ninth ring hold them all? Their number is numerous. Or perhaps it is just the black and silver that make the whole thing seem so desperate and dangerous.

Two guards approach the wagon. "Get down from there, ya piece of shit," says one, grabbing Duncan's arm and pulling him to the ground.

"What is the meaning of this?" Sara shouts. "He has been helping me in the Fields."

"Aye. We know," says the other guard. He takes hold of her arm and pulls her off as well. "Ya need to come with us, miss," he says. "Ya be under arrest."

"For what?"

"Conspiracy and heresy against GOD the Almighty."

Duncan is on his feet. He looks up to the hospital cupola where stands Doctress Deirdre looking down on them. He cannot see her face, but he knows it is her. The woman is as shadowy a figure as a ferryman.

CAYDEN LOOKS back over the bedraggled revolutionaries. The sinner's march stands in the bitter winds of the eighth ring in front of the Silver Sea. They shiver from the chill, but also from the dread of proceeding any farther. The army is silent, each individual staring down what lies ahead. The wind steals away any whispers, taking them into the domed and hardened crawlers' nests that cover the valley. This be not a sea of water, but of spun silver thread from giant arachnid-like creatures—ancient experiments that resemble humankind with flesh and torsos—which have claimed every tree and boulder in the region. The webs glitter and pulse in the wind as if alive.

"We must venture through," says Rossa. She is standing beside Claire with the bridle in her hand. Key rides the horse. "It'd take too long to go around. Old Man, ya say ya know a path through? A safe path?"

"Aye," Old Man says, his back as straight as a soldier. "The crawlers abandon their cathedrals every ten years and move on to another, building and adding anew. There's such a one just there." He points to the opening of a tunnel beside two silver-shrouded willow trees.

"These crawlers look to be somethin' terrible fierce," says Lawl. "And Passions know, we done faced enough monsters already. How ya gonna get this lot through the caves without a panic?"

"They've got me and me scythes," says Cayden. "Besides, if these tunnels are abandoned, we should have naught to fear." He stares at Old Man with a challenging glare.

"Will ya be my hero, then?" Lawl gives the ferryman a teasing smirk.

"Anytime, handsome," says Cayden. He delights in the looks on the faces of those around him. "Aye," he says. "The ferryman is learnin' to joke."

"He's got a point, though," says Lorien from his steed. "None look ready to head in, but we cannot wait around. GOD's Army is on our tail. If they don't get us, the hungry men will."

"Well, then," says Gemma, who has remained silent for some time. "Let's give them courage." Without a pause, she starts down the hill toward the abandoned crawlers' nest and waits for the others there.

Cayden smirks and gives a short "Ha!" then he follows her. The entire march is now filing into the crystal cathedral. They are silent, in awe and fear. No one dares take a deep breath. The Silver Sea is beautiful but laden with peril. Even the horses and hounds seem to sense the danger. Hooves and feet echo as loud as drums in the dark corridors of the crawlers.

Cayden allows himself to wonder at the sight in front of him. The trees, so high and majestic, are shrouded in silvery twine. It is as if the entire valley were blown crystal glass, as if the march was venturing into the largest palace that has ever been built, stretching on and on for miles. Old Man is in the lead. He knows what paths to take. He listens for hisses and scurrying. Cayden lets him to it, though he does not trust this new marcher yet. He will be ready if needed, but until then… such beauty and such danger…

"Some courage you've got," Cayden says to Gemma. He has wrested his eyes from the magnificence around him to see her walking nearby. They are in a narrower path now where it is wise to walk in twos and threes at most. "You're a small thing. A crawler'd eat ya right up."

She smiles at him. "No. Nothing will happen to me. Not in here. We had to get through it, and I knew they'd follow me if they were going to follow anyone."

"So, you're finally playin' your part."

"With hesitance." Madden is shaking behind her. "It's okay, boy," she says to the hound. "We'll get through it."

"For a big dog, he's a big baby, eh?"

"He's still a puppy in most ways, I think. How long do you think we'll be walking the Silver Sea?"

Cayden shrugs. "I didna see an end to the gleam when we came upon it. I have a feelin' we're gonna be in here a while. But by my countin', we should be at the ninth ring very soon. It won't be long now. What do we plan to do then?"

She looks at him. "We bring it to its knees, Cayden, and then see what's beyond. There are twelve rings, you know. Twelve, not nine."

Twelve. Cayden feels that new desire curl up like a snake ready to strike. Some call it curiosity.

"Cayden," Gemma says. "Promise me something. Promise me that no matter what happens, no matter who dies in the battle that's coming, promise me you'll take the march and you'll go on. Promise me you'll see the hidden rings."

Cayden is silent for a moment. Gemma is watching him intently. He wants to ask what she knows. What prophecies has she heard to say such dire things? But he only nods his head and says, "I promise."

He looks into her eyes, and he wants to kiss her. But he does not.

Night has fallen. The sinner's march has departed the Silver Sea, resting on large hills of grass high above. Rossa is watching Key as he sleeps soundlessly against Cruncher—who is not sleeping so soundlessly. Fire dogs, it seems, are gassy, grumbly sleepers.

Rossa is thankful they had no incidents with the crawlers on their passage through the Silver Sea. Not one monster in sight, nor one vicious bite. They passed a couple ancient skulls, but they did so quietly, trying to ignore their importance or augury. And if a crawler tried to snatch Key from Claire's saddle? What then?

"I woulda chased the damn bugger down whatever tunnel it dragged him," says Rossa to herself. "I didna come miles and miles to have the one thing I was ever truly after, the one thing what's safety I care for more than any other, be snatched away by a demon with too many legs.

"So, why do ya keep goin'? I ask meself. You've got the boy, why not head on back to the city?

"And just what exactly would I be headin' back to? I got no family there. Not no more. They gave me up, remember? Me own brother gave me up and then me father beats me and throws me out on the streets when that traitorous, dumbass brother of mine gets his arm scythed off by a ferryman. They're probably all dead by now anyhow. They couldna stay out of trouble, me family. Always gamblin' what little they had. From what little I hear, the whole Immortal City is fallin' apart. The world be endin' again. How many second chances does a species deserve? If it weren't for ya, sweet child," she said, smiling at the sleeping gypsy boy, "I'd say a plague on us all and be done with it. But ya give me hope, ya do. You're like your mom in that way, aye.

"And what is all this riffraff we've gotten ourselves mixed up with, eh? Sinners and convicts, orphans and horsemen, a hero, and a ferryman. A ferryman! Never thought I'd see the day when I'd be marchin' anywhere with a ferryman, at least not on the same side. I got a feelin' in my core that once we reach the ninth ring, the whole blasted Immortal City is gonna collapse. We'll have nowhere to go but out and what be out there beyond the last wall? Aye, that's the question.

"My, my, little one, how you've shaken the world. But I doona mind it. My world needed some shakin', I s'pose. All my old skin, the woman that used to be me, is done shed now, and I'm brand new again. A queen, they say. A fuckin' queen. And of what? I'd laugh if it didna terrify me so.

"So, why di'nt I turn back once I found ya again?" She is silent for a moment. The camp around her is growing more still as the night takes it. "Because ya deserve a better life. Because we all do. And because GOD's done pissed me off too many a time for me to back down now."

She sees the child smile, though his eyes are yet closed. She hopes some of her words have made it into his dreams.

"Sleep with the Passions, my boy," she whispers. "They be all we got now."

GEMMA IS fascinated by the Silver Sea below. She stands alone on a hill, yards from the other marchers as they slumber, or try to. It is cold, yet Gemma is not guarding against it. Her arms are at her sides, and she is watching the beautiful light display in the great web cathedral, marveling at the bright bursts of white and green. Sometimes a burst of deep blue flares like a star and then dies away. Old Man has told her the lights were signs of birth and death. The crawlers glow white when feeding, green at birth, and dark blue at the moment of death. These colors are remnants of their ancestors' souls from long ago when they were yet human. The Silver Sea is busy with its natural order this night. Gemma wonders if she will flicker as gloriously when she dies.

She hears a rustling in the trees behind her and knows before he speaks it is Old Man. "Is it time?" she says.

She turns to face him. He is dumbstruck by the question, though he does not lose his soldierlike poise. "Miss?"

"You've come to take me to my death, correct?"

"H-how did…?"

"It does not matter." She approaches him and touches his face gently. "Let's get on with it."

His eyes are watering. "I'm sorry, miss," he says. "I had no choice."

The brush around them shakes and falls, and Mags Hensil and the Sisters of GOD surround her. They are in full white garb, Mags now wearing a fanning crown of gold and amethysts. "He's quite right," says Mags. "No choice. Bring her."

Gemma is being led through a path to a clearing not far from where she was standing. Old Man holds to her arm. Mags leads, and the Sisters follow. Gemma says nothing. The night is hushed and breathless. Not a word is spoken until they arrive in the clearing. There they tie her to a large tree. Old Man objects, but Mags strikes him into silence.

"Poor Gemma Kerr," Mags says, her face retaining all the emotion of an unhappy ivory statue. She stands before the tree with folded hands. "If only you had played the part GOD set forth for you, this would not be necessary."

Gemma sees the Sisters drawing out their crossbows and arrows. Old Man's jaw drops, his eyes widen.

"Your mother and father have failed, Gemma. They have both been torn apart by GOD's dogs. Oh, yes. He let loose the hungry men into the manse and locked the door. You should have heard your mother screaming. Screaming for mercy. Begging for forgiveness."

Gemma smiles. "You're a liar, Mags Hensil," she says. "I know the first ring is in ruins, and I also know GOD will soon be dead."

Mags's face twists like a cloth bag in a blinding wind. She gestures for a Sister to bring her a crossbow, and she then fixes it on Gemma. Without warning, she shoots an arrow into Gemma's thigh. The girl cries out in pain.

"Stop this!" Old Man exclaims. "This is not what you said you were going to do with her. You said—"

He falls to his knees, an arrow from one of the Sisters' crossbow buried deep in his back. He looks up at Gemma, his face one of deep regret, reaches out for her, and then he collapses to the earth.

"Even at your death you speak blasphemy, girl," says Mags. "You shall find no release for your soul."

Gemma refuses the pain in her thigh. She raises her head, even as the tears stream, and smiles, resting it back against the tree. "My soul is already released," she says.

"Sisters," Mags says with decisive nonchalance. "Let us strike this sinner down."

One by one, the arrows pierce her flesh, but she does not feel them. They are but pebbles to her. Her eyes are on the sky. She is past the clouds and with the stars. And from that height, she sees her own body, that which she had for so many years called "Gemma Kerr," slump forward riddled with arrows.

She sees how Mags Hensil lifts her head by the hair to make certain she is dead and say, quite unconvincingly, "Satisfactory."

She hears the rumble through the brush, and sees the great white hound jump into the fray and tear one of the Sisters apart as the others scream in horror. She sees another Sister who starts to run felled by Cayden Lothair's scythe. From both of their lifeless bodies, Gemma watches as screaming, confused souls rise, still clawing at their grounded forms, unwilling to move on. The horsemen surround the remaining Sisters of GOD and take their bows.

"We're too late," Rossa cries, horror-stricken.

Mags Hensil is bellowing, held still by horsemen. "You've killed two Sisters of GOD!" she screams. "Heresy! Heresy! GOD shall have His vengeance!"

Rossa knocks her out with her sword hilt, and the woman falls to the ground like a bag of Holy rocks.

Cayden Lothair unties Gemma from the tree and cradles her body to the earth. He rocks her. "She knew," he whispers. "She knew."

Rossa looks away, her face crumpling. The horsemen stare in disbelief. The Sisters of GOD huddle together. Madden looks beaten.

Gemma is with us now. She has done her part, and now it is up to the others. We smile at her. It is not a smile she can see, but instead a smile she can feel. There are but three hundred souls. That is all there ever have been. And Gemma is part of ours.

A PROPER funeral would be a pyre, but the march has no time. Gemma's body is buried on the hill in the clearing above the Silver Sea. All one hundred and fifty-three of the surviving marchers have part in the burial. Each takes one claw of dirt from the earth and passes the pick on to the next. The ground is hard and cold. There is a fierce breeze. Gemma is wrapped in a long wool blanket once owned by Gol of the forest folk and lowered gently into her tomb.

Key is standing with Lawl and Rossa. He knows what part to play. When Cayden nods to him, he beats a song of mourning. Not a whisper disturbs the ceremony. Even the captive Sisters stay silent. Key is certain this has nothing to do with any respect they feel toward Gemma, but rather for fear of being gutted by Cayden Lothair or Queen Rose. Key has that desire himself. He wishes the Sisters would say something. His anger is nearly interfering with his playing.

After the ceremony, the marchers begin to stir. "What do we do now?" some are asking. "Where do we go? Our hero is dead."

They are heartbroken.

"We go home," some are answering. "We have lost."

"No," Cayden says. His voice carries over the march. They turn to him. "We keep goin'."

"Why?" a man of the original sinners says. "So we can lose more? I have been with the sinners since the beginning. I stayed with them after Colm Archer was captured, after Usker Lance was slaughtered, after the hungry men and the fire dogs, I stayed. But this… she was our last hope."

"She still is," says Cayden. The crowd is staring at him, listening. "Ya would turn your backs on her? On all she stood for? If ya turn back now, this will all be for naught, all the sacrifices your friends and families have made, then GOD wins. The Immortal City is crumblin' around us."

Mags Hensil gasps. Her hands are tied as she stands between the horsemen and the original sinners.

"Ya can go back, aye," says Cayden, "but to what? Ya will surely die when ya return and your death will have no meaning then. But if we keep goin', if we keep to Gemma Kerr's vision… yes, ya still may die. But at least you'll die fightin'."

Key looks up at Rossa's face. She is stirred by the ferryman's speech and breathes deep.

"When we were in the Silver Sea," says Cayden, "Gemma says to me that whatever happens I was to keep goin'. She wanted someone, lots of someones to see what lies outside the Immortal City. Ya can all go back if ya want, but I'm headin' on. I'll fight the whole bloody ninth ring if I must. And what's that say about ya if a ferryman desires to fight on, but ya sinners don't?"

"You'll not fight alone, ferryman," says Rossa, approaching Cayden and putting a hand on his shoulder. "I'll be comin' with ya."

Others slowly take up in agreement.

"Aye," says Lawl. "The love of me life is in that wretched place. I plan to be his hero. And I know just what smirk to wear, too."

The original sinner nods. "Forgive me my doubts, Brother Cayden. I wavered momentarily. Of course, I will march with ya. But what about the Sisters here? What do we do with them?"

"Feed 'em to the damn crawlers," says Lorien.

A chorus of approval resounds in the circle. Rossa walks into the center and stands by Gemma's grave. She raises her hands, and the marchers hush. "We shall take the Sisters with us," she says. "We shall show them mercy, and then we shall show them their GOD… dead."

The marchers like this notion even more. The forest erupts in raucous cheers.

"All of this is folly!" hisses Mags Hensil. "How dare you speak thusly of GOD. It is repugnant. And after all He has done for you."

"He has done nothin' for us, dear Sister, but eat our souls while we yet walk. He builds enmity between people where none should exist. He be a greedy, jealous demon who must be cast down. We have built His perch too high. We have given Him too much power over us. His words be only words, and yet with one of them, He can end the life a sweet child, of an entire district, no questions asked."

"Heresy! Heresy!"

"Saying the word alone will not light me afire, Sister. Ya need a spark, and I'm afraid you're all wet."

"Give up," shouts Mags. Her white makeup is cracking, showing decay. "Give up now. The ferrymen are on their way."

"The ferrymen are here," says Cayden.

"You? You are no ferryman. You've abandoned the way of GOD. I curse you, Cayden Lothair, and I spit on the grave of this whelp you've just buried."

"I wouldna do that," Cayden warns her.

But Mags is not listening. Key watches as the Sister coils back and spits forth the largest ball of phlegm he has ever seen. It lands just short of the grave. Mags is smiling and content with her actions… for a very brief moment.

"What?" says Mags to Cayden. "Are you not man enough to do anything about that?"

"It wasna me I was warnin' you about," he says.

Mags is caught unawares as Rossa rips her crown of gold and amethyst off, taking with it great clumps of hair. Then Rossa strikes the mad queen across her face with the abrasive headware. Her mouth snags on the gold corner and rips clear up her cheek. She falls to the ground in screaming agony, crimson painting her white robe.

Key is astounded, his mouth agape.

"Bandage her up," Rossa says with the crown still in her hand. "We need to be movin' on."

BLOODFLOOD

THE ONLY room in use at the House of Kerr is the front parlor where Esther keeps an eye on Bana, occasionally poking at the embering fire with an old cane left behind by one of their wealthy friends when they used to have visitors. The rest of the manse is closed off and even colder than before. Echoes freeze in the air, and any light is snuffed out quickly and angrily by shadows. The halls and chambers would creak and groan if anyone was there to hear them complain. Only the parlor has life in it now, and that is dying a slow death as well.

Esther woke up facedown on the red velvet sofa, drool staining the pillows and a nearly finished bottle of wine upright on the floor beside her. She woke with the knowledge that Gemma was dead. Something went clip in the night. No. Something went snap. Yes. It was more snap!

She was silent and still for a while, uncertain if she had the tears enough for her grief. The world was red. Red velvet. Bleeding. And she realized she was angry more than grief-stricken, and she knew what she had to do.

Esther Kerr has risen now and is readying Bana in the bed chair Lawl had concocted for him. "Are you comfortable, dear?" she says as she slides a pillow behind his back to prop him up. "I want you to be very at ease. We are going for a little adventure, you see… What's that, dear? Well, you see, our sweet daughter, sweet little Gemma, has been killed, and I'm afraid it's all our fault. Of course, yours more than mine, but I'll take some of the blame. Oh, darling. There is no point in crying now. You paid absolutely no attention to her when she was here."

She stacks his oxygen canisters on the back of the bed with the rest of the apparatus in a handy container Lawl constructed just for them. They protrude to either side of the bed chair like bulbous metallic wings.

"There's no reason to worry anymore, darling, about anything… What? What are we doing? Well, we are going to go… settle things. That's all."

She picks up the wine bottle, which still contains a modicum of flavored backwash, and she drinks it down, then throws the bottle out the window. Bana's eyes are quite large. He is whining and trying to move, but Esther covers him in thick blankets and grabs spectacles for them both.

"Out for a stroll!" she says as she pushes the parlor doors open with the bed chair.

It is cold outside, but she does not wear a coat. Now that the Kingdom Guards have abandoned their posts, she is free and the abrasive air is keeping her vigorous and attentive.

The first ring is in utter ruins. The manse directly across from the Kerrs is a hollowed-out mess, fire having completely gutted it. Esther knows the only reason her home was not lit up along with the others is because she is Gemma's mother. She imagines there is some Holy adjective describing her. When they make a religion of her daughter, she hopes the paintings are flattering.

Esther bumps and rolls her husband down the steps, paying no attention to his groans. Once on level ground, she hums happily as she bobs and weaves past detritus and dead bodies. Past murdered guards and citizens, spoiled loot, and lost children. There is still some fighting. She hears it as background music far away.

A guard rushes past her and pauses. "Lady Kerr," he says. "You should be back in your manse."

She ignores him and keeps walking, pushing Bana as if they are but on a stroll in the park.

"Everyone is out today, Bana," she says. "How lovely! Just look at how much fun they're having. Though I do wish they'd find some place more convenient to sunbathe. I suppose lying in the middle of the street is some new fad, eh?" She laughs. "These young folk and their trends. And would you look at those precious children singing by that fire. My, they put a lot of emotion into their songs! And how about that! The guards are dancing in the air with the revolutionaries. Some type of stage show, I suppose, though someone should tell them we can see the strings. It does not sincerely look as if they are flying if one can see the strings."

Esther gasps in delight, though she does not dawdle. "Wonder of wonders!" she says. "Look at that big bear on the leash over there. I imagine those twin handlers leading him have quite the job. Still, they look as if they can deal with that bear fine. My my my! All those muscles on those boys. And look, Bana, darling! There's a ringmaster. It must be a circus, and doesn't she look happy? Oh, delight of delights! I'm certainly glad we got to see all of this, aren't you? I said, aren't you?"

She lowers her head for a listen, then stands up straight once more, laughing and cackling and quite broken.

"We must remember," she says, "I say, we simply must remember to tell GOD what we've seen when we get to the Tower. A bear on a leash! Delightful!"

THE OPERATING room is overcrowded for Deirdre's taste. Two of these people should not be in here: the patient and the mad dog in the corner.

The former doctress Sara is trying to calm herself. It is a heartbreaking sight. She looks at the ceiling in defiance, though Deirdre knows the girl is terrified. Her chin and neck are held stable by a biting piece of metal, and her arms and legs are restrained. She knows the routine for lobotomizing people. Deirdre herself had taught her. And now Deirdre is being forced to lobotomize Doctress Sara.

Deirdre is silent. She does not have to say a word to her nurses. They function as a collective machine. The girl that used to be Orna will be assisting Deirdre in the procedure. Two other nurses stand at the ready. Deirdre looks into Sara's eyes, seeking forgiveness for what she is about to do.

"Get on with it, fucking bitch!" barks the dog in the corner. He is drooling, and his teeth are bared. His pupils have shrunk to the size of dust particles.

Hegart found out. Another doctor was spying on Deirdre this whole time. This someone told Hegart what Deirdre conspired to do with Doctress Sara and one of the sinners. Deirdre was leading the Senator General on a tour to get reacquainted with the hospital when the betrayer spoke up, a young doctor hoping to make a name for himself and get into Hegart's good graces. Unfortunately, Hegart has no graces, good or ill. After running the doctor through on the spot, he turned like a wild, slobbering dog on Deirdre. She refused to tell him where the body was buried, so he broke her nose and promised her worse. "But first," he said, "I'm going to watch as you scoop that cunt's brains out of her head."

And here they are. Deirdre is in pain as she pulls the surgical mask over her face. Her good eye is red with tears. She has not seen to her nose properly yet, but what is the point if worse is to come? She takes a breath and starts the saw. Sara's eyes water, and she looks into Deirdre's. The dog drools. He even laughs.

But the door to the operating room crashes open. Deirdre pulls back.

"Senator General Hegart," says a breathless guard. "There's a riot, sir. An uprising in the barracks."

Interesting, thinks Deirdre.

Hegart growls and rises. "Keep working," he snarls at Deirdre as he leaves the room for more active prey.

Deirdre wastes no time. She puts the saw down and tears off her mask. "Help me with these restraints, girl," she says to the girl who was Orna. "You, in the corner. Strip. Give Doctress Sara your uniform and cap."

"You'll get yourself killed," Sara says, free of the cutting metals.

"I'm already dead. That monster can't do much else to me than he's done."

The naked nurse hands Sara her clothes, and Sara hurriedly slips out of the operating gown into the nurse's uniform.

"I hope you're a good actress," says Deirdre. "You'll need to be a nurse for a bit. Give me your feeble face… Good. That'll do. You need to go to the Thorn Fields. Take the trail you were on earlier and just keep going. Orna will drive you."

"What's beyond the Thorn Fields?"

"Girl, how should I know? But it's not this, and that's all that matters. Now go!"

"Thank you," Sara says. She wraps her arms around Deirdre's neck, and the embrace warms Deirdre. It takes all her willpower to separate herself from the young doctress.

"Go!" Deirdre commands. The girl hurries away.

And what will she tell Hegart? Why, she will tell him the truth. She let the girl go. He will kill her. She knows this. Yet it will be a good death. A death with reason. She heads up to the cupola. She will wait for the Senator General there. Until his ominous arrival, she will stare down the orange sky.

AND THIS is how the riot began.

Duncan was led in front of the other sinners, a walking portent. They were lined up in slovenly rows in front of the barracks, the wind chilling them to their bones. The guards cased each line, slapping the backs of the sinners' heads with ferocity and screaming expletives into ears. Degradation and humiliation are their favorite weapons. They have always loved tears more than blood. A cut with the right word will never heal.

Duncan stood stoic, his face as defiant as the guards who held him, held his arms tightly, twisting whenever they felt the whim or a change in wind. Strange, Duncan thought, that I am to be executed so soon. Surely, GOD has some say in the matter, and yet no one around him looked very much like a god.

Duncan found Tully in the sinners before him. Three rows back. The skinny man made certain Duncan saw him. He stepped out of line and got a hard thwack on the back of the head for it. But that was all Duncan needed in the way of assurance. He had to bite his tongue to keep from smiling.

Then the first guard fell.

A small dustup happened behind Duncan. He glanced over his shoulder while his own holders were looking. One of the guards in the rear had been downed. Blood leaked from a small hole in his forehead, his eyes still open and appearing as confused as everyone else. The guards, whose postures quickly changed from proud bullies to fearful quarry, began to look around for the culprit, but they would never find him. The small ersatz pipe gun was being passed between the assigned assassins in the group with such liquid ease, a ferryman would be pleased.

Suddenly, one of the guards holding Duncan fell. Duncan heard the sharp whistle pass close to his head before the guard stiffened and crumpled. The other guard loosened his grip on Duncan, and Duncan slid from his grasp and broke his nose with a sickening crunch. The spurting geyser of blood was the signal flare the sinners needed.

Those in the know went on the attack. Those who had no idea what was happening either slid away to hide or angrily joined in the revolt. They shifted their makeshift weapons from their sleeves and pants legs into their palms. Tully tossed Duncan Sary Cledes's leg bone, which he had strapped to his own thin leg. The tip had been sharpened extensively, and Duncan began slashing and sinking it into chests and throats with animal zeal. Cries from the guards arose all over the camp. They were not expecting this. Never had there been a revolt in the ninth ring. By the time sinners were brought here, they were scared, tired, and beaten. Easy to bully and command.

The barracks and the grounds around them became a battlefield. Duncan saw Tully jump on the back of a guard, wrap his legs around the man, and then slide a triangle clamp over the guard's thick neck, breaking it instantly. Others used the guards' own prods and shanks against them. Some went half mad in their revenge, laughing with every slice and slash, every half decapitation and full death.

This will end badly for us, Duncan thought. When Hegart hears what's happenin' and comes to squash us, we'll all be thrown alive into the mixers. But at least we've made our stand. We are no longer comfortable with bein' complacent. Lawl would be proud of me. I wish I coulda seen him once more before this life ends. But next life... Next life it'll be just me and him.

And he runs a stunned guard through for simply standing there and reminding him of his own former self. Complacency will get you killed.

ESTHER IS struggling, pushing Bana up the Tower's winding ramp. The structure has no stairs, for what use are steps to GOD? Esther is grateful. Stairs would only be more of a struggle. The building is mostly deserted. The Kingdom Guards are nowhere in sight, having, Esther assumes, fled or been drawn out to fight. No ferrymen are around, and the remaining Children in Red cower in corners, too frightened to move or leave the only home they have ever known. Esther sees them in the dim light, and in moments of lucidity, she tells them to go find a new home.

"Your GOD cares for you not, children," she calls out, breathless. "Get out. Get out now or you will die." She doesn't know if any heed her words, but she pushes on. Bana whines in a long, continuous stream now that echoes and bounces off the stone and concrete. He is such a child at times, she thinks.

The massive double doors to GOD's great room are open. The room is as dim as the rest of the Tower except at the very top where one of the blinds has malfunctioned and is letting in a thick, creeping stream of light. The gleam bounces off the high chair and its resident even as He hisses, as if hissing will defend Him from melting. The room has a definite displeasing odor as well. The funk of waste.

Bana continues his whining song as Esther pushes him forward and stops at the base of the high chair. She hears GOD's hisses through His speaking horn turn into something resembling more a gasp of recognition.

"Oh, good," says Esther. "You see us. I was afraid we'd need to wake you. We all know how grumpy you can be when woken. That was how your dear old mother died, if I remember correctly." She looks around. "Not much has changed since I was here last."

She is squeezing the handles on the bed chair. Her knuckles are white. Her jaw shakes with rage. She is now studying the empty council seats in front of her.

"It seems your anger is as fierce as ever. Your councilors are all gone... well, not all. You still have Bana." She pats her husband on his padded head. "Would you like to see him better?"

He answers with an excited intake of air.

"Very well." Esther is unwrapping Bana, taking off his spectacles and blankets and the shawls wrapped around his head. These things are for safety. His precious skin, so thin and fragile, needs the protection against the light and the elements.

A creaking comes from above as GOD leans forward. Esther can just make out His pale, horrid face in the sparse light. His Lordship looks like a blighted turnip.

Esther folds the blankets and shawls and puts them on Bana's lap. He still whimpers. "Yes. Quite moving, isn't it?" Esther says. "And I must say," she looks from one to the other, "the resemblance is remarkable. Tell me, Your Lordship, after so many years, how looks your father?"

HEGART IS standing proud in the ninth ring, the new and future GOD of the Immortal City, as it begins to snow. Clad in his thick, black coat, he no longer worries about the excessive saliva spilling from his mouth. The public is easy to manipulate. He could bottle and sell his spit as special elixir, and they would drink it by the gallons.

The futile uprising has been easily quelled. The ground is a steaming swamp, soaking up blood from sinners and guards alike. Those sinners who are not dead are now on their knees in front of him, their hands on their heads where Hegart can see them. The Kingdom Guards are useless, thinks the Senator General. They stand in ignominy. They shall be disbanded and replaced by an army of ferrymen.

But where are the ferrymen? He just now notices the absence of shadow and black from his legions.

"You have made things," says Hegart to the sinners, "so much more difficult than they needed to be. Your deaths will not be quick and easy, I'm glad to say. No. I will take great pleasure in ripping you apart or dipping you headfirst into vats of acid."

He slurps back some of his juices and slides his tongue over his sharpened teeth.

"Yes. The ninth ring will be flooded with a sea of blood, and the air filled with the song of your pain."

No response. No pleas of mercy. Not even from those who did not take part in the fight. Hegart is not pleased by this. He wants a show.

He locks eyes on Duncan and Tully. "As an example of what I mean to do, your leaders shall be the first to go." He steps forward and pulls Tully up off the ground by his neck, the thin man's feet inches off the cold earth. "I am disgusted with you, dear brother," he spits. "Our father would be so disappointed."

He throws him to the earth.

"The father ya killed, dear brother," says Tully. He has no fear in his large eyes. Only contempt and condescension.

Hegart's face twists. "How dare—"

Before he retaliates with word and fist, however, a guard is racing toward him on horseback. "Senator General," the guard says. "They've come. They're here."

"Who?" yells Hegart.

"The sinner's march, sir."

Hegart grins most viciously. "Kingdom Guards," he says. "Bring these sinners to the front and line them up outside the hospital. I want them to see their hope's destruction before they meet their own ends."

Hegart jumps onto his steed and rides. What a marvelous turn of events, he thinks. This will be a battle to record in his GOD Book. How GOD slayed the heathens. How GOD laid the way for true and lasting order. GOD is jealous and vengeful.

He waits, mounted on his horse, as thousands of his guards fill in the grounds around him and the hospital. The sinners, as ordered, are forced to watch from a distance on their knees, hands again on their heads. The air is crisp, and the snow is covering the earth. The clouds above have sucked all the sound away, leaving the hushed awe of winter. Hegart's grin grows as the small, insignificant sinner's march appears through the dead orchard trees. They are shadows, but becoming more defined as they approach. There are one hundred and fifty, at most, and they seem to be led by a woman on a horse.

Hegart laughs. "A woman," he says. "And a boy with a drum. Why, this sinner's march is little else but a roving band of whores and orphans."

The Kingdom Guards laugh.

And then Hegart sees Cayden Lothair. His smile fades somewhat. One good fighter among one hundred and fifty.

"Leave the traitor for me," says Hegart. "I'll wear his cock as a necklace."

THROUGH THE dead orchard he is marching, climbing over limbs and the splits in the bows of trees, as if these wooden hands are giving him up to the ninth. They are all marching assuredly, every one of them a bomb of defiance and resilience. Cayden is glad to be of their number even as he hears the death knell. The snow is falling harder, but that only encourages them. Chill meets chill, and the hairs that stand up on the backs of their necks are hobnailed with expectation. Key keeps a steady rhythm on his drum, with Lawl nearby. The orphans and forest folk are quite set and ready to meet their fates, taking as many guards down with them as possible. Madden and Cruncher are stalking, and Rossa leads them all on her steed, Claire, with Lorien and his horsemen close behind. Even Mags Hensil and the Sisters of GOD are made to march, though in the back and led by ropes. Mags's wounded face is bandaged and her mouth is forced closed. This, a first.

The march stops at a good distance from the hospital. The orchard surrounds them still. The air seems breakable. Cayden takes in the great wealth of guards before them. This will be his death. The guards have more show than skill, but they also have more numbers.

"Stay strong," Rossa tells them from astride Claire. "Keep your courage. They have numbers, aye. But we have the right." She looks sideways at Cayden, her eyebrow arched. "And right always wins, aye?"

"Aye!" Cayden shouts loud enough for even Hegart's army to hear.

"Aye!" the sinners echo. "Aye, aye, aye!" The refrain is continuous refrain, and while it evokes laughter from Hegart's guards, it offers nothing but hope to the sinners. They scream it until it dissolves into a great roar.

Lawl has brought along a set of magnifyers with him from his bag o' tricks. "Brother Lawl," Cayden says, "may I see those?"

He puts the magnifyers to his eyes and makes a noise of some fright, which startles those around him.

"What is it?" Lawl says. "What do ya see?"

"Nothin' but a very ugly man. The Senator General is smilin' and droolin' somethin' awful."

The sinners laugh.

And yet as Cayden speaks, Hegart's grin diminishes slightly. He focuses his attention on something beyond the ferryman. Cayden hears a commotion to his aft and turns to see a swath, a field, a great flood of marchers—marchers he has never seen before. Indeed, marchers from other districts all over the Immortal City. The sound of joy cannot be contained in the sinner's march at this sudden and great shift. Hope pings. Cayden looks to Rossa, but she is just as baffled.

And then Cayden sees her look up at the sky. A fleet of bright red balloons are sailing for the ninth ring. Cayden uses the magnifyers and sees they are manned by marchers and orphans with weapons.

Cayden looks back at Hegart just as the final traces of a smile disappear from his face only to be replaced by... fear? Why would Hegart fear sinners and balloonists?

And then the ferryman sees the ferrymen to his side, coming up parallel like a black rug over the now white ground. They got his message at Erung Ferry's tomb. They understood. There were at least two hundred of them, their black capes flapping in the wind, staring with anger in the direction of Hegart's army. One of them looks to Cayden and nods, and *en masse* the ferrymen unsheathe their scythes. A great, thunderous cheer rises in the march.

Cayden hands the magnifyers back to Lawl and looks to Rossa. Her smile is beautiful, her chest heaving with excitement, her eyes wide with victory. She raises her sword. "Sinners!" she cries. "Let's bring GOD to his bloody knees!" And in a voice that shakes the ring, "Charge!"

Cayden feels a surge of love. Love for the cause, for those he is fighting with, for those he is fighting for, for those who have passed.

Like Gemma. Like his own father. And with each step forward, he can see his father and his father's namesake, Erung Ferry, marching beside him, singing.

AND WITH a deafening roar of a thousand battle cries, the marchers descend upon the army at the ninth ring. Orphans, balloonists, horsemen and forest folk, the homeless, the turned-out, the spit-upon and spied-upon, the heretics and immoralists, the ex-guards and the ferrymen all fighting as one. And we are there with them.

ESTHER LEAVES Bana down below as she climbs the ramp—however unsteadily due to her intoxication and loss of wits—to retrieve GOD. She takes her time, delighting in the fear her doddling is creating in His Worship, until she at last stands over His chair and is looking down upon Him.

"Impressive height," she says, looking over the edge of the desk at her minute husband below. She leans forward and searches the switches and keys of the Power of GOD until she thinks she sees the right one. "But to see clearly, I think one needs a bit more light."

The window shades shake and rumble as they rise, flooding the room with sun. They haven't been retracted in so long, they are constipated and slow. The golden gilded edges of every piece of furniture and wall decoration in the chamber rejoice and glow, a celebration of excess. GOD and Bana begin to howl like aggrieved spirits.

"I agree," Esther says. "Quite gaudy." She gives a tsk-tsk.

GOD is in such pain, He does not notice Esther unplugging Him from His feeding tubes. She takes GOD's chair by the handles and wheels Him down the ramp. He flails and rages, hissing violent commands.

"Be still now," Esther warns. "You don't want me to accidentally let go of your chair, do you? Why, you would go quite out of control down this ramp." This calms Him, but He still breathes heavily and hissfully. "But then, I suppose control has never been your strong suit, has it? The plague you and my husband and the others released to gain power, wasn't so easy to control after all. You and Bana didn't expect to be infected. No. You believed so vehemently in your GODhood, you believed yourself quite immune."

Esther strains to keep the chair from escaping her grip and racing down the ramp. Yet she envisions the clash of the two soulless blights in her head, and it makes her laugh.

"But you see, darling deity, I might be the only one aside from our precious Bana here who knew you, who knew GOD when He was just a girl. When He was just the third-sex bastard child of Bana Kerr, the product of Bana's affair with… that woman. You could have had quite a normal life. Maybe even a good life. But you wanted my life. You wanted my husband to be your father. You gained power in the Guardians of Democracy and came to the conclusion that someone genderless was better, at least where Bana's affections were concerned. And maybe you were right. He always has been rather sexist in his views of females and third-sexers."

They come to the bottom of the ramp, and Esther stoops down so she may talk to GOD face to face. "Do you know the only time Bana and I ever touched was when we created Gemma." Her heart breaks, and her voice cracks. "My Gemma…"

Her thoughts paralyze her momentarily, but she is brought back around by Bana's incessant droning behind her. She stands again and turns the blights and their chairs toward each other. "Anyway, that dreadful gender-milking ensued. But then, unfortunately, you saw gender wasn't the answer after all and that Bana still only saw you as a woman, not his daughter. So, you began the soul retractions from a method found in some older-than-ancient book in a now-lost library. But that didn't work either. You still have at least the ghost of a soul, or else this passion to see Bana and be accepted by him would have died years ago."

She bends down once more, peering into GOD's feeble, pale face. "You, my dear, are no deity. You are simply insane. You've sacrificed yourself for a man who, I can tell you, is not worth it. And by the way, he was proud of you, but until now… Until this very moment, he never knew you were his child. I never told him your mother had come to the manse pleading for me to hire her so she could feed you."

GOD roars, trying to say something, but it is all a jumble of letters and phlegm.

Esther walks behind Bana's chair and, with a grimace, snaps a tube on his oxygen tank. Walking back to stand between the father and daughter, she digs a small unlit fire stick out of a pocket in her gown. Bana and GOD scream. GOD screams the loudest.

"We, this trinity, are all horrible people," says Esther, and she lights the stick.

She feels such warmth, such absolute warmth, as the Tower of GOD does fall.

KEY IS dazzled, excited, and terrified as he scampers around the battlefield, beating his drum. He can do little damage with the antique blade he uses, but a little damage is better than none at all, and he has always been very good at dodging. He finds himself too often looking up in awe at the great red balloons as they fire arrows down on the Kingdom Guards. A few of the guards have tried to down the balloons, but they have not succeeded. Good throwing arms are rare when being attacked on all sides, and the enemy has little time to put together a javelin force or catapult.

Key runs beneath the bulbous shadows, keeping up with Lawl who is using both sword and what he calls "chemical warfare" on the enemy. This consists of poisonous plants mixed in water and pulverized in a container from the bag o' tricks, then sprayed directly into the faces of the guards who get too close. From what Key can hear, it is quite painful. But Lawl has become adept at sword use as well, and he is swinging mightily.

The child looks to see Rossa to his right. She fights astride Claire. Lorien and his horsemen fight beside her. A few have been cut down. Rossa herself has a gash on her leg, but she fights on, her teeth gritted as she hacks her way past those who mean to do her harm. Her rage is magnificent, and she yells with every swipe.

"This way!" Lawl shouts to Key, grabbing the boy by the collar and pulling him toward a host of ferrymen laying waste to a pack of guards.

Cayden Lothair is among them, and he is just as good as his brethren. Better. He sees Key and slashes through a charging guard, tearing the man in half. "That was for you, my friend!" he shouts and continues with the fight.

Two ferrymen die in front of him, and Lawl pulls Key in another direction. People are falling all around him now. A guard still alive but on the ground tries to bring him down, but the child severs the guard's hand with three hacks from his dull blade.

Lawl lifts Key onto Madden's back with Eight and her brother Two. "Free the prisoners!" Lawl screams. He swats the hound on the rear, and they are off as Lawl continues fighting. Key has not the chance to say anything on the matter. He is holding onto Madden's fur with one hand and with the other doing his best to inflict some damage on the guards as they race by. Two is laughing something fierce. "Good dog! Good dog! Good dog!" he cries with each bounce. Madden is bleeding from numerous cuts, but he is not slowed.

The view from the hill at front of the hospital is a living tapestry of war. Blood and guts and steel. The prisoners are still on their knees, surrounded by guards. Key does not know how they will manage to break through. But then, he does not need to worry on such things. Madden seems to know exactly what to do. The great hound topples three Kingdom Guards at once, and Cruncher leaps into the fray and tears into another. Chaos ensues as the prisoners once again rise to their feet, even those who did not fight before, and take to battle. Madden finishes tearing out a guard's throat as the children slide off his back.

The great hound races to Tully, and as if expecting this, the thin man with the large eyes jumps up on the beast's back with a wide grin, shouts something Key cannot hear, and races off toward the battle.

Key sees another of the freed prisoners grab a large bloody bone from what looks to be a pile of scraps and weapons, ready to fight. Yet as he does this, Key realizes they are cornered. The prisoner with the bone, Cruncher, Eight, Two, and himself have nine guards surrounding them, ready to carve them up. Cruncher growls, but he is wounded and limping. "Stay close," says the man with the bone to the children. "When I say duck… DUCK!" he screams, and they do.

Nine guards are instantly beheaded by four ferrymen from behind. Their bodies fall like potato sacks. Key and Cruncher immediately follow the man with the bone down the hill. The ferrymen adopt Two and Eight. In fact, as Key looks around, he sees all the children have been adopted and are being protected by at least one ferryman, some even fighting alongside them.

Cruncher is keeping up with Key, though wounded, and Key is doing his best to keep up with the man with the bone. Guards surrender and plead for their lives. Key sees Lawl up ahead, and he is different somehow. The look on his face is an expression of utter joy. In fact, he is in tears. The man with the bone embraces him, and they kiss before both turning to fight off a couple of stubborn guards. Then they pull Key to them and enfold him into another embrace. Their happiness makes him happy. Their whispered words of joy and relief make him smile. And by the time they pull away from each other, the battle is over.

Senator General Hegart stands yards away surrounded by Rossa on her horse, Cayden Lothair, Tully, and a dozen angry ferrymen. Hegart is snarling and drooling. He holds his sword ready to strike down anyone who dares approach him. He shoots glances from one face to another.

"Your war is lost, Hegart," says Rossa. "Your time and your GOD's time are over. The Immortal City is fallen."

Hegart rages at those words and intends to strike her down at least, but he is caught by a ferryman's hook and a sword pierces his side. Hegart spins around in pain, and Cayden impales his genitals. Tully, with Madden just behind him, asks for a scythe and Cayden obliges. By now, the Senator General has a crowd watching him.

Tully leans down to where Hegart has fallen and says, "This be for our family, ya ass."

With that, he slides the scythe into his brother's chest.

DOCTRESS DEIRDRE Maire has watched the battle from the cupola, at first like some death herald, a silhouette, somber and solid, and then, as the battle turned, as things began to unfold in a surprising way, she felt cleansed by the snow falling outside. Cleansed of all that shadow. She felt the tiniest tug of a smile when she caught sight of the balloons, and then, when the ferrymen poured from the orchard like sticky black molasses, she even laughed. The sound of it caused the two nurses following her around as if attached to her to jerk to attention. Perhaps even they sensed some change in the winds. They are mindless after all, not soulless.

Abrythnia stands beside Deirdre now, and together they watch as Hegart is slain. But his death does not fill the doctress with any sense of satisfaction. There should be more than mere death to atone for what he has done.

"He is not dead, my dear," Abrythnia explains. "The soulless cling to life most vigorously."

"Nurses," Deirdre says, keeping watch on Hegart's limp body now spilling blood on the hospital grounds. "Please go fetch the Senator General. He should not die in such a manner on the battlefield. He deserves… something more memorable, I think."

BEYOND...

STEAM RISES from the blood and the flesh as the snow falls. A natural blanket of quiet intensifies the sound of humanity. The battlefield is inundated with emotion. Fear, grief, anger, relief, and, at last, joy. Over the bodies of the dead and dying, amidst the horror and heartbreak, there are reunions. Marchers and sinners alike who had been taken prisoner, embrace those who have come to their rescue, some family members and friends thought long dead. Cries of surprise and disbelief echo through the ring as lost children and orphans find mothers, fathers, sisters, and brothers. Tears of sadness and tears of joy may look the same, but they are by no means kin. One stings. The other cleanses.

Those orphans who have found no family waiting for them in the ninth ring discover instead a silent comfort with their ferrymen protectors and are content to help keep watch over the captured Kingdom Guards and the Sisters of GOD, who were tied to the orchard trees during the battle.

Rossa walks around the battlefield with Claire, Key, and Cayden, seeing to the wounded, comforting those in their final minutes. There are tears, but there is also pride to be seen in those who are dying. Others are being told of the grievances done against their friends and family while they have been imprisoned. Tully holds on to Madden fiercely as Gemma's death is explained to him by Lorien; Duncan tells Lawl of the death of his beloved aunt, Gran.

SENATOR GENERAL Hegart hears all of the words as echoes spoken around him as he lies dying. They pass through his ears like wind through a tunnel. Above him, he sees a sky heavy with orange clouds. They are moving, falling. Large snowflakes fall onto his eyes, blurring his vision. This is a dream, this has all got to be a dream.

He rages in and out of consciousness. He sees the mindless nurses surround him, and he is lifted. He is being carried. Yes. Deirdre will fix him. She will care for him. And once he has recovered, he will smash the world. He will rape it. He will be the fiercest of all the gods. The sky turns red in his anger, and he faints away once more.

Then he is awake again, but fastened to a bed in the hospital. He is confused. Hegart tries to escape the restraints, but he cannot move so much as finger. He tries to say something but cannot speak. The nurses mill about him like worker ants.

He realizes then in a shock of blinding ice fear, *The bitch has paralyzed me.*

As if called, the doctress steps into view. She is smiling, and that unnerves him. She is smiling. "Now," she says, "now we are even, sweetie pie."

She is fastening the straps on his arms and his legs, as if he could still somehow climb out of this paralysis.

"A precaution," she says. "You can never be too careful with the dregs that are brought in here. You told me that many, many years ago." She says something to a nurse, then returns her attention to him. "We're going to fix you right up, even without the Power of GOD to help us. Yes. It seems the Immortal City has at last fallen, and GOD's Tower with it. But don't you worry. I know what a masculine fellow you are, not afraid of a little pain." She winks. "You will live. I intended to lobotomize you when you were brought up here, but I think not now. No. It's best you keep all your faculties, your sharp wit, your plotting mind. Only you will not have the body, the freedom, to act on these grand machinations. You will be quite incapacitated, Hegart. I, on the other hand, am leaving the ninth ring... for good. Most people are, so you will be quite alone. But I am not heartless. I plan on leaving you in the care of these fine nurses."

A large nurse behind Deirdre stares at him, unflinching. Her brain-dead eyes show a flash of manic soul.

Deirdre's smile fades, and she leans in close to his face. "I want you to feel each hunger pang individually as you slowly starve to death. The nurses will keep you alive so long as they themselves have nourishment, but once that runs out..." She shrugs. "They too will either flee this place, leaving you here to decay with it, or they might just start snacking on you. Who's to say, really?"

She pulls up. "And one more thing. We're going to take those nasty teeth out as well. You won't need them anymore. And I'm sorry to tell you, but we are fresh out of any anesthesia for any of this."

Blinding white ice.

She disappears from his view like the fading sun to be replaced by the large angry nurse holding a pair of fang-like retractors. Hegart is screaming at the doctress. His mind is a frenzied, pleading mess.

IN THE Thorn Fields, Duncan sits back on the ground, holding on to his ankles as he waits for Lawl to respond. They have been there for some time. Duncan has told him everything now. He can do little else but anticipate the fury and hope for clemency.

The air around Gran's grave is as sharp as the thorns and thistles. The snow has stopped falling. It lies two inches deep on the ground. Lawl sits beside the grave on folded knees, his back to Duncan. Not a word has been spoken between the two since Duncan told him how he betrayed Gran. Every silent second is torture. He did not make excuses, for what good would they have done? Hurt is hurt, betrayal is betrayal. But love… love is stronger.

"Ya need to give him time," says Gran. She has been sitting beside Duncan, mostly quiet. He is not surprised she is there. He has come to accept that in this new world, dream and reality now swap places on a daily basis.

Duncan gives her a sideways glance and smiles. "Ya look good, Gran."

She is younger now, vibrant. The silver in her hair is more affectation than age.

"Aye, I do." She is sweet. Her eyes absolve him. "And I be free."

"Are we all crazy?" he says. "The whole world sees the dead walkin' around, talkin' at them. Have we all been driven insane?"

"Naw. Quite the opposite, in fact. The world is just now startin' to wake up and see things correctly, more fully. Nothin' is impossible. The world becomes…"

"Vivid."

"Aye. Vivid."

They sit in stillness for a while longer, and then something remarkable happens. The sky above them fades, but clears. The ever-hanging clouds depart, their orange tint fading to yellow then dust pink then a remarkable deep blue. And there are stars. Bright, bright stars. Duncan, embracing his knees now, watches the beautiful aerial clearing with glassy eyes.

"Look," he says to Lawl in a slight whisper of wonderment, as if speaking too loud would scare them away. "Look at the stars, Lawl."

Lawl has seen them. He is now looking over his shoulder at Duncan. His face is lighted by the moon. It is not a hard and angry face, but gentle. He stands and walks to Duncan, holding out his hand.

FORGIVENESS

THE EXODUS occurs days later. The marchers and the sinners were in need of a rest free of fear. People needed to be fed, and the doctors saw to all those who required tending to. They buried their dead, and children were let to play as children should. The ferrymen volunteered to clean up the Factory, for they were the only ones who had the stomach for it.

When at last people started to leave, some still chose to remain behind and wait for any others who had heard of the ninth ring's great fall and wondered what lay past the Immortal City. The walls were falling, it was said, one by one, and a wind of freedom was gathering people into new marches and cavalcades. They suffered from crime and looting, of course. The soulless and insane will always commit atrocities, but with a large enough force, Lorien assured Rossa they could be handled.

"My horsemen and I," he said to her as they sat astride their steeds and looked out over the grounds, "will remain behind. We will keep an eye on our captured Kingdom Guards and wait for other seekers from the inner rings. And then someday we will join you, wherever you are. I cannot leave just yet. I still have my horses to reclaim."

"Be careful," she told him. "Not only are there everyday marauders, there are still free guards and hungry men. And we may find other strange beasts we do not yet know of. Who can say what monstrosities our jealous GOD came up with?"

"They'll be no match against our new force," said he. "Most of the ferrymen plan to stay behind and pick up from where their lives were stolen from them. And the forest folk as well. They know these lands and love them more than any city dweller could. I imagine the Passions might even return someday. Would make for a great fairy-tale ending."

Rossa smiled at the thought. "Let us hope it be written."

Tully, too, told the doctress Deirdre Maire of his plans to remain behind with Madden. "At least for now," he said, big eyes as bright as the sun in the now cloudless sky. "Madden will be with me. I wouldna mind doin' a bit of adventurin' here before I head out there into the unknown.

And I want to see Gemma Kerr's grave by the Silver Sea. She meant a lot to me, ya know."

Deirdre, still stoic and unsmiling, nevertheless now had a softness to her expression, a certain relenting contentment. "You come find us, though, Mr. Tully," she said to him. "When you are through with your adventuring, you come find me. It would be nice to have someone to talk about better times with."

And so, this day, a grand procession of a thousand makes its way to the Thorn Fields with scythes and swords and fire, led by a redheaded queen on a gray horse and a former assassin. They are followed by a grand assortment of folk: orphans, Lawl and Duncan, a drummer boy and his fire dog, a few curious forest folk, two dozen ferrymen, original sinners, new marchers, the Sisters of GOD taken prisoner, Deirdre Maire and a couple other doctors, two mindless nurses, and a traveling show that once had a bear. The mother and her twin sons who ran said show had released the creature into the first ring.

Clearing a path to the wall they all know has to exist is slow going and difficult work, but their spirits are high and the chilled air is electric. Never have more smiles graced the ninth ring. They see the wall at last, tilting and impaired, but high enough to see greetings over the thick branches of briars. There is much celebration, and Key provides musical entertainment.

It is morning now. Rossa and Cayden climb the outer steps of the wall and stand atop the structure, looking out over the undiscovered country beyond.

"The tenth ring," Rossa says, slight surprise in her voice. "Gemma was right. There is somethin' beyond the nine. And it looks as wild as an orphan's hair."

"Decidedly more tamable, though," quips—yes, *quips*—the ferryman.

"I think the Sisters need to see how their GOD has lied to them."

Mags Hensil is initially belligerent when she and her Sisters are brought to the top of the wall by the ferrymen who guard them. Her torn mouth is now stitched, and she will have an ugly scar as a reminder of her downfall. Her attention is focused on Rossa, hateful intent. She does not care why she has been brought up the steps. But then the wails from the Sisters startle her. The six of them fall to their knees as they take in the blasphemy that lies before them. They tear at their clothes and hair, these women who have given their lives, their voices, to an absolute truth.

Mags stumbles forward. She steadies herself on the ruined stone wall. "This cannot be," she says, gesturing outward. "Sisters, this cannot be."

And Mags Hensil has died, even before the Sisters of GOD, in a violent rage, rush her, tipping her over the wall before the ferrymen are able to subdue them. Only two of the Sisters choose to venture on with the march. The other four remain at the wall and eventually, tiring of their Sisters' voices and the memories of the things they have done in the name of GOD, they will either kill themselves or plot to kill one another. But that is all speculation. We do not know the future. We swear it.

NOT TOO far from the ninth-ring wall, the marchers come across Doctress Sara and the nurse Orna by a campfire. Deirdre seems surprised to receive such an embrace from Sara. Sara seems surprised anyone is left alive.

Time has not been kind to the tenth ring's ruins. They are but piles of rock and fragments of statues, some now concealed in so thick an assemblage of vines and moss, they resemble trees. Any road that was once here is now swallowed by the extravagant plant life. Everything here is larger, fuller, more abundant in size and number, more imposing and even deadlier. The trees reach higher than any in the previous nine rings. The few forest folk who have come on the journey climb them and keep watch for the wall. They too are awed by the tapestry of new mysteries opening up to them. The tenth ring is home to many wild monsters and myths, some seen in dreams, others never imagined. Dinotonks, snovelfarks, and rendwolves were once thought fairy stories, but they are, it seems, quite real.

Cruncher is bitten by a snake with two heads, but, the fire dog that he is, he bites it right back. He is sick for a day but, much to Key's relief, mends.

Some of the forest folk and the children claim to see Passions as well darting hither and nither.

"They're just keepin' their eyes on us, s'all," explains Eight. "Makin' sure we mean the trees no harm. There be other faces we seen besides the Passions, but it's best we don't talk about them." She nods at her brother Two.

"Scary faces, scary eyes," says Two.

Others besides the children have said they have seen the scary faces as well. They do not want to speak of them, either. The ferrymen promise to keep guard over the camp. They seem to know there is little difference between what is and what is only told as story.

The eleventh ring is much the same as the tenth, with one major exception. The marchers have at last come upon the source of the River Hung, not from a large ocean or the mouth of a river god, but from the sky. They stand in wonder on the banks of a large lake at the foot of the greatest mountains anyone has ever seen. These mountains must have cliffs, but who can see them? The river falls, roaring from some cliff or peak hidden high, high, high in the white clouds above.

"But where," asks Rossa, "is the twelfth ring? We've trusted the River Hung to lead us onward with every step. Now we are at the very beginning of the river and no wall in sight."

DAYS HAVE passed, and the marchers are becoming restless, their hopes of ever seeing what lies beyond the Immortal City being mocked by the birds that fly over their heads. If only the balloonist had come with the march, then he could have gone ahead and reported back what he had seen. But, as he explained, the balloons are well past their prime. The Battle of the Ninth Ring was their last hurrah.

Cayden feels the mounting disquiet personally. He does not say it aloud, but every night, he whispers a sort of apology to the girl hero. "Gemma Kerr, Sweet Gemma Kerr," he says. "How will we survive without her."

They have followed the mountains but can find no sign of the wall. And asks Lawl, "What if the mountains are the wall? What if just beyond them…?"

Rossa shakes her head. "But if that be so, Mr. Lawl, how will we ever find the way past them? Just look at 'em, sir. The mountains are so high with so many cliffs and crevasses, 'twould be a bloody terror. The gate to the twelfth ring could be anywhere in all that rock."

"Aye," says Lawl. "I didna say it was a solution, Queen Rose. Only a guess."

They are camped now at a large stream, which has branched off from the lake. Cayden sleeps with his eyes open, a habit from his ferryman days he knows he will never lose. The marchers are sleeping or silent in huddled groups around him in the woods. He himself is wrapped up in the muscular embrace of the slumbering twins, Anger and Spite. He has worn them out tonight.

Only the sounds of winter birds and the crackling of campfires fill the cold air. His breaths are ghost dancers. Even asleep, he studies each tendril. Cayden finds he is sometimes more alert as a dreamwalker than a daywalker. And then, standing in the middle of the creek like a river goddess, he sees her. Gemma Kerr smiles and waves for him to come meet her in the rushing waters. And strangely, he rises, yet he does not move. He turns around briefly to see himself still sleeping against the tree with the twins, his own eyes staring up at him, and he decides that having a soul will take some getting used to.

"You're going the wrong way," Gemma says once he is standing beside her in the icy stream. "Go back to the lake. The gate is not far. It is under the moon."

"I miss ya," he says, heartbreak in his voice. "Won't ya come back to us? Won't ya show us the way?"

She smiles and that alone is worth a thousand nightmares. "Someday," she says. "But I get to have my adventures first, remember? Then I'll call you to me. Go back to the lake, Cayden, and look under the moon."

So, the march, enlivened once more by Cayden's tale, heads to the lake of the River Hung. After many hours of searching, Cayden finally sees Gemma once more as she climbs up a steep incline to an insignificant wall of rock. She points to what seems a natural formation resembling a half moon. Beneath it is a small cave.

"Built most likely to keep the location of the Immortal City secret from enemies," says Lawl.

The tunnel is thin, allowing only a few through at a time. Cayden and two other ferrymen go first, and the others follow. Arriving in the twelfth ring, they are greeted by the gleam of white stone. The cave empties onto a great bleached stone precipice on which to stand and survey their surroundings. The twelfth ring is a country of white steps, which descend gently lower and lower into a waiting mist. Every so often, structures reminiscent of offices or shops will crop up, and the steps are cracked here and there by nosey trees or curious brush. But this is not a land for habitation. This is a land for coming and going.

And the march descends, for they are going.

Though they have provisions from the eleventh ring, they do not need to make use of most of these. The twelfth ring is a land of narrower circumference. The march reaches the mist before noon the next day, and they spot the final gate of the final wall at dusk. A strange new scent stirs from beyond, clean and refreshing, and as the march nears the gate, they hear the sound of waves beating on a shore.

The gate is crumbling. Half an archway is all that remains. The white stone steps sink into white stone walkways and these fade into a white sand beach beyond the arch. Slowly, the marchers trickle out of the gate, out of the Immortal City, and glimpse for the first time what eyes have not seen in epochs. The ocean is large and blue and more expansive than many of them can yet wrap their minds around. They cry with delight and fear, awe and anxiety, cheers and weeping. And laughter. Yes. There is much laughter.

Mountains sit astride the wide shore. Mountains not part of the Immortal City, lying just outside its walls. They come out like arms to either side of the gate and sweep wide and tall until they form a bay. And the sky, the sky delights in shades of blue, the darkest on the far horizon, fielded with stars, and there be great spheres hanging in it as well.

As they are taking these wonders in, the marchers are startled once more by the sight of masts suddenly rising from the blue water—sterns of sailing vessels with carved sea spirits and Passions. At least twenty-five such ships are now rising just off the ancient dock. And out of the deep, climbs like the crawlers a shadow crew with no more defined features than silhouettes, and they are setting the sails, every vessel coming to life, all the riggings as if new. When done, they stand on the decks, flickering dark spectrals.

"They are waiting," says Gemma.

The entire march sees and hears her now, even those who have never dreamed. They gasp in unison. She stands on the dock, dressed pleasantly in a tunic and brown pantaloons. The wind blows her hair.

"Waitin' for what?" Rossa asks, bending down and massaging Claire's neck to calm her. "Where are they thinkin' of takin' us, sweet Gemma?"

"Anywhere," she answers. Her eyes are on fire. "There is so much to see."

Cayden looks to the far horizon. "What is it like?"

"It's… unbelievable. The adventures you will have!"

And now, at last, we show ourselves. Who we are. Who we have been. Who we will be. We are all one yet we are all part of the three hundred souls. We are the ancient and the newborn. We are the living, and we are the dead. We do not have a god because we are god, every one of us, and we are wholly divine. We shape the world with our thoughts. We shake the world with our actions. We smile at our friends, our connections. Gemma to Cayden, Claire to Rossa, Gran to Duncan and Lawl, Aidan to Key, Usker and Colm to the marchers, and Abrythnia to Deirdre Maire.

"Are you ready to go?" we say.

Rossa's eyes are misting. "Well," she says to her friend the ferryman, "what do ya suppose we do now?"

Cayden breathes deep, and he smiles. "I suppose we wake up."

"Aye," says Rossa. "Then let's wake up. One, two, three…"

ERIC ARVIN resided in the same sleepy Indiana river town where he grew up. He graduated from Hanover College with a bachelor's degree in history and lived, for brief periods, in Italy and Australia. He survived brain surgery and his own loud-mouthed personal demons.

Facebook: www.facebook.com/eric.arvin.5

galley proof

ERIC ARVIN

Fiction writer Logan Brandish is perfectly happy in his peaceful small-town routine with his best friend, his cat, and his boyfriend—until he meets the editor of his next book, the handsome Brock Kimble, and the lazy quiet of everyday living goes flying out the window. Faced with real passion for the first time, Logan becomes restless and agitated, and soon his life and his new manuscript—a work in progress he'd always thought would be completed—are in a shambles.

But as Logan is learning, you can't always get what you want… at least not right away. To take his mind off the mess, he takes a trip, but even the beautiful Italian, um, scenery can't keep his thoughts from his erstwhile editor for long. Logan just might have to admit there are some things you can't run from.

www.dreamspinnerpress.com

WOKE UP
in a
STRANGE
PLACE

Eric Arvin

Joe wakes up in a barley field with no clothes, no memories, and no idea how he got there. Before he knows it, he's off on the last great journey of his life. With his soul guide Baker and a charge to have courage from a mysterious, alluring, and somehow familiar Stranger, Joe sets off through a fantastical changing landscape to confront his past.

The quest is not without challenges. Joe's past is not always an easy thing to relive, but if he wants to find peace—and reunite with the Stranger he is so strongly drawn to—he must continue on until the end, no matter how tempted he is to stop along the way.

www.dreamspinnerpress.com

Eric Arvin

Subsurdity

vignettes from Jasper Lane

The suburbs have never been this HOT!

SubSurdity: Book One

Jasper Lane is a well-off neighborhood, not much different in appearance than most, with a tree-lined drive, manicured lawns, and crystal clear ponds. But underneath the pleasantry, a completely different world lurks.

Cassie Bloom, the grand dame of Jasper Lane, has a missing son and husband and throws gay porn parties that are the social events of the year. Her best friend, a transsexual named Vera, owns a nightclub. Melinda Gold is the resident religious fanatic whose views clash with that of her son Patrick. Sandy and Steve Jones are the stereotypical all-American couple (except Steve acts in gay-for-pay porn unbeknownst to his pregnant wife).

Rick Cooper just moved in, and despite his qualms about another relationship (having literally lost an eye in the previous one), he falls for ex-soldier, James. And David and Cliff are the most "normal" couple on the block... never mind that David helped Cassie with some past nefarious deed and that Cliff is the biggest gay porn star in the biz. Throw a dog named Gayhound and a dead body into the mix, and Jasper Lane may just be the gayest neighborhood in town!

www.dreamspinnerpress.com

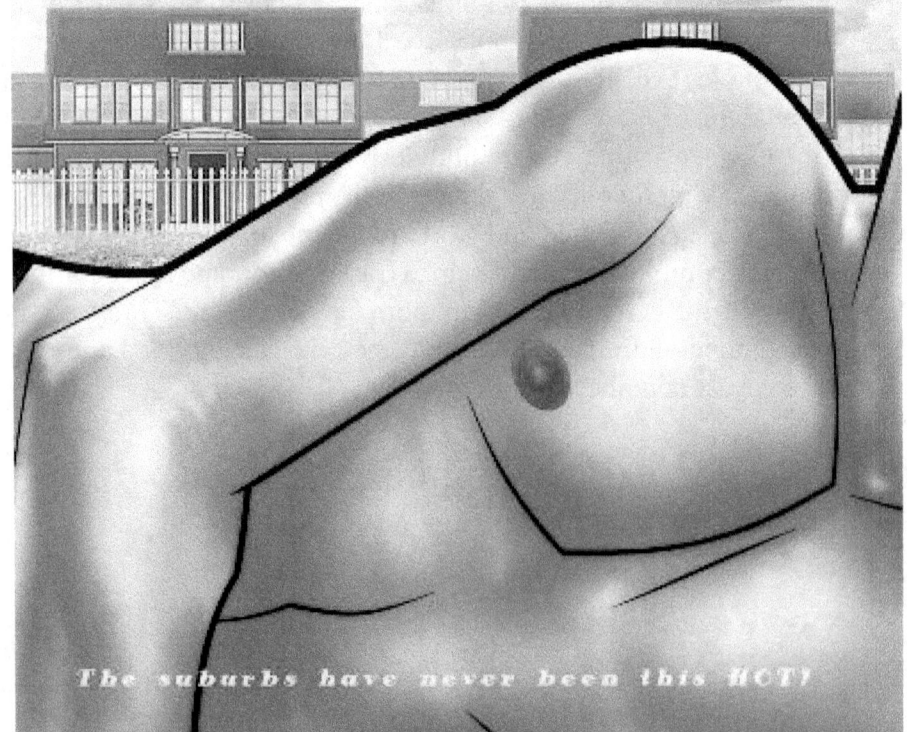

Eric Arvin

Suburbilicious

vignettes from Jasper Lane

The suburbs have never been this HOT!

Sequel to *SubSurdity*
SubSurdity: Book Two

Take another turn down Jasper Lane, the well-off neighborhood where gay porn parties, fresh cheesecake, and friendly busybodies welcome newcomers while a dog named Gayhound helps with the landscaping.

Cassie Bloom is thrilled her son Jason is home, but she's worried about the secrets buried around the house, especially when a scary-looking stranger starts spying on her! Rick and James are basking in the blush of love—or is it the flush of jealousy as Rick's rugby teammate starts hanging around?—and the flamboyantly gay Terrence is off bonding with his newly discovered son, Christian. Melinda, divorced from her stuffy husband, is looking to dip her toe in the dating pool, but she's got one problem: her potential date's embarrassing last name.

Steve and Sandy Jones are now proud parents, but Sandy's got to find something to do with herself, and running for office in the Gay Porn Wives Club may be just the ticket. And remember, it's a do-unto-others mentality on Jasper Lane, so when lesbian couple Asha and Keiko move in and Sandy helps Keiko get a directing job at Steve's gay porn film company, it's par for the course!

www.dreamspinnerpress.com

Eric Arvin

SuburbaNights

vignettes from Jasper Lane

Sequel to *Suburbilicious*
SubSurdity: Book Three

On Jasper Lane, Cassie Bloom is gearing up for Halloween; Becky is expecting, and her father is overbearing and paranoid; Rick and James are their usual happy selves, though James has developed a porn obsession; Terrence is putting together an all drag cheer squad; and David is helping Cliff transition from adult film star to bodybuilder. Of course, that's just what's going on at the surface. This is suburbia, and its underbelly is teeming with secrets.

Like what's up with that rather odd family that moved in down the street—the family with the big cross in the front yard who look nothing alike. Like where Cassie's son, Jason, has disappeared to and why he hasn't called. Like what on Earth Nanna Hench is doing with a scooter, a megaphone, and a clown car full of religious zealots.

When Cliff suddenly disappears, Jasper Lane goes on high alert. Terrence posts fliers, and Rick and James scour the gym. David is determined to get his husband back, but when he goes missing too—and with Cassie and Melinda on a road trip to find Jason—it's up to Terrence to solve the mystery and save the day.

www.dreamspinnerpress.com